ALL THE SILENT BONES

NEW YORK TIMES BESTSELLING AUTHOR

GREGORY FUNARO

All the Silent Bones
Red Adept Publishing, LLC
104 Bugenfield Court
Garner, NC 27529
https://RedAdeptPublishing.com/
Copyright © 2025 by Gregory Funaro. All rights reserved.

---

1.   http://StreetlightGraphics.com

For my wife, without whom I could never have written this.

And for my late uncle Ray, who was loved more than he ever knew.

"The past is a foreign country; they do things differently there."
—*L.P. Hartley*

Prologue: A Box of Bees

Jimmy Kauffman's funeral took place on a windy Sunday in December. The mercury in the old thermometer outside the church rectory touched thirty-two during the service that morning, but hours earlier, when Ronnie Matarese stumbled home and into his darkened kitchen, the weather app on his iPhone showed thirteen degrees.

Or eighteen. With the cocktail of Molly and Irish Car Bombs and a few other things pumping through his system, the sides of the three or the eight or whatever the hell it was wouldn't stop opening and closing. Ronnie stared at it blankly, his brain needing a couple of seconds to put together why he had checked his phone in the first place. Pure reflex. His apartment was freezing.

"The fuck?" Ronnie flicked the wall switch beside the door, and the kitchen lights came on. He staggered over to the thermostat above the table. Forty-eight degrees. He leaned closer. The fire symbol for heat was missing at the top of the screen.

He turned back to the door, which was the only way in or out of his second-floor abode. No sign of forced entry, and his laptop still sat on the table where he'd left it.

Debbie. The bitch actually had the balls to turn off his heat, a parting gift after cleaning out her shit. Ronnie's lips curled. He should've taken back her keys. Fucking whore never stopped busting his balls. Not even on the day of her father's funeral.

Ronnie slid the thermostat switch to Heat. The kitchen lights flickered, and the fire symbol started blinking. He tossed his phone and keys on the table, moved into his bedroom, and flicked on the wall switch. His TV was still on top of the dresser, but the window was open. Ronnie closed it. Fucking Debbie, all right. Nothing was missing, and the window was too high up for someone to use the trash cans. In the glow of the streetlight, Ronnie could see their dim shapes in the strip of darkness by the fence where he usually parked his Mustang. Good thing it was still in the shop. He would slit Debbie's throat if she ever took a key to it.

Ronnie shivered, stuffed his hands in his pockets, and closed his eyes, grateful for the cold and the rush of adrenaline that had sobered him some. He felt sharper now. Still angry, yeah, but mellow too. He had his OGs to thank for that—Angel, mainly, for scoring the Molly and keeping him straight when all the bullshit with Debbie had threatened to push him back on the pipe. *Lucky bitch.* Any other night, if she'd pulled something like this, he would have gone after her. Not tonight, though. Nothing would bring him down—not even the cunt's father, sixty years old and dead of acute alcohol poisoning. *See you in hell, Jimmy Kauffman, you pickled old fuck.*

Ronnie chuckled and began swaying as he hummed the chorus to "Gangsta's Paradise," the song he and his OGs had closed down Paddy's with. Yeah, still some anger in there with the mellow, but it was the kind of anger Ronnie liked, quiet and cool, the kind he could focus like a laser—like when Debbie's big mouth was just begging for a backhand. The last time had been one hundred percent her fault. She'd earned herself a black eye and a split lip. Even Angel agreed she'd deserved it. *Who the fuck did she think she was, shit-talking his mother?* Especially while he was playing *Call of Duty.*

Ronnie's stomach lurched, and his eyes widened. His PlayStation 5. If the bitch took it...

He whirled for the door then staggered back a step when he saw a guy sitting in the chair near the closet.

Ronnie squinted and blinked as his brain tried to determine if it really was a guy or just a pile of clothes made to look like one, something Debbie had left to fuck with him. The guy didn't move, and he was bundled in black from head to toe with his face concealed almost entirely behind a pair of sunglasses and an old-fashioned hunter's cap with earflaps. Then Ronnie's eyes landed on a pistol with a big suppressor pointed directly at him, and he knew the guy was real.

"Hi, Ronnie," the man said.

Ronnie's eyes darted toward the door.

"I wouldn't try it, but hey, that's me." The man motioned toward the bed with the pistol.

Swallowing hard, Ronnie sat on the edge of the mattress and clutched the blanket with his right hand. "The fuck is this? I ain't done nothing."

"It's not what you've done but what you will do," the man said. "Something much worse than whacking around Jimmy Kauffman's daughter."

Ronnie sat there with his face all scrunched and his brain telling him no fucking way. Debbie's father was just some old union guy. He wasn't connected like Ronnie was. True, the Matarese family didn't have anywhere near the kind of muscle they did back in the day, but no one did, save for the DeLorenzos and the Boston crew. And Ronnie was in tight with them.

"You don't remember me." The man lowered his sunglasses to reveal his eyes.

Something ignited in Ronnie's brain, a spark at the end of a fuse, snaking its way through all the booze and drug-addled slop and leading him back to his youth, to a pair of cold blue eyes behind the tiny square of security glass in his door at the Rhode Island Training School—the RITS, as everyone called it. He had done his one and only bid there at sixteen, six months for dealing Vicodin and possession of a stolen firearm. Not his first offense, judge threw the book at him, no connections saving his ass that time.

Ronnie had learned his lesson, though, or at least, how not to get caught. He never saw the inside of a prison cell again. But he still saw those blue eyes on the other side of the glass sometimes in his dreams. Eyes that had watched him like a hawk from the catwalk above the rec area. Eyes that had never shown a trace of fear, not even when their owner single-handedly broke up a fight between three guys, mowing them all down like a human machete.

Fuck. Machete. Yeah, that was his name. The guy in his bedroom was Bobby "the Machete" Bonetti. He was a tenth-degree black belt or something. Ronnie and the other juvies used to call him Bruce Lee behind his back, but to his face...

"Bossman?" The word passed Ronnie's lips in a whisper—a fizz, not even a pop at the end of his fuse of recollection.

Bobby slid his glasses back up over his eyes. "When I was a kid," he said, looking around, "I used to live in a place like this with my mother. Two bedrooms on the first floor of some triple-decker over in Silver Lake. Whole neighborhood has gone to shit now."

Bobby turned back to Ronnie, who caught a glimpse of himself, just the smudgy gray outline of his head, reflected in his old correction officer's sunglasses.

"Shit," Bobby said. "My mother used to beat the shit out of me when I was a kid. Not literal shit, but something gets beat out of you just the same, right? Where does it all go, I wonder. Does it just evaporate? Or does it hang around and settle into things?"

Ronnie's tongue felt stuck, but other fuses were being lit now in his brain, rapid-fire synapses sputtering to life and fizzing out again in muddy, dead-end answers to *What the hell is he doing here?* Never mind that he hadn't seen Bobby Bonetti in almost fifteen years; the son of a bitch was talking crazy. Ronnie wasn't too wasted to notice that.

"She didn't always beat me, though, my mother. Sometimes, she did other things. Like this time when I was eight years old. It started with a dream I was having. I don't remember much else except for opening this cardboard box on my kitchen table. The inside was deep and lined with black stones fading down into a circle of darkness."

Ronnie's brain was fully awake now, all systems go with the singular purpose of talking his way out of this, whatever *this* was. It wasn't the first time he'd been in a situation where he had to defuse a bomb before it went off, like when he'd still been dealing crystal on the side and one of his clients started tweaking.

"What are you doing here, Bossman?" Ronnie flashed a charming smile to accompany the forced sweetness in his voice, the same tone he used after his fights with Debbie, when they lay together in the dark and he called her honey and promised to never hit her again. Ronnie's instinct was to try to pull the same shit on Bobby, but when his old corrections officer leaned forward with his elbows on his knees and both hands on the pistol, Ronnie's throat closed so tight that he couldn't speak.

"In the dream," Bobby said, "I leaned into the darkness for a closer look, and this smell came back at me. Kind of like your smell, Ronnie—cigarette smoke, sweat, dogshit breath. Cherry Robitussin was mixed in there too. I gagged and tried to push the box away, but my arms wouldn't work right, then from out of the darkness at the bottom, there appeared this buzzing swarm of bees." Bobby Bonetti sat back in his chair again, the pistol leveled and steady.

Ronnie swallowed. His throat felt like sandpaper, and his heart, lodged and pounding there, made it hard to breathe. But still, he did his best to keep his voice smooth. "Look, Mr. Bonetti. I don't know what you think I—"

"Next thing I know, the bees are everywhere. I remember trying to scream but not being able to breathe, then this big bee lands on my head and stings me. That's when I woke up—right when the bee stung me. The room was dark, and I was gasping for air. I just sort of, you know, threw my hands up to where the bee was but instead grabbed my mother's wrist. She had me by the hair."

So maybe this *was* about Debbie. Ronnie had yanked her around by her bleached-blond hair plenty of times during their five-year on-and-off relationship. *What else could it be?* Other than Debbie's bullshit, he was doing well. He had just been promoted to shift supervisor down at the warehouse, and he never batted an eye when the DeLorenzos asked him to launder their stolen merch. Yeah, this *had* to be about Debbie.

"I hear what you're saying." Ronnie smoothed the blanket beside him. "It ain't right the way I treated Debbie. And you have my word, Boss—Mr. Bonetti—I swear, if I so much as lay a finger on that girl's head—"

"So I try to get my mother off me," Bobby went on as if Ronnie hadn't spoken, "but her grip was too strong, and she literally drags me out of bed by my hair. Had me all hunched over and scrambling for the door. My room was right off the kitchen like this one, and in no time, we were in the back hallway. My mother, she throws open the cellar door and snaps my head back, shoving me toward the top of the stairs. 'Do you hear them?' she whispers in my ear. My scalp was on fire, and I was crying, but still, I managed to say, 'Yes.'"

"Mr. Bonetti, I get it. I swear I—"

"You see, Ronnie, my mother used to think there were elves living down there in our cellar. Elves. Why, I have no idea. Her mind was so fucked up sometimes. But the night I'm telling you about, she tells me only love can make them go away then asks me if I love her. I didn't reply fast enough, so she snaps back my head. At the same time, I brace myself against the doorframe, my toes curling over the top step. I beg her not to throw me down the stairs. 'Do you love me?' she asks again, twisting my hair, and I tell her I do."

Ronnie Matarese felt a darkness descend upon him, even as he understood that it had always been there, pouring out from those eyes behind the sunglasses and into his apartment. A darkness as indifferent and as cold as the one that had greeted him when he'd returned home. A darkness that feared no light and could not be reasoned with. A darkness that was neither happy nor sad but *just was*.

Bobby "The Machete" Bonetti had not visited Ronnie to warn him or give him a beating. He had come to kill him. Ronnie suddenly knew this as surely as he was sitting there, and he was both terrified and furious that he hadn't realized it sooner, when he still might have had a chance to escape. More than anything, though, Ronnie was sad. He wasn't ready to die—he wasn't even thirty—but there was no turning back from the elves at the bottom of these stairs. *That* was what this crazy SOB was trying to tell him.

Ronnie began to cry, softly at first then harder as Bobby finished his story.

"So my mother, she lets me go, but I just held on to the doorframe and didn't dare look back. She was still there. I could hear her breathing. And in my mind, I watched her, mouth open and eyes blinking as she looked around like she usually did when she came out of one of her episodes. A minute later, I hear the sofa springs in the parlor. She'd been sleeping in there for weeks because the elves hid under her bed, she sometimes thought. But still, I didn't move. I just stood there, staring down at the darkness in silence."

Ronnie searched Bobby Bonetti's sunglasses but saw only murder in the smudge of his reflection, light and shadows on a face that looked like a skull. This was not the way he was supposed to go out, sniveling on his bed like a pussy and not knowing why. And *that* was the hardest part. Not knowing why. Not knowing what he had done—no, not had done but *would do*. And just as quickly as the darkness had descended, Ronnie saw a light. It was faint at first but coming fast, like when he was speeding through the cross-harbor tunnel up in Boston.

"You said you were here because of something I *would* do," Ronnie said, making no attempt to hide the desperate, trembling hope in his voice. "Not because of something I did but because of something I would do. That's what you said, right? What is it? Tell me what you think I'm gonna do, and I swear on the souls of my dead parents that I won't do it. Please, I'm begging you, Mr. Bonetti. You have my word."

"I would give anything to have that kind of silence again," Bobby said. "A silence so precious that, when it's broken, it stings you like a box of bees."

Then Bobby shot him.

Part I: The Old Neighborhood (1979)

Chapter One

The summer before Ray Dawley started sixth grade, Bobby Bonetti moved in down the street from him on Lexington Avenue. Not the fancy one in New York City, but the crowded stretch of capes and colonials in Cranston, Rhode Island. The neighborhood was called Eden Park, which Ray always thought was kind of dumb because the place didn't look like a park at all, except for maybe the pond at the bottom of his street, but even that was polluted, everyone knew.

Still, Ray figured his neighborhood was a lot nicer than the one from which Bobby and his mother, Carla, had moved. Best of all, Ray and Bobby were already pretty good friends. Their mothers both worked as nurses at the hospital, and for the past couple of years, Carla had been bringing Bobby along when she visited. Ray had never gone to Bobby's house, though—some "dago triple-decker," Ray's father called it—over in Silver Lake, a blue-collar Italian-American neighborhood west of downtown Providence. Carla usually brought pastries from some bakery there, and after Ray and Bobby stuffed themselves, they would play outside while their moms smoked Kools and gossiped over Gallo wine. Carla also had a side hustle painting Welcome signs—most with flowers, some with cats—and when she brought them over, Ray's mom would always buy one.

"Another Carla Bonetti masterpiece," Ray's dad would grumble when he came home from work. "How much that gypsy take you for this time?"

"She's been through a lot" was all Ray's mom would say before tossing the sign into the coat closet with all the others she'd bought over the years.

Ray's dad never came right out and said he didn't like Carla Bonetti, but when he found out she and Bobby were moving into one of the duplexes at the bottom of the street, he sat out on the screened porch all night, drinking Narragansett and sucking Marlboros down to the nubs.

A big broad-shouldered fella, Frank Dawley worked as a supervisor at Brown & Sharpe in North Kingstown. Ray knew they made tools there, but he wasn't sure what kinds, only that they were more complicated than screwdrivers and stuff. Ray's dad never asked for his only son's opinion on things, but if he had ever asked him about Carla Bonetti, Ray would have told him he didn't like her much either, mainly because she was so different from his mom.

Sue Dawley was plump and fair and wore her sandy-blond hair in a bun, even when she wasn't working. She had a gentle, breezy way about her, whereas Carla Bonetti giggled too much and smiled as if she knew a secret or something. Ray figured she was pretty, in a way, with her black hair falling in thick, wild ringlets about her shoulders, but her eyes were dark and restless. She was also the skinniest woman he had ever seen, her bony arms wrapped tight with bulging veins that always made him think of needles.

Bobby Bonetti was dark and skinny like his mother—"Bobby Bones" the kids called him—but that was where the similarities ended. Bobby had straight black hair that was slick and as shiny as the piano in the cafeteria, and his eyes were big and blue and sad in a way. Ray noticed that Bobby was a lot quieter around people besides him, and Bobby's laugh was always wheezy and stifled, like a kid cutting up in class who didn't want the teacher to hear.

That wasn't to say that Bobby didn't cut up now and then too. One time, right after the Bonettis moved in, Ray was up in Bobby's room, helping him unpack, and in one of the boxes, he found an old Zippo and a pair of dog tags that had belonged to Bobby's father. Ray had learned at some point when he was old enough to understand such things that Bobby's parents had never married before his father was killed in Vietnam. Ray could tell Bobby felt uncomfortable whenever the subject came up, but Bobby usually just blew it off by making a joke or doing something stupid.

"Get a load of this, Ray." Bobby snatched the Zippo, lay on his back, and threw his legs over his head. Then he put the lighter in front of his butt and flicked the wheel. *Whoosh!* A fart shot out of his ass like a flamethrower.

The whole room instantly stank, but Ray laughed so hard he almost puked.

That night, after Ray told his parents about the Zippo thing at supper, Ray's dad asked to speak with him on the screened porch. The only furniture out there was a few lawn chairs and an upside-down paint bucket, on top of which Frank Dawley always set his empties. By the time Ray finished helping his mom dry the dishes and stepped out onto the porch, his father was already three deep into his six-pack. Ray pulled up a lawn chair and sat beside him.

"Listen, Ray," his father said. "I don't mind you hanging out with that Bonetti kid, but I don't want you going in his house no more 'less you're with Mom, understand?"

"Why not?"

"Because I said so should be enough, but since I'm buzzed, I'll indulge you this one time. Some people got a darkness around them, hanging in the air, like that burning fart you think is so funny. It gets in their hair and their clothes, and eventually, no matter how hard they try, they can't get clean of it. You spend enough time with them, before you know it, that darkness is hanging on you too. Understand?"

Ray didn't understand at all. Bobby was a good kid, way better than his friend Eddie Sayers and even Matt Kauffman. Ray said as much, but his dad just looked at him sideways, his eyes little more than black slits in the twilight as he took a long pull from his cigarette then dropped it into the empty beer can he was using as an ashtray. It made a hissing sound like a snake.

"You just stay out of that house like I said. Understand?"

Ray nodded and proceeded to disobey his father for the rest of the summer. Bobby Bonetti was the only kid in the neighborhood who had an Atari, which had been purchased for him by his uncle Tommy. Tommy Bonetti was over at Bobby's house a lot to keep an eye on him when Carla was working, but Ray never told his father that. Somehow, even at eleven, Ray knew that the darkness of which his dad spoke hung on Tommy Bonetti more than anyone.

Ray figured Bobby's uncle was around twenty, maybe. He was dark and skinny like Bobby's mother, with long feathered hair and a neatly trimmed mustache. But he was quiet and never smiled, and his eyes had a way of landing on Ray that made him want to be quiet too. He never said two words to Ray, but still, Ray would make it a point that summer to stop by whenever he saw Tommy's red Camaro parked outside. Being around Tommy made him feel cool, like maybe he was part of a secret club. And when Tommy looked up at him from his sandwich or whatever he was doing and jerked his chin to say hello, Ray would act tough by just jerking his chin back before heading up to Bobby's room to check out what Tommy had brought his nephew.

Tommy was always bringing Bobby stuff: Atari cartridges, records, a color TV for his room once, and paper bags full of quarters to play Space Invaders at the bowling alley. Ray always wished Tommy would hang out with them, but he never did, and he never stuck around long after Carla got home. Then, one day, shortly after sixth grade started, Tommy Bonetti stopped coming around altogether.

Ray asked Bobby why, but Bobby just shrugged sadly and said his uncle had to go away for a while.

A few days later, Ray and Bobby were fishing down at Blackamore Pond with a pole Bobby's uncle had given him for his birthday back in May. The spot was a small patch of shoreline off a trail in the woods, just below a high retaining wall for one of the nicer houses on Shirley Boulevard. Bobby had just caught a decent-sized sunfish when Eddie Sayers and Matt Kauffman showed up.

"Lemme see," Eddie said.

The fish was still dangling from Bobby's line, and as he handed the pole to Eddie, Ray got that tense, heavy feeling in his stomach that he often got when he hung out with Eddie Sayers—not quite fear, not quite excitement, but more like the *should-I-really-do-this?* feeling he got when he waited in line for the roller coaster at Rocky Point. Years later, Ray would always remember Eddie Sayers as if sitting next to him in the front car, just a big faceless grin beneath a red mop of windswept hair. Eddie's voice was high, too, like he was shrieking going down the dip, and he was a fast talker.

Matt Kauffman was the opposite. He had a tentative, almost halting way of speaking, and he moved slowly, as if he hadn't a care in the world, which Ray thought was strange since his father was always looking for an excuse to whack him around.

"You guys wanna see something cool?" Eddie jabbed the fish at the end of Bobby's line with his finger.

The fish twisted and flipped its tail. Bobby shrugged and smiled tentatively with his hands in his pockets, looking like a new kid still unsure of how he fit into things. Ray could tell Bobby didn't want Eddie messing with his fish, but he didn't say anything either when Eddie unhooked it and set it in the dirt. The fish began flopping around, and Eddie gently stepped on it with one foot as he slipped a jackknife from his back pocket.

Bobby's smile wilted, and his brow furrowed beneath his bangs. "Hey, we were gonna throw it back."

Eddie opened his knife and kneeled over the fish. "I know. I ain't gonna kill it."

Eddie held down the fish with one hand and—with no emotion whatsoever, Ray thought—began sawing off its tail. There was a squishy, crunching sound as the blade bit through the bone, then the tail was off. Eddie threw the bloody knife on the ground, snatched up the fish, and ran toward the pond, where he tossed the poor fish in. It made a splash about three feet from shore.

As the surface of the water grew still again, Ray's waiting-in-line-for-the-roller-coaster feeling turned into something sad. Like someone had just hung a sign on the gate saying the ride was closed. The fish was just floating near the muddy bottom, gills beating slowly and little blood tendrils leaking from its stump.

"The hell you do that for?" Bobby asked.

Eddie picked up a stone. "Relax, princess. My cousin told me their tails grow back. I just wanna see how it swims without it."

Eddie chucked the stone at the fish. It made a plopping sound, but the fish only lolled to one side as the ripples swept over it. Ray swallowed hard and swiveled his eyes to Bobby, who just stood there, frowning down at the water.

Matt chuckled. "Must be in shock or something."

Matt Kauffman was a year older than Ray but still went to Eden Park Elementary because his asshole father had held him back in second grade so there would be more of a gap between him and his older brother, Jimmy, coming up in hockey. Ray never understood that, but as with so many things Kent Kauffman did—the whacking, the hockey, the spending his sons' paper route money on booze—Matt seemed to shrug it off as a part of life, just like when Eddie did stupid shit.

Bobby, on the other hand, never did stupid shit when the four of them were together. He hardly even spoke, which was why it took Ray's brain a couple of seconds to catch up with his eyes. He didn't even see Bobby move past him, and in a blink, it seemed, Bobby picked up Eddie's jackknife and tossed it so far out into the pond that Ray barely saw it splash.

"The hell you doing?" Eddie asked, slack-jawed and eyes wide.

Bobby shrugged. There was something in his eyes that Ray had never seen before—something dark and hard and tired.

"You're gonna pay me back for that!" Eddie cried.

"The fuck I am."

Eddie balled his fists, and his freckled cheeks flushed red. He'd used his stocking money for that knife—sent away for it to *Boys' Life,* he'd told Ray, and had waited practically all summer for it to come. And whereas only seconds before, Ray had thought the roller coaster was broken, the car was now back on the tracks and going way too fast. Bobby and Eddie were going to fight, not the pushing and shoving kind of fight, but a *real* fight, where someone took one in the face. Ray looked at Matt, who just stood there, mouth open and eyes darting around uncertainly.

"Oh, I get it," Eddie said, voice tight and lips tense. "Fuckin' degenerate just like that uncle of yours." He nodded at the fishing pole. "He steal that piece a shit like everything else he brung you?"

Bobby just glared at him.

Eddie waved his hand dismissively. "Whole family's a bunch of degenerates. Heard your uncle got picked up for jacking cars. Was all over the papers, my dad said. Whole parts ring he had going. Not anymore, though. Only part Uncle Tommy be getting in jail is a big dick in his—"

Eddie never made it to "ass." One punch, square in the nose, was all it took for Bobby to shut him up. And when it was over, Ray wasn't even sure what had happened, only that Bobby had moved fast, then Eddie was sitting in the dirt, hands cupped over his nose with blood running down into his collar.

"You broke my nose!" Eddie wailed.

Ray could only stare at him in shock. The feeling in his stomach was way different now, all pukey and rising. The car had fallen off the roller coaster, people were screaming, and blood and body parts were flying everywhere.

Ray experienced everything next as a blur, a sudden shift in the light that made the woods, the pond, even the blueness of the sky look darker than before. More tough-guy words were thrown around, then somehow, Ray managed to wedge himself between Bobby and Matt to keep them from going at it too. All that was over pretty quick, then Matt helped Eddie to his feet.

"Traitor!" Eddie spat at Ray, then he and Matt traipsed away through the woods.

But what was left behind, the shift in the light, the darkness, re-mained there at Blackamore Pond long into that winter—and for many winters afterward, Ray Dawley came to understand when he was older.

Even Bobby Bones would agree with him on that.

Chapter Two

Three months after the thing with the fish, on a cold Tuesday morning in December, Bobby Bonetti sat up in his darkened bedroom and flicked on the clock radio his uncle Tommy had given him. A commercial was on for some early Christmas deals at the mall. Yeah, Christmas this year was probably gonna suck. Bobby had seen enough movies about prison to know they didn't let you out to buy your family presents and stuff. But still, it was hard to feel bad about things like that on a snow day.

Bobby was like ninety-nine percent sure it would be a snow day, the first one all year. There had to be at least a foot out there now, and it was *still* snowing. His mother had left the light on out back, and in the tiny square of yard on their side of the duplex, the old picnic table looked like an igloo. Still, like every other kid at Eden Park Elementary, Bobby needed to hear Salty Brine officially announce, "No school, Cranston!" before he would allow himself to start jumping around and shit.

Bobby rolled his eyes as another commercial came on, this one for some new car wash in Warwick. *Who the hell washes their car in December?* Even Uncle Tommy wouldn't expect him to do that. He had asked Bobby to look after his Camaro while he was in jail. He told Bobby not to let it get too dusty and to make sure to run the engine for half an hour every few days. He even said Bobby and Ray could sit in the front and listen to the radio as long as they promised not to fuck around. Bobby figured the car looked like a mountain out there in the driveway under all the snow, but the stairs were creaky, and he didn't want to wake up his mother by going down to the living room to check.

Not that she would be pissed off or anything. She was doing real good since they moved to Cranston. No more chugging Robitussin and not even a whisper about elves in the cellar. Even the scars where she sometimes dug her nails into Bobby's forearms had begun to fade—the bite mark on his ass, too, even though it was kind of hard to tell because he had to stand on a chair and twist around to see it in the bathroom mirror.

Then again, Bobby did miss living downstairs from his grandmother and Uncle Tommy—especially Uncle Tommy. He felt safer knowing he could always crash up there in his sleeping bag if things got really bad. Bobby wasn't sure if his uncle knew about the bite mark, which had only happened that one time last year when his mother had pulled down Bobby's pants to spank him for swearing. "Forgot to take my happy pills," she'd said and promised never to do it again.

"Sixteen before six here on your PRO-FM dial, and it is a mess out there, folks."

Bobby froze. Okay, this was it. First some traffic bullshit then good ol' Salty was off and running. Bobby hardly dared to breathe, not even when he heard "No school, Foster-Glocester!" which Salty didn't even need to say because those lucky bastards always got school cancelled, even when it wasn't really snowing. Scituate, Burrillville, Woonsocket, Smithfield—why couldn't this prick just go alphabetically? Asshole was making him hold his breath like a schmuck. Then boom, Bobby *finally* heard those magic words every kid at Eden Park Elementary was waiting to hear.

"No school, Cranston!"

Bobby screamed into his pillow then quickly dressed and was downstairs in the living room before he could say, "Suck my balls, Eddie Sayers!" Dumbass had told everyone at school yesterday that the weathermen didn't know shit and it would probably be just a few flurries. Prick wouldn't have lasted five seconds at Bobby's old school in Providence with that mouth. After the thing with the fish, it had taken less than a week for them all to start hanging out again, but still, that none of the other kids at school found out was a miracle, what with Eddie always trying to sound like a tough guy.

Bobby drew back the front window curtain. Plows hadn't come by for hours—the mounds under the streetlights were all wavy looking and smooth. But they were pretty big, which meant shoveling out his driveway would take forever. That sucked, but at least Ray would help him. He told Bobby yesterday at lunch that he didn't have to shovel his own driveway because his father had a snowblower, which meant he could be down at Bobby's as soon as it was light. Good ol' Ray.

After a blur of Cream of Wheat and layering up, Bobby sat by the front window, sweating his balls off for what seemed like forever until he saw his best friend coming down the street with a shovel propped on his shoulder. In the still-steadily falling snow, Ray was just a smudge at first, but as he got closer, Bobby could see that the snow in the street was above his ankles. The whole thing was like a dream come true. Bobby squeezed out his front door and was knee-deep in snow a second later.

"S'up, Ray."

"S'up, Bobby."

Ray was bundled up from head to toe and had on a Boston Bruins hat that was also a ski mask. Bobby thought it made him look like a bank robber. Pretty cool, but Bobby liked the hunter's cap he was wearing better. His nana Mary had given it to him a couple of years back, saying it had belonged to Bobby's grandfather, who had died before Bobby was born. The cap was super warm because it was lined with fur and had earflaps he could pull down and tie under his chin if he wanted. Sometimes, when his mother was at work, Bobby would wear the cap inside and pull down the flaps and pretend that his grandfather was talking to him from heaven. He would tell Bobby how proud of him he was and how he wished they could have hung out and stuff before he died. But Bobby was already way too hot from waiting to wear the earflaps.

After only ten minutes of shoveling, Ray stuck his shovel in the snow and rolled the ski mask up onto his forehead. His cheeks were all red and blotchy, and his lips were blue. "My dad thinks we're idiots for starting before the snow stops, but I told him it's better to get paid once and shovel twice than to let Eddie and Matt move in on our territory."

"You tell your old man to go fuck himself too?"

Ray laughed. "Every day."

Hanging out with Ray was fun because he could take getting his balls busted and went along with Bobby's ideas for doing stuff just as much as coming up with his own. He was really good at keeping secrets too. A couple of months back, when Bobby was sleeping over, he told Ray about the time when his mother almost threw him down the cellar stairs. He could tell Ray felt bad, but Bobby made him promise not to say anything—they even spit in their palms and shook on it. Man, having a friend like Ray was almost as good as having a brother, maybe even better, since brothers, especially older ones like Jimmy Kauffman, could be real douchebags sometimes.

Bobby hated that prick. Jimmy Kauffman was in the ninth grade but still not above giving his brother, Matt, and his friends wedgies and shit now and then. Jimmy and his friend Chuck Finola had caught Bobby only once so far, not long after he moved in, as a sort of welcome to the neighborhood, Ray had said. They didn't have to worry about Jimmy and Chuck today, though. The older kids didn't bother shoveling anymore, and their only competition was Matt and Eddie.

Ray had broken everything down for Bobby during lunch the day before at school. Matt and Eddie had two houses, and Ray had three. They all basically charged five bucks a house, but Matt and Eddie got ten for doing Mrs. Chabot's because her back patio was so big. Ray admitted that he had felt kind of sad when he found out Eddie and Matt had started shoveling without him last year, but in the end, it all worked out because Ray found his own houses and ended up making more than twice what those assholes made because Mrs. Ruggieri paid him double and he didn't have to split it with anyone.

"Yeah, but if I shovel with you, you'll make way less," Bobby had said.

Ray had just shrugged and went on eating his shepherd's pie. Good ol' Ray.

Bobby figured the two of them were a lot alike when it came to showing a guy he was your best friend without really having to say it. Ray even gave Bobby his drawings without him having to ask, the most recent being Farrah Fawcett from this picture he'd copied from *Tiger Beat*. Ray was the best drawer Bobby had ever seen. He'd even gotten Farrah's tits right and everything.

By the time Bobby and Ray had finished the Bonettis' driveway, it had stopped snowing, and Bobby's mother insisted they have some hot chocolate before they headed out for the day. The rest of that morning was a blur of steamy breath and tired muscles, of sweat trickling down their backs and tossing around ideas of how to spend their money, which ended up being ten dollars each. Bobby felt guilty for taking half of Ray's haul, but Ray insisted, saying it was still more than Matt and Eddie made.

After they finished with Mrs. Ruggieri's, Ray's mother fixed them some grilled cheeses and tomato soup for lunch. Then the boys were outside again, where they ran into Matt Kauffman and Eddie Sayers, who was dragging the toboggan he had gotten for Christmas last year down the street.

"Just in time, ladies," Eddie said. "We're heading down to Black-amore, if you wanna come. The hill there is prime."

"Pond's frozen solid," Matt said. "Jimmy and his friends cleared away a big patch of snow near the shore to play hockey before some asshole cop came by and told them to screw."

"They're shoveling their asses off over at Aqueduct now," Eddie said, "so we'll have the whole place to ourselves."

Bobby exchanged an uneasy glance with Ray. Not more than fifteen minutes ago, Ray's mom had told them not to fuck around at the pond. There were springs or something there that bubbled up and made it so the ice was unsafe, especially with all the snow on top. "Some kid drowned in there a few years back trying to walk across," she'd said, "so you boys stay away, understand?"

When Ray told this to the other guys, Eddie rolled his eyes and scoffed. "It's not like we're gonna be sledding far onto the ice. And even if it breaks, which it won't, it's no worse than if you fell through at Aqueduct Field. Besides, if some kid drowned down there, what's his name? Where's the memorial to him?"

Bobby thought that was a good point, but still, he didn't like risking it when they could just walk over to Aqueduct Field and go sledding with everyone else. Yeah, it was a bit of a hike, and the hill there was for babies, and there was a good chance Jimmy Kauffman and those other assholes would hassle them some. But still, Bobby would rather hang out anywhere other than Blackamore Pond. All he could think about when he passed it was that poor fish Eddie had killed back in September. Well, Bobby was only half sure Eddie had killed it because after everyone left that day, he didn't see the fish anywhere. Probably died farther out from shore, he figured, lonely and for no reason.

"You don't even have to go on the ice at all if you don't want," Eddie said. "But hey, pussies will be pussies."

Bobby looked at Ray again, who just shrugged, then the four of them headed off together. Even with the plows, there was still at least a good inch of hardpack on the street, and Bobby almost suggested sledding down the hilly part at the bottom of Lexington instead. But for some reason, he just kept quiet like always when Matt and Eddie were around, and soon, they had looped over onto Blackamore Avenue, climbed over the guardrail, and were standing in the woods at the top of the hill.

The hill was about thirty yards long, steeper near the top then flattening out for the last third in a little beach area. As far as the ice went, Jimmy Kauffman and his crew hadn't gotten very far. They'd only cleared a patch of maybe ten by ten, beyond which the snow blanketed the pond so seamlessly that Bobby couldn't tell where the water ended and the land began. The sky was still gray, and because of all the snow and the fog on the opposite shore, he could hardly make out any trees over there and only a handful of lights from Reservoir Avenue at the top of the embankment.

Eddie bounded down along the side of the slope so as not to ding up the run then began stomping around on the ice. "Totally safe!" he called up to the others. Eddie hurried back up to the top again and snatched the toboggan from Matt. "Watch how it's done, pussies."

Eddie threw the toboggan out in front of him and dove onto it. He flew headfirst down the hill on his stomach, whooping and hollering the whole way, until he reached the ice, where he twisted the toboggan and skidded sideways to a stop just before he hit the snowline. Eddie stood up with a shit-eating grin, flipped everyone the bird, then began heading back up the side of the run, dragging the toboggan behind him.

"Those assholes did us a favor for once." Matt nodded at the ice. "That ridge of snow will stop you from going too far out."

Bobby and Ray smiled at each other, and by the time Eddie had joined them again, Bobby didn't feel anxious at all about what they were doing.

"You like that slide technique?" Eddie asked breathlessly as he handed Matt the toboggan.

Matt said something about sliding into Eddie's mother then was down the slope and on the ice, where he twisted a bit too late and ended up crashing into the snowline so hard that the toboggan slid out from under him.

Eddie howled with laughter. "You gotta twist right *before* you hit the ice!" he called down.

Matt just ignored him and trudged back up the slope. "Who's next?" he asked, his eyes swiveling between Bobby and Ray.

Ray nodded for Bobby to take the toboggan. Just as Bobby was about to jump on, Eddie reiterated his advice about twisting before he hit the ice.

"Like this." Eddie demonstrated by throwing out his hip. "That way, you won't fuck it up like dumbass here."

"Just let him do it," Matt muttered.

Eddie chuckled, and a moment later, Bobby was speeding down the slope on his stomach. He twisted the toboggan near the bottom like Eddie said, but it must have been too soon because he hit a bump and went flying off. For a second or two, Bobby seemed to be floating in space, then he hit the ice, and the whiteness of the world exploded into stars. He had a sense of everything blinking out, then the stars were fireflies, dancing and dissolving in a ring of darkness around Ray's face looking down at him.

"Jesus, you okay?" Ray asked, eyes wide and steamy breath pluming from his mouth.

Then Bobby felt the pain, sharp and pounding like a fist behind his eyes. He raised a glove to his forehead and muttered that he'd turned too early. A minute later, he sat up with Ray at his side. The world was all white again with only a handful of regular flies buzzing around, then the other guys were there too. Matt looked scared like Ray, but Eddie looked pissed off—or happy. Bobby couldn't tell.

"The hell you doing?" Eddie asked. "Why didn't you turn like I told you?"

"Shut up, Eddie," Ray said. "He hit his head. Blacked out, I think. You sure you're okay, man?"

Bobby touched his forehead again. Even through his glove, he could feel the knot forming above his right eye, just below his hairline, where his head had taken the brunt of the impact.

"It's not my fault." Eddie sounded more scared than pissed off now. "You guys heard me, right? I told him how to do it, how to twist just before you hit—"

"I'm okay," Bobby said, standing up. The pain had tapered off to a dull ache in the back of his head, and not a single firefly was dancing anywhere.

There was a bit more back-and-forth among the guys, including Matt asking Bobby to recite his address and phone number—which he had seen some guy do in a movie once, he explained—then Ray handed Bobby his hunter's cap. In all the commotion, Bobby hadn't realized it had fallen off.

"Better than a helmet, that thing," Ray said. "Next run, I'd keep it tied, though."

Bobby nodded, but as soon as Eddie and Matt started back up the slope, he began to feel really stupid. And scared. Like so scared he could almost cry.

Once the others were out of earshot, Ray leaned closer and whispered, "We can take off, if you want. I'm kinda sick of this already."

Bobby shook his head. The last thing he wanted was for Eddie to think they were pussying out.

As if on cue, Eddie called down, "Come on, you pussies!"

"Go ahead." Bobby slipped his cap back on his head. "I just need to catch my breath."

Ray held Bobby's eyes a moment longer then started up the slope. Good ol' Ray. The stupid-scared-crying feeling was not as bad with him around. But just as Bobby was about to head off after him, he spotted something white moving near his feet. At first, he thought it was an old sneaker frozen beneath the ice, but when he looked closer, the sneaker solidified into a fish unlike any he had ever seen—a fish so white it practically glowed. It had long flowy fins like an angel's wings, and its big black eyes and pulsing O for a mouth remained sharp while the rest of it fluctuated in clarity, as if dissolving, receding, and coming back into focus all at once.

Bobby's eyes darted back to Ray, who was halfway up the slope, then back to the fish, which leveled off and began moving under his feet. Bobby spun around, and as the fish swam away from him, he noticed that its tail was missing. A warm, tingling rush of joy bubbled up inside him, and he began to run after it. As with so many things, Eddie Sayers had been wrong. The fish's tail had never grown back, and that dumbass hadn't killed it after all.

But is it really Eddie's fish? It had to be. How many fish could there be swimming around Blackamore Pond with their tails cut off? But this fish was white and seemed to be getting brighter the farther away it swam, which was impossible. A normal fish couldn't glow like that. Unless it was a ghost.

So cool. Bobby ran faster. He was seeing the ghost of Eddie's fish. And instead of blood streaming out the back of it, there was a trail of blue sparkles. Bobby could see them shimmering and dissolving beneath the ice just as clearly as he'd seen the fireflies minutes earlier. But still, even if the fish were a ghost, how could he see it beneath the snow?

Crack!

In a split second of whirling white terror, Robert Bonetti realized that he had ventured out onto the ice way too far. The snow was up to his knees, and he was dimly aware of Ray and the other guys screaming at him to come back. But before he could turn around, the world opened wide and swallowed him whole.

Chapter Three

Eddie's first thought when he saw Bobby running out onto the ice was that if he fell through and drowned, Eddie would be blamed for it and go to jail. His second thought, almost right on top of the first, was simply to run away. But for some reason, he just stood there at the top of the slope, half confused, half in awe, as a third thought blocked out everything else. He wanted to see if the ice would hold.

The other guys must have followed Eddie's gaze because, all at once, they started yelling at Bobby to come back. But Bobby wouldn't listen. He just kept plowing through the snow, then *crack*, he was gone.

Everything that came next happened very fast. Eddie bounded down the hill, then he was out on the ice, dragging along his toboggan with Matt a few yards ahead and Ray Dawley out front. *Ray Dawley*, the biggest pussy of them all, at least when it came to climbing trees or going all the way to the end inside the big drainpipe on the other side of the pond. But there he was, leading the way then crawling on his stomach like some Army guy in the movies.

"I see him! Hang on. I'm coming, Bobby!"

Matt got down on his stomach, too, and took hold of Ray's ankles. Eddie was still too far away to grab Matt's. He had frozen in his tracks a yard or two over the snowline. When Matt, his eyes all panicky, whirled around and screamed for Eddie to hurry, a sickening groan emanated from somewhere deep inside him, and Eddie dropped to his hands and knees and began crawling toward the others. His muscles felt unresponsive and heavy, his lungs so tight that he could hardly breathe.

Choking and splashing sounds came from ahead, and Eddie spotted a thin crescent of black water just beyond Ray's Boston Bruins cap. Then one of Bobby's gloves shot up in a spray of ice and snow.

"Come on. Hurry!" Matt cried.

Eddie lurched forward and grabbed Matt's ankles. Matt was on his stomach, holding Ray's ankles. Ray was on his knees, struggling to hang on to Bobby's arm. With a barbaric cry, Ray heaved Bobby out of the water and onto the ice.

Seconds later, the three of them were on their feet again, panting and grunting and dragging Bobby away from the hole. His water-logged clothes made him feel ten times as heavy, and by the time they reached the toboggan, Eddie's arms and legs were so tired, he could barely feel them. He held the toboggan steady while the other guys rolled Bobby onto it. Eddie figured Bobby was still alive because he was shivering, but his eyes just stared vacantly at the sky. His skin was blue, and he wasn't saying anything.

Eddie snatched in a breath that felt like needles, and he dragged his sleeve under his nose. He was crying, he realized, but then some old guy in a fedora started yelling at them from atop the hill, and he snapped out of it. Someone must have called 911, too, because it seemed as soon as they dragged Bobby back to shore, the cops and rescue guys were there, wrapping him in blankets. The rest of the neighborhood showed up a short time later, and the rescue guys loaded Bobby into the ambulance on a stretcher.

Eddie could only imagine how the whole scene must have looked to them, what with their tracks leading out to that black hole in the middle of the ice. But none of the parents, not even Eddie's mother, yelled at them before Carla Bonetti disappeared with Bobby into the back of the ambulance. He was still shivering, but at some point, had started blinking and mumbling too.

"He's in shock," one of the rescue guys said. "Gonna be okay. The hell were you guys thinking? Don't you know that ice isn't safe?"

Eddie just shrugged, looked down at his snow boots, and begged himself not to cry again. Then the cops sat the three of them down on the guardrail and started questioning them.

"We didn't wanna go out on the ice, sir," Ray said, and Eddie instantly felt a little better because he could tell that Ray was trying not to cry too. "We were sledding is all. I swear. But then Bobby fell off and hit his head. He said he was okay, but he must not have been, really, because he started running off in the wrong direction."

Eddie wanted to speak up and tell the cops how Bobby didn't listen about twisting and how Bobby kept running even after everyone screamed at him to come back.

"I saw the whole thing," the old guy with the fedora chimed in. "Boy just took off across the ice like he had a death wish. These three here are heroes, I tell you. Bona fide heroes."

Bona fide heroes. The old guy in the fedora first coined it, but it was a reporter from the *Providence Journal* who wrote it down. He called Eddie after supper that night. "Your friend's going to be okay," he said. "Hypothermia, still in the hospital for observation, but he's talking now and real grateful for you guys. He's having a hard time remembering things, so can you tell me again what happened, son?"

Eddie felt sort of numb. He'd told his story at least a dozen times and didn't need some reporter to fill him in on how Bobby was doing. He had been standing right there by the phone earlier when his mother was talking to Mrs. Kauffman, who had gotten the scoop from Mrs. Dawley, the only mom in the bunch who was friends with Bobby's mother. "Crazy Carla," Janet Sayers always called her, to which Eddie would just nod and pretend to smile even when his mother wasn't looking. He figured it was good practice for when his mother *was* looking and he needed to hide what was happening between his legs.

Sometimes, just the mere mention of Carla Bonetti's name would give Edward Sayers a woody—and not just because of that article his cousin Billy had shown him in *Penthouse Forum* about the Italian mafia wife who'd seduced the luckiest pizza delivery boy on the planet. Nah, even before that, Eddie'd had it bad for Carla Bonetti. She was younger and prettier than all the other moms. Eddie especially loved the way her hair fell on her collar bones and how the veins stood out on her neck when she was looking away from him. But when she looked back—eyes smiling, lips full and red and stretched wide over those pearly whites—that really sent him over the edge. Sometimes, when he was lying in bed, doing the thing Billy had taught him that summer, all he had to do was think about those lips between his legs, and he would blow his load, after which, he would just lie there in the dark with a sad, achy feeling in his stomach. A feeling of wanting to put his arm around Carla and feel her head and the softness of her hair on his chest. Eddie had never been close enough to smell those long black ringlets, but for some reason, he thought of lemons—a clean and perfect smell.

His achy, wanting feeling for Carla Bonetti was never worse than that night after the thing on the ice, so bad it made Eddie cry. And not just because of what he overheard his mother telling his father, who was stuck in Boston at some real estate convention because of the storm.

"Don't worry, Rick," Eddie's mom had said on the phone. "Ol' Janet's holding down the fort. Pamela is sleeping over at Lisa's, and Eddie's already in bed. Hardly touched his supper. Still in shock, I guess. You'd be real proud of him, Ricky. That Bonetti kid would've drowned. Crazy, I'm telling you, just like his mother."

"Crazy, my ass," Eddie told Carla in his mind. "She's just jealous of you, baby." Carla's hair tickled Eddie's nose as she snuggled into him. "You want to see crazy, maybe I should tell ol' Janet what I overheard Dad saying not long after you moved in—that time when ol' Ricky boy was watering the lawn and Kent Kauffman showed up."

Eddie had been reading a comic book on his bed when the sound of the men's voices and the pops of beer tabs drew him to his window. Kent Kauffman stood on the sidewalk, unshaven, hair tousled, half a six-pack dangling by his side, and his gut peeking out from under his wifebeater. Totally the opposite of Eddie's four-eyed penny-loafer father.

"Gail kick you out again, Kent?" he asked.

"Yep. Was thinking of heading down the street. You see that number who moved in with her kid? Single and ready to mingle, looks to me."

"Might join you. Those Silver Lake bitches like to suck it, I hear."

The men laughed and started talking about the Red Sox, but Eddie sat there for a long time after they parted ways, trying to decide who was the bigger slime, Kent Kauffman or his father. Eddie finally settled on Kent Kauffman, who had shown up at Blackamore Pond with the rest of the neighborhood, half in the bag and wearing the same dirty wifebeater under his Army jacket. Fucking slime, all right. Eddie had seen the way Kent looked at Carla when she was climbing up into the ambulance, how his eyes crawled over her ass to the bare parts of her legs between her coat and snow boots.

But from what Eddie could tell, Carla had eyes only for him, eyes that were red and sad and betrayed. She gave him a fleeting glance just before the ambulance doors closed, one that said, *I could have loved you, Eddie, but now...*

Did Carla know that Eddie froze up? Did she think him a coward because he was the last one out on the ice? Or maybe, just maybe, she assumed Eddie was the one who put Bobby up to it, especially if Bobby ever told her about the fish thing and what he'd said about his uncle Tommy. Eddie hoped to Christ that Bobby hadn't. He felt guilty about the fish now—why was he always doing stupid shit like that?—and Bobby had had every right for clocking him one. Fucking mouth, always getting him into trouble.

Still, he wanted to tell her how sorry he was, not just for what he'd said about Tommy but for what everyone else in the neighborhood said about her too. They didn't understand her like he did, which was why Eddie had swiped her panties that one time when the other guys were playing Atari in Bobby's room.

Eddie had ducked out to take a leak and, on a whim, peeked into the hamper in the bathroom. The panties were right there on top, almost like they were begging Eddie to take them. He stuffed them down his shorts and kept them nestled in his crotch until he could be alone with them in the bathroom. They didn't smell like lemons, just a little like sweat. Eddie did the thing Billy taught him right into Carla's panties. It nearly killed him having to get rid of them, but ol' Janet was a first-class snoop, so it was a good thing the panties didn't clog the toilet when Eddie flushed them.

Eddie never thought about stealing Carla's panties again, but in the days following the thing on the ice, he thought about her more than ever, it seemed—especially at Bobby's homecoming. Everyone made a big deal about it. And even though Eddie and the other guys were grounded, their parents let them attend his party. There, Eddie was introduced to a bunch of Bobby's relatives, and some newspaper guy took the boys' picture standing around Bobby in his bed. Bobby's body temperature was back to normal, but he'd been diagnosed with a mild concussion, which was why he couldn't remember anything. Eddie felt sort of queasy looking at him. The bruise on Bobby's forehead was all jagged and black like the hole in the ice.

With everyone around, Eddie didn't get to talk much with Bobby, and Carla didn't say much to Eddie, either, except for how grateful she was that her son had such good friends, and that was mainly when she was talking to other people while doling out the coffee and pastries. Eddie wanted to go to her, to tell her that he would have been the first in line out there on the ice had he been thinking clearly. He was certain Carla would take his face in her hands and kiss his cheeks so hard that she left red marks. Then at some point, when they found themselves alone in the kitchen, Carla would tell Eddie to come by later after everyone was gone and Bobby was asleep. They would have soda and some cheese and crackers and listen to the 5th Dimension album Eddie knew she had, the one with "If I Could Reach You" that Eddie's mother had too. Eddie would confess he sometimes listened to the song under the dining room table while dreaming of him and Carla slow dancing. Carla, moved to tears by the depth of Eddie's affection, would put her hand on his cheek and kiss him softly, her lips sweet like lemonade.

But none of that happened, and Eddie didn't say shit, not even when that slime Kent Kauffman put his arm around Carla and said, "Hey, if there's anything you need."

Eddie both wanted to kill the bastard and admired the hell out of him for that. Scumbag had even shaved and combed his hair for the occasion. Thankfully, Kent left with his wife and Eddie's mother after about ten minutes, the ladies gossiping all the way up Lexington Avenue, no doubt, while poor Kent lagged behind, sucking on his Marlboros and wishing he could put a bullet in the backs of their heads.

Or was Eddie the one wishing all that? Sometimes, but usually only when ol' Janet tuned his ass with his father's belt because his grades sucked or because he left the milk out on the counter. Or when ol' Ricky boy called him a retard and said that he wouldn't hire him at the agency if he was the last man on Earth. And he couldn't forget ol' Pammy girl, Eddie's horse-faced older sister who was presently blackmailing him into doing her laundry because she caught him doing the thing Billy taught him in the bathroom on Thanksgiving.

Oh yeah, Eddie had a special bullet for each of them someday. But on the afternoon of Bobby's homecoming, there were only thoughts of Carla Bonetti coupled with a weird, exhausted feeling of trying to hide it and act normal. Even Ray, who was Bobby's best friend out of the three of them, didn't seem to know how to act. And not long after the streetlights came on, the living room got too crowded, and Eddie found himself outside leaning against some cars with Matt and Ray. They hadn't really talked about what'd happened, and Eddie wondered what the other guys thought.

After a long silence of them just standing there with the party sounds getting louder and softer, louder and softer, Ray said, "Glad he's gonna be okay." He looked up at the second-floor window, which was for Carla's bedroom, not Bobby's.

"Yeah, me too," Matt said. "Dumbass scared the shit outa me."

Ray shook his head. "Must be messed up, not being able to remember what happened."

Matt shrugged. "Lucky him."

"Sorry I froze up and started crying," Eddie threw in. The words slipped out before he even realized he was speaking.

When he looked up at his friends again, their mouths were open, and their eyes were staring back at him all buggy. There was a second when Eddie got that *Oh shit* feeling, like when he knocked over a picture or something in the living room because Pam was chasing him.

Then Matt blinked as if he were coming out of a daze. "You serious? Kid woulda dragged us all in if not for you."

"No shit," Ray said. "Like the anchor in a tug of war. Eddie the anchor."

Eddie let out a shaky breath that sounded like he was both laughing and crying at the same time. He probably would've started full-out bawling again, too, had Ray's father not come out and motioned with his finger to Ray that it was time to go.

The three boys were still grounded the next day, so Eddie didn't see Ray and Matt again until Friday morning, when school started up again. They had a big assembly where some cop gave them each a junior police medal after bitching everybody out about winter safety and shit. The story about the ice and the picture of them all standing around Bobby's bed came out that evening in the *Providence Journal*. "Snow Day Saviors," the article was called.

The following Monday, Bobby returned to school. The bruise on his forehead was smaller and all yellowy around the edges, but everyone treated him the same as always, maybe a little better.

Eddie, on the other hand, wasn't sure how to act around him, and not just because of the thing on the ice and the way Carla had looked at him from the ambulance. Something inside Eddie Sayers had changed. He had never given two shits about Bobby Bonetti when Bobby lived in Providence and used to visit Ray. But after Bobby moved in down the street, Eddie always got this gnawing, burning feeling in his stomach whenever he came around. Eddie never hated Bobby, though. Even after Bobby chucked his jackknife out into the pond and bloodied his nose, Eddie kept waiting for a bullet with Bobby's name on it to appear in his head next to the ones he always imagined for his family. But it never did. And not until Bobby returned to school did Eddie begin to understand why.

Everyone was out at recess, and Eddie was standing alone by the fence, watching Matt and the other guys running and sliding down this stretch of ice that always formed beneath the cafeteria windows. Eddie usually loved recess during the winters, especially when there was snow and the teachers would let the kids get away with anything. But today, it was as if the cold, lonely grayness of the sky had poured down into his body, and all he could think of was being with Carla and listening to the 5th Dimension.

"They don't come back," Bobby said, his eyes glaring at Eddie from under his hunter's cap.

Startled, Eddie blinked back at him, confused. He had no idea how long Bobby'd been standing there.

"Fish tails," Bobby said. "They don't come back when you cut them off."

His lips curled back over his teeth in a smile that made Eddie's insides shrivel. He could see it in Bobby's eyes, the black and soulless hole in the ice that had always been there. *That* was why Eddie could never bring himself to hate Bobby Bonetti—because to hate someone, a guy had to be brave and risk the other guy hating him back. And Bobby Bonetti was much too dangerous for that.

Eddie somehow knew this even at eleven. And just like his second thought that day on the ice, all he could think about was running—this time to Carla Bonetti, whom he would whisk away to his bedroom, sheltering her there forever from the darkness that had found her son that day in Blackamore Pond.

Part II: The Liars' Club

Chapter Four

The two things Shelly Kauffman would remember about the night her husband was murdered were the Bunnymen and the buoy. The latter had tolled in the distance like a church bell, but the day after, in the psych ward of the Newport Hospital, the fifty-five-year-old widow would tell the nurses it was the Bunnymen who summoned Matt Kauffman to his doom, luring him away with lips like sugar beneath a killing moon.

Echo and the Bunnymen, an 80s band whose songs "Lips Like Sugar" and "Killing Moon" bookended a Spotify playlist that Matt had made specifically for their trip—the Cure, the Smiths, and a bunch of other bands from their college courtship four decades earlier. Dear Matthew. They were in Rhode Island for his brother Jimmy's funeral, and he still made an effort to be romantic. Even booked them a room in a bed-and-breakfast in Newport—quaint, Victorian, with a fireplace and antique furnishings. Just perfect, and so close to the harbor that they could practically spit on the Goat Island lighthouse from their third-floor window.

Still naked under her bathrobe, Shelly stood gazing out at the lights, the smell of bleach mixing with her husband's Bleu de Chanel as he pressed himself against her from behind. The room was hot, and the window was cracked open—the frigid December air popping her stomach into gooseflesh as Matt slipped his hand under her robe and twirled his finger around her nipple. Shelly shivered. She was still tender from their lovemaking, during which Matt had reached around and pinched her nipples so hard that Shelly had screamed into her pillow. The memory of him like that—her hair twisted in his fist, the slap of his thighs as he pounded away at her from behind—instantly made her wet again, and she rocked her hips back into the hardness she could feel growing again in his jeans. Their lovemaking had been so unexpected and yet long overdue, animallike in its abandon but somehow forbidden amid the somber lipstick traces on Matt's face—funeral kisses from relatives whose names Shelly had already forgotten.

But Matt's kisses had hardly been somber when they got back to their room—hungry and fumbling at first like in college, then confident and deliciously demanding like the young lover he had become by their honeymoon. She could not remember the last time she'd felt such an uncontrollable desire from him. Even before the kids, they had fallen into an *Everybody Loves Raymond* kind of sex—tired, predictable, and barely able to be squeezed in with work and all the other crap going on. But when Shelly and Matt climaxed together during the opening chords of "Killing Moon," for a fleeting moment, she swore she was back in her dorm room at UNH.

Matthew Kauffman. The third and last lover Shelly Boyle had ever known. Her soulmate, and now her time traveler. And as he lay there on top of her, back in the present with his love spent and his breath heavy in her ear, Shelly hoped that he understood, hoped that he remembered why, against all odds, they had made it work through all the bullshit that came with two children and nearly thirty years of marriage. Their love was alive again. Shelly could feel it—watered and taking root in the same soil with which they had buried Matt's brother, Jimmy, only hours earlier.

James Kauffman, professional alcoholic and first-class asshole, was finally dead just shy of sixty. Acute alcohol poisoning was the official ruling, but Shelly suspected it was really hatred that had eaten away at him from the inside. Despite his father's dreams, Jimmy had never made the NHL—he'd been plagued by a pair of knee injuries at Quinnipiac and began self-medicating. He'd flunked out during his junior year, and after a failed stint in the minors, wound up working at Electric Boat with his father. Divorced three times, with a son presently serving five years for B and E and a daughter who, last Shelly had heard, had traded her needle for methadone and a bagful of backhands from some mafia clown.

Good riddance to the whole clan, Shelly thought. And thank God her mother-in-law wasn't around to see what model citizens her grandchildren had become. Poor Gail. From the moment they met—Thanksgiving break, 1988—Gail had always held a special place in Shelly's heart. Something so sad and yet so grounded in those tired and lonely eyes, even in the days before the brain cancer finally closed them for good.

As for her father-in-law, Kent, Shelly's hatred of him began on that same Thanksgiving Day, when after one too many Dewars, Kent started laying into Matt about his poor performance in UNH's first home game versus BU. Worst was when Matt broke his leg skiing senior year, after which Kent didn't speak to him for months because he'd blown his shot at the minors. That had been the nail in the coffin for son number two—just said fuck it to the whole hockey dream, took a job at Credit Suisse, and moved to New York City to be closer to Shelly's family.

And that should have been the beginning of a long journey of self-reflection for Kent Kauffman, but much like his son Jimmy, the bitterness only seemed to eat away at him from the inside. Things eventually smoothed over enough for Kent to attend Matt and Shelly's wedding, but the peace would last only a few years. It all came to a head on Christmas Eve, when old Kent, who was partying like it was 1999 (which it just so happened to be, by the way), finally told Shelly what he really thought of her.

"Fuckin' A, Shell," he slurred from the kitchen doorway as Shelly helped her mother-in-law take down the plates for dessert. "All that work I done, and that prick throws it away for a suit and a suburb down in Jersey. I swear, that snatch of yours must be magical. Like a slot machine shooting out gold coins when you cream."

That was the last time Shelly ever saw Kent Kauffman alive—laughing it up and screaming that he was just kidding after Matt threw him on the couch and Jimmy had to pry him off. The next time Shelly returned to Rhode Island was in the early 2000s to visit Gail when she got sick. Seven months later, it was her funeral. As for old Kent, he would drop dead of a heart attack in the frozen foods aisle at Shaw's ten years to the day after his wife. It was then that Shelly began to notice a change in Matt—just a glimmer at first, but growing in intensity these last few years like a light fast approaching in a tunnel.

It started with the nightmares. Over the years, Shelly had lost track of how many times Matt had woken her up in the middle of the night moaning, "*I'm sorry, I'm sorry!*" before Shelly shook him awake. "It's all my fault," he would mutter, still half asleep, to which Shelly would respond with some version of "No, it's not, you guys were heroes. Go back to sleep." She knew to say this because, at some point, Matt had told her that his nightmares were about the whole "Snow Day Saviors" thing. Shelly encouraged him to see a therapist, but he didn't want to hear it and would actually snap if she pressed him too much. And so Shelly endured their marriage with a nagging anxiety that, someday, her husband would opt to jump in front of his train at Penn Station instead of taking it home.

But all of that, the nightmares and Shelly's worries, seemed to evaporate on the very day Kent Kauffman died—as if, to make up for all his bullshit, old Kent switched off a light in Matt's head before exiting the building for good. Then came the other things—little things, that only a wife would notice. A lightness in his voice, fewer curse words when they were stuck in traffic, the sing-alongs with their kids' shitty music. Then, Shelly began to notice the bounce in his step, the sparkle in his eye, and a spontaneity that hadn't been there since college; the weekend in Vermont after they dropped off Jenny at Bennington; surprising Matt Junior with Celtics tickets during his first year at BU; flowers, chocolates, jewelry, a butt plug once as a joke; all of it coming faster and faster down the tunnel until today, when they made love as if it were the end of the world.

But it wasn't the end, it was the beginning. And now that Jimmy Kauffman was dead, Shelly and her husband were out of the tunnel and into the light for good. The past was gone, buried six feet under with a man who'd called Shelly a cunt and took a swing at her husband ten years ago. Kent's funeral was the last time they had seen Jimmy Kauffman alive. But now, Shelly and Matt never had to see the son of a bitch again—never had to come back to Rhode Island either. They were finally free.

Well, *almost.*

"I'll be back by eleven, I promise," Matt said, rubbing his hardness against Shelly's ass. "You rest up for round two, okay?"

Shelly rocked her hips back into him, and Matt cupped her breast in one hand and slid the other down to her groin, where he traced his finger back and forth across the top of her pubic line.

"Tease," Shelly said, and the buoy went *ding-ding* in the distance.

"For whom the bell tolls," Matthew said, nibbling her ear. "Shakespeare, right?"

"John Donne, you dumbass."

Matt laughed, gave her neck a quick peck, and moved over to the nightstand, where he slipped on his watch. In the streetlight from outside, he could have been twenty again—slim, fit, his hair still as full as the first time they drove down to Rhode Island from New Hampshire. *This* time, however, they had driven up from New Jersey. Checked in at 3 p.m. the previous day and still had enough time to do some shopping before taking in a late dinner at the White Horse Tavern, which for years, had been on Matt's bucket list. The light. The spontaneity...

"And it'll be just the three of you tonight?" Shelly sat down at the edge of the bed. The sheets were on the floor, and as Shelly pulled them up over her legs, the musty odor of their sex wafted up at her and made her sad—like back in college, when she harbored that secret childish fear that she would never see Matthew Kauffman again after they made love. *Christ, almost thirty years of marriage, Shelly, get a grip.*

Matt shrugged and, moving to the coat rack, blended into the shadows there as he slipped on his heavy woolen coat. "Yeah, Ray said he hasn't talked to Bobby since he moved back. I was surprised not to see him today, but it is what it is."

Shelly smiled. "It is what it is" was to her husband what "To be, or not to be" was to Hamlet. But Shelly found no humor in it. She was simply grateful that Matt would not be seeing Bobby Bonetti this trip. One more thread severed from the past.

"Be back before you know it." Matthew opened the door, and a shaft of light fell across the bed. "Don't get dressed."

Shelly giggled. "Wasn't planning on it."

They exchanged "I love you"s, then Shelly was alone in the dark. She lay back on the bed and let her bathrobe fall open. Her flesh looked almost silver in the streetlight—and damn good for fifty-five and pumping out two kids. But soon her eyes drifted up to the patch of darkness at the ceiling, and her thoughts to Bobby Bonetti.

In the near forty years she and Matt had been together, Shelly had only met his childhood friend a total of four times—once at their wedding, once at Eddie's, then two more times at the funerals for Matt's parents. But Bobby Bonetti had behaved the same way at all of them—polite, soft-spoken, but somewhat somber. Shelly thought him handsome in a Keanu Reeves-ish sort of way. Sad blue eyes, full head of longish black hair. A little on the short side, but still, the strong, silent type she might have pegged him as had he not been the stuff of Matt's nightmares.

The stuff of nightmares. That was how Shelly thought of Bobby Bonetti, but Matt truly seemed not to care and would just dismiss his wife when she asked about him. Usually, it went something like: "I don't know much about him anymore. He was working as a corrections officer at the training school, last I heard. Honestly, we never really talked after eighth grade, when his mother got sick and he moved back to Providence."

"Why did you invite him to the wedding then?"

"I don't know. You save a guy's life..."

Of course, there were times over the years when Shelly thought Matt might be lying—or at the very least, that there might be more to the Snow Day Saviors story than the framed, yellowed newspaper article on the Kauffmans' kitchen wall. And during those early years, Shelly would listen for clues when Bobby's name came up during the holidays or on the rare occasions they hung out with Ray Dawley and Eddie Sayers. But they were no help either. Same for Google when that became a thing.

Then again, what did she expect? Matthew Kauffman had never been one to talk about his past. And why would he? Their life *now* was all that mattered: their marriage, a picture-perfect kind of love, maybe even the groovy kind Phil Collins sang about in that god-awful song Matt had been singing to her ever since college just to piss her off. Back then, Shelly Boyle had rolled with the artsy crowd. An English major, complete with the requisite horn-rimmed glasses, black turtlenecks, and flowy hippie skirts down to her Doc Martens. She never would have been caught dead with Phil Collins on her Walkman, which blared a steady rotation of alternative music with a spattering of Grateful Dead just to endear her to the granola crowd.

As for what endeared her to Matthew Kauffman, Shelly would never know. She was a far cry from the blond sorority types the hockey players usually went for. And if not for her roommate, Missy McLeod, a social butterfly if there ever was one, Shelly certainly would never have ended up at that shithole apartment house where half the hockey team lived. The "Puck House," it was affectionately known as because of all the "pucking" that went on there.

"You are not spending homecoming in this room, holed up like Emily Dickinson!" Missy had said as she literally dragged Shelly out the door. One hour and three beers later, there was Matthew squeezing his way toward her through the crowd, all smiles and saying something douchey. Well, not nearly as douchey as Shelly might have expected from a guy at the Puck House. But for some reason, it took Shelly a second to realize this.

"Hey, how'd you like *The Grand Illusion*?" Matthew asked, his voice hoarse and smelling of beer above the blaring Def Leppard.

Shelly just blinked back at him through her steamed-up glasses.

"You're in Bill Nicolas's Intro to Film class, right?"

Embarrassed, Shelly burst out laughing, her brain finally catching up as she turned to Missy to explain that, yes, *The Grand Illusion* was a film they had recently screened in her Intro to Film class. Missy was gone. Shelly frowned, but rather than her stomach sinking as it normally did when Missy ditched her, it squeezed when she realized the implications of what Matt had just said.

He had noticed her. Which was absolutely amazing because Shelly had noticed him too. Many times. The blond, somewhat contemplative-looking lad who chewed on his pen too much and always sat three rows ahead of her in Murkland Auditorium. And two classes ago, when Professor Nicolas called on Matt, who eloquently defined mise-en-scéne like some second-year PhD student, Shelly began to suspect that there was more to this book than just its handsome hockey-player cover.

Matt would prove her right that night at the Puck House, after which he walked Shelly back to campus, the two of them still discussing the finer points of Jean Renoir's direction. Matthew Kauffman. Handsome and confident but not cocky. Intelligent, a good conversationalist, but also a good listener. And goddamn it, a gentleman too. Didn't ask to come up to her room, didn't even try to kiss her good night. And much to her surprise, Shelly was actually bummed about it.

Still, that was the beginning of it all—a blur of sitting next to each other in class, late-night talks over cheese fries, and movie dates on the couch. It would be nearly a month before they finally slept together, but even so, none of their friends thought it would work. Matthew was a communication major and liked sports, whereas Shelly's feminist, pot-smoking English set was one of the few things that genuinely irritated him. Shelly eventually lost track of how many of her friends he offended with his eye rolls and jerk-off gestures when one of them was talking all Gloria Steinem or something.

Had it been anyone else, such a display of "toxic masculinity," as the young ladies called it nowadays, would have sent Shelly running for the hills. But when it came to Matthew Kauffman, for some inexplicable reason, Shelly Boyle, God help her, had grown to love everything about him.

Not his friend Bobby Bonetti, though. No, she didn't even *like* him.

That was Shelly Kauffman's last thought before she drifted off to sleep. Her husband's, too, she would imagine days later, when the echo of screams she never heard played louder in her head than any Bunnymen.

Chapter Five

That night after the funeral, Ray Dawley made a bet with himself. He sat at the window on his front porch, drinking a beer and watching some guy and his dog at the far edge of his property. The dog, a poodle or something, sniffed around at the edge of the streetlight's glow, near the chain-link fence between Ray's lawn and his neighbor's. Bundled up from head to toe, the guy stood on the sidewalk, holding the leash and shifting his weight as he looked around uncomfortably. Ray didn't recognize him—couldn't see his face because of the shadows and his jacket zipped up over his chin—and the guy couldn't see Ray because the porch was dark.

If he doesn't pick it up, I'll call the whole thing off.

As if on cue, the dog squatted and left Ray a present on his lawn.

Winner, winner, chicken dinner. He sipped his beer and wondered what his father would have done back in the day, but Ray couldn't remember him ever getting pissed off about things like that. He couldn't remember people walking their dogs at all, come to think of it—only disembodied barking and the vague smell of shit coming from behind the neighborhood fences.

As far as Ray knew, he was the first person from Lexington Avenue to repurchase his childhood home, a brooding two-story Dutch colonial with gray shingles and a detached garage. Where massive oak trees had once lined the streets, the curbs were now buckled and bare. The sidewalks were cracked, and the once-bright, neat-angled houses looked saggy and gray. The people who lived in them were gray, too, nameless ghosts of neighbors he once knew: the Chinese family in the old Kauffman place, the lesbians with the box garden where Mrs. Ruggieri's rose bushes used to be, the dumbass who parked his motorcycle on Rick Sayers's once impeccably manicured lawn.

A handful of folks from when they were kids were still around, old-timers with faded Rotary stickers on their storm doors and rusty air conditioners in their upstairs windows. The men all had hunched shoulders but still watered their tomato plants and hung their flags on Memorial Day. The women still watched *Wheel of Fortune* with the volume too loud in the summer, but they ignored Ray now instead of waving when he passed by their yards. Ray considered himself an old-timer, too, but deep down, he knew he had more in common with the ghosts. A shadow of his former self that his neighbors sensed but couldn't see.

Like this asshole with his dog.

The dog finished its business and, like some little shit fairy, disappeared into the dark with its owner. During his first marriage, Ray would have promptly scooped up his little gift in a plastic bag and chased after the guy. During his second marriage, he would have just yelled at the prick to come back. But now, just shy of a year into his third, Ray Dawley didn't have the energy.

Shit Fairy pays everyone a visit, sooner or later, he figured.

Ray reached for his phone, and the screen blinked on with the time, 6:15. Beer chilling in the fridge, pizza on its way, and Natalia and Maggie at his mother's—the three of them huddled on the couch, already deep into their first episode of *Say Yes to the Dress*, no doubt. Spending the night there had been Natalia's idea. "Stay up as late as you want, babe. I'll get Maggie to school. A boys' night will be good for you."

Ray sipped his beer. Who was he kidding? No way would he call off his reunion with Matt and Eddie. Still, he couldn't understand why he'd agreed to it—and at *his home* of all places. Then again, that had been Natalia's idea, too, and as with most things, Ray had a hard time saying no to her. Not because he was pussy whipped, of which Eddie would most certainly accuse him later that evening, but because Natalia's ideas were usually good ones. Never mind that she knew him better than anyone.

Yeah, a trip to some loud restaurant for shitty beer and buffalo wings would have been excruciating. Natalia had wanted to save him from all that. Just like she had been saving him from things ever since they got together five years ago. That had been Natalia's idea too. Ray had been working as a theatre professor in some third-rate program down in East Bumfuck, South Carolina when he got Natalia's DM. Just a casual invitation for a drink, it seemed, after a decade of liking their kids' pictures and piecing together each other's divorces on Facebook.

Hi, Ray. Loved that picture of you and Maggie down at Beavertail. She's getting so big! You visiting your mom? Would love to catch up over a drink, if you're game.

Ray was game, all right. He'd had a thing for Natalia Morris ever since high school but had never found the balls to ask her out, in part because he was afraid of her. Natalia was so serious all the time—understandable, given that her younger sister, Gina, had committed suicide. Ray and Natalia had been in tenth grade at the time, and Gina was in eighth. Ray knew Natalia was suffering back then, but what scared him was that he also knew he could love her so desperately for it. He wanted to protect and save her, while at the same time, he was keenly aware that he didn't know how.

Ray confessed as much during their drink—which led to three more and an Uber straight to Natalia's bed. As they lay there together, naked and breathing softly in the dark, Ray Dawley wanted nothing more than to come back to Rhode Island after thirty-plus years of doing everything possible to get away. It would take another four years of long distance and a brutal custody battle with Maggie's mother before he could make it official, but now, *somehow*, here he was—married to the love of his life, his daughter with him for good and his stepson away at Brown, and living in his childhood home, to boot. That had been Natalia's idea too. Sealed the deal just before they got hitched.

"Last summer, only family, didn't forget about you guys," Ray had told Matt and Eddie after the service. They probably hadn't registered anything after the thing about the house.

People move out of Eden Park, not back, their faces said.

But Natalia just smiled and squeezed Ray's hand. No use explaining how the neighborhood was getting better. A lot of yuppie types were moving in because the property taxes were half what they were in Barrington, which was why they didn't mind shelling out the money to send Maggie to Moses Brown. "Yada, yada, boys' night," Natalia had said instead.

Ray got up from his chair and, moving to his entryway, pawed at the wall just inside the door until he flicked on the outside light. He turned back toward the window and finished his beer like that—looking out at the brightness flooding his walkway and wondering if he deserved to be so lucky.

Chapter Six

"**I** *don't feel much like talking*," Bobby's mother said. *"I want to go swimming."*

"Wait. Was it Papa and Nana who told me to come by here tonight? The angelfish, maybe?"

"I don't know. I'm going swimming now, so I'll ask her."

"You know if she got the present this morning? I tied it to a brick because of the ice. Wasn't able to throw it out as far as I usually—"

"She always gets them, sweetheart. Always..."

Bobby frowned. He hated when his mother blew him off. But more so, he was anxious to know what had possessed him to drive through his old neighborhood that night. A premonition, he would conclude later, divined from what he saw in front of the church that day—Ray, Matt, and Eddie. Their faces like tea leaves foretelling the future. Like the voices that sometimes spoke to him from his grandfather's hunting cap.

Bobby slipped the cap off his head and set it down in the darkness beside him, his fingers reading the details like braille—the frayed edges of the brim; the crude stitching he had done himself on the left earflap; the fur, worn away in some spots and hardened with age in others. *Like sharks' teeth,* Bobby thought. He had seen a documentary once in which this marine biologist said some sharks could have up to fifty rows of teeth. Thing was, they weren't attached to their gums like human teeth. No roots, which was why shark teeth were always left behind when they bit into something.

Bobby had no roots either, but he never left anything behind. So what the hell was he doing in his old neighborhood, parked around the corner just far enough to see Ray Dawley's house, especially so soon after getting rid of his pistol in Blackamore Pond? Sunday night, he could be making a few extra bucks tending bar at the Santa Maria Di Prata Club. But instead, Bobby had lied to his uncle Tommy and said he was meeting some friends to watch the game. Didn't need to add much else. Uncle Tommy never asked questions. Been that way going on three years now, ever since his old girlfriend threw him out. Tommy was a good roommate all around. Split the bills, cleaned up after himself, and wasn't home much except on Sundays for football and *60 Minutes.*

Bobby checked his watch—a quarter past six. No second-hand ticking like on the TV show, no Anderson Cooper introducing a story about some crazy fuck freezing his ass off while casing the house of his childhood friend. Bobby sniffled and blew his nose in a wad of tissue from his jacket pocket. Still nursing this cold going on two weeks. *Seriously, the fuck am I doing?* It had been almost two hours since he'd seen Ray's wife and daughter coming out with their overnight bags, their faces featureless in the waning twilight before taking off. Maggie and her stepmother, Natalia—*Dr. Morris*, Bobby always called her during their therapy sessions.

Bobby was certain Dr. Morris hadn't seen him parked there when they left. Same as she didn't really see him during their sessions, either, for which Bobby used the alias Dave Ruggieri. Solid Italian name, typical goombah paying in cash, no need for a social security number to pin him to his health insurance and risk Dr. Morris discovering that he had grown up with her husband—which was why Bobby had started seeing her in the first place. To be closer to Ray.

Maybe that was why he was parked around the corner from Ray's house, his black Honda Accord blending in with all the other alien cars in the neighborhood that night. Friends and cousins and coworkers all gathered to whine about the loss of Tom Brady as the Bills handed the Pats their asses. Had it been daytime, the only thing that might have drawn anyone's attention was the darker-than-legal tint of Bobby's windows—a medical exemption he got due to acute light sensitivity that eventually put him on disability from the RITS. Dr. Morris knew about his condition because he sometimes wore sunglasses during their sessions. A delayed result of hitting his head on the ice at Blackamore Pond, the doctors figured, but Bobby had told Dr. Morris it was because of a botched laser surgery back in the mid-nineties, around the time his mother took her own life.

His mother. That was really the only thing Bobby talked about with Dr. Morris that was true. "Rhonda," he called her during their sessions—a name he made up on the spot but later attributed to the fact that his father used to like the Beach Boys. When Bobby was a kid, his mother had one of their albums featuring the song "Help Me, Rhonda." She used to play it sometimes when they were alone together after the thing on the ice. But Bobby never told Dr. Morris that.

And of course, Bobby never told Dr. Morris about the voices he started hearing in the hunting cap soon after his mother died—*real* voices, not pretend ones like his grandfather's when he was a boy. Voices that led him to guys like Ronnie Matarese, voices that explained why they glowed and trailed sparkles when they moved—like the tailless angelfish that had led him into the depths of Blackamore Pond.

Bobby sniffled, put the cap back on, and stuffed his hands into his jacket pockets. His fingers and toes were almost numb with the cold. Nothing compared to the cold in Blackamore Pond forty-plus years ago. But still, Bobby could feel it entering his pores and reaching into those deepest parts of him, all the way down to the dark bottom, where something black and shapeless and awake now stirred. Something rising from the muck, from all the sediment and decay that buries things discarded and long forgotten, like all the pistols he had thrown into the pond over the years.

Ray Dawley's outside light flicked on, and as Bobby watched, the rising sensation grew stronger and settled into a sense of weightlessness—a warm, peaceful feeling of floating underwater, which remained with him long after the pizzas were delivered and Eddie Sayers and Matt Kauffman arrived.

Bobby tied the earflaps under his chin. No voices called to him, but it was confirmation nonetheless—a light now at the surface, visible even from way down here in the darkness where he swam.

Chapter Seven

Before heading over to Ray's, Eddie Sayers drove his F-150 to the Pontiac Food Mart for a pack of Marlboros then to the bottom of Blackamore Avenue, where he parked, pulled up the hood of his Patriots sweatshirt, and took his first drag in over a decade. The smoke felt like warm honey pouring into his lungs. As he exhaled into the sliver of night above his driver's-side window, he imagined himself as a monk making an offering to the past—an incense-laden prayer, not of the faithful but of sacrifice. Something deep inside him given up for—*what?*

At fifty-five, Edward Albert Sayers had his suspicions, but as he took his second drag, the bitterness of it on his tongue spoke only of why he had quit smoking in the first place. Katie. It had been eleven years since their divorce. Should have been the beginning of a new era—daughters out of high school, parents living in Florida, and Eddie a detective lieutenant in charge of his own division. Get in shape, bang some chicks, do whatever he wanted finally, that had been the plan. But goddamn, his remorse over the end of their long run together *still* caught him by surprise sometimes.

After all, it wasn't as if he and Katie had ever been happy—not even in high school, when Eddie used to park his car in this very spot, a half block from her house, and beg her to rub one out for him before saying good night. The begging continued into their marriage, when Eddie was lucky to dip his wick once every few months. Miracle they had two kids, the way the frigid bitch always came up with excuses. And when she didn't, she just lay there like a bag of hair. After years of hearing the word "issues" tossed around, "trauma" became the common refrain. An abortion sophomore year with some guy she was seeing before Eddie. *"Instead of being so selfish, how about trying to be supportive once in a while, huh, Eddie?"*

He tried—Jesus flippin' H. Christ, how he tried—but it wasn't like he didn't have his own issues. His job was brutal at times, and it became near impossible for Cowboy Eddie to keep his little horsey in the stable. He eventually lost count of how many times he'd cheated—a steady rotation of badge bunnies who he tossed away like the condoms he used. But when Katie left him for her boss at the DMV, it cut deeper than he ever would've imagined. Like he had just been driving along all these years, listening to some song on the radio, then it suddenly cut out, leaving him with only his thoughts and the hum of the tires for mile upon mile of maddening silence.

At least, that was how Eddie saw it as he absently fingered the radio controls on his steering wheel. One thing was sure: eleven years, fifty pounds, and dozens of bottles of minoxidil later, here he was, pumping himself full of nicotine and wishing the days of badge bunnies weren't so long gone—anything, really, to break the hum of the tires. Katie should have been long gone too. Just a spot getting smaller and smaller in his rearview mirror, he thought, looking up at it as if he might see her, young and pretty and waving goodbye in front of her old house up the street. But Eddie had to go and retire, didn't he? And now the bitch was coming after half his pension.

Eddie took another drag and offered it to the night. Thirty years with Cranston PD, twenty-seven years of marriage, two kids, and this was the thanks he got. Never mind their lawyers had already worked out the financial bullshit eleven years ago. Eddie agreed not to go after the half mil Katie inherited when her aunt died, and Katie agreed not to go after half his pension. Cut-and-dried, easy as pie. But Eddie should have known nothing was ever easy with Katie Higgins. Claiming she was entitled not only because her uncle, who had been chief of police back then, had pulled the strings to get Eddie on the force, but also because of the mental abuse she had suffered during their marriage—signed their settlement under duress—that was the new song she was singing. She even brought up the story about this fish he cut up one time at Blackamore Pond—just one more example of his inherent cruelty, her lawyer said, that went back decades. Never mind that Eddie had confided in Katie about all that in high school because he still felt so guilty about it. The coldhearted bitch. Her fucking lawyer too. The hearing was set for eight o'clock tomorrow morning, but Eddie would ride this one solo. No way he was paying another dime in legal fees, especially when it was pretty much guaranteed Judge Capuano would end up throwing the whole thing out—big fan of the cops, statute of limitations, and all that. Still, the fact that Katie's motion was even being heard...

But was that why he had stopped here to make his offering to the past? Or was it because he was dreading the reunion at Ray's house even more than seeing his ex-wife in court tomorrow? The douchebag had been back in Rhode Island since the summer and never even texted him. Not like they were still close, but it was the principle of the thing. Ray hadn't even told him he had gotten married. Third fucking time, Natalia Morris, valedictorian of their class and now some big shot psychiatrist. Eddie could tell when they were talking outside the church that she barely remembered him. But Eddie remembered her—like most people, probably—as the girl whose sister hanged herself. Gina Morris, two years younger than all of them. Poor kid was only in eighth grade. Story was, Natalia was the one who found her. Fucked her up for a while too.

At least, that was what Eddie had heard. They had rolled with separate crowds back then—Eddie with the chuckleheads, Natalia with the dexters. Ray sort of floated with an in-between crowd for a time, then the theatre dorks his senior year. Weird, though, that the two of them should hook up in their fifties and move back into Ray's childhood home. Then again, Ray had always been weird—"artsy-fartsy," Frank Dawley had called his son the last time Eddie saw him alive. Ran into him at Stop & Shop. Damn, almost twenty years ago that was.

Then there was Matt Kauffman. Eddie hadn't really spoken to him at all since asshole Kent died. But would Eddie be able to keep his mouth from running like the old days? Probably, since Ray would be around, but man, when it was just him and Matt, it was almost like a reflex, the two of them swapping stories about all the ass they'd pulled. Matt's wife had no idea what a dog her husband was. Or maybe she did but turned a blind eye. Business trips mainly, a blowjob at the office Christmas party. At least that was what Matt had told him ten years ago when they'd gone out after Kent Kauffman's funeral.

Eddie took a final drag of his cigarette, tossed it out onto the pavement, then turned on his lights and drove away. Maybe it wasn't the reunion he was dreading after all, he thought as he swung past Blackamore Pond onto Lexington Avenue. Maybe it was simply the way the phone call he'd received an hour ago from John Seabrook still sat with him. Seabrook, one of the detectives from Eddie's old division, had wanted to know if he'd noticed anything out of the ordinary at Jimmy Kauffman's funeral—specifically with regard to the dearly departed's daughter, Debra.

Come to find out, Debra's boyfriend, Ronnie Matarese, had been found dead in his apartment over on Dyer Avenue with a bullet between his eyes. Ronnie, the squirrel-brained son of former crime boss, Rocco Matarese, was known to the Cranston Police in name only and didn't seem to play much of a part in what little remained of his family's once-powerful organization. Either way, Eddie told Seabrook, it was not his problem anymore. Still, when the call was over, Eddie felt the old instinct dropping in—cold and heavy, like an anchor in his stomach. *Why would someone want to whack a small-timer like Ronnie Matarese?* Nothing missing, no forced entry, looked like a targeted hit, Seabrook said. His girlfriend, Debra, had a solid alibi. The police were questioning a few witnesses from the night before, but no suspects as of yet.

Not my problem, Eddie repeated. So why the anchor dragging him down, it seemed, as he drove up the hill? Was it because he would soon be hanging out with Matt Kauffman, the uncle of the victim's girlfriend? Or was it because Eddie had always been an anchor in a way too? Eddie the Anchor—that was what Ray Dawley had called him that day after the thing on the ice, and what Eddie Sayers had been ever since. The last in line, the only one of them never to leave Rhode Island, stuck in the mud at the bottom of the ocean. Or was it the bottom of Blackamore Pond?

Yeah, Bobby Bonetti never left Rhode Island, either, Eddie thought as he pulled to a stop in front of Ray's. But as he looked again in his rearview mirror and saw only darkness there, he reminded himself that Bobby Bonetti had never been one of them.

Not before the thing on the ice, and certainly not after.

Chapter Eight

When Matt Kauffman arrived at Ray Dawley's, he half expected to see Lorraine Bracco waiting for him in the driveway—standing there with her arms folded, smiling and leaning against her car like in *Goodfellas*, when Henry Hill was released from jail. Matt had even put on Tony Bennett's "Boulevard of Broken Dreams," the song that underscored the scene when they went to Pauly's house to celebrate Henry's homecoming—a reunion that was also a goodbye to Henry's former self when he looked Pauly in the eye and lied to him about dealing drugs. That was the turning point, the beginning of the end for Henry Hill. After that, he could never go back.

Matt Kauffman was at a similar turning point, he thought—a homecoming, a reunion, a celebration that was also a goodbye to his former self. The beginning of the end of his friendship with Eddie and Ray—a lie wrapped in promises of keeping in touch when, deep down, Matt planned to never set foot on Lexington Avenue again.

Shelly would have just rolled her eyes if he had tried to explain the whole Henry Hill thing—or at the very least, she would have encouraged him to make a more erudite allusion. Forever the snobby English major, his wife. One would think that, after all these years, she would just let him have it, those feelings and thoughts that he couldn't help tying to movies—especially since that was how they first met in college. A conversation about Jean Renoir's *The Grand Illusion*, the irony of which was never lost on him. *The Big Lie* was a more appropriate title for their marriage. A seedy tale of deceit and infidelity amid the well-to-do of Millburn, New Jersey.

Christ, if Shelly ever found out how close he had come to leaving her, to just throwing away the life they had built together for his coworker, Lisa Davenport—whose presence, along with her husband and kids, had graced the Kauffmans' humble abode many times. They'd even taken a couple of family trips together. Maine. Florida. Yeah, if Shelly ever found out, she would probably just mosey on down to the Millburn Station and throw herself in front of the inbound express. Not her husband's first dalliance, either, but the first time he had been in love. The affair went on for almost two years before Lisa called it quits—a change of heart that had left Matt broken just days before his father's death. After the funeral, however, it was as if something inside him just turned off and there was only Shelly again. Faithful, always there. Matt couldn't explain it beyond feeling he had been given a second chance and didn't want to blow it.

And now, ten years later, Matt had been given another second chance. He had been released from jail like Henry Hill. His former life was almost gone. One last hurrah before the Cranston Matthew Kauffman said goodbye forever. *Surreal being back here,* he thought as he entered Ray's, "The Boulevard of Broken Dreams" still playing in his head. No big Italian dinner waiting for him like at Pauly's, but plenty of laughs and backslaps just the same. And after a quick tour of the house—of which only the kitchen and upstairs bathroom seemed to have been updated—the three of them found themselves in the downstairs den, scarfing down Big Cheese Pizza and Miller Lite and joking about the shitty job Kent Kauffman had done stuccoing the walls over forty years ago.

"You can actually trace his drinking that day," Matt said. "See how the half-moon pattern started off fine in one corner of the room and gradually got messier as it progressed toward the other?"

"Impossible to strip without knocking out the wall entirely," Ray explained. "The house has had two owners since my parents sold it back in the late eighties, and the shit's still there. The hell was my mother thinking?"

"The hell *you* thinking?" Eddie glanced around. "I don't get it, you wanting to move back here. Then again, you were always a whack job, Dawley. Reading Stephen King and shit when the rest of us were jerking off to *Playboy*."

"Yeah," Matt said. "I always figured you'd go into art or something, Ray, the way you used to draw. I still don't get the whole theatre path."

"Me neither," Ray said. "Not anymore. Seems like some other guy. A character in a movie I saw as a kid. I can see the guy's face, but I don't remember the story."

"Still," Matt said, "twenty plus years, must've been hard giving all that up."

Ray sipped his beer. "Not really. It was more about what I was moving toward than what I was leaving behind. Natalia, blending our families. Moving was a small price to pay. Besides, the whole discipline has changed—academia in general, really. Too political. Can't say boo without offending someone. Harm. That's the word the students throw around all the time now. 'Your words, this play harmed me, Dr. Dawley.' Everybody's looking to be a victim, someone always causing them trauma. That's the other word I used to hear a lot before I threw in the towel. Trauma."

Eddie popped a hunk of pizza crust into his mouth. "Trauma my ass." He chewed. "Let those pussies you teach—"

"*Used* to teach. I'm retired like you, tough guy."

Eddie swallowed. "Yeah, well, let those pussies spend a week with me. I'll show them trauma. All that bullshit in the colleges now, a smack in the mouth is what they need. And I'm not just talking about the students neither."

Ray nodded thoughtfully. "I might just agree with you on that, Professor Sayers."

"There, ya see?" Matt slapped Ray's thigh. "You can take the boy outta Cranston, but you can't take Cranston outta the boy."

Ray chuckled. "You insensitive bastard. Don't you understand that I've been traumatized? All my suffering, every bad choice I ever made can be attributed to someone else doing me harm. Professor Sayers is right. I *am* a whack job, but I take absolutely no responsibility for it. Stephen King is to blame. He needs to be cancelled immediately for all the trauma he caused me. Or was it Connie? I get them confused now. *The Shining*, my second marriage. Same thing, really."

Eddie laughed. "Yeah, man, I hear you. Plenty of times I wanted to take an axe to Katie's head. She and Connie must be cousins or something. Going after a guy's pension is one thing, but your kid? After you basically raised her on your own all those years? You ain't kidding, Ray. Fucking miracle you didn't go *Shining* on her ass." Eddie tipped his beer at Ray and swigged it.

Ray sighed. "It's my own fault." He stared down at his can. "So many red flags. Connie could have been poking me in the eyes, I was so blind. Narcissist. That's another word thrown around a lot these days, but Jesus, if the shoe fits between your ass cheeks. Polar opposite of Hana. I don't know, maybe that was the attraction, another way to escape the guilt. I always blamed myself for what happened."

"Hey, hey, hey," Eddie said, "you cut the shit, you hear? I'm a lot bigger than you now and have no qualms about kicking your ass if you keep talking like that."

Ray smiled sadly, and a heavy silence fell upon the room—like a big history book dropped on the coffee table between them. So much history, for which, over the years, Matt had only been a detached observer. Emails, texts, a random phone call. Bits and pieces of Ray's life were strung together like a movie trailer in Matt's mind.

The following preview has been approved for all audiences by the Motion Picture Association of America.

Fade-in to wistful violins and a scene of Ray and Hana Kim both reaching for the coffee in the break room. An architectural firm in New York City, where Ray is temping between acting gigs. Love at first sight, we can tell, and soon the couple gets married at City Hall. A rom-com, we think, of which the only thing missing is Julia Roberts. Clips of Ray and Hana walking in Central Park and moving in together, sitting on the floor amid their boxes and Hana laughing as Ray drops a dumpling in her lap while trying to feed her with chopsticks. Then, we see them lying in bed in each other's arms.

"You have always been a teacher at heart," Hana says over the music, which becomes even more melancholy as we cut to her working late as a graphic designer in Boston—tired, scenes of her douchebag boss giving her more work as Ray slogs away at Tufts in pursuit of his PhD. More scenes of them struggling, Hana at the kitchen table, fretting over bills, Ray teaching bored-looking undergrads and typing away into the wee hours of the morning. Still, we can tell the love is always there, embodied in a slow dance, just the two of them alone in their kitchen as the music crescendos with a quick cut to a head-on collision in which Hana is killed by a drunk driver. She had rushed down to Providence after work to catch a play Ray was directing. Sad organ music underscoring his devastation as he moves in with his parents for a year before getting his degree and taking a position at the first place that offered him one. Some shit school in South Carolina. "Only temporary," he tells Matt at Gail Kauffman's funeral. Anything to move forward after Hana.

Moving forward. The music is darker now, the cinematography more frenetic in its depiction of Ray's second marriage. Flashes of him on nowhere dates and one-night stands before he goes the online route. A profile picture of Connie Blake underscored with an ominous, Darth Vader–like death march, an unsettling juxtaposition to the whirlwind montage of romance splashing across the screen. An elopement to Aruba, glimpses of happiness when Maggie is born, but then Connie, a pharmaceutical sales rep, leaves Ray on his own most of the time while she travels for her job. Quick shots of Ray changing diapers, sitting up all night with Maggie coughing, snapping at students because he's too exhausted to teach, while Connie jumps into bed with one of her clients. The music abruptly stops when Ray discovers an email exchange between them then picks up again when it becomes clear that Ray is anything but heartbroken. The music is faster, more determined now as Ray files for divorce and Connie, terrified that he might expose her affair, consents to giving Ray physical custody of Maggie.

Cue the montage for Ray's third marriage. Maggie getting bigger now—toddler messes, art projects, elementary school concerts, and figure skating. The music hopeful, the imagery brighter as Ray opens the DM from Natalia Morris. Once again, romance and passion splash across the screen—rare, precious moments stolen during their long-distance courtship. Connie, having changed professions, files for custody of Maggie. Quick cuts of lawyers pointing fingers during a brutal court battle that nearly breaks our hero. But with his one true love by his side, in the end, he is victorious. In the final shot of the trailer, we see Ray and Natalia standing in their front yard, sun setting in the distance and the camera pulling away as they put their arms around each other and gaze up at their home.

Fade to black, et le fin.

All this played through Matt's mind in a millisecond, after which he raised his can and said, "Hey, here's to happy endings, Ray. You deserve it."

"Hear, hear." Eddie raised his can too.

Ray toasted them back with a sad smile, and the three men drained their beers. Ray collected the empties, vowing to return with another round after he took a leak, and disappeared into the kitchen.

Matt watched him with a mixture of admiration and guilt. The truth just seemed to pour out of Ray—same with Eddie, for the most part—but Matthew Kauffman was full of secrets. The *Goodfellas* one about saying goodbye, yeah, but others too—lots of them, he realized as his eyes drifted up to some pictures on the wall. Class photos of the kids, Ray and Natalia exchanging their vows, the four of them on some big boulder in the woods. In this last one, Ray and Natalia sat, all smiles under their baseball hats, with the kids standing over them, making goofy faces. Everyone looked younger, the picture taken maybe four or five years ago. Matt had plenty of his own pictures like that at home but couldn't look at them without seeing what was underneath—something buried in the wall behind the smiles, deep beneath the plaster and old laths; something one could only see if they stripped everything down to the studs. They were the silent bones of a house, built upon secrets and lies—his flings over the years, Lisa Davenport, how he had spoken to a lawyer about leaving Shelly. There were other things too—secrets from before Shelly that he had never told anyone but that still clung to him like the stucco his father had slapped on Ray Dawley's walls over forty years ago.

"Hey, dumbass," Eddie whispered, snapping his fingers. "I asked you a question."

Matt just blinked at him—the flash of a secret, the face of a young girl glimpsed only briefly through a crack in the wall before it was plastered over again and hidden behind the smiling picture he always displayed in public. "I'm sorry, what did you say?"

Eddie chuckled and shook his head. "Never mind." He snagged another slice of pizza. "Fucking lightweight. Two beers in, and you're already hammered."

Chapter Nine

Two hours and five beers later, Matthew Kauffman was well on his way to being hammered, all right.

There had been a moment, right after Eddie called him a lightweight, when Matt had almost called it a night—when the stucco walls and the smiles from the family pictures felt as if they were closing in and suffocating him. Matt found one picture particularly oppressive—a childhood photo of Natalia and her sister, Gina. His heart began to beat very fast, and his body heat gathered around his collar when his eyes landed on that one. But then Ray returned with their third round, sat in front of it, and somehow, there was Henry Hill again—the inspiration of how calm and sincere he had been when he looked Pauly in the eye and lied to him about dealing drugs. And at that moment, Matt resolved not to flee in panic. No, he had to see the lies, the secrets through to the end.

Some deep breaths and another beer helped, then Ray broke out the throwback Atari 2600 console that Natalia had given him for his birthday. Time seemed to lose all hold on Matt then, as if one of the ships in *Space Invaders* caught him in a tractor beam and dragged him all the way back to the summer of 1979. And after a few more Millers as well as almost puking from laughing so hard at Eddie's shit talking, Matt had no more thoughts of leaving early—not even when the conversation inevitably came around to the only kid on the block who'd had an Atari back in the day. Bobby Bonetti.

Ray and Matt had last seen him ten years ago at Kent Kauffman's funeral. Eddie, however, had run into him a few times at Stop & Shop since then. Didn't have much to say other than he was still doing karate and on disability from the RITS. A condition or something that made his eyes too sensitive to light. Eddie wasn't sure what it was called, only that he had to wear sunglasses basically all the time, it had gotten so bad.

"Other than that, he looks the same, honestly," Eddie said, preoccupied with his game. They had switched out the throwback's joysticks for paddle wheels, and Ray and Eddie were sitting on the floor, deep into a playoff round of *Circus Atari*, which involved bouncing a pair of guys off a seesaw and into a scrolling banner of balloons overhead. Matt found the crudeness of the sound and graphics comforting—the tinny *boing-poof-poof* of the stick figures as they crashed into the red, blue, and yellow dots. *Circus Atari* had always been his favorite—Matt had been unbeatable back in the day. Now, not so much. He had lost the first round to Ray, but was truly enjoying watching his friends play—the flatscreen TV, the windshield of a spaceship hurtling him into the past as he sat back with his feet up on the coffee table. Like Captain Kirk in *Star Trek* sipping Saurian Brandy with the Enterprise on autopilot. That was another of Matt Kauffman's many secrets—he had been a closeted Trekkie ever since he was a kid.

"There's so much distance there, you know?" Ray said. "After Bobby's mother had that breakdown and he moved back to Providence, I didn't see him again except a couple of times when we ran into each other drinking in high school. He was running with a pretty rough crowd then. Glad he turned out okay."

"Yeah, he was never the same after the thing on the ice," Eddie said.

"You guys ever think about that?" Ray asked. "What happened that day and, I don't know, how it might have affected you?"

Eddie shrugged and shook his head. Matt opened his mouth to speak then quickly closed it—a squashed impulse to tell his friends about the nightmares he used to have. His father standing at the edge of the hole, laughing maniacally and pushing Bobby underwater with his hockey stick as Matt and the other guys tried to save him. But then, *someone else* grabbed the hockey stick and began climbing out onto the ice. Someone Matt did not want to see, someone he didn't even want to think about when he was awake—which was why he thought it best to keep his mouth shut rather than risk another panic attack. *Warp factor five, Mr. Sulu.*

"I thought we would have seen him there today," Ray said. "Only at weddings and funerals, right? Wonder why he didn't show."

"You could always give him a call and ask," Eddie said sarcastically, the *boing-poof-poof* intensifying now.

Ray chuckled. "I wouldn't know what to say."

Matt fingered the rim of his beer can. *Yeah, what do you say to a guy whose family has known ties to organized crime?* A couple of years after he was married, Matt learned from Eddie that Bobby's uncle Tommy had been named as a suspect in the murder of some guy whose bones were discovered by a construction crew like fifteen years after the fact. The story ended up making the national news and everything. Charges never stuck, but still, a lot came out about the Bonetti family's mob ties. *Yeah, you can't stop characters like that from showing up at funerals and shit, but you definitely don't invite them to hang out with you. Not anymore, not even if they're your nieces and nephews.*

"Still," Ray said, "feels weird, us playing without him. Can't even say Atari without thinking of those days up in his room, you know?"

"Goddammit," Eddie said as his last guy missed the seesaw and crashed into the ground with a staticky splat. "Okay, Ray, you have thoroughly succeeded in fucking up my game. What's next? I say *Night Driver* since we already got the paddles connected." Eddie looked at his watch. "Plenty of time to whip both your asses before Shelly starts hounding Matt to come home and rub her feet."

Ray laughed and stood up. "That reminds me."

He disappeared into the living room, and Matt heard what sounded like a cabinet opening and the clink of glasses. He checked his watch too.

"Yeah, cut me off, bartender," Matt said. "I need to sober up before I head back."

Ray returned, setting a tray with a bottle and three lowballs on the coffee table. "Not before you sample my wares, Lord Kauffman."

Matthew's jaw nearly hit the floor when he saw the label—*Bowmore 25 Islay Single Malt Scotch Whisky, Twenty-Five Years Old*. His heart began to beat very fast. The last time he had tasted a Bowmore was ten years ago, when he and another VP from Credit Suisse had shown this bigwig from Zurich a night on the town. Company had footed the bill, of course, but when Matt went to purchase his own bottle of Bowmore a week later, he discovered the vintage they had shared ran upward of five hundred dollars.

"Holy shit," Matt said. "Ray, this is too much."

Eddie examined the bottle. "What? This good stuff?"

"It had better be, given what Natalia paid for it." Ray took the bottle from Eddie and uncorked it. "Only tapped once so far." He filled each glass with a neat two-finger pour. "When Natalia and I took our belated honeymoon up in Vermont. It's meant for special occasions. Don't worry, gentlemen, the boss insisted."

As Ray set down the bottle and handed them each their glass, Matt felt his insides shrivel. Christ, had Henry Hill experienced this kind of guilt when he betrayed Pauly? No, not that cold-blooded son of a bitch. Come to think of it, why was Matt so dead set on putting the past behind him anyway? Was it really because there was nothing left here now that his brother was dead? Or was it because of all the secrets, all the bones buried but not forgotten?

"To fifty years of friendship." Ray raised his glass. "And if we're lucky, fifty more."

Matt and Eddie echoed Ray's sentiments. They all knocked glasses, then the three of them took their first sips together. Matthew felt as if he had died and gone to heaven. The smooth, malty smokiness, with notes of vanilla and pepper—and something he could not quite put his finger on yet—felt like liquid gold going down his throat. He took another sip. Licorice, that was what he tasted. Matt smiled as he sat back in his chair, feet up on the coffee table, the glass on his stomach—just as he had seen his father do a million times back in the day.

If Matt had inherited anything from Kent Kauffman, it was a weakness for whiskey—which, instead of a crutch, he had carefully cultivated over the years into a sophisticated but rare indulgence. Of course, ol' Kent wouldn't have known a Bowmore from a Beam if it'd jumped up and bit him in the ass. But still, for a moment, maybe for the first time ever, Matthew was grateful to be Kent Kauffman's son—grateful for his friends, too, and their history together here on Lexington Avenue. *Yeah, fuck you, Henry Hill,* Matt thought. Secrets or no secrets, he could never say goodbye to his former self, to Ray Dawley, and to his best bud growing up, Eddie Sayers.

"Warp factor ten, Mr. Sulu," Matt muttered as Eddie launched into a game of *Night Driver*.

The Enterprise's viewscreen was black now, the primitive-looking nose of a car swerving back and forth at the bottom as Eddie tried to stay between the undulant hash-mark guideposts that represented the road. Another sip, then another, then something flashed before Matt's eyes. A memory, another secret he hadn't thought about in years—brought on, no doubt, by the booze and the video game and all the positive vibes suddenly flooding his brain.

Matt remembered driving with his father in the Garden City Shopping Center when he was eight years old—late on a Sunday afternoon, it must have been, because it was getting dark and the parking lot was empty. He sat on his father's lap and steered, the reflection of the car in the storefront windows sweeping past, the glare from the streetlights swimming up over the windshield as they drove round and round.

"Don't tell your brother," Matt's father whispered. "I never let him do this."

Matt could smell the whiskey on his father's breath, could feel the muscles in his legs tensing as he worked the pedals—his hands, so big and calloused and red knuckled from punching who knew what, hovering just above his son's hands on the steering wheel. For a moment, Matt thought he saw his father's smile reflected in the windshield, then there were only the hash marks of the *Night Driver* game, pixelated trees and houses and cars that looked like skulls coming at him—all of it growing dark and fuzzy at the edges. Matt shook his head, but the darkness kept encroaching.

"Damn, this game's making me dizzy," Eddie said, his voice hollow and far away, and the windshield flashed white with the game's tinny sound of a crashing car.

"What you get for driving drunk," Matt muttered—to Eddie or his father? Matt wasn't sure now as his eyes drifted up to Kent Kauffman's booze-fueled stucco job. The half-moon pattern was showing cracks again—a glimpse of someone in the wall peeking out at him. Or were they coming out of the ice again? Matthew Kauffman wasn't sure about that either, but their face would be the last thing he ever saw—just before he blacked out, then hours later, when someone stirred him from his slumber and murdered him at Blackamore Pond.

Chapter Ten

That night, at precisely eleven o'clock, Shelly Kauffman texted her husband from bed, asking when he would be home. The response, which she got almost immediately, both irritated and alarmed her. She could see on her tracking app that he was still at Ray's.

Hey, babe. Drank way too much. Need to sober up before I head back. Will text you when I leave. Love you and don't wait up! xoxoxo

Strange. Matt always put an "I" before his "love you"s and never used "xoxoxo."

Shelly thumbed the contact icon at the top of his text and was about to press call, but then she thought better of it and, going back to Matt's message, gave it a thumbs-up instead. She could just hear Eddie Sayers calling her a nag and did not want to give him the satisfaction of being right, never mind spoiling her husband's good time—the last good time that he would ever have with his friends from Lexington Avenue.

It was a thought that, despite her husband's absence, brought Shelly Kauffman comfort, and soon afterward, she fell asleep to the distant sound of bells.

Part III: The Gathering Storm

Chapter Eleven

Tommy Bonetti stole his first pack of cigarettes when he was ten years old.

The crime took place at Skip's Market—which, in the late 1960s, was located a block away from the Bonettis' triple-decker on Webster Avenue. Tommy's accomplice on that crisp October day was his friend Freddie Maroni—a chubby, slow-witted brute with a fascination for matches and burning insects alive. The boys partook of their stolen wares behind Freddie's garage. Freddie coughed a little but did okay. Tommy ended up puking all over his sneakers.

"The hell happened to you?" his brother, Mario, asked when Tommy sat down for supper later that night.

Tommy shrugged—he still felt sick, and his sneakers were caked with puke.

Mario shook his head. "Bad news, this one."

Mary Bonetti stopped what she was doing at the stove and made the sign of the cross. "Don't say that," she cried in her thick Italian accent. "Bad news comes in threes!"

Whether Mary Bonetti ever suspected her youngest son had been smoking that day, Tommy never knew, but later that night, when he was lying in bed and the phone rang, he knew even before his sister answered that the second bit of bad news was about to drop.

"Oh my God, he's dead!" Carla screamed. "He's dead. I knew it, he's dead!"

Come to find out, Bobby Carnevale, who had been going with Carla since the summer, had gotten himself killed on his first day in

Vietnam. Decades later, Tommy would learn from watching *60 Minutes* that 997 soldiers were killed on their first day and 1,148 were killed on what should have been their last. Tommy would remember those numbers always, along with many others, some of which he only calculated in his head—like the approximate date Bobby Carnevale knocked up his sister before leaving for boot camp. August 23, 1967. That was the third bit of bad news, blurted out by Carla herself right there in front of everyone only seconds after she hung up with Mrs. Carnevale.

Jesus, Mary, and Joseph, what a scandal. A good Catholic girl like Carla Bonetti? Seventeen, unmarried, and eight weeks pregnant with a dead man's child? A son, everyone would learn when little Bobby was born the following May. But by that time, the Carnevale family wanted nothing to do with the Bonettis and accused Carla of pinning her bastard on their dead son because she wanted money—which was hilarious, since everyone knew the Carnevales were a bunch of welfare pigs.

But that was all right. A lot of other people in the neighborhood had stepped up to help. They even had a bunch of presents waiting for Carla and Bobby when they came home from the hospital. Tommy hadn't cried since his father died, but he came close to it—from happiness, go figure—when his sister brought his nephew home and let Tommy hold him. Tommy would remember that day as the happiest of his life. A day when their house seemed brighter, when anything seemed possible just because this new kid had come along—his powdery hospital smell mixing with the eggplant frying in the kitchen. All the presents piled up around him in the parlor, everything—even the air, it seemed—was wrapped in white and silver and glistening like something holy.

Tommy had a present for Bobby that day too—an ABC block that he had lifted from a local toy store. He figured it would have been good for either a boy or a girl. In the coming weeks, Tommy would steal more toys for his nephew—a rattle, a ring of big plastic keys, some roly-poly guy that chimed—but then the owner of the toy store caught him, called his mother, and Mario ended up giving him one hell of a beating.

That was all right. Tommy was used to getting beatings by that point—from his brother, yeah, but also from some of the bigger kids who he went after for calling his sister a *"putana."* No one ever talked like that in front of Mario, though. At twenty years old, six foot three, and nearly three hundred pounds, Tommy's big brother was a giant in Silver Lake. But everyone down at Bonetti's Autobody still called him Little Mario because he inherited the business from his father, Big Mario, when he dropped dead the year before. Took a heart attack while stopped at the intersection of Union and Pocasset Avenues—his body slumped over on the steering wheel, the car stalling out with the horn blaring until someone pulled him off.

That was all right too. Tommy was grateful, in a way, that his father wasn't around to see his only daughter unmarried and preggo. Plus, being kind of like the man of the house, especially when it came to looking out for his nephew, made Tommy feel important. But after Carla graduated nursing school a few years later and started working at the hospital, she moved with Bobby into Mrs. Ursillo's old place downstairs and didn't seem to want Tommy around as much anymore. Tommy asked his mother about it, but Mary Bonetti would just scowl and clutch her rosary beads and mutter something in Italian that Tommy couldn't understand.

Eventually, it was Tommy's sister-in-law, Eva, who clued him in as to what was going on—she and Little Mario were living up on the third floor at the time. One day, when Bobby was five, Tommy went downstairs with a couple of baseball gloves to teach him how to play catch. But Carla just told him to go away through the back window because they were watching *Gilligan's Island.*

"Don't take it personally, kid," Eva said.

The green of her lawn chair and her jumper were like camouflage with all the tomato plants behind her, so Tommy hadn't noticed her sitting there in the shade of the garage.

"Your sister's gotta be her own mother for a while." She fanned herself with a copy of *Vogue*. "You'll understand when you have kids of your own."

Eva was actually a pretty cool gal to have around when she wasn't having one of her headaches. She didn't say stupid shit like most girls, and that plump face of hers was always smiling in a way that made Tommy feel seen. But the feeling never lasted long. He was nearly sixteen now and in charge of Sal "the Gagootz"'s books at the pool hall. A lot of bad characters hung out there, and by that time, Tommy had come to realize he was a bad character too—especially after Freddie got killed in a car accident and Tommy started feeling pissed off all the time. Carla telling him to go away only made things worse.

With seven years between them, Tommy and his sister had never been close, but things really took a turn for the worse when Tommy was six and Carla started looking after him because their mother went to work part-time at the jewelry factory. It started with pinches to Tommy's gut and flicks on the back of his ear for no reason but then escalated to smacks on the head. Sometimes, when Tommy didn't do what Carla said, like getting down on all fours and begging for his lunch like a dog, Carla would dig her nails into his forearms or lock him in the bathroom until he started crying. Things came to a head when Tommy was eight and Carla spit in his face because he wouldn't get out of her chair. Tommy got so mad, he chased her out of the house with a butcher knife. Carla ran all the way to the shop to get Big Mario, who stormed home with his face and hands all smeared with grease and beat the shit out of Tommy with his belt.

But that was all right. Tommy didn't have to stay with his sister anymore after that. He learned a lot about cars from hanging out with his father at the shop. And after Big Mario died, Tommy could pretty much do whatever he wanted. Anything was better than being around Carla. But after Bobby was born, the anger, the hatred he had toward his sister seemed to disappear—or, at least, seemed to get tucked away, like on the top shelf of the broom closet, hidden behind his dead father's shoe-shining stuff.

Tommy would always look back on those early years when Bobby was living with him as the happiest of his life—a time when the outlines of his world were so sharp, he never had to think about things like where he might fit into it all. He still got in trouble sometimes, sure, but there was always a vague sense of keeping things under control, a steady march toward something better that, although unclear, would someday appear in front of him like the presents in the parlor when Bobby was born.

However, after Carla moved downstairs, things got complicated. Tommy was a good-looking kid. He liked cars and nice clothes, and sometimes, a girl would distract him for a while. But eventually, it seemed he only had time for worrying about his nephew. He didn't think his sister would ever make Bobby beg for his food and shit, but still, sometimes late at night, when he heard Carla screaming, he would start downstairs only to be stopped by his mother—her eyes watery, her rough jewelry-shop hands like a vise on his wrist.

"Don't interfere," Mary Bonetti would always say.

For the most part, Tommy listened. The last thing he needed was to push Carla even further away. Besides, other than the nail marks on Bobby's arms, the kid seemed happy. But then this one time, Tommy accidentally walked in on his nephew taking a piss and saw what looked like a bite mark on his left butt cheek. It was only for a second, then Bobby, startled and embarrassed, pulled up his pants and hurried out of the bathroom.

A couple of days later, when Carla was home alone, Tommy—age twenty-one now and working for the Matarese family—sat down across the kitchen table from his sister with a loaded revolver.

The same revolver with which he had made his bones murdering Don DeFusco in the back of Sal's Pool Hall two weeks earlier, after which he and another associate, Lou Barboza, buried him near some golf course in Massachusetts.

"I'll make this quick." Tommy set the revolver on the table. "If I find out you are doing things to Bobby like you did to me, I will kill you myself."

There was a time when Carla Bonetti, even with a loaded gun pointed at her, might have called her baby brother's bluff. But that was before Tommy had started running a chop shop and carrying out hits for Bruno Matarese. Maybe she saw in her brother's eyes what the capos had seen when they took him on—something dead and yet singular in its purpose.

"I want to make things better for him too." Carla dropped her eyes, and a single tear fell onto the flowered tablecloth. She rubbed her thumb at the stain. "The pills are working—making me happier, I swear, and the painting helps."

Tommy's eyes swiveled to some Welcome signs on the table that Carla had painted—thin wooden boards, some with flowers, some with cats.

"I wanted to tell you and Ma about this place in Cranston down the street from this girl at work, Sue Dawley. It's off Pontiac Avenue, across the street from Blackamore Pond. Sue's got a kid Bobby's age. Other kids in the neighborhood too. Good kids, Tommy. Something better for him."

Tommy knew about some of the delinquents Bobby had started hanging out with, and as more of his sister's tears stained the tablecloth, for a moment, Tommy almost felt pity for her. No one could say Carla Bonetti had had it easy these last ten years, same as no one could say she hadn't dedicated her life to her son. Got her nursing degree in record time, worked her ass off at the hospital, never dated.

Not like she didn't have any takers either. Not bad looking, his sister—a spoiled brat and a nut, but not bad looking.

"I'm asking your permission, Tommy," Carla said. "Something better for him, and you can come over anytime you want. I'm gonna need your help looking after him, like you used to. The landlord said he's thinking about selling someday—rent to own, he said maybe. I was thinking maybe you'd want to go in on it with me. Maybe you and Ma can even move in next door."

Tommy traced his finger along a tulip in the flower pattern on the tablecloth. He pretended to consider Carla's proposal, though he knew that to deny Bobby such an opportunity would be selfish—especially if Tommy could keep an eye on him.

Tommy rose from the table and picked up his revolver. "I'll think about it," he said, moving to the door.

Carla called his name, and he stopped.

"I'm sorry if I ever caused you pain," she said. "I always loved you. Even when I didn't know how."

If Tommy Bonetti had been someone different, Carla's words might have touched him—might have reached way down like sunlight into the deepest pits of him and stirred something there. But as Tommy mounted the stairs up to his apartment, he understood that all that was left inside was darkness and a hatred for everything and everyone around him. A hatred so cold that he could kill his own sister and sleep like a baby that night—because she had killed him, too, in a way. All of them had.

For the first time, Tommy Bonetti saw it all so clearly: the monster that was Silver Lake. A monster with tentacles made of people that entered the lungs like smoke and slowly suffocated a person without him knowing until it was too late, until he was old and broke and looking out the window at some kids in the schoolyard, wishing he'd had someone around at that age to tell him what he didn't know. To drag him off the street corner by his collar and send him with a kick in the ass back to school. Or maybe just to sit with him at the kitchen table and help with his homework. Someone who wasn't so tired from work or so pissed off at everything that they would encourage him with his knack for numbers. Someone to give him a pat on the back once in a while and hang his test on the refrigerator even when he got a B. If he'd had *someone like that*, yeah, then maybe the monster of Silver Lake couldn't stand being inside him and, like some exorcised demon, would flee his body with a legion of dying voices speaking in tongues he no longer understood.

The next day, Tommy gave Carla permission to move to Cranston, and once it all went down, things really seemed to turn around for them—especially Bobby, who, every time Tommy saw him, had a brightness in the air around him, a sense of beginning, of anything being possible. Even after Tommy got pinched for running the chop shop, Bobby still seemed happy when Carla visited with him at the prison—the light in his eyes so powerful, Tommy thought, that it could have bleached away the decades of filth staining the visitor's table between them. Yeah, Tommy Bonetti had done right by his nephew. He had saved him from the monster of Silver Lake.

Then a different monster appeared. Tommy read about it in the paper before he got the scoop from Carla—"Snow Day Saviors," the article was titled. Tommy would always remember that, same as he would remember the picture of Bobby—a shadow across his face, his smile just a little grainier than those of the friends gathered around his bed, as if the photographer's flashbulb couldn't quite reach him. Carla visited a week later on a Saturday—alone, for the first time without Bobby—and Tommy began to feel afraid.

"He's different," Carla said, her eyes red and tired, "something lost. I don't know. I'm just worried even you can't protect him now."

"What are you talking about? Kid's probably still spooked from almost dying."

Carla shook her head. "My boy left our house that morning, and someone else came back. I don't know how else to explain it to you."

"You're talking batshit, you know that?"

Carla shrugged, her eyes fixed, it seemed, on some scratches near the corner of the table—little half-moon gouges, like the ones her nails left in his forearm when he was a kid. Bobby's too.

Tommy's heart beat heavily. "Don't forget our talk."

Carla smiled sadly. "I'm a good mother," she said, a sense of detachment in her voice, in her eyes. "All the guns in Silver Lake won't change that."

That was the last thing Carla said to him that day, and after she left, Tommy understood why he had been so afraid. The faraway look, the nutty way Carla spoke reminded him of how she sounded when she tried to make him beg for his food when he was a kid. Detached, unemotional in her cruelty. The way she slurred a bit reminded him of his former associate, Joe Turchetta, when he was all pumped full of smack. Tommy was certain Joe had dropped dime on him—payback because Tommy had refused to route the slimy prick's cars through the family shop after the Matareses cut off dealing with him. Tommy took the fall like a good boy and kept his mouth shut—even when the Feds dangled the immunity carrot if he helped finger old Bruno for Don DeFusco, who the Feds said had been working for them as an informant before he disappeared. Like Tommy hadn't known that when he put a bullet in the back of his head.

But Tommy didn't say shit and resolved to quietly serve out his five-year sentence—which would probably only be two and a half, with good behavior—and settle things with Joe Turchetta when he got out. Now, that seemed like a lifetime away after what Carla had told him. The hardest part was that she was right. He couldn't do anything for Bobby while he was stuck inside. No one else to keep an eye on him or to watch out for something weird, like the kind of shit that presented itself when Carla auditioned for him with her best Joe Turchetta impression.

But Tommy didn't think it was smack pumping through Carla's veins. No, it was a drug that her brain produced naturally. Tommy was so spooked, he used one of his phone calls to tell Mario and Eva to look out for anything weird. *But would they even know what to look for?* After all, Carla put on a good act next time she visited. So did Bobby. Everything back to normal on the surface—the smiles, the joking around, the bruise almost gone on the kid's forehead. But something else was gone too—the light in Bobby's eyes—and in its place, something worse than the monster of Silver Lake. Something cold and dead. Something dangerous and all too familiar because Tommy had seen it staring back at him in the mirror many times. Bobby Bonetti had the eyes of a killer.

Tommy refused to believe it, refused to even entertain the idea that falling through the ice or hitting his head or whatever the hell happened could have made his nephew into a killer. No, it was just his nut-bag sister messing with his head—the dead-end helplessness, the bleak totality of his sentence finally getting to him. And as the weeks turned into months, Tommy reassured himself that, next visit, Bobby would show up with the light in his eyes and everything would be hunky-dory like before. But the months turned into years—sixth grade became seventh, seventh became eighth—then in April of 1982, Tommy got a phone call from his brother.

"It's Carla," Mario said. "I don't know what the hell's going on, but looks like she'll be in Butler for a while. Cops picked her up night before last. Said she was just walking down Reservoir Avenue, half-naked and muttering something about caterpillars in her blood."

"The fuck you mean, caterpillars?"

"Christ, I don't know, Tommy. I'm just telling you what they told me. Docs said she did it to herself. Bite marks and blood up and down her wrists. She was all bandaged and sedated when I took Ma.

Some kind of breakdown, everyone's saying. I don't think she even knew we were there."

"What about Bobby?"

"What about him?" Mario asked, his voice tired and tight with the exhale of cigarette smoke. "He's just as scared and clueless as the rest of us. Said he was asleep when it happened. Didn't even know she was gone, he told the cops. Blood everywhere, Tommy. The place is like a slaughterhouse."

Tommy took a deep breath, his mind racing in two directions—into the future, for what would happen to Bobby, and at the same time, into the past, digging through his memories like dirt until he hit something solid: the bite mark on his nephew's ass. Tommy closed his eyes and leaned his head against the wall, against the cold, damp stone that felt like a tomb. "What happens next?"

His brother sighed. "I don't know. Docs won't say how long she's gonna be there. She can kiss that job at the hospital goodbye, though, I can tell you that. No way they'll take her back after something like this. I guess we'll just have to figure it out. Get Bobby settled at Ma's, then when you and Carla come home... Christ, I don't know. I can't think that far ahead. Haven't slept in two days, Tommy. Blood everywhere. I've never seen anything like it."

Tommy got out of prison three months later on a Friday, upon which the whole world, it seemed, gathered in Mary Bonetti's tiny backyard to celebrate. Friends, family members, some guys from Tommy's old crew, most of whom he hadn't seen since he went in. But Tommy had eyes only for his nephew, who had arrived somewhat late because of a trip to Rocky Point with his karate group at the Y. And once everyone was deep into their sausage and peppers and telling stories that Tommy had heard a million times, Tommy sat next to his nephew on some lawn chairs in the backyard and asked how he was doing.

"Good, good," Bobby said. "Real thankful Mario and Eva helped me finish out the school year in Cranston."

"That's good. Mario told me you're really getting into karate and shit, huh?"

"Yeah, all that's good."

"Looking forward to starting school next week with your old friends Mark and Mike?"

"Yeah, but judging from Mark's yearbook, Silver Lake chicks are a lot uglier than the ones at Park View."

Tommy laughed. "What about your friends back there, the ones in the paper with you that time? You gonna miss them?"

Bobby shrugged. "Yeah, I guess. We sort of drifted apart when we got to Park View. I figure at least Ray and me'll keep in touch. But after what happened with Ma, I don't know if his parents want us hanging out anymore."

As Bobby stared down at the grass, Tommy searched his nephew's eyes for some indication of sadness—regret, shame, *anything* that might betray the detachment in his voice—but there was nothing.

Tommy put his hand on Bobby's shoulder. "You know, I never told you how proud of you I am."

"For looking after your car, you mean?"

"No, for keeping your head through all this. Not just what happened with your mom, but everything else from before. I see more than you think I do. The way you been fighting your own battles all these years. That was the last thing Big Mario ever taught me before he died—a real man fights his own battles—but I'm not so sure about that anymore. Sometimes, I think you just need someone in your corner. A guy standing at the edge of the pond, maybe, holding you back from running out onto the ice no matter how safe it looks. I'm gonna be that guy for you now. I'm not going back inside ever again. And when your mom comes home, we'll all have a talk—you know, sit down and figure out the living arrangements so I can look out for you like before, like I should've been doing all along. I'll be standing right there on the shore with you from now on, okay? I promise I won't let you fall through the ice again."

Tommy swallowed back a lump and forced a smile that made his cheek twitch. And as the voices of the gathering hung in the humid air between them, Tommy realized he had probably just spoken the most in a single clip that he had in his entire life. The words had just poured out of him, like fire from a dragon, during which he had searched his nephew's eyes for a sign that what he said had caught hold—the beginning flickers of a flame that Tommy could blow on and stoke until the fire burned inside his nephew on its own. But Tommy saw only darkness reflected back at him. Even when Bobby smiled and said thanks.

Chapter Twelve

Tommy had been dreaming of pigs when their squeals startled him awake.

At sixty-six, he still held out hope that someday he would be admitted into the Heavy Sleepers Club, of which every other guy in his family was a member these days. Take his brother Mario, who, now, in his mid-seventies, could literally just fall asleep right there at the dinner table during the holidays. Tommy didn't think he would ever be that hardcore, but Christ, what he wouldn't give to sleep through the garbage trucks and not wake up every time his nephew got up in the middle of the night to piss.

Shifting in his recliner, Tommy looked at the time on the cable box beneath some travel show on PBS he'd switched to when it became clear that Brady and the Bucs didn't have a prayer against the 49ers. *12:06.* He switched off the TV with the remote and blinked at the door. In his dream, the details of which were already fading, the pigs had gotten into his garden out back—their squeals sounding a lot like the squeak the back door to the garage made. Bobby must be home.

Silence now as Tommy waited for him to pass by the doorway to the den. And when he didn't, Tommy got up and went out to the kitchen. He found Bobby standing at the sink with his back turned, coat still on and wearing that stupid hunting cap. His shape was little more than a silhouette in the light above the stove. Bobby was drinking a glass of water and staring at the window as if he could see Tommy's pigs outside in the dark. A goddamn pin dropping could wake up Tommy Bonetti when he was sleeping, but he couldn't hear the faucet turn on when he was awake? Getting old sucked. Almost as much as both the Pats and the Bucs losing on the same day.

"That Josh Allen is gonna dominate next year," Tommy said, reaching for the milk in the refrigerator.

Bobby turned to him, his face almost entirely in shadow now because of his cap and the way the light hit it. "What'd you say?"

"The Bills." Tommy fetched a glass from the cupboard. "They'll go all the way, I think."

Bobby nodded absently, and Tommy poured his milk.

"How about you take off that clown hat before I waste my breath again?"

Bobby took off his grandfather's hunting cap, tossed it on the table, then slipped off his coat and draped it over the back of a chair. Tommy returned the milk to the refrigerator and sat. He nodded at the chair across from him, and Bobby sat too. Tommy didn't turn on the lamp above the table because sometimes, especially late at night, the light hurt his nephew's eyes. But Tommy didn't need to see his face to know he had been lying earlier about going to watch the game. After the ass ramming Josh Allen gave the Pats, the mere mention of the quarterback's name should have sent a diehard Pats fan's head shaking instead of nodding.

Yeah, after all those years dealing with lowlifes—not just in prison and working for the Matarese family, but also at the restaurant he'd managed and part-owned for almost a quarter of a century—Tommy could spot a liar coming a mile away. Whose car broke down or whose grandmother died for the fifth time. Which bartender was skimming the till or dealing weed. Tommy had seen it all.

"How come you lied about watching the game?" The lilt of anxiousness in his voice took him by surprise and made him realize he was more wounded by Bobby's deception than he'd thought.

Tommy had been looking after Bobby in some way or another ever since the kid was in ninth grade. Mario and Eva too. Made sure he finished school and steered clear of the Silver Lake delinquents and stuck with the karate. Tommy worked with Bobby at Mario's shop after they all moved to Cranston in the late 80s, trained him as a bartender at the restaurant and later got him the job at the RITS through a connection. Tommy didn't feel Bobby owed him. But still, a football game? Why would his nephew lie to him about something like that?

Bobby shrugged. "I'm not sure. I ended up in my old neighborhood in Cranston, just sitting there in my car across the street from Ray Dawley's house. Couple of hours, then I just been driving around, thinking."

"Dawley. The kid from the paper? That thing on the ice?"

"Yeah. I saw all three of them standing outside the church this afternoon at Jimmy Kauffman's funeral. Brother of my friend Matt—one of the guys from the paper that time along with Eddie Sayers..." Bobby's eyes had fallen to the table shortly before he drifted off. He sat there like that for a few seconds—eyes down, almost catatonic—then seemed to catch himself and, with a smile, shrugged again. "I don't know. I ended up bagging the funeral, so I didn't talk to them. Shame about Jimmy Kauffman, though."

Jimmy Kauffman. Tommy was even better with names than he was with numbers, and this one rang a bell. Before switching over to his travel show, Tommy had heard on the eleven-o'clock news that the grandson of his former boss, Bruno Matarese, had been found executed in his apartment over on Dyer Avenue. The reporter had mentioned something about police being called to the residence before—a couple of domestic disputes involving a Debra Kauffman, the victim's girlfriend, whose father's funeral had been earlier that day. When asked to comment as to whether the girlfriend might be a suspect, the reporter said the police had not ruled anyone out yet.

Police. Tommy used to call them pigs back in the day. Might explain his dream—they were all over the place behind the reporter.

He would call a friend of a friend on Cranston PD tomorrow to get the scoop, but it looked like Matarese was murdered earlier that morning between three and five o'clock, right around the time Bobby got home.

Fucked-up coincidence, right?

"And this morning?" Tommy asked. "You didn't get home until after four."

Bobby slipped a napkin out from the tin holder on the table and blew his nose. "I don't want to lie to you again," he said, his voice pinched as he wiped his snot. "So maybe you should just ask me where I left my green bathrobe."

Bobby smiled, and the hairs stood on the back of Tommy's neck.

Forty years earlier, a couple of days after Tommy was released from the ACI in August of 1982, Bruno Matarese sat him down at a table in the back of Acorn Social Club with a tray of lasagna his wife had made. They had just returned from visiting his sister in Sarasota, Bruno said, and he was happy to be home. At his age, which was seventy-four at the time, people learned to appreciate the little things in life, especially their health. Tommy agreed, though he thought Bruno looked like shit. He was still fat as all get out, but his hair was thinner and his breathing wheezy. The corners of his wide, bullet-shaped lips twitched when he smiled, and his eyes looked bloodshot and glassy and too small for his enormous skull—which, with its orangey tan, sat like a pumpkin, neckless and heavy, above the fleshy V of his open collar.

1982, the world had changed a lot since Tommy had gone in. Ronald Reagan was president. Disco now sucked, and Volvo-driving yuppies were everywhere. Given all the trouble the RICO Act had caused organized crime over the last decade, Tommy figured it was about time all the bullshit caught up to old Bruno, who had already done six of a ten-year bid in the mid-seventies for conspiracy to commit murder. Ever since then, the Feds had been trying to pin everything but Jimmy Hoffa on him.

No surprise then, when Bruno sat down with Tommy on that afternoon in August, the mood was happy but also tense with the palpable awareness of time growing short—Bruno's time, things changing, the end of an era. *Like when you're at the beach,* Tommy thought, *and you see storm clouds gathering on the horizon.* Bruno had also asked the horse-faced Lou Barboza to join them. Lou, who for years had been the outfit's top trigger man, had explained earlier that the boss was paranoid that the club was bugged. So when Bruno held the knife over the lasagna and asked Tommy if he wanted to cut his own piece or have Lou do it, Tommy got the message. He cut his own piece, then Lou slipped Tommy a matchbook with an address written on the inside.

And just like that, Tommy had permission to whack Joe Turchetta—who, besides being a regular at the local methadone clinic, had moved on from auto parts to prostitution and was in deep with rival Angelo Ricci's crew.

It all went down two weeks later in Joe Turchetta's first-floor apartment near Union Avenue. Tommy and Lou surprised Joe, asleep in his bed, during a late-night rerun of *The Twilight Zone,* which played throughout the murder on a TV in the corner. Lou held down Joe's feet while Tommy strangled him with the belt from a green terry cloth bathrobe lying on the floor. The men tied the bathrobe over Joe's head and took him outside, but as they were putting him in the trunk of his own car, Joe started moaning and twitching. Lou went back inside, grabbed a butcher knife from Joe's kitchen, and stabbed him repeatedly until the blade broke off and tore open a gash in Lou's hand. Tommy quickly bandaged it with the belt from Joe's bathrobe then followed Lou in Joe's car to an overgrown lot behind an old factory on Branch Avenue in Providence. There, Tommy and Lou buried Joe in a shallow grave—still in his green bathrobe, the broken knife blade still in his stomach—then Tommy followed Lou again to a junkyard in Johnston owned by Lou's brother-in-law. They disposed of Joe's car in the crusher, and that was the last anyone would ever see of young Joseph Turchetta until the mid-nineties, when a picture of his bones and the green bathrobe and the broken knife were splashed all over the news after being discovered by a construction crew.

Now, sitting across the table from his nephew forty years after Joe Turchetta's murder, Tommy got Bobby's green bathrobe message loud and clear. *Don't ask me about my bones, and I won't ask you about yours.* Same way he got the message when Bruno Matarese sat him down in the back of the Acorn Social Club with his tray of lasagna. As Tommy had suspected that night, there were indeed storm clouds on the horizon. Old Bruno would die two years later of a heart attack, after which his son, Rocco, managed to fuck things up so royally that, by the early 1990s, the DeLorenzo family had taken over and the hub for the New England operations had moved to Boston.

Yeah, Tommy had a sense of something coming back then, just as he had a sense of something coming now—something dark and ominous, like a dragon circling over the head of the stranger sitting across from him.

Chapter Thirteen

Around half past midnight, Bobby stripped down to his underwear, put on his hunting cap, and sat on the edge of his bed in the dark. He was exhausted but didn't want to risk falling asleep before someone in the hunting cap told him what was going on. He remembered very little after leaving Ray's—just long stretches of darkness broken by flashes of places to which he wished he belonged: the old houses on Benefit Street, the Van Wickle Gates at Brown, the big statue of Roger Williams overlooking Providence.

But had Bobby really driven around looking at all those places like some pussy-ass tourist feeling sorry for himself? Or were they simply images thrown at him from the void of the hunting cap? A vague sense of wanting to see them one last time before—well, before what? That was the question. The thing he had felt at Ray's? The sense of something coming, of something rising from the muck deep inside him?

"The fuck, come on," Bobby whispered, then his nana Mary, her voice distant in the hunting cap, told him to watch his mouth. "I'm sorry, Nan, but I don't know what's going on. Why don't I remember anything after—"

A muffled cough startled him, and Bobby fixed his eyes on his bedroom door. No light underneath. Tommy was still in his room, from the sound of it. Bobby had heard his door close a few minutes earlier. He hated the way they'd left things, but of all the nights to start asking questions. It was so out of character for Tommy Bonetti. Just one more thing about tonight that didn't make sense.

"Bobby, I'm-a gonna take care of you." His grandfather's thick Italian accent sounded much closer than his grandmother's.

Bobby turned from the door and leaned his elbows on his knees. He pressed the hunting cap's earflaps to his head and breathed in deeply. When Big Mario spoke, you better listen. Bobby had learned this lesson the hard way going on three decades ago, when his grandfather had warned him what would happen to his mother. But Bobby hadn't listened. Just his imagination, he thought; a throwback to his childhood when he used to pretend to talk to his grandfather. Then, the angelfish *showed* Bobby what would happen in a vision. *Just a dream,* he thought when he fell asleep wearing the hunting cap. A flash of his mother's naked legs and the angelfish swimming between them in the bloody water. Bobby called her the next day—everything was fine, new medication was working wonders. A week later, Bobby found her in the tub with her wrists slit, eyes black, mouth open, and skin as white as the angelfish belly up in blood.

The glowing and the sparkles started after that with the boys from the RITS. *Only* with the boys from the RITS. "Aura" was the closest word Bobby could find to describe what he saw. That was around the same time his eyes started getting sensitive and he had to turn off half the fluorescent lights when he taught at the karate studio. Bobby wasn't sure what was happening until one kid, whose aura was so bright Bobby could hardly stand to look at him, murdered his grandmother not even forty-eight hours after he was released.

Bobby would keep an eye on them after that, sometimes for years. Some auras stayed bright when the kids got out, while others dimmed then blinked out altogether. Then some, like Ronnie Matarese, who had never glowed at all, would appear to Bobby out of nowhere. Divine intervention—Bobby just happened to see him a week earlier at the Warwick Mall, Ronnie's aura so bright that he looked like a ghost among the throngs of shoppers on Black Friday.

Bobby never understood this—why sometimes guys glowed then stopped, or started when they had never glowed at all at the RITS. So Bobby would wear the hunting cap, sometimes for hours on end, waiting for someone in there to tell him what to do. His grandfather, his mother, his grandmother too. It was Big Mario who gave him the lowdown on Ronnie Matarese—which was why, as Bobby sat there on his bed, not even twenty-four hours after the hit, the angelfish's appearance took him by surprise.

She appeared to him glowing white and swimming in space, but instead of trailing sparkles like that day at Blackamore Pond, the angelfish swept into view the image of a dirty linoleum floor. Bobby lifted his eyes and was immersed in what appeared to be a scene from a movie—a gritty, violent movie about some stripper named Tammy, affectionately called "cunt" by her new boyfriend, Ronnie, as he kneeled over her and stabbed her repeatedly in the face. The angelfish swam around them then darted under the kitchen table, where the stripper's little girl cowered, screaming and crying. Ronnie howled like an animal and lunged for her, the cheap Christmas tree on top of the table falling over, the plastic ornaments scattering everywhere as he dragged the little girl out by her ankles and—

Bobby tore off the cap. He didn't need to see any more—Big Mario had already told him what would happen if Bobby didn't act. And Bobby *had* acted, so why was the angelfish showing him all this again? She had never done that before—her visions were always of the future, not the past. Rapes, murders, a child abduction once, and a school shooting. Bobby had stopped fourteen of the scumbags over the years, but the cops had no idea that their murders were connected. All bottom feeders, their bones silently buried deep beneath the muck of their own little ponds. Ronnie Matarese was as dead as the rest of them now—the stripper and her daughter, safe—so what the fuck was going on?

Bobby tossed the hunting cap on the floor, lay back on his bed, and closed his eyes again. No use asking the angelfish what it all meant. She never spoke. Same as his uncle Tommy—at least until tonight.

Yeah, Bobby thought. *Everything was business as usual until tonight.*

Chapter Fourteen

Monday morning at five, Ray's alarm went off as usual with the opening notes of "Summer Breeze" by Seals and Crofts—a guilty pleasure of his going back to his childhood, which reminded him of just that: a summer breeze blowing the curtain sheers in his old bedroom upstairs. That room belonged to Maggie now. The curtain sheers had been replaced with blinds by the previous owner, and last summer, Ray had kept on the central air most of the time. *Funny,* he thought. *Even in your own house, the past is a foreign country.*

Ray pawed blindly for his phone on the table beside him, turned off the alarm, and blinked at the screen in disbelief—only realizing gradually that it was his *second* alarm that had awakened him, not his first. The four-o'clock alarm was the big guns—"Welcome to the Jungle" by Guns N' Roses—which usually sent him springing out of bed and flailing for his phone to avoid an elbow from Natalia. *How the hell did I sleep through that?* The five-o'clock alarm was only supposed to be a backup, a nudge to get his ass in gear if he wasn't already sitting in front of his computer. Or if he was, to stop looking at random shit on the Internet and get to work on his book.

His book. Although he had retired from teaching, Ray had been picking up some online writing gigs here and there while he worked on his book—an unabashed and scathing takedown, he hoped, on the state of academic theatre, which he figured would be summarily dismissed. No one wanted to hear from an old guy like him anymore. And if Dr. Dawley had a problem with it—or heaven forbid, any *feelings* other than guilt—he hardly deserved any sympathy, what with his five-plus decades of complicity in the systematic oppression of, well, *anyone* who wasn't a straight white male. What was even more disturbing was that his former colleagues no longer even tried to hide their bias.

"I refuse to look at another CV from a straight white male!" Karen Barton had cried as she pounded the table during their last search committee meeting.

When Ray had the audacity to point out that literally ninety percent of the faculty were straight white *women* like Karen, and that maybe she should step down in the interest of diversity, Karen had a meltdown, complained to their chair—a straight white woman—who kicked it up to the dean—also a straight white woman—and a formal reprimand was inserted into Ray's personnel file for "fomenting a hostile work environment." When Ray voiced his concerns about Karen's remarks, which were clearly discriminatory and a violation of HR policy, the dean dismissed him. She also told Ray that he needed to go through sensitivity training, to which Ray gave her the finger and turned in his resignation the next day.

"Yay, another straight white male running for the hills," Karen Barton was said to have remarked—unless, of course, they were her straight white husband, then she would fight tooth and nail to get him hired. The hypocrisy, the double standard was truly astounding.

Was Ray Dawley bitter? Probably. Was carrying around this kind of shit at fifty-five unhealthy? Definitely. Did he ever intend to publish his book? Meh. Ray hadn't published or edited a single journal article since he'd attained full professor. But Natalia encouraged him to write it anyway. "Don't let that part of you die unless you're sure you want to bury it forever."

Typical shrink thing to say, and Christ, how he loved her for it.

As Ray sat up and leaned forward with his elbows on his knees, his head began to pound like someone was jabbing an ice pick between his eyes. "Jesus," he muttered, gazing first upon the bottles—*bottles?*—on the coffee table, then at Eddie, who lay, mouth open and snoring, on his back on the floor with a throw pillow under his head. The jacket for Ray's vintage KISS *Destroyer* album was on the floor beside him, and the vinyl had been placed on the old-school turntable next to the Atari. The power for the turntable was on, but the TV was off.

Ray's eyes swiveled back to the coffee table and registered two shot glasses with the lowballs as well as a bottle of tequila next to the empty bottle of Bowmore. *Shit.* Natalia would kill him for drinking the whole thing—but *tequila*? Whose idea was that? Last thing Ray remembered was Eddie playing *Night Driver* before they—*what?* Clearly, they had done some serious partying, but Ray couldn't have been so hammered that he didn't remember any of it. *And where the hell is Matt?*

A chill gripped the back of Ray's neck, and in a rush of panic, he stood too quickly. Stumbling sideways, he reached for the wall, his fingers clawing at the rough half-moon ridges of stucco amid waves of numbing darkness. *I'm going to faint,* he thought as the darkness began to shimmer—then his headache returned with a vengeance, and the room dissolved into focus.

Ray breathed in deeply and smacked his lips. His mouth was dry and tasted like someone had shit in it. His legs felt shaky and slow to respond as he staggered down the hallway into the small toilet closet under the stairs. Ray stood at the sink in the dark and splashed cold water on his face. He dried himself on the hand towel and went into the kitchen, moving aimlessly, it seemed, until he turned on the lights in the adjoining dining room and remembered he was looking for Matt. Ray checked under the table—*seriously?*—then moved into the living room, where he closed the door to the liquor cabinet—*Christ, Natalia is really going to kill me*—before heading back into the den. Ray stepped around Eddie and looked out the window. Matt's car was gone. *What time did he leave? And why the hell can't I remember saying goodbye?*

Ray slumped onto the sofa, listening for a moment to Eddie's snoring and thanking God that Natalia wasn't around to see this shit. Maggie and Jeremy too. Divorce is never pretty for kids, but it's ten times worse when one of the steps is a fuckup. Ray wouldn't quite categorize himself as such just yet, but he had to admit that retiring at fifty-five and writing a book that would probably never get published while his wife brought home the bacon didn't do much for his self-esteem.

"That's just the patriarchy and your white privilege and your white rage and your toxic masculinity talking," Karen Barton might have said, to which Natalia would have replied, "Hubby still can't get it up for you, eh, Karen?"

Ray chuckled, and his eyes drifted up to a picture of his wife on the wall. Their wedding day, Ray in the picture, too, looking down at her hands as he slipped the ring onto her finger. The black and white had been taken by Jeremy, who was one hell of a photographer, though he didn't know it yet. Kid managed to capture the moment perfectly, the curve of his wife's face, the softness of her smile—her dreams, her hopes, her excitement for the future like the sun shining in her big, beautiful brown eyes. Ray didn't look half bad, either, which in and of itself was a miracle of modern photography, since he was truly the most unphotogenic person on the planet. Not an asset when one was trying to be an actor. Ray had once comforted himself with the knowledge that he was a man of the theatre, and who the hell needed film, anyway, but it was all bullshit—just one note in a whole symphony of bullshit to which he had marched steadily for over two decades until he met the love of his life—a life that he never dared to think he deserved after Hana.

Hana. Dear, dear Hana. Ray almost felt ashamed saying her name in his head, never mind looking back on his life and seeing her as a player in it—a lone actress on a dingy stage whose brilliance could not be dulled by the shit show of a production going on around her. It had been almost twenty-five years since her death, and Ray still didn't understand how it had happened—how he could kiss her goodbye after the production of *Romeo and Juliet* he'd directed then, a half hour later, be driving home and see her car crushed like a tin can on the side of the road. How the cops and the EMTs could hold him back, how their eyes could be so heartless and angry as he pleaded with them to let him hold his wife, then so somber and sympathetic when they asked him to identify her body on some metal table at the morgue an hour later.

"It meant so much to me that you came," Ray had said to Hana after the show.

"It was worth it" was Hana's reply.

That was the last thing she ever said to him. *It was worth it.*

As he sat there, looking up at the pictures of his family, Ray had an image of himself just closing his eyes, lying back like Eddie there on the floor, and breathing his last breath. Would it have all been worth it if he died right now? The loss of Hana and the two decades of soul-shredding academia? The ninth-circle-of-hell marriage to Connie and the spiritual and financial toll of the custody battle?

"You bet your ass it was worth it," Ray muttered as his eyes landed on a picture of Maggie—age ten, hair in pigtails, her smile all braces as she cradled a pumpkin she had just chosen from the patch stretching out behind her. *Christ, was that really four years ago?* Maggie, always so smart and so strong. Even during the divorce, when she was six years old and would break Ray's heart every time she had to go with her mother for the weekend—her hand on the window, the way she looked back at him with tears in her eyes. When Maggie returned and Ray watched Connie drive away, he always wished it had been her in that car instead of Hana, the shadow of whom Connie blamed for Ray's inability to truly give her his heart.

In a way, Ray supposed she was right, and only in hindsight did he realize that he had fallen for Connie Blake because she was so different from Hana—just one more attempt to distance himself from his grief, from the crushing guilt that had plagued him since her death. It wasn't without a trace of guilt, either, that Ray entered into his relationship with Natalia—who, despite coming into the picture after Ray had raised Maggie for nine years, went above and beyond to forge a relationship between them. That wasn't to say Maggie had no initial jealousy, but it didn't last long, and very soon, Maggie gave herself over to the kind of maternal presence that Connie could never show her during her every-other-weekend visits.

As for Ray and Jeremy, the bond just never materialized. Ray, at first, blamed Jeremy's age, then Jeremy's father, who saw Jeremy regularly, whereas Maggie's mother, about a year before the big custody battle, moved to California and now only got three weeks in the summer and alternate holidays. But when it came right down to it, Ray had no one to blame but himself for the hands-off approach he had taken with his stepson—a repetition, he now realized, of the tack his own father had taken with him, and which only resulted in wasting what little time he'd had before Jeremy went off to college.

"I'm sorry," Ray muttered, his eyes moving from picture to picture. To his wife for being a shitty husband sometimes. To Jeremy for being a shitty stepfather pretty much all the time. And to Maggie for... well, for so many things Ray didn't know where to begin. For the divorce, for dropping her off at day care when he could have spent time with her, for snapping at her when he was tired, for screaming at her when she made a mess, but mostly, for just being himself.

Ray felt his throat tighten and the steady pressure of tears building behind his eyes. God, he missed his daughter—he missed *all of them*—and Ray Dawley suddenly felt more alone than he had in a long time. He wished he could just go upstairs, turn off Jeremy's reading light, kiss Maggie's sleeping forehead, then slip into bed next to Natalia and fall asleep with his arm around her. A sob escaped his lips, and he swallowed hard. *What the fuck is wrong with me?* Jeremy was literally twenty minutes away at Brown in one direction, and Natalia and Maggie half that in the other. *So why am I so emotional?* The booze, the hangover, and a lack of sleep, he told himself—but that was bullshit too. Ray had always been a little too emotional for his own good.

"*You tho thensitive,*" Connie said in his head, and Ray felt a wave of nausea.

Christ, he thought. *How could one man carry around so much love and hatred in him at the same time?*

Chapter Fifteen

When Eddie opened his eyes, three thoughts pummeled his brain, one right after the other. His first thought was that Katie would kill him. His second thought was that he would just do it himself—would go home and grab the forty-five in the nightstand and put a bullet between his eyes, anything to stop the pain in his head. The third thought, which came to him as he looked around and realized he was lying on the floor at Ray's house, was that the only place he would be seeing his ex-wife was—*court, I'm going to be late for court!*

Eddie twisted onto his side and, using the coffee table for leverage, pulled himself up onto his knees with his eyes on the windows. Still dark outside—which was a good thing, he registered on some level—but his limbs were stiff and achy, and his headache suddenly felt like a jackhammer in his skull. What an idiot. He never should've had that Scotch. *Gonna look like a goddamn bum today in front of the judge*—that was, if he could ever get his fat, creaky old ass down to the courthouse.

Eddie groaned and, half crawling to the sofa, climbed up and sat on it with his head in his hands. He closed his eyes, dragged his tongue over the fuzz on his teeth, and rubbed his forehead. Christ, last time he had a hangover like this was the morning after his buddies took him out to celebrate his divorce. A night at the Foxy Lady topped off with a lap dance in the VIP lounge, during which Eddie passed out. *But last night... what the hell happened?* Last thing Eddie remembered was playing *Night Driver* then—

"Morning, sunshine," Ray said, and Eddie opened his eyes to a cup of coffee floating in front of him. "Black. Because you're too fat for cream and sugar."

Eddie took the coffee from Ray and cradled the cup in his hands. The warmth felt wonderful. His fingers were like ice. "What time is it?"

"Almost five thirty." With his coffee, Ray sat in the chair across from Eddie. "I know you got that thing at eight, so I wasn't gonna let you sleep much longer."

Eddie sipped his coffee—not strong, not hot enough, but it felt good going down. "And Matt? He take off already?"

Ray nodded. "Alarm woke me up at five. He was already gone. Shelly's gonna kill him. Wish we could be there to watch."

Ray smiled and sipped his coffee as Eddie, again, replayed the events from the night before in his mind. Nothing much in his memory banks after Ray broke out that bottle of Scotch.

"Bowmore," Ray said, as if reading his mind. "What we get for polishing it off and dipping into that tequila."

Eddie looked at Ray sideways—*Are you kidding me?* his expression said.

Ray just shrugged. "I know, right? What the hell were we thinking? There were only two shot glasses on the coffee table when I cleaned up, so I figured it was your idea after Matt left. Same with the KISS record."

Ray nodded at the entertainment console, and Eddie saw the *Destroyer* jacket propped up against it. *But tequila?* No wonder the inside of his head felt like a construction project on I-95. Then again, Eddie had drunk a lot more on the night his guys dragged him to the Foxy, and even then, he didn't feel like this the next day. This hangover was unlike any he had felt before. The pain in his head not sharp but dull and thick. The strange mental sluggishness and not remembering shit. Christ, a decade-plus after that night at the Foxy, Eddie still remembered most of it. Yeah, big difference between some fake tits in his face and three middle-aged dudes playing Atari. But the fact that Eddie couldn't remember a single goddamn thing after Ray served them that top-shelf Scotch was weird. *Really* weird. Like Ray roofieing him kind of weird.

The back of Eddie's neck prickled, and the onset of diarrhea curdled through his stomach. Something was wrong—*very* wrong—and Eddie felt his pockets for his phone. Ray snagged it from atop the entertainment console and tossed it to him. Eddie swiped open his notifications. A couple of headlines from his news and Patriots apps, a text from a buddy about how Bill Belichick sucked balls, but nothing from Matt.

"What time you say he left?" Eddie hoped Ray didn't notice the tension in his voice.

Ray narrowed his eyes. "You got shit in your ears? I told you. He was gone when I woke up. Don't remember much after the Scotch, honestly, so I was hoping you could fill in the blanks. I haven't drunk like that since... well, since I don't remember when."

Eddie stared down into his cup of coffee and suddenly felt repulsed by it. His heart was pounding now along with his head, and he could feel the heat of panic gathering around the hood of his sweatshirt. He needed to get out of here. Now. Eddie set his cup on the coffee table and rose unsteadily. "Look, Ray, I gotta get going. Gotta get home and—"

"Yeah, sure, I get it—"

"Shower and make myself presentable for that thing."

"Of course, yeah. Big day ahead."

Ray set down his coffee and fetched Eddie's jacket from the living room. Eddie slipped it on.

"You okay to drive?" Ray asked.

"Yeah, fine. I mean it, thanks for everything."

"Of course."

"Great seeing you, buddy. Don't be a stranger."

"Yeah, you too. You got my number now. I'll text you."

"Sounds good."

Ray and Eddie clasped hands and gave each other a quick bro hug. Ray flicked on the outside light, then Eddie was out the door and in his truck. The cold darkness, the sound of the F-150's engine starting up, and the air blasting on was sobering, and as the pain in his head subsided somewhat, all of a sudden, Eddie felt like a fool. Why would Ray roofie him? Could thirty years on the job really have made him that paranoid? He just woke up, for Christ's sake. Things would come back to him eventually. And Matt's car was gone. He probably made it back to Newport in plenty of time to bang his wife—or maybe some side chick he had here in Rhode Island. Eddie smiled. Wouldn't put it past him, the dog.

So what the fuck am I panicking about?

Tequila. Yeah, that was it. Eddie Sayers hated tequila. Like with a passion. Like so much that even just thinking about it made his stomach turn. Ray of all people should have known that. And if he had forgotten, Eddie most certainly would have reminded him about the time when they were in tenth grade and Jimmy Kauffman paid Matt with two six-packs of Coors to write a college paper for him. The three of them polished off the beer in the big drainpipe down at Blackamore Pond, then Eddie had the bright idea to raid Ray's liquor cabinet while his parents were out at some wedding. Blueberry brandy and a bunch of other liqueurs that he only sipped because they tasted like shit. Except for the tequila. Eddie drank *a lot* of that and ended up passing out in Ray's cellar, face down, in a puddle of his own puke. Boy-oh-boy, ol' Rick and Janet sure rained a shitstorm on his ass when he came stumbling home at dawn, looking and smelling like he just got mouth fucked by Jose Cuervo.

Eddie's eyes swiveled to Ray's door. He would never have agreed to drink tequila unless he was out-of-his-skull blitzed. And if he had been *that* far gone, shouldn't he still be a little drunk now? Or at least smell like he did when he went stumbling up the street four decades ago?

Had Ray's outside light not turned off a second later, Eddie might have gone back inside to hash out what happened. Something was *way* off, his gut told him, but his childhood friend roofieing him just didn't jive with it.

Must have been the Scotch, Eddie told himself. Maybe he had been missing out all these years. Maybe that was what life was like on the top shelf, and why high rollers like Matt Kauffman were willing to shell out so much for a bottle of Bowflex or whatever he called it. Because it made people forget—not just the night before, but things like wives who didn't put out for decades then left for their boss only to come after half of a guy's pension a decade later.

"Fuck it," Eddie muttered, throwing the truck into gear. He had bigger fish to fry today. As he drove up Lexington Avenue, past his old house then past Matt's, Eddie made a mental note to text him later to wish him safe travels back to New Jersey. He would text Ray, too, to apologize for leaving so abruptly and to ask him to go grab breakfast soon.

They were still friends, after all, and though Eddie hated to admit it, he could use a friend like Ray Dawley these days. Someone who knew him like family, someone who would always be there. True, Eddie had never been as close to Ray as he was with Matt, but maybe that was because Ray had always seemed out of reach. Too smart, too artistic, his heart something that Eddie couldn't even begin to understand. And a heart like that—so different than Matt's, so open and honest and vulnerable—well, that was not the kind of heart to roofie someone.

Matt Kauffman on the other hand...

Yeah, maybe *that* was what was bugging him.

Because if Ray Dawley hadn't roofied him, then that left only one other person.

Chapter Sixteen

Matt told her not to wait up, but Shelly did anyway—until about one, she estimated, when the Peter Jacobson podcast she had been listening to eventually lulled her to sleep.

Three more episodes had played through by the time the intro music woke her up at 5:22 in the morning. Still no Matt. Cruelly ironic, really, since her husband was the one who had initially suggested they give Jacobson a try a couple of years ago—to bust her chops, more than anything, Shelly knew, since Jacobson had a rep for being a pillar of the right-wing patriarchy. Matthew quickly lost interest, but Shelly... Well, despite Jacobson's sometimes-infuriating anti-feminist rhetoric, she had to admit the prick did offer some helpful advice on relationships. Soon, Shelly found herself listening to Jacobson during her morning runs and at the gym—his words inducing in her a rage-filled but validating adrenaline boost that screamed, *You see, Matthew, I am right!*

As Shelly lay there in the dark, refreshing her husband's location on her phone for the third time, she was tempted to text him a link to one of Jacobson's podcasts on respect and courtesy. *Back to school, asshole!* would be a fitting caption. Shelly couldn't believe it. The bastard was *still* at Ray's. Probably passed out on the floor in his underwear after a night of air guitaring and flying elbows off the sofa. Maybe he even had a concussion. *Serves him right, the dumbass.*

Shelly clicked off her phone and exhaled tensely at the darkened patch of ceiling. Sunrise was still over an hour away, she figured. Maybe that was her husband's rationale for crashing at Ray's. More and more, he had been complaining about driving at night, so she could see him thinking a forty-plus-minute drive back to Newport in the dark, smelling like a brewery, wasn't a good idea. But still, the excuse offered Shelly little comfort, as did the promise she had made to herself that she would not text him. No use sending *that* out into the virtual universe, a declaration in writing that Shelly Kauffman really had become the desperate, needy housewife she had always feared she would be.

Then again, she had only herself to blame. She should've known better, should've insisted on them all going out to dinner, including Ray's wife, his goddamn third. Shelly had never quite known what to make of Ray Dawley, who was so different from Matthew, never mind Eddie Sayers. Not a bad-looking guy, Ray, but somewhat strange, even for Shelly, who had rolled with plenty of artsy types back in the day. Something just seemed *off*, almost like Ray was a different person every time they got together. Which Ray Dawley would it be? The quiet and aloof Ray? The witty and charming Ray? The crude and buffoonish half-brother of Eddie Sayers? Shelly swore he had a split personality and had even told Matt as much on their ride up.

Her husband had just smiled and shrugged. "Maybe that's the appeal to Natalia."

Natalia. Shelly wouldn't have minded getting to know her and already liked her *way* better than Connie, Ray's second wife. Dr. Natalia Morris. Smart, classy, attractive, and yet approachable. Shelly had felt an instant connection with her, the two of them sticking out like a pair of sore thumbs amid the rough-skinned, cigarette-smelling broads who attended Jimmy Kauffman's funeral. Maybe Shelly could just text Natalia to call Ray to find out if Matt was okay.

Well, of course I'm okay! she could hear her husband snapping. *Christ, Shelly, you track every goddamn move I make!*

Yeah, Shelly, another voice that sounded a lot like her mother's chimed in. *Maybe you have too much time on your hands. Maybe you should go back to work now that the kids are away at school instead of waiting around all day for your husband to come home and fuck you.*

Shelly's stomach squeezed. Waiting around. That was really the only thing she was good for these days. Just waiting around for her husband to call the shots—when they took their vacations, whose wedding they couldn't attend because of his job. When they could have sex—*because of his job.* Yep, their whole marriage was just one big Ferris wheel revolving around his job. *But that's okay, Shelly-belly, because your job is to just sit right there on that Ferris wheel and go round and round wondering when your husband is coming home.* Just like the nine-year-old whose father told her he was going out to get a pack of cigarettes after dinner and never came back. *Really? Is that what Shelly Boyle's near-thirty-year marriage to Matthew Kauffman boils down to? Just some deep-seated, epic reenactment of trauma?*

Christ, what she wouldn't give to talk to someone, to confess that maybe Dr. Jacobson's lectures hadn't helped her as much as she thought. Maybe Natalia had an opening this morning. Maybe Shelly could just take an Uber to Providence, and the two of them could meet for coffee and make Matthew worry for a while. No way would she call him and start begging him to come home like she did when her father called a couple of weeks later from Florida to say that he loved her and was coming back and just needed some time to put things together. Turned out, the only things Greg Boyle ever put together were the barrel of a shotgun and his mouth.

"Good riddance," Shelly's mother had said. "We're better off without him."

But Shelly never felt that way—and still didn't, forty-plus years later. Yeah, Dr. Morris would probably just roll her eyes at Shelly's daddy issues. What a cliché. Still, if only she had her number. That was another stupid mistake Shelly had made outside the church yesterday—she didn't get *any* of their numbers, not even Ray's. Shelly figured she could find Natalia's practice online, but did she really want to leave a voicemail to say—*well, what?* That she was worried her husband hadn't come home even though she had been tracking him every five minutes since he left—*and, hey, I know we hardly know each other, but if you haven't left for work yet, can you maybe check on him, then we can meet for coffee so I can make things even more awkward by telling you how I've been second-guessing every choice I've ever made for way longer than I'm willing to admit?*

Wow. Was Shelly Kauffman really that desperate?

Chapter Seventeen

An hour after Eddie Sayers left, Ray Dawley sat down in his den to write. He settled in as he usually did with a fresh cup of Keurig brew beside him, his feet propped on a throw pillow on the coffee table, and his MacBook atop another pillow on his lap. The computer was closed, but the blinds were open, the darkness of the outside world bleeding away into the pale of winter, into the color of death.

Ray had already exchanged his good-morning phone call with Natalia, who said she hoped he'd had a good time and reminded him that she had an eight-o'clock patient. She wished Ray good luck on his writing and told him that her three o'clock had cancelled, so she could pick up Maggie. Ray thanked her and told her he loved her. Told her to tell Maggie that he loved her, too, and said that he would take care of dinner. Fish or chicken or something healthy, he assured her.

However, as soon as Ray opened his computer, he knew the day was lost. The previous three cups of coffee—as well as the shower and shave and the fresh set of clothes—had done little to help his concentration. The hangover, yeah, but more so, it was the sense of dread that came upon him when, as he glanced out the window, a police car and tow truck sped down the street in the direction of Blackamore Pond, lights on and engines revving.

Ray Dawley had never been one for morning walks—he preferred the late afternoons, when the air smelled of other people's suppers, when the light spoke of things winding down rather than starting up. But when he saw the unmarked black police car speed by his house a few minutes later, Ray figured today was as good a day as any to try something different. Well, that wasn't *really* what he figured, but it was what he kept telling himself as he swapped his slippers for his sneakers and donned his parka and Patriots hat.

And yet, as soon as he stepped outside into the frigid twilight, something even colder than December settled into his bones—the heaviness of the inevitable, a sense of mounting, miserable certainty that grew stronger with every step as he hurried toward the pond. He could see the flashing blue lights, just a hint of them at first, reflected off the houses farther down the street. A police SUV, lights on, zoomed past him, then Ray reached Summer Street, and a whole sea of flashing blue police cars exploded into view at the bottom of the hill.

Ray was full-out jogging by the time he reached the crowd of onlookers gathered near the corner of Lexington and Concord. The entire Cranston Police force was there, it seemed. Some state vehicles too. Marked and unmarked cars clogged the street. Cops were everywhere keeping people away, and the tow truck Ray had seen passing his house earlier had been backed into the short access ramp for the pond. From where he stood, Ray could see its front end and the strip of flashing lights creeping forward past the fence that belonged to the adjoining property. A pair of plainclothes detectives stood near the guardrail that hugged the curve onto Blackamore Avenue. One was smoking a cigarette and pacing while the other just stood there with his hands in his pockets and his eyes fixed on whatever the tow truck was pulling out of the pond.

Ray had heard the whir of the truck's winch as he'd approached, but only became aware of it when it cut off with a loud clunk, and the detectives disappeared with some uniformed officers down the ramp. As kids, Ray and his friends would sometimes compete to see who could skid their bike closest to the water's edge, but all that had ended in seventh grade, when Eddie, who had Matt riding on the back of his bike, failed to brake in time and rolled right in. Eddie always blamed Matt for jumping off too soon, which he said messed up his pedaling and earned him a beating from his mother when he returned home soaking wet and smelling of pond scum right before they were supposed to go out to dinner. Ray hadn't thought about that in years.

"That you, Ray Dawley?" Chuck Finola, half smiling, approached, his eyes little more than slits in the flickering blue of his booze-bloated face.

Ray and Chuck had shaken hands and said hello at Jimmy Kauffman's funeral the day before, but not much else. Growing up, Jimmy had been best friends with Chuck, who used to live around the corner on Concord—still did, judging from the pajama bottoms beneath his hooded Patriots parka. If Ray had a nickel for every time this prick had given him a wedgie...

"Hey, Chuck, yeah," Ray said, aware of the tremor now in his voice and a dull ringing in his ears. "Forgot to mention yesterday that I moved back into my old house." Chuck's expression brightened as if he were preparing to say he'd never left, but Ray didn't give him the chance. "What's going on?"

Chuck sighed and shook his head. "Someone took a wrong turn, looks like. I'm the one who called it in when I was walking Duke. He never does his business by the water, but this morning, I dunno, maybe he sensed something. Dogs, right? You couldn't see the car at all if you were just passing. Even up close, it was hard to see without a flashlight. Ice is still pretty thin, so it broke right through, I guess."

"They find anyone inside?" Ray's question gave voice to the fear that he had tried to deny ever since he stepped out of his house—the reason why he had taken his walk, the reason why he remembered Matt jumping off the back of Eddie's bike after all these years. Matt. *Jesus Christ, don't let it be Matt.*

Chuck shrugged. "Was dark, Ray, and the flashlight on my phone sucks. Pond's half-frozen, but still, most of the car was underwater, looked like. Cops won't tell us shit, but I can't imagine anyone drowning. Not deep enough, ya know? Dumbass probably took a wrong turn and ditched his car after the engine stalled."

"What kind of car is it? You see a plate?" Ray's voice shook, and the dull ringing had moved from his ears into his bones, vibrating there like a death knell with the cold, dreaded certainty of what was coming. Ray hadn't noticed what make and model car Matt had been driving when he pulled up to the house, only that it was a high-end black sedan. A Lexus, maybe.

Chuck sighed and shook his head. "I'm telling you it was dark. Saw the Lexus logo, but the plate was underwater. By the time I got Duke inside and came back, cops had taken over and started keeping people away. Tow truck showed up about twenty minutes ago, but... Ah, shit, that thing there ain't a good sign."

Ray—his ears and bones buzzing so loud now that he had hardly heard anything after "Lexus"—followed Chuck's gaze and saw a boxy-looking gray van pulling up from around the corner on Blackamore Avenue. It stopped alongside the guardrail and turned off its lights. Rhode Island State Police Mobile Crime Laboratory, he read in the flashing blue as the rapidly spreading daylight seemed to poison everything. Yeah, Matt drove a black sedan that was probably a Lexus, but so did plenty of other people—people who wouldn't need the homicide division if they had driven drunk into the pond. They would just send an ambulance. Like they did for Hana.

"Guess I was wrong," Chuck said, echoing Ray's thoughts. "They don't bring out the big guns like that 'less it's a homicide. Must be a body down there after all."

Oddly, Ray felt a spike of hope. His hangover, his lack of recollection of the night before must be making him paranoid. *Who the hell would want to murder Matt?* And even if he'd decided to drive back to Newport drunk—which Ray now highly doubted—he never would have made a wrong turn into the pond, no matter how hammered he was. Matt could drive the neighborhood blindfolded. They all could.

Ray's frigid fingers were already reaching for the phone in his back pocket before his brain caught up with them. Why hadn't he thought of calling Matt right away instead of standing here wasting time talking to Chuck Finola, who was now bitching about how the cops shouldn't be blocking everyone's driveways? Ray nodded, half-listening, then raised a finger to excuse himself as he moved away and dialed Matt's number, his eyes never leaving the area at the top of the ramp as the call connected. Ray feared—foolishly, he would realize later—that he might hear Matt's phone ringing above all the commotion or maybe see some movement indicating that the cops did, but then Matt's voicemail kicked in, and Ray ended the call.

Still, Ray took it as a good sign. Or at least half of him did—the bright side, the glass-half-full side. Of course it went to voicemail. Poor bastard was probably snoring away his hangover next to Shelly right now—if she didn't make him sleep on the couch, the snobby twat. *Come to think of it, if Matt's phone were underwater, it wouldn't have rung at all, right? It would have shorted out, and my call would have gone straight to voicemail, right?*

But then the glass-half-empty part of him chimed in—a voice that Ray usually ignored because it often spoke of truths too difficult to confront. The same voice that told him not to believe Connie when she denied cheating on him months before he found her emails. The same voice that, even now, told him to stay put and see his old friend Matt when all he wanted to do was retreat to his den and hibernate like some grizzled old bear.

Yeah, for once, Ray Dawley was listening to the glass-half-empty part. The tow truck had inched forward halfway into the street, but Ray still couldn't see shit behind it, and now some cops from the

Mobile Crime Lab hurried over with their equipment bags. Flashes of photographs taken on the ramp soon followed, and Ray felt himself transported back a quarter of a century ago, when he stood at the margins of a scene much like this one on the side of I-95. Hana's car, crushed and flipped over on its roof in a ditch. Her body on the ground nearby, the soles of her dressy black boots sticking out from under the sheet like the truth he sensed about to peek out at him from under some big blanket of denial in his mind.

Just then, one of the cops—a kid with baby cheeks rosy from the cold—came out from behind the tow truck and fetched some rolls of police tape from the trunk of a car near where Ray stood.

"Excuse me, Officer," Ray said, "but can you tell me what's going on?"

"We've got an active crime scene, sir." The cop slammed shut the trunk. "You should go home like a good citizen and let us do our job."

Like a good citizen? You officious little prick.

"Can you at least tell me if the car has Jersey plates?" Ray asked, upon which the seriousness of the cop's full attention confirmed his fears. The car was Matt's. Ray knew it as sure as he was standing there, freezing his ass off. He felt something in him split—the dark half, the part of him that had known all along what was coming, controlling a mounting hysteria on the inside, while the bright half, the hopeful, glass-half-full part of him kept his gums flapping. "I'm worried it might be a friend of mine," Ray went on. "So can you just tell me if the car has Jersey plates? I might be able to help you."

"Why you worried it's your friend?" The cop's narrow eyes and baby cheeks moved closer.

Ray didn't like the way this little prick was looking at him—like he was suspicious or something—but the bright side just kept him talking. "Look," Ray said, lowering his voice, "my friends and I were drinking at my house last night up the street. One of them left while I was passed out. Matt Kauffman is his name—visiting from New Jersey. I'm worried the guy in the car might be him."

"This guy was at your house?"

"Yeah, along with Eddie Sayers," Ray said, lips tight. Something inside him hardened—something connecting the bright half and the dark half and numbing him to the confirmation this rookie prick had unwittingly given him. "Detective Eddie Sayers," Ray added, holding the cop's beady blue eyes. "You know that name? He was at my house too. Ray Dawley. I'm one of his oldest friends."

"Stay here." The cop hurried back toward the ramp.

"The fuck else would I go?" Ray muttered.

Chapter Eighteen

Bobby pulled into the parking lot adjacent to Dr. Morris's building and backed into a space so the front of his car faced her windows.

Dr. Morris's office was on the first floor of a renovated Victorian on Waterman Street, just around the corner from Wayland Square—a hodgepodge of bougie shops and kale-croissant cafés that Bobby would never have been caught dead in. Still, he enjoyed his weekly visits to the East Side, this foreign country where the past so seamlessly blended with the present, where things were rarely torn down but instead repurposed.

That was because Bobby felt repurposed, too, when he came up here. Not so much today, because he was running behind. An accident on 95 near the Thurbers Avenue exit. Some wake-and-bake dumbass not looking where he was going, Bobby figured. Par for the course ever since Rhode Island legalized marijuana. Couldn't drive anywhere nowadays without smelling it, especially heading into Providence.

Normally, Bobby would have taken the long way—entering Waterman Street from Benefit and driving up College Hill—so he could watch the students. Long before Bobby started seeing Dr. Morris, he had often roamed the Brown University campus pretending that he belonged there. The faces, the clothes changing over the years. The notebooks replaced by smartphones as the students disappeared into the old brick buildings—into forbidden illuminati chambers where intellectual designers renovated the interiors of their heads. Bobby envied them—wished he could take pieces of their lives and fit them into his body, into his past like new rooms with hardwood floors and walls painted with possibility.

Possibility—a concept that had always eluded Robert Bonetti. But not Dave Ruggieri.

Bobby blew his nose, stuffed the tissue in his pocket, and exited his car. The lot behind Dr. Morris's office was small and only had a few spaces, so Bobby always parked next door behind a more modern-looking building for some real estate agency. The two lots were separated by a chain-link fence with a break in it. On the side of the fence where he parked his car, he was still Robert Bonetti, but as soon as he stepped through the opening into the lot for Dr. Morris's office, he was Dave Ruggieri.

Bobby entered the building through the back door, sat in the tiny, dimly lit waiting room, and took off his sunglasses. The overhead fluorescents normally hurt his eyes, but because Dave Ruggieri was her first patient on Mondays, Dr. Morris always turned on the small lamp in the corner for him. Another therapist and some acupuncture guy worked on this floor, too, but at this hour, only Dr. Morris's white-noise machine ran down the hall. Everyone else opened up shop at nine, but Dr. Morris had made an exception for Dave because of his shift at the RITS.

Bobby checked his watch. Almost eight. Dave Ruggieri was always on time, just like Bobby. But *unlike* Bobby, Dave was divorced, had two boys in college, and liked to fish in his spare time—bits and pieces of a biography he had borrowed from Jerry Cotoia, another corrections officer with whom Bobby had worked at the RITS. Dave had just broken up with yet another girlfriend, a possibility that Bobby found unappealing.

Unlike Dave, Bobby found women annoying, especially when fucking them—the sounds they made, the smell of their breath, the sliminess of their snatch. Bobby figured he was asexual, something Dave had thrown out to Dr. Morris when he told her he was losing interest in sex. Normal for guys his age, she'd said, though much of Dave's sexual nature had to do with his relationship with his mother.

His mother. The only thing Bobby and Dave had in common, and which had come up during their first session together when Dr. Morris asked Dave about his treatment goals. Dave was an insightful guy and had done some research on trauma. He figured on some level that his problems stemmed from his mother—what she did to him as a child and what ended up happening to her. Bobby had to admit that it helped to be able to talk about those things as Dave, mainly because Bobby could imagine he was a kid again, talking to Ray Dawley, the last real friend he ever had.

Bobby was insightful like Dave, which was why he figured he had started seeing Dr. Morris to be closer to Ray—though he hadn't quite been able to articulate that to himself when he'd made his first appointment. Back then, he just had a vague sense of finding something that had been lost. *A friend?* Not really. *You can't have friends unless you tell them the truth about the stuff that makes you tick.* But still, being with Dr. Morris was like going back in time, like repurposing the past into the kind of possibility that had always eluded him.

That possibility didn't elude Dave Ruggieri. Even just sitting in Dr. Morris's office gave Dave a feeling of possibility, as if he were absorbing it from the refinished floors and freshly painted walls. Sometimes, an object or something—a lamp, a book on one of the shelves, the way the light hit the ficus leaves in front of the window—would draw Dave's attention, and he would lose track of what he was saying, only to find Dr. Morris's smiling, heart-shaped face floating in space on the other side of the glass coffee table.

There was also this big painting of some birds above the love seat on which her patients sat. Three branches stretched across the canvas with a handful of birds on each one. Most of the birds had blue in them, but they all looked different somehow. Dave would often pause briefly to look at the painting before he sat or when he was leaving. One bird on the bottom branch was the only one in the painting with its head turned away so he couldn't see its face. That bird was Dave's favorite. Same for Bobby, who would always make a brief appearance to remind Dave to be like the bird, to not show his face, before he sat on the side of the sofa with his head directly in front of it.

"Good morning, Dave," Dr. Morris said, all smiles as she peeked around the corner into the waiting room.

She motioned for Bobby to follow her, but it was Dave Ruggieri who did so—Dave who relished the smell of her perfume and the way her ass swayed in her jeans as she led him down the hall and into her office. Dave who wondered what her tits looked like under her blouse and what kinds of sounds she made when her husband was dicking her.

And who knows? Maybe Bobby Bonetti would have wondered all this, too, if he had been interested in such things.

Chapter Nineteen

Even as her patient sat down for his appointment, Dr. Natalia Morris felt like two different people. On the outside, she was the professional who had just reviewed David Ruggieri's case notes, but on the inside, she was still the flailing, insecure stepmom who had snapped at her stepdaughter an hour earlier.

The incident had been particularly rough because Ray's mother had been there, hovering outside the guest room with disapproving eyes. Never mind that Maggie had refused to drag her ass out of bed—which was ridiculous, since they had all turned in early the night before after an excruciating marathon of *Say Yes to the Dress*. Never mind that Maggie had almost made Natalia late for work and that the only reason they were staying at Sue's in the first place was so *her son* could have a boys' night with his friends. All that was irrelevant, of course, and lost in a single moment of impatience that would forever deem her unworthy in Sue Dawley's eyes. Cancel culture on the domestic front as if she had made some stupid, drunken tweet.

On some level, Natalia knew it wasn't that bad, but Christ, it sure felt like it—in part because, after five years, she still didn't know her role as Maggie's stepmother. They basically had two speeds—BFFs or awkward because they were both afraid to screw things up. Especially Maggie, who, if Natalia showed even a hint of irritation toward her, would shrink away and walk on eggshells until the air around them magically became relaxed again. Of course, one didn't need an MD in psychiatry from Duke to see that Maggie suffered from anxiety and abandonment issues because of her narcissistic mother. And sometimes, when Connie would call Maggie fat or selfish during their FaceTime calls and hang up on her, Natalia would sit on the couch with Maggie's head in her lap, stroking her hair in silence until she sensed the tears her stepdaughter was holding back had subsided. Strange, but those were the easy moments. What was harder, what was virtually impossible, was when Natalia tried to offer Maggie the kind of structure and responsibility that Ray had never instilled in her. *Never mind discipline, never mind chores, how about just cleaning your room and not leaving toothpaste globs in the sink? How about just flushing the toilet after you piss and not leaving the wrappers for your sanitary napkins all over the place like some goddamn Easter egg hunt?*

What made things worse was that Ray offered zero guidance on how to navigate these sorts of things other than a "Maggie loves you" and "You're doing a great job." Never mind that he hadn't made even half the effort with Jeremy, the hardest part was that Natalia felt as if she were going through it all alone—not to mention that all her efforts were taken for granted.

Take last night. *Had Ray even wondered how things went at his mother's?* He sure as hell didn't ask during their good-morning call—just the usual coordination of logistics and an "I love you." Distracted, hungover probably, his mind on his book and just assuming, as always, that his dutiful wife had everything under control. And heaven forbid Natalia should ever try to talk to him about such things. After the initial anger and defensiveness, Ray would look at her with Maggie's eyes—the worry, the fear that he had made some irreparable mistake, that he had once again chosen unwisely and his wife, *his fucking third*, would betray him in some way. Hana had died on him. Connie had cheated on him. So what kind of rug pull did Natalia Morris have in store?

Natalia closed her office door, and as Dave sat down, she glanced at the bird in the upper righthand corner of the painting above the love seat—the one spreading its wings as if it were just lighting on the branch. Natalia often looked at that bird when she was about to sit down, when she needed to put aside her personal life and focus on her patient. She felt silly for relying on a visual prompt to settle in. But when she took her chair, crossed her legs, and flipped to a fresh page on her notepad, the stuff with Maggie seemed further away—on the ground below the branches and unable to reach her.

What also helped that morning was that she genuinely liked Dave, in part because he was so earnest about getting better—unlike so many of her other patients these days, who only wanted affirmation for some self-diagnoses they got from Google. What was more, Dave wanted her to challenge him and give it to him straight. Refreshing, to say the least.

After some small talk about the weather and the cold he'd been nursing, Natalia wrote his initials and the date at the top of the page. "So, what's on your mind? Any place you'd like to begin today?"

"What we talked about last time, I guess."

"About your lack of focus during karate?" she asked.

Dave shook his head and smiled weakly.

"Oh, about visiting your mother's grave, you mean. Are you saying you gave it a shot?"

"I wanted to, yeah," Dave said. "But I pussied out again."

Natalia nodded and made a note. Dave Ruggieri hadn't visited his mother's grave in over twenty-five years, he had explained a couple of months back. Understandable, Natalia had said, given what his mother had done to him.

"Well, let's talk about that." Natalia switched her legs. "Why do you say you pussied out?"

"Well, I didn't go, did I?"

"No, but maybe that's because you're not ready—that is, if you understand why I suggested you try such a thing in the first place."

Dave sniffled and dragged the back of his hand under his nose. "Yeah, I get it. Closure, right?"

Natalia smiled and moved the box of tissues from the table beside her to the coffee table between them. Dave pulled out a tissue, blew his nose, then crumpled it into the waste basket beside the love seat.

"I suppose that's a way of looking at it," Natalia said. "But closure implies the end of something, and we're really just beginning. That's all you can ask of yourself right now. Just take the first step—when you're ready, I mean. As long as you agree with me that visiting your mother's grave is a good idea."

"Yeah, I can see how it might help. How being there and, what, absorbing the fact, unconsciously, that she's six feet under might help me move on. But what's keeping me from going, I think, is that, you know, the rest of my family is in that plot too. My grandparents, their son who died as a baby who I never knew. I don't know—I mean, I know they're all dead—but still, it feels weird being around them and thinking about that stuff, you know? Growing up, families like mine, you didn't talk about mental health and abuse and shit. Unless you were going to confession, maybe. Even then, I would never say anything, not even to a priest, you know?"

Natalia nodded. *Preaching to the choir, my friend,* she wanted to say, and an image flashed before her eyes. Her sister, Gina—young, pretty, and hanging dead from their father's chin-up bar in the garage. Natalia's eyes darted up to the bird in the top-right-hand corner of the painting, then there was only Dave again.

She inhaled deeply. What Dave's mother had done to him as a child was truly despicable, but the area around which Dr. Morris needed to tread very, very carefully was what began between them around the time Dave reached puberty. That was when things took an even darker turn, for which Dave now blamed himself.

"That might be a good place to start, then," Natalia said. "No matter how much I tell you you're not to blame, it doesn't mean anything until you believe it—until you actually see the past, instinctively, from the point of view of the victim, not the abuser."

Dave sniffled and looked around. "Like renovating the inside of my head, huh?"

Natalia smiled. "That's a good way of looking at it, yes. The memories inside the head will still be there, but everything will look different to you, like with a fresh coat of paint. The idea is, if we work on the blame, we can eventually tackle the shame."

Dave smiled. "You're a poet, and you don't know it, Doc."

"Just one of my many talents."

Dave's smile wilted, and he held her eyes—a little too long, Natalia thought. Her stomach squeezed, and blood rushed into her cheeks.

She looked down at her pad and, pretending to make a note, scribbled, *Dead bodies in a concentration camp.* She visualized them stacked like cordwood outside an oven at Auschwitz. Gray, naked, emaciated. Natalia often thought of things like that to keep herself from blushing when one of her patients was flirting with her—or, in the case of Dave Ruggieri, stared into her eyes as if he were searching for some hidden meaning. Dave was handsome, no denying it—a little short, five-eight maybe, same height as Natalia—but other than that, entirely her type: dark, with chiseled features and tragically hopeful blue eyes. But it was the way he sometimes looked at her—raw and open and childlike in his appraisal—that made her feel... well, *naked* was the only word she could think of to describe it.

"So, let's start with a hypothetical," she began. "Let's say you didn't have a choice. Let's say someone kidnapped you and just plopped you in front of your mother's grave. What do you see happening?"

Dave sniffled and screwed his face up in a way that made him look older, made him look his age. "I don't get you."

"Well, you said your grandparents are there, right? Do you see them watching you?"

Dave shrugged.

"You don't have to do this, but do you think it might help if you could orient yourself in relation to where they were? Like, do you imagine them looking up at you from their graves or down from above—you know, from heaven, maybe?"

"Yeah," Dave said, thinking. "Definitely heaven, yeah."

"And your mother? She's looking down on you too?"

Dave chuckled and shifted uncomfortably in his seat. "No, she's in the ground, probably. Looking up at me through the dirt. Through the lid of her coffin, I guess."

"Good, so she can't touch you, right? And your grandparents, well, they're in heaven. So if you wanted to just go there and think about stuff, they'd have no idea what was in your head. Even if you wanted to talk to your mother, if you got down real close to the ground and whispered, they would probably have a hard time hearing you, don't you think?"

Dave sniffled again, snatched another tissue, and wiped his nose. "I get what you're saying, Doc. But with their bodies in the ground, I don't know, it still feels too close for me to actually start talking about stuff."

"What stuff?"

"You know. Elves and caterpillars and shit."

Natalia sat back in her chair and, with her pen, directed Dave's attention toward the ficus by the window. "There's a plant growing on your mother's grave," she said. "Before you can speak to her, before you can speak to anyone, you need to count the leaves—quietly, and to yourself—from top to bottom like we usually do. Go ahead, start counting, and when you reach the bottom, you can tell everyone—your mother, your grandparents, even me—what happens when the elves come out of the cellar."

Natalia watched closely as Dave began to count, mouthing the numbers one by one until he reached the bottom, upon which his eyes glazed over and he began to speak.

Chapter Twenty

In another lifetime, Bobby Bonetti sat at the top of the stairs in his hunting cap and pajamas. He was watching his mother below in the living room. She stood with her back to him in the shaft of streetlight coming from the window, her body swaying gently as "Help Me, Rhonda" played on the record player. It was late, the house was dark, and Bobby could tell his mother didn't know he was there. In her white nurse's uniform, she appeared to be glowing—like the angelfish.

Bobby waited for the song to finish, and when it began again, he crept down the stairs and, standing behind his mother, slipped his arms around her waist and nestled his cheek against her back—her perfume, the bleached crispness of her uniform like spring as they swayed together to the music. He never would have even contemplated doing such a thing before he fell through the ice, but now, one month later...

"Where is my son?" his mother whispered, folding her arms over his.

"Dead," Bobby whispered, closing his eyes. "The elves dragged him down to the bottom of the pond."

"Elves can't swim."

"Sure, they can. They switched him out in the darkness down there and sent back some other kid who looks just like him."

Bobby didn't know what he meant by that, or why he said such things, but the words just kept coming out as if someone else were making him talk—like he was a ventriloquist dummy for that Wayland Flowers guy on *Hollywood Squares*, only Bobby didn't know who the person moving his mouth was. Just a shadow, a faceless black shape of a kid he sometimes saw under his skin when he looked in the mirror.

Bobby figured his mother saw the shadow kid too—especially when they were sitting at the table and she looked at him as if she were worried he was sick or something. This was the first time she had ever asked him where her son was, though—which Bobby figured was because of her episode. He had known as soon as he saw her from the top of the stairs that she was in the middle of one, her first since they had moved to Cranston.

However, unlike those times in Silver Lake, Bobby wasn't scared at all. Just the opposite, he was excited and wanted to see if his mother would try to hurt him. Maybe she would try to bite him again on his ass or push him down the cellar stairs like when she heard the elves. *But elves are fast,* Bobby thought, *and difficult to catch on land.* They were creatures made of night and shadow that talked in whispers like the wind in winter branches. And when someone caught them, they gouged out the person's eyes and tore open his throat. Even worse was when they kidnapped children—kids like Bobby, who they dragged down into cellars and open graves—down, down, down to the bottoms of old wells and dark ponds, where they sucked out the soul in gaping kisses then climbed into the kid's skin so they could pretend to be him and live in the light. Bobby didn't know why all this ran through his head, but somehow, he knew it to be true.

"Who are you?" Bobby's mother asked, her hands tensing over his, and Bobby felt himself sink into her.

"Just Bones now," the shadow guy, the ventriloquist, the elf inside made him say.

Bobby's mother began to weep.

Chapter Twenty-One

"Who are you?" Natalia asked, and Dave sighed wearily. "Just Bones now."

She leaned forward. This was where she needed to be careful. On one level, the ease with which she could lead Dave into his disassociated state was alarming, but for him to move toward synthesis of his multiple identities, Natalia was confident that Bones was the problem—though he hardly ever reared his head during their sessions.

Dr. Natalia Morris was an expert on dissociative identity disorder—which, for Dave, was clearly the result of the physical and sexual abuse he had suffered during childhood. Although instances of such mistreatment were tragically more common than most people could comprehend, true DID was so rare that David Ruggieri was only one of a handful of genuine cases Dr. Morris had come across in a quarter century of clinical practice. Not the most extreme example, either, but certainly one of the most fascinating in that Bones not only was an elf who lived under Dave's skin but also had been present, in one way or another, since shortly after puberty, as if the maturation process itself had triggered a mechanism within Dave's brain to help him cope with his abuse.

"Long time no see, Bones," Natalia said. "How are you today?"

Bones shrugged and raked his fingers back through his hair. "All right for now, I guess, but I know what you want to talk about, and I'm tired, honestly."

"We don't have to talk about Dave's mother, if that's what you mean."

"Hey, you're the one with the diploma on the wall, so whatever you think is going to help Dave will help me too. I'm not going anywhere, so I don't give a fuck, really."

Natalia made a note of Bones's initial response. Like many DID identities, Bones had an entire history separate from Dave's. Precisely how he entered Dave's body as a child was still somewhat unclear to Natalia—in part because, as Bones had explained, he had become just that: Dave's bones. The skeleton, the silent framework upon which the rest of him was built. As a result, Bones had forgotten most of what his life was like before he entered Dave—to help Dave get revenge on his mother, he explained. Bones was from a shadow world that paralleled this one, in which kids didn't take shit from anyone and gave it back tenfold to whoever tried to give it to them. Especially their parents.

"No one is saying you need to go anywhere," Natalia said.

Bones rolled his eyes.

"I mean it. My only goal is for you and Dave to work together and understand each other. I know you think you made him do those things to his mother, but that is the most insidious part of Rhonda's abuse. She made Dave think *you* were the abuser, not her."

Unlike other cases of DID that Natalia had treated, Dave's was unique in its manifestation of dissociative amnesia. During their sessions, Natalia had been able to tease out each identity without the others knowing it. However, outside her office, it seemed that Dave's identities watched and communicated with one another, even argued sometimes. Bones thought Dave was a pussy, but he liked him all right, but Machete, holy shit, Bones *hated* Machete. Though Bones was from the shadow world, a world in which the sun never shone, he had been able to see just fine in the human world until Machete came along and got laser surgery. Now everything looked bright and hurt his eyes. What was worse, Bones had explained, was that Machete wanted to stop other kids with elves inside them from doing things like Dave had done. And that really pissed him off.

"You have no understanding of the shadow world," Bones said. "I killed the pussy part of Dave. He only came back to life because of me, because I found him down there in the dark. I taught him how to lie, how to make it look to everyone else, even his mother, that he was still Dave."

"Do you lie, Bones? To me, I mean?"

Bones smiled knowingly. "About some things, maybe. You know, like on TV, where the names and places are changed to protect the innocent."

"And Dave is one of the innocents?"

Bones made a wringing motion near his eye to indicate crying. "Not anymore. I killed that part of him when I got inside. I killed the boy who tried to pretend his mother didn't dig her nails into him or squeeze his balls when he wouldn't listen. The boy whose mother beat him for making a mess and once bit him on the ass for who knows why. Or the time when Dave was five years old and wet his bed. His mother got so mad, she shoved his head in the toilet so he would remember where to piss and almost drowned him. She would have done it, too, I promise you, had Dave's grandmother not been there. But Dave's grandmother was a pussy too. She didn't do shit to stop Dave's mother. All of them in that house were pussies except for Uncle Tommy."

Natalia wrote down, *Uncle Tommy*, the only person besides Dave's mother who all the identities had mentioned by name.

"So, I killed that part of him, yeah," Bones went on. "The innocent pussy part. I taught him how to stand up for himself—same as I taught him how to crush the pills and mix them in Rhonda's booze and cough medicine just to see what would happen."

"But you didn't know it would make her do what she did."

Bones shrugged. "Not the first time. But I kept doing it afterward so she would do it again—so she would come into Dave's room at night and crawl into his bed. So she would tell him how happy she was that he didn't die in Vietnam and ask him to give her another baby because the elves took their first one away."

"Dave loved his mother," Natalia said quietly. "After everything she had put him through, it was the only way he could feel close to her."

"No, Dave knew it was wrong, but I made him keep doing it for almost two years until something broke in Rhonda. And you know what? Dave laughed. We both did. The two of us just sitting on the stairs, laughing as she paced the living room in her bra and panties, ranting and raving about caterpillar blood as she chewed open her wrists. You know why the cunt did that? Because elves have caterpillars for jizz, worms of darkness that spread out inside when they fuck you. I was inside Dave when he put that darkness in his mother—a darkness so deep that it became one with her blood. Chew your wrists or slit them open a decade later, makes no difference. She couldn't escape the darkness pumping through her veins. A darkness that I, Bones the badass elf, the A number one motherfucker of all time, made Dave put there."

Bones beamed. Natalia understood that Dave's unconscious mind had crafted the Bones identity from a detail of his mother's delusions to cope with her abuse. She also understood how Bones was directly related to the changes he felt during puberty. But still, even with a quarter century of dealing with the worst trauma imaginable—family members who did the unspeakable to their own children—it was hard to stomach the way Bones spoke of what happened with Dave and Rhonda.

"And is that why you keep messing things up for Dave with other women?" she asked. "Because you can't put the darkness inside them anymore? Or is it because you're jealous, and you don't want Dave to have something normal between a man and a woman?"

Bones frowned, and his eyes became slits. "I don't give a fuck about all that," he said, wounded. "As long as he does bad things to other people, what do I care?" Bones leaned forward. "Don't you get it, Docky-Doc? After so many years, I was so close to breaking him down, to controlling him completely. I mean it. The only thing that kept Dave from turning out like those kids at the RITS was his uncle Tommy. But by the time Dave was in his twenties, Tommy was finally losing his hold on him. Goddamn, I was so close, Doc, then that motherfucker Machete comes along. And all because Dave's mother slit her wrists. What a pussy."

"Who's the pussy? Dave or Machete?"

"Machete!" Bones cried, his eyes suddenly wide and wild. "That pussy ruins everything! What's easier, you tell me, luring some kid into a cellar and taking over their body? Or just going after them like Machete when they can't go anywhere? Pussy move, when they're already caught like fish in a barrel."

"Like at the training school, you mean?"

"The RITS, yeah. You know how hard it is for elves to stay inside kids when you got guys like Machete around, scaring and setting them straight? And if they die before they do something bad, *really bad*, then the elves inside them die too. Pussies like Machete, they fuck everything up!"

Natalia held Bones's eyes for a moment. "Has Machete ever killed anyone? Boys like Dave, I mean, who have elves in them?"

Bones smiled impishly and kissed the air. "You should ask Machete that."

Natalia smiled and wrote down, *Dead bodies strewn about after a plane crash*—not because she was uncomfortable, not because her heart was hammering and her pen was shaking, but because she needed a moment to decide where to go next. Should she continue speaking to Bones or engage with Machete? So far, in the five months she and Dave Ruggieri had been working together, Machete was the only identity who spoke to her of the truth about elves.

And *that* was what both terrified and excited her.

Chapter Twenty-Two

Bobby blinked at the plant near the window and, as he swiveled his eyes back to Dr. Morris, reminded himself that he was Dave Ruggieri. "I'm sorry, what was I saying?"

Dr. Morris smiled. "You zoned out again. We had been talking about visiting your mother's grave. You said you were going to give it another shot this week, just a quick drive-by to get your feet wet, then we started talking about fishing."

"Oh yeah." Dave remembered everything now, as if their entire conversation had been downloaded all at once into his brain. More of the bullshit life that he had stolen from Jerry Cotoia, something about chartering a fishing boat for him and his friends when the weather got better.

Dave was about to make some more small talk, but then he caught Dr. Morris eyeing the clock on the wall behind him. Dave glanced over his shoulder at it too. Almost nine o'clock.

"Holy shit," Dave said. "That flew by."

Dr. Morris smiled, but Dave thought her eyes looked different from before—suspicious, calculating, and entirely devoid of the sympathy that had been there when they spoke of visiting his mother's grave. He also sensed that something had passed between them—something hidden behind an empty black curtain of forgetting. This made Dave feel uneasy and exposed. Only afterward, when he was driving through the East Side as Bobby again, did he begin to understand why. Dr. Morris knew a secret.

Part IV: This Foreign Country

Chapter Twenty-Three

If the past is a foreign country, then here, on the other side of the crime scene tape, it must be another world. And yet, precisely how Ray Dawley had arrived on this distant planet was still somewhat of a mystery to him. An hour earlier, he had been on Earth, settling in to write in the comfort of his den. But now, here he was, out in the merciless morning of some half-frozen world, sitting on a guardrail and staring down into a paper cup of cold coffee with over a dozen drawn-faced, tired-eyed aliens buzzing all around.

One of them was Detective Sergeant John Seabrook—a big, thick-necked guy with glasses and an uncanny resemblance to George Foreman. Seabrook was good friends with Eddie Sayers, he had explained, and worked under him in his old division until the son of a bitch retired. They already had a good idea who the deceased was—registration in the car, face matched the driver's license they found in his wallet—but still, it would be helpful if Ray could give them a positive ID and maybe some details before the medical examiner took over and they moved everything to the lab.

"It's my understanding that you might be one of the last people to have seen the deceased alive. We'd appreciate any assistance that you might be able to provide in this matter, Mr. Dawley."

"Please, call me Ray," he had said as Seabrook and another detective whose name Ray didn't catch led him to the car. On some level, Ray had wanted to tell them that he understood, that he had been this route before and was just grateful that the police weren't treating him the way they did when his wife was killed. But Ray kept all that to himself as he approached the car, which was still hooked to the back of the tow truck and leaking water out the front. All four of the Lexus's doors stood open, and a policewoman who had been taking pictures wished Ray good morning as she stepped aside for him. Seabrook had introduced Ray to the medical examiner, Dr. Rita Gonzalez, who stood on the other side of the door, shining a flashlight on the body in the driver's seat.

"That your friend?" she had asked.

Ray felt something dark and putrid welling up inside him even as the bright side, the glass-half-full side, whispered with its last, dying breath that this had to be some kind of joke, that at any moment, Eddie Sayers would pop out from the narrow strip of woods on the shore behind him, howling with laughter and crying, "Gotcha, Dawley! Oh man, you shoulda seen your face!"

But there had only been Ray's voice, muddy and distant, as he identified the body and tried to wrap his mind around the horror before him. Matt Kauffman, who had been laughing it up in Ray's den the night before, was dead—strangled, it appeared, in the driver's seat of his car. His neck had been tied to the headrest with a length of rope. His open eyes bulged from their sockets. His face was bloated, and his skin bluish white. Stuffed in his mouth, unmistakable in the beam from Dr. Gonzalez's flashlight, was the tail of a very large fish.

"Yeah, that's him," Ray had said. "That's Matthew Kauffman."

"You sure?"

"Yes, I'm sure."

But now, sitting on the guardrail in this alien world, Ray wasn't sure at all. Nothing seemed real anymore. Never mind that his friend was dead. Never mind that it appeared someone had strangled him. *But a* fish *stuffed down his throat?* Ray had actually smelled it before he'd seen it. Now, all he could smell was his coffee and the whiff of booze from his pores. He was sweating, a feverish heat collecting under his hat and coat like when he used to shovel driveways up the street four decades earlier.

The snap of a twig startled him—some cops scouring the woods on the other side of the guardrail—and Ray looked again at Matt's car. From where he sat about twenty yards away, Ray could no longer see his friend. A canopy had been set up over the driver's side, and the forensics team had begun bagging evidence from the interior and placing it in a plastic storage bin.

"Get you a refill, Ray?" Seabrook was filling his cup from one of the coffee urns that had been set up on the table near the mobile crime lab.

Ray shook his head, and Seabrook handed the cup to his partner, Detective Costa—a hollow-eyed, snaggle-toothed guy with a mustache and skin like Swiss cheese.

Costa sipped the coffee then leaned in closer to Ray with his foot on the guardrail. "I know this is hard, but can you tell me again what happened last night—the last thing you remember, I mean? I'm not following the sequence of events after you guys started playing"—he checked his notepad—"*Night Rider*, you said?"

"*Night Driver*, yeah. And look, I'm not trying to be a dick, but I've told you guys three times already, I don't remember much after that—what time Matt left. We must've been passed out. Eddie and I. We polished off a bottle of Scotch and half a bottle of tequila. Never mind all the beers."

Seabrook sat beside Ray on the guardrail and lit a cigarette. "I hear you. Been there plenty of times myself with Eddie too. Only Irish boy I know who can't hold his liquor."

Detective Costa snickered, but Ray just exhaled wearily.

"Look, I'm just trying to get a bead on what time your friend left. You sure you were passed out? You think maybe you were just so hammered you don't remember it?"

Ray's stomach squeezed. "I don't know, maybe. Whole night is a blur now. Why don't you just ask Eddie? Maybe he remembers more than I do."

Seabrook checked his watch. "Yeah, we been trying to get ahold of him, but I figure he's knee-deep in that hearing now. Unbelievable, some broads. Work your whole life just to find some peace, and they won't let you have it."

Ray breathed in deeply and sipped his coffee—cold, tasted like shit, didn't even want it, but anything was better than just sitting there, sweating and talking to these guys with his thumb up his ass. If they considered him a suspect, why not just come right out and say it? Jesus Christ. Matthew Kauffman. Strangled to death with a fish in his mouth. This couldn't be happening. "I'm sorry," Ray said, his throat tight. "I wish I had more to tell you. Have you found his phone yet? I thought you guys could do that in like two seconds or something these days."

"We've got someone working on locating the phone." Costa looked at his notepad. "Working on tracking down the wife too. Shelly. Your friend didn't tell you where they were staying in Newport?"

Ray shook his head. "Eddie and I were just busting his balls last night about how she tracks him. Probably been calling him all morning. They were only in town for a few days. His brother's funeral was yesterday, and now—"

Ray's voice choked off. Shit, was he really going to lose it in front of these guys? Just like he did forty-something years ago when the cops questioned him on this very same guardrail after Bobby Bonetti fell through the ice? It was all too surreal, too unbelievable to cry. No, if Ray started crying, he might not be able to stop. Strangled with a fish in his mouth. *Are you kidding me?*

"Hey, Dan, can you excuse us for a sec?" Seabrook asked Costa.

The men exchanged a look that Ray found irritating—rehearsed, like the look on those insipid TV crime dramas following some trite good-cop, bad-cop routine—then Detective Costa nodded and disappeared around the other side of the tow truck. Seabrook took a long drag from his cigarette and exhaled slowly.

"Eddie often talked about growing up here," he said, looking around. "You guys got a few years on me, but I figure it's the same, the friends you make when you're a kid. I got a bunch I still keep in touch with too—a bond that, for whatever reason, is still there, you know? Course, unlike you, I never left. Grew up on the other side of town. Graduated Cranston West in the late nineties. You guys were East, right?"

Ray nodded. Seabrook was trying to soften him up for something, he could tell. *How about just getting to the point?*

"Goddamn shame, honestly." Seabrook looked over at Matt's car. "A thing like this happening to someone you've known your whole life. You did say you guys sort of lost touch though, right? You think maybe Kauffman could've been into something you don't know about? Snort a little coke, maybe hit the pipe now and then?"

"Are you kidding me? Matt? Guy never even smoked weed, as far as I know."

Seabrook smiled. "Okay, I hear you. I'm just trying to pin down what your buddy might've been doing down here. A drug deal is always my first bet, but let's put that aside for a second and think about how the killer could've gotten to him."

"After Matt left my house, you mean?"

"Yeah. The way I see it, we only got a couple of options. First thing I'm thinking is, for whatever reason, your buddy called someone to meet him down here, then things went bad. The other option, Kauffman's killer maybe surprised him somewhere else and forced him to drive down here. I suppose this could have been random—that your buddy had just driven down here and happened to be in the wrong place at the wrong time. But stuffing a fish in his mouth? You get where I'm going?"

Ray felt a curdle of nausea in his stomach. "Yeah, that this was intentional. That Matt was a target."

"Not necessarily," Seabrook said in a plume of smoke. "Late at night, your buddy's horny, texts some side piece he's here in Cranston or maybe a pro through some app. Who knows? His wife tracks him, right? GPS isn't always accurate. The phone would still register near your house if he's wanting to pay for a blowjob." Ray made a scoffing sound. "Hey, I've seen it before. You'd be surprised the trouble some of these married guys will go to for a little adventure."

"That doesn't sound like Matt," Ray said. "And what, you're saying he and some hooker had a falling-out, so her pimp strangled him and stuffed a fish in his mouth?"

Seabrook smiled, cleared his throat, and spat the phlegm into the brush behind him. "Yeah, I suppose you're right." He took another drag. "Any other reason you can think of why your buddy might've driven down here?"

Ray sighed and rubbed his eyes. "Nostalgia, missing his brother, maybe? We spent a lot of time down here as kids. Maybe he wanted to take one last look before he drove back to New Jersey. Or maybe to just clear his head."

"Okay," Seabrook said. "So, let's say someone jumps him as he's leaving your house, maybe is even waiting for him in the back seat of his car, then forces him to drive to the pond, where he strangles him. ME will need to confirm that, but from what I can tell, looks like that's how it went down. After that, the killer stuffed that fish in his mouth and rolled his car into the pond. Kauffman's wallet had over a hundred dollars in it, so robbery wasn't a motive. Pond's half-frozen, water's pretty shallow, so the killer didn't care about hiding the car. Unless he's a stupid son of a bitch. But judging from that fish, I'd say he was pretty intentional about the whole thing. Wanted to send a message."

Ray felt the hackles rise on the back of his neck. "You mean like a serial killer or something?"

Seabrook leaned closer. "Listen, Ray," he said, his voice lower now, "I could get in trouble for this, but since you're a friend of Eddie's and it's probably gonna come out anyway, goes without saying what I'm about to tell you stays between us, okay?"

Ray nodded.

"Your friend's brother, the one who died—"

"Jimmy."

"You know his daughter, Debra, had been dating this small-time mafia hood?"

Ray shook his head.

"Dirtbag named Ronnie Matarese. Beat the shit out of her last week. Not the first time either. Bada boom, bada bing, what do you know, Ronnie is shot to death early yesterday morning in his apartment. Execution style, one bullet, right between the eyes. That's not been made public yet."

Ray swallowed hard. His throat felt like sandpaper. At the funeral, Ray had only spoken to Jimmy's daughter briefly to express his condolences, but even Natalia had noticed how the girl's makeup had been unable to hide the bruising under her eye and the scabbed-over split of her busted lip.

"Matarese's murder was all over the news last night," Seabrook went on. "Just a punk riding on his name, family not even close to what it was in the old days. But this Debra, Matt Kauffman's niece? Kind of weird, don't you think? Her boyfriend and her uncle being murdered not even twenty-four hours apart?"

"Are you saying you think the murders might be connected?" Ray's heart hammered, and the hair on the back of his neck felt like a collar of pins and needles.

Seabrook shrugged and took another drag from his cigarette. "Weird, is all I'm saying. Media already connected the girl to Matarese. Police records of domestic disputes, that sort of thing usually makes someone a prime suspect. But imagine the field day those vultures are gonna have when they find out your buddy in that car there is little Miss Debbie's uncle."

Ray swiveled his eyes in the direction of some news vans that had begun lining the hill on Lexington Avenue a half hour earlier. Even now, a couple of cops were getting into it with a reporter on the Blackamore Avenue side, but from where Ray sat, he couldn't see what was happening behind the mobile crime lab.

"So you're telling me you think Debra killed him?"

"Girl has an alibi for Matarese. Probably her uncle too. But that doesn't mean she didn't hire someone. Someone mobbed up, maybe, like Matarese."

"So this was a mob hit, you think?"

"Maybe. Or at least made to look like one. You've seen *The Godfather*, right? Remember when they killed that guy and sent the Corleone family some fish in his bulletproof vest?" Seabrook jerked his chin at Matthew's car. "This thing remind you of that?"

"But that's just the movies." Ray's voice rose with anxiety and disbelief. "I mean, mob guys don't really do that sleep-with-the-fishes shit. And even if they did, why would someone want to murder Matt?"

"Well, that's what I'm asking you." Seabrook met Ray's eyes for the first time. "Your friend ever mention anything about his niece? Some falling-out they had over money maybe when her old man died?"

"Christ, I don't know." Ray's head spun. "Jimmy didn't have a pot to piss in. Been living in some Section Eight dump over in North Kingstown for years—basically drank himself to death, Matt told me. Why don't you ask Debra all this?"

"We'll talk to her again. But you see her getting cozy with anyone at the funeral?"

"New boyfriend, you mean?" Ray asked. "Someone who might've taken care of business on her behalf?"

Seabrook nodded, and Ray racked his brain, playing over the mourners he had seen outside the church. But their faces, with the exception of Chuck Finola and a few others from his childhood, had already begun to fade. Ray sighed and shook his head, then Detective Costa appeared from around the tow truck and hurried over to them.

"We've located the victim's phone." His eyes landed on Ray. "We could get a search warrant, Mr. Dawley, but it would save us a lot of time if you'd just give us permission to come inside."

Ray's heart dropped. "My place?" was all he could muster on legs made of jelly.

Seabrook took a final pull from his cigarette, ground it into the pavement with his shoe, and stood beside Ray. "One sec, Ray," he said and pulled Costa aside to speak with him in private.

Ray just stood there, suddenly panicked as his bright side began yapping away again, forcing his brain to look at things logically while at the same time telling him to stay calm. *The cops traced Matt's cell phone to my house, but so what?* Easy enough to explain. Poor guy was so hammered he must have forgotten it when he left—just staggered out to his car, and that was when his killer surprised him.

But as Ray watched Seabrook and Costa conferring, his cynical, glass-half-empty side kicked in. What if the detective's spiel about all that mob bullshit was just that, some bullshit smokescreen to keep him occupied while the cops traced Matt's phone to the very place they suspected it might be all along? Ray's house. *You know what that means then, right, Ray? Guess who's their prime suspect? That's right, I'll take Dumbass Cranston Boys for a thousand, Alex.*

Ray swallowed back an urge to laugh, to just give himself over to a sort of suppressed madness he could feel welling up inside him. A sense of I told you so, of knowing all along that his homecoming, his marriage to Natalia, and the life they had planned had been too good to be true, that sooner or later, the rug pull would happen. An hour before, he had been sitting in his den with a new dawn brightening around him, and now here he was, on his way to jail for a murder he did not commit.

Jesus, calm down, Ray told himself as Seabrook shot him a look then lit another cigarette. Why did he always do this? Go from zero to sixty in two seconds? *Might I remind you, Ray, you didn't do any-thing. Same as you didn't do anything when you got called on the carpet by the dean. Same as you didn't do anything to make Connie cheat on you or Hana die. That's where all this is coming from, right? Your whole life, one moment, everything is pristine and covered in snow, and then the next, the ice breaks, and you're underwater.*

Detective Costa disappeared again behind the tow truck, and Seabrook returned.

"Sorry about that, Ray," he said. "This cell phone stuff is still in that tricky gray area of exigent circumstances, know what I mean?"

Ray didn't, but he nodded anyways.

"But yeah, Dan is right. If you give us permission to retrieve the phone from your house, we don't need to waste time getting a warrant, and that'll be better for everyone." Seabrook jerked his chin at the news vans. "Only a matter of time before they report on that—location where a warrant's been served, know what I mean?"

"He must've dropped it outside or something." Ray heard the tremor in his voice—the scared child, the eleven-year-old kid who tried not to cry when he told the cops what happened with Bobby Bonetti over four decades ago in almost this exact same spot. "But yeah, go ahead, search the whole house for all I care."

Seabrook half smiled, and Ray saw something soften in his eyes. *Pity? Compassion?* Either way, Ray Dawley felt a softening in him too—an ebb in his tide of panic that maybe he wasn't a suspect after all.

As if reading his mind, Seabrook said, "We really appreciate your help, Ray. We'll find who murdered your friend. I promise you that."

Two minutes later, Ray was heading back up the street, mercifully unnoticed by the news crews and the Chuck Finola crowd. The plan, Seabrook had told him, was to meet Ray in front of his house. The detectives would slip away in an unmarked, drive up Blackamore, loop around on Pontiac, then park a few houses up from Ray's on Lexington so they wouldn't draw attention. Scene had been handed over to the forensic team anyway, other neighbors being questioned, body would be on its way to the morgue soon, so still plenty of roadkill for the crows to pick at, Seabrook had assured him.

So just cooperate. Ray hurried past the vans. *Remember, you didn't do anything, so there's nothing to fear.* But that was his problem, wasn't it? He had *always* been afraid—even as a kid, when he followed Eddie and Matt up shoddily nailed planks to someone's treehouse or into the darkest reaches of the big drainpipe at the pond. Yeah, Ray had always hung back, had always been the last in line—but not that day out on the ice. No, *that day*, Ray had been first. So there must be something inside him, right? A reserve, a well of courage that he could draw from when it counted.

As Ray approached his house, he tried to picture that well of courage inside him—imagined himself cranking up a bucket of the stuff and gulping it down. Ray inhaled deeply, slipped out his phone, and dialed Matt's number, moving closer to the hedges as he listened for the ringtone. A second later, he saw Seabrook and Costa, their faces grave, heading toward him on the sidewalk.

"Timing is on our side," Seabrook said. "A request for a wellness check from Kauffman's wife was called a few minutes ago. She tracked his phone to your house. Dispatch is handling it now. Newport Police will take care of notifying her in person."

"Jesus, Shelly," Ray muttered, his mind refusing to entertain what she was about to go through—what he knew all too well from firsthand experience—then he led Seabrook and Costa inside his house. Ray was dimly aware of the air tensing as they glanced around the living room, then he motioned for them to follow him into the den, where he dialed Matt's number again.

"We pretty much spent most of the night in here," he said, then the theme song from the James Bond movies started playing somewhere near the windows.

Before Ray could move toward the sound, Detective Costa slipped past him and followed the ringtone to the sofa.

"I see it," he said. The phone was wedged between the seat cushions.

Ray hung up, and Costa put on a pair of latex gloves he'd had in his jacket pocket.

"That's where he was sitting last night," Ray said. "That's the last place I saw him before he left."

Costa slipped the phone out from the sofa and brought it to Seabrook. The two men examined it for a moment, then Seabrook said, "You wouldn't happen to know the code to unlock it, would you, Ray?"

Ray shook his head. His heart was pounding again, and he felt short of breath. "Shelly might, but isn't there a fingerprint lock? Can't you just bring the phone down to... you know...?" Ray's voice tapered off awkwardly. How should he say it? The pond? Matt? His cold, dead thumb?

"We can try," Costa said. "But usually, the person needs to be alive."

"Something to do with an electrical charge people give off," Seabrook said. "Body chemistry, I don't know."

Ray swallowed hard. *Well, shouldn't you get moving?* he wanted to say as the two detectives just stood there looking at him, then, thank God, Costa's phone rang. He slipped it out of his pocket, looked at the caller, then exchanged another of those TV looks with Seabrook.

"Need to take this," Costa muttered, then he disappeared outside with Matt's phone.

Seabrook stuffed his hands in his pockets and looked up at the pictures of Ray's family on the wall. "Stepson's away at college? Wife and daughter at your mother's?"

"That's right."

Seabrook's eyes drifted down to the throwback Atari still on top of the console and hooked up to the TV. "So, here we are then. No one else but you, Eddie, and Kauffman in the house, then, at some point, your friend leaves. Your alarm wakes you up around five, then Eddie wakes up—when, did you say?"

"About twenty minutes later. Am I a suspect, Detective?" Ray's question had slipped out before his brain had decided to ask it, and he answered himself just as quickly. *A murder victim's cell phone is found at your house? Yeah, I'd say that makes you a suspect, Mr. Dawley.* And yet, oddly, the jumpiness Ray had felt only seconds earlier was gone. In its place a sense of calm resolve to confront the inevitable settled over him, drawing from that well of courage, he hoped, because—Ray kept reminding himself—he didn't do anything wrong.

"I don't know yet." Seabrook held Ray's eyes. "This was the last place anyone saw Matthew Kauffman alive. His cell phone was found at your house, but if you were the killer, man, you'd have to be a certified moron to let a detail like that slip. Problem is, it justifies a search of the premises."

"A search for what?" Ray asked, his mind already transporting the Chuck Finola crowd from the bottom of the street to the sidewalk outside his house. *Meet your new neighbor, everyone—you know, the whack job who bought his childhood home and is now the prime suspect in his oldest friend's murder.*

Seabrook thrust his hands in his pockets and leaned against the doorway to the living room. "We'll dust for fingerprints," he said. "Also look for anything that might tie this place or someone here to the murder scene. The rope in the car, for example"—Seabrook looked down the hallway toward the kitchen—"Maybe a fish in the freezer."

Ray sank onto the sofa. Jesus Christ, this couldn't be happening. Never mind the neighbors, what about his wife and daughter coming home to a bunch of cops crawling all over the place?

"You've been more than cooperative so far, Ray," Seabrook said. "You give me permission in writing to do a search, to seize anything we might want to analyze, and we can avoid the publicity of a search warrant. Costa or someone from the forensics team can sign off as a witness, and we can do this real quiet—can even be out of here before your daughter gets home from school."

"Yeah, of course. Do what you want. I don't give a fuck."

"This isn't a crime scene, Ray. So it won't be like at the pond. You have my word on that. If you didn't do anything wrong, you've got nothing to worry—"

Seabrook's cell phone rang, and he slipped it out of his pocket, his eyes leaving Ray's only to see who was calling. "About time," Seabrook said when he answered. "No, forensic team has taken over, and I'm at your buddy's. Uh-huh. Yeah, I thought of that too. How fast can you be here? Okay." He hung up.

"That was Eddie?" Ray asked.

"Yeah. That was Eddie."

Chapter Twenty-Four

Eddie hung up with John Seabrook, drove his truck to the attendant booth, and paid for his parking just like any other schmuck at the district courthouse that morning. No more reserved spaces for law enforcement, no more special treatment *period*, not even from Judge Capuano, in front of whom Eddie had testified during domestics countless times over the years. That son of a bitch. Eddie had arrived in the courtroom showered and shaved and suited up like the old days, like he owned the place, only to be sent away by Cap with his tail between his legs.

Oh yeah, Katie had done him dirty, all right. She and her lawyer had produced some threatening emails Eddie had sent her during the divorce—which Eddie would have known about had he hired an attorney and requested an evidence exchange, Cap said. *What a dumbass, how could I have forgotten about all that?* Cap didn't want to hear anything about context or about the agreement surrounding Katie's half million in inheritance from her aunt. Instead of throwing out the case, he'd issued a continuance so Eddie could hire an attorney. Should've known, should've just bitten the bullet and dropped the five grand for the retainer. *Fucking Katie. Never ends.*

And yet, as Eddie swung his truck out of the lot and onto Clifford Street, all that bullshit seemed like a walk in the park compared to what he was dealing with now. Last thing he expected coming out of the courthouse was a bunch of missed calls from the guys in his old division. The first call Eddie returned was to Dan Costa, who had tried him a half dozen times and left a message about getting back to him ASAP. Somehow, Eddie knew it was about Matt, but he never imagined what Costa ended up telling him. Matthew Kauffman had been found strangled to death down at Blackamore Pond. There was more, Costa said, but Seabrook would fill him in once he got his ass over to Ray Dawley's. Costa said he needed to secure a search warrant, to which Eddie told him to get one for a blood and urine test, too, if Ray didn't consent.

"The hell we need that for?" Costa had asked.

"I have reason to believe I was drugged" was Eddie's reply. He would willingly submit to a toxicology test, but if Ray refused, then they would need a warrant to confirm what Eddie had suspected then rejected earlier: Ray Dawley had roofied him.

Eddie still couldn't remember shit from the night before and, while waiting in the drive-through at Dunkin' Donuts, did a quick search on his phone for the symptoms of being roofied. Blackouts, amnesia, and extreme sedation when mixed with alcohol. Oh yeah, Eddie Sayers had been roofied, all right—*that* was why this hangover felt so different than any other he had experienced over the years. Other than Matt, who was now dead, who else could have slipped him something if not Ray Dawley?

Eddie explained as much to John Seabrook when he called him next. "Wait for me to get there before you ask him about it, understand? I'll know if he's lying."

And now, as Eddie headed down Clifford Street for I-95, he reminded himself, as he always did during a murder investigation, that he had one of two choices. He could give in to his emotions and be a part of the problem, or he could put on his big-boy pants and help find a solution. True, the victim this time around was his friend, probably the best friend he had ever had, but Eddie needed to keep his head. Besides, he was angry, and Detective Sayers always did his best work when he could focus that anger and hone it like a surgeon's scalpel dissecting the clues—same as he did when he had decided to become a cop nearly forty years earlier.

Eddie still remembered the moment as if it were yesterday: Sunday, May 25, 1986, after the interview Ralph Richard gave on some local TV show. Ralph Richard had just been acquitted three days earlier for the sexual assault of his four-month-old daughter, Jerri Ann, back in 1984. Initially, the case had been treated as an abduction, but when poor little Jerri Ann's battered body was discovered among some trash a block away from her home, suspicion fell on Ralph and his wife, Donna.

Eventually, the couple was charged and were scheduled to be tried separately—Ralph for sexually assaulting his infant daughter, Donna for her murder. Come to find out, Ralph was some dirtball drug dealer, and his wife, well, her stupid story just never added up. If only they had let Eddie Sayers into the courtroom, things would've turned out differently. Eddie had studied every detail of the case during Ralph's trial—which, incredibly, resulted in a not-guilty verdict, though the sick fuck's semen had been found on his infant daughter's body. Eddie, along with everyone else in Rhode Island, was in shock. Same when Donna's charges were ultimately dropped following her husband's acquittal.

But all that wasn't what made Eddie want to be a cop. No, it was that Sunday-morning interview with Ralph Richard and his attorney. Ralph was lying. Eddie knew it as sure as he was sitting there eating his Cheerios. Bastard even had the balls to fake cry for the camera and everything. Same shit he pulled in front of the jury, Eddie figured, and those dumbasses *bought it*. Not Eddie Sayers, though. And from that moment, his course was set. No more pieces of shit raping little girls and bashing their brains out as long as Eddie Sayers had something to say about it. He enrolled in classes at CCRI the following fall, and three years after that, Katie's uncle got him into the academy, and his path was clear—just like his path now was leading him straight to Ray Dawley.

No, not Ray! Eddie's gut screamed. *Anyone but Ray.*

But if not Ray, then who? The only other possibility was Matt. But Matt was dead, and Ray was alive, so Eddie kept coming back to Ray. Maybe there was a side to his old friend that he had been blind to all these years. Could the biggest pussy of them all be responsible for the horror show Edward Sayers suddenly found himself starring in?

Eddie felt as if he were going insane and had to remind himself again to stay calm—to focus, to hone the blind rage that he had felt so many times over the years when he looked into the dull, remorseless eyes of those who had done the unspeakable. Things that most people couldn't even imagine. Things that Eddie Sayers would carry around with him like poison for the rest of his life because they had forced him to see the world for what it really was: a bottomless, churning cesspool of evil, of dumbasses and liars, of thieves and cons and murderers—some so bad that they would rape a four-month-old girl and bash her brains out and toss her in the trash while others went on with their lives like nothing had happened. That was, until something *really important* came along, upon which they would swap out their selfie sticks for crocodile hashtags and protest signs bashing the very people who had dedicated their lives to protecting them.

Yeah, *that* was the world in which Eddie Sayers lived and breathed. And this time, the cesspool had claimed none other than Matthew Kauffman as one of its victims. But Shelly—Jesus Christ Almighty, Shelly and the kids—they were the real victims now. What the hell could he say to them? What could he possibly offer in a world where things like this weren't supposed to happen to people like them? It wouldn't help them to know that this was the way the world really was, that they were just plain lucky not to have been swept up into the cesspool sooner. Worse, Eddie couldn't fathom looking Shelly in the eye and saying that he would always be there for her and the kids when he knew damn well that no one could ever ease the pain, the emptiness, the never-ending wondering of *why* that would define their lives from now on.

Why? Well, that's the question, isn't it? Why, why, why would Ray Dawley drug me then drive Matt down to Blackamore Pond to strangle him—if that is in fact what happened? No, the whole thing just didn't make sense—never mind that Eddie was getting way ahead of himself.

Yeah, Eddie thought as he swung his car onto the on-ramp for 95, before he could even begin to ask why, he needed to be sure of *who*—and Eddie would be there when John Seabrook questioned Ray. Eddie would know right away if his old friend was lying—just like he knew it with Ralph Richard forty years earlier on TV.

And if Ray's telling the truth?

Well, then Eddie Sayers would have to cross that bridge when he came to it.

Chapter Twenty-Five

Tommy had just finished lowering his last jar of pickled peppers into the pot of boiling water when he received the text message from Pete Scungio.

The old enamel canning pot on the stove had belonged to Tommy's mother, but he had tweaked her pickled pepper recipe into something all his own. Tommy had learned from trial and error that the sweet spot for his peppers, which even his asshole cousins in Warwick agreed were the best, was about three weeks from jar to table—the perfect amount of time so the peppers stayed crisp and the taste of celery and mustard seeds didn't become too overpowering. The seeds had been Tommy's idea, a little twist on his mother's vinegar brine of peppercorns, onions, and garlic. And don't forget the dash of turmeric. That was the secret—just one of many that Tommy Bonetti would take with him to the grave.

The text message from Pete had to do with another of Tommy's secrets. Tommy had texted him earlier about Ronnie Matarese, but Pete's friend on Cranston PD said he couldn't say more than what was already on the news because, go figure, Cranston PD had their hands full with *another* body—this one found in Blackamore Pond at the bottom of Lexington Avenue. Pete said he would text again later when he learned more, but Tommy wasn't sure he wanted to know anything now. Hadn't Bobby told him he'd been hanging around his old neighborhood last night? And hadn't he all but confessed to the Matarese hit when he made that cute little green-bathrobe comment?

The water in the canning pot began to boil again, and Tommy set the timer on his phone for fifteen minutes. Normally, he would just keep an eye on the microwave clock, but he felt loopy and unfocused from lack of sleep and didn't want to risk leaving the jars in too long if he got distracted. Tommy sure as hell felt distracted. The fuck did his nephew get off bringing up that green-bathrobe shit? Tommy had tossed and turned all night before finally falling asleep sometime after four. Miraculously, the garbage trucks didn't wake him that morning, but by the time he stumbled out into the kitchen, Bobby was already gone—off to his usual Monday therapy session, he figured.

Still, even after spending the morning on his peppers, Tommy couldn't shake what his nephew had said to him the night before—*Mind your own business,* in so many words—but it was the implication of that business that bothered him. Was Bobby doing hits for the DeLorenzo family? And if so, how long had this little side hustle been going on?

No, no way Bobby would be that stupid—not after what he saw Tommy go through when that construction crew found what was left of Joe Turchetta and his green bathrobe thirty years earlier. Lou Barboza, who had recently turned State's witness against Rocco Matarese, tried to finger Tommy for it. They even took a sample of his DNA, but since only Lou's blood had been found on the knife, the case against Tommy fell apart. Lou would go into the witness protection program for over a decade before he was picked up as part of a sex-trafficking ring in Arizona. The DeLorenzo family had him whacked in prison soon after.

But Ronnie Matarese getting whacked? Well, unless there was something going on that Tommy hadn't heard, it didn't make sense. Kid was just a punk. And Bobby being involved, well, that didn't make sense either. One, *how would they even know each other?* And two, Bobby was in his mid-fifties now and didn't need that shit. He had a good thing going with his disability and the bartending gig at the club. *Why would he want to get mixed up with the DeLorenzos?*

Tommy chuckled to himself and wiped his hands on his mother's old apron, keenly aware that he was becoming more and more like her with every passing day. Look at him, standing there, worrying like some fucking old lady whose son was out too late. At least he had the excuse of being tired. Tommy needed a solid seven to eight hours of sleep now to feel sharp—unlike when he was still managing the restaurant and sometimes would be up for two, three days straight. Usually, he had Tara to thank for that. What with her constant nagging, he would often just spend the night in the office rather than come home and be subjected to her bullshit.

No, he just didn't have that kind of stamina anymore—especially around the holidays. Tommy was the family's go-to guy for Christmas now, so he needed to start prepping early and a little at a time. He basically did everything for Christmas Eve these days—the spaghetti *aglio e olio*, the marinated squid, the snail salad, the fried smelts, and whatnot—but after Eva's shit show last year with the baked stuffed shrimp, Tommy planned on taking over that too. Thankfully, Christmas Day would be a lot easier. Mario was bringing his homemade wine, as usual, and Eva was bringing a stuffed veal roast that she was buying premade, so the biggest things ahead of him after today were the Christmas cookies and his mother's Italian wedding soup, which he would store in the garage freezer along with some side dishes that he planned on prepping early too.

But hey, at least he enjoyed it, he told himself as he checked his jars on the stove. At sixty-five—retired, divorced, no kids, and a half dozen or so ex-girlfriends still pissed at him—he had nothing better to do with his time than cook for his family and worry about his nephew. And yet, as much as he tried to tell himself how ridiculous the whole DeLorenzo thing sounded, Tommy couldn't shake how much his conversation with Bobby the night before had spooked him. Before he realized what he was doing, Tommy was on the floor, reaching for the pistol bag under Bobby's bed.

Tommy felt guilty snooping around like an old lady in Bobby's room, which had originally been his room when he'd bought his mother their little two-bedroom ranch in 1988. By that time, Mario and Eva had a place of their own, Carla had been in the nuthouse going on six years, and Bobby was living in a little apartment above the karate studio where he taught. Bobby would eventually move back home to look after his grandmother when she got sick. And after she died, he never left.

As Tommy's fingers found the handle for the pistol bag, more than ever, he felt like his mother, who had sawed off the footposts on this very bed over a half century earlier because Tommy used to hang his clothes on them instead of in his closet. *How many times did Mary Bonetti search my room?* he wondered—but she never found a custom nine-millimeter suppressor like Tommy did when, sitting on the floor, he opened his nephew's pistol bag.

Yeah, back in the day, Tommy Bonetti never kept the same gun in his house for long, and *never at all* if it had been used in a hit—which was why, when he dug farther into his nephew's pistol bag and found only his earmuffs and his safety glasses, he was almost positive that Bobby had ditched his gun after whacking Ronnie Matarese. And *that* was a problem.

Chapter Twenty-Six

As Eddie was parking his truck on the street behind Ray's car, Dan Costa hurried out of the house to meet him. Ray's old Honda Civic had been in the driveway when Eddie had left that morning, and now, an unmarked that he figured belonged to Seabrook and Costa sat in its place. Farther up the driveway, barely visible from the street, a CSI van had been backed in almost to the garage. They were keeping things quiet because Ray was cooperating, Seabrook had told him.

Eddie breathed in deeply and, fixing his eyes on Ray's car, muttered, "I am confident, articulate, and relaxed. Car." Mrs. Aurecchia, the old lady who'd run Eddie's special reading group back in elementary school, had taught Eddie this mantra to help calm his nerves. The trick was to look at the cars parked outside or to just think of his favorite while saying, "I am confident, articulate, and relaxed. Car." C stood for confident, A was for articulate, and R was for relaxed. At first, Eddie thought the whole thing was stupid, but eventually, all he would have to do was think about a red Corvette Stingray, and he wouldn't feel so nervous reading in front of the class—never mind forty-plus years later when he had to play it cool in front of a murder suspect.

Eddie shut off the engine and got out as Dan Costa came around to the driver's side.

The detective shot an anxious glance back toward Ray's house. "We got a couple of guys from CSI in there now," Costa said. "I don't know, man, your buddy seems pretty shaken up."

"I bet."

"Thing is, he hasn't asked once about a warrant or a lawyer—just gave us his consent to do whatever we want, including the blood and urine tests."

"The fuck," Eddie said, irritated. "I told you guys to hold off on asking him about that until I got here."

"That's what I'm telling you. It was his idea—maybe someone slipped you guys something in the pizzas, is what he said."

"Pizzas my ass."

"He telling the truth about that? They delivered after you guys got there?"

"Yeah, but you guys find those liquor bottles? That high-end Scotch and the tequila?"

"Dawley led us right to them. Empty Scotch bottle in the recycling bin out back, right on top of the pizza boxes. Tequila half-empty in the living room liquor cabinet. Gave us his consent in writing, doesn't give a shit if we tear up the whole house, he said. That sound like someone who's guilty to you?"

Eddie felt a flush of anger in his cheeks. "I never said he was guilty, Dan. I just want to make sure you go into this with a clear head. Only the three of us were in the house last night, understand?"

Costa shrugged and looked down at the pavement. "Yeah, well, anyway, he's on the porch with Sarge."

Eddie headed into the house. Ray Dawley's porch had three places to sit. An armchair in the corner, a tattered love seat under the living room windows, and an old rocker near the front door. Seabrook was on the love seat, but Ray, who had been sitting in the armchair, sprang to his feet as soon as Eddie entered and, with tears in his eyes, threw his arms around his friend and hugged him.

"Jesus Christ, Eddie. Matt—"

Eddie stiffened and awkwardly returned the embrace. Ray's emotion had caught Eddie off guard, leaving him somewhat rattled and suddenly uncertain as to whether he would be able to tell if Ray was lying.

"Yeah, man, I know, I know." Eddie patted Ray firmly on the back.

The men separated and sat down—Ray in the armchair, apologizing as he wiped his nose on the back of his hand, and Eddie in the rocker opposite him near the door. The porch felt hot and tight, the space heater in the corner going full blast. Eddie unzipped his coat and loosened his tie.

"Thanks for coming, Eddie." Seabrook flipped to a fresh page on his notepad. "We got a pretty good idea from Ray what happened up until you guys started playing *Night Rider*—"

"Jesus Christ, *driver*," Ray muttered. "The game is called *Night Driver*."

"Right," Seabrook said. "After that, well, what about you, Eddie? You remember anything after you guys dipped into that Scotch"—Seabrook swiveled his eyes to Ray—"Bowmore, you said it's called, right?"

Ray exhaled wearily and nodded.

"Yeah, that's when things get fuzzy." Eddie's heart beat fast, and he felt short of breath.

Costa was right. Ray didn't look guilty at all. His eyes were red from crying, and his expression reminded Eddie of when they were kids talking to the cops that day on the ice—earnest, desperate, afraid.

"Last thing I remember is playing Atari," Eddie went on. "Then, all of a sudden, it's five thirty, and I'm on the floor with a hangover and a throw pillow under my head."

"A throw pillow?" Seabrook asked.

Ray gestured, open-handed, to Eddie. "You see?" he asked, his voice cracking. "What'd I tell you? Eddie was on the floor with a pillow under his head, and I was in the chair. Friggin' KISS album somehow ended up on the record player too. I don't remember any of that—not even taking out the tequila. Which is why I'm telling you someone must have drugged our pizza."

"We'll have someone follow up on that." Seabrook looked at his notes. "You said delivery was through DoorDash, right?"

Ray turned his watery red eyes on Eddie as if Seabrook hadn't spoken. "Tell him, Eddie. You been around the block. How can we not remember anything unless someone roofied us?"

Eddie opened his mouth to speak, but nothing came out. If Ray were guilty of roofieing him, no way he would have the balls to just lay out exactly what he did as part of some act he thought might relieve him of suspicion. And the emotion, the fucking sincerity. Guy used to be an actor, yeah, but if he was this good, he would be in Hollywood right now, not Cranston.

"Only way we can know for sure now is that toxicology test," Seabrook said with his eyes on Eddie. "Ray here had that idea, too, along with taking a polygraph. We'll need to do all that down at the station—"

"Please," Ray said, "let's just get it done as soon as possible. I need to call my wife. She has no idea what's going on. And my daughter—"

"We'll have you back in plenty of time before Maggie gets home," Seabrook said, his eyes still on Eddie. "Won't be too much longer around here, I figure." He was looking at Eddie as if to say, *Well?*

Eddie swallowed back something that felt like an impulse to laugh—or maybe cry, he wasn't sure. On the one hand, he thought Ray didn't need to take a lie detector test—he was innocent, Eddie was almost sure of it—but on the other, if Ray hadn't roofied him, then it must have been Matt. *But why? And how does that connect to his murder?* Eddie fingered his collar. The porch was like a sauna. He could feel the sweat trickling down his back and took off his jacket. "Come on, Ray, help me out here," he said, aware of a tremor in his voice. "Can you remember anything else we haven't touched on yet?"

Ray threw up his hands. "Only that you hate tequila. I'd completely forgotten about that until I came back with these guys. You got sick from tequila when we were kids—remember when you raided the liquor cabinet in the living room? You swore you'd never touch that shit again, which means the tequila must've been my idea. I probably pressured you, Eddie, but I swear on Maggie, I can't remember!" Ray's voice cracked with emotion, and he snatched in breath.

He was on the verge of losing it again—Eddie, too, it felt like—and he glanced at Ray's car parked out front. Eddie repeated his CAR mantra in his head—*I am confident, articulate, and relaxed*—but it didn't help. Rising from his chair, he motioned for Ray to follow him. "You excuse us for a second, John?" The words had come out of Eddie's mouth before he understood why he was saying them—only that he suddenly felt claustrophobic and needed some air to clear his head.

He and Ray were outside on the front lawn a few seconds later—Ray, standing there, shivering with his hands stuffed in the pockets of his hoodie, Eddie close to him with a hand on his shoulder. He'd neglected to put on his jacket, but the cold felt wonderful. Sobering.

"This is so fucked up I don't know where to begin," Eddie said. "But I think you're right. We were drugged. Only question is who did it, understand?"

"Eddie, I'm not stupid," Ray said, his voice tight. "I know you guys think it's me—I mean, it's my house—but I swear on my daughter—"

"Okay, okay, we're not even there yet." Eddie forced a calmness into his voice. "John is a good guy. I mean it. He's not gonna just zero in on someone unless things point that way. Know what I mean?"

"Just tell him to let me take the polygraph—"

"They're going to do all that, okay? As long as you didn't do any-thing, you got nothing to worry about. Shit, at this point, I'm just as much a suspect as you."

"Yeah, but you didn't see him, Eddie. Didn't even look like Matt, the way he was murdered. And that fish in his mouth—"

"Whoa, whoa." Eddie's heart skipped a beat. "What do you mean 'fish'?"

"Your buddies didn't tell you that?"

Eddie shook his head, and something dark and heavy and vague-ly familiar began pooling in his stomach.

"Fuck," Ray said, "I don't know if I'm supposed to talk to you about this—"

"Come on, cut the shit. It's me."

Ray looked at Eddie with such tired helplessness that Eddie wasn't sure if he should hug or smack him.

"Seriously, Ray?"

Ray sighed and avoided Eddie's eyes. "I don't know if Seabrook was feeding me a line of bullshit, but he said what happened to Matt has all the markings of a mob hit. He was strangled, yeah, but some-one also stuffed a fish in his mouth. And not a whole fish either, I heard one of the CSI guys telling Costa before you showed up. Just the tail."

"Just the tail?"

"Yeah. Guess they didn't know that at first—until they pulled it out of his mouth, I mean. Seabrook told me Matt's niece, Debra, was tied to this mafia guy who got whacked a couple of nights ago. Maybe Matt's murder is connected through her in some way, he's thinking. Because of the fish tail. You know, like in the movies, when the mob wants to send a message."

Eddie nodded absently. His legs felt weak, and he could hardly hear his friend through the buzzing in his ears. Ten minutes earlier, he had been wondering whether Ray Dawley was a murderer, but now, Eddie felt as if he had stepped into some goddamn *Twilight Zone* episode in which things just kept getting weirder and weirder.

Ray's eyes narrowed with concern. "You okay, man?"

Eddie turned away from him and vomited into the bushes. He was dimly aware of Ray asking again if he was all right but could only focus on purging himself of the darkness in his stomach. Matt's killer had sent a message, all right. And Eddie Sayers had a feeling that message was for him.

Chapter Twenty-Seven

Twenty minutes after Shelly requested the wellness check, a pair of state troopers and a woman dressed in a long parka entered the parlor. The clock on the mantel chimed the quarter hour. Shelly Kauffman was good at noticing details like that. Times, places, where things were. She sat in a leather wingback chair by the fireplace, thumbing absently through an issue of *Better Homes and Gardens*. But when she saw the look on the troopers' faces, Shelly set down the magazine, stood, and reached for the handle of the rolling suitcase beside her. The troopers removed their hats.

"Mrs. Kauffman?" one of them said—handsome, square jawed, broad shouldered, and with smooth skin like copper. No name tag, just the number 212 over his left pocket. Shelly nodded, and something clicked. That had been the number of her homeroom in ninth grade. It was also the temperature at which water boiled. Shelly had never made that connection until now.

Her hand slipped from the suitcase. It had been dark outside when she'd packed and come downstairs to avoid a delay in departure when her husband returned. No discussion, no apologies accepted, just the silent treatment all the way back to New Jersey, that had been the plan. However, when eight o'clock rolled around and still no Matthew, Shelly began texting and calling him. A half hour after that, she made the call to the Cranston Police. Change of plans, it looked like now. But that was all right. Shelly Kauffman was good at adapting, acclimating, accommodating, and a bunch of other A-words too.

"We are here to deliver bad news," Homeroom Trooper said.

Again, Shelly nodded. She felt something shaking inside her—a rattling lid on a pot of hysteria about to boil over. But hey, that was all right too. She would have everything under control in a moment. She was good at things like that—keeping things under control, making sure they didn't boil over on the stove. Hadn't she been preparing for this all morning? She had known something bad had happened when the dispatch officer, unable to hide the anxiousness in her voice, made Shelly repeat the name of the bed-and-breakfast where she was staying.

"Your husband, Matthew, died last night in an apparent homicide," Homeroom Trooper said. "He was found in his car, which had been driven into a pond in Cranston."

Shelly nodded again. "Blackamore Pond?"

The troopers exchanged an anxious glance. Understandable, since Shelly's voice was trembling now and sounded far away.

"Yes, ma'am," Homeroom Trooper said. "At the bottom of Lexington Avenue."

"Where he grew up," Shelly said, dimly aware that she hadn't stopped nodding since Blackamore Pond.

The troopers exchanged another glance, then the woman who had arrived with them stepped farther into the parlor.

"Mrs. Kauffman, my name is Marilyn Bryant," she said. "I'm a crisis intervention specialist located here in Newport."

Shelly just kept nodding. The woman had blond hair and a sharp nose like Shelly's homeroom teacher in ninth grade, but Shelly couldn't remember her name—only that it wasn't Miss or Mrs. Bryant. No one went by "Ms." back then or cared about their pronouns. Numbers, the temperature of things were more important—212, like the pot that Shelly could feel now boiling over inside her, sending hot liquid through her veins. How strange that she could remember the 212 and nothing else. But hey, that was all right too. She could always check her old yearbooks when she got home.

Shelly had saved them along with her class pictures going back to kindergarten.

"Mrs. Kauffman, I'm here to help you through this," Marilyn Bryant said. "I'll accompany you to the medical examiner's office in Providence. That's where they've taken Matthew."

"And you're sure it's him?" Shelly's voice trembled, so far away now that she worried these people might think it was coming from the fireplace, maybe even from her old homeroom back in New Jersey. Millburn Junior High School, room 212. "Did you check his yearbook picture?" Shelly asked. "Mine's in a box in the guest room closet. Matthew's are in there, too, I think."

Marilyn Bryant moved closer and took Shelly's hand in hers. She was wearing formfitting black gloves—Isotoners, Shelly guessed, looking down at them.

"I know this is a shock," Marilyn Bryant said, "but you need to come with me."

It was then and only then that Shelly felt the tears streaming down her cheeks. *The pot on the stove is boiling over, 212,* she thought as she touched the wetness on her face. "Oh my God. This is really happening." Her fingers, glistening with her tears, were the last thing she saw before the parlor's old plank floor rushed up at her. After that, everything went black.

Chapter Twenty-Eight

Bobby felt the click sometime around noon, just as he entered the final sequence of his number four long form. If one of his students had ever asked Sensei Bonetti to describe the click, he most likely would have said, "You'll know it when you feel it." He had heard it called other things over the years. Flow state. The zone. The experience of being so immersed in an activity that one lost all sense of time and place.

For Bobby, however, the click was an actual moment when, as he blocked and struck and took down his imaginary opponents, he felt a stillness come over him. A sense of being at one with the air he breathed, of moving through space like a soul released from its body. No more tiredness in his muscles, no rubber mats beneath his feet, no chill of his sweat-soaked gi or even an awareness of the frayed black belt around his waist. A sense of weightlessness, of just being there, as if his movements were simply extensions of the light and shadow around him.

Bobby started calling it "the click" after he saw Ray Dawley in a play in high school. *Cat on a Hot Tin Roof* was the name. Boring piece of shit about some chick named Maggie, who basically spent the entire play bitching at her husband because he wouldn't fuck her. Ray played the husband and pretty much just drank and walked around on crutches the whole time. Bobby didn't know much about acting, but he thought Ray was all right since he sounded like he was just talking whereas everybody else was yelling. But it was something Ray's character said about why he drank that helped Bobby understand why he did karate. Ray kept saying he was trying to get "the click," which Bobby took to mean the moment when the booze kicked in and he was suddenly at peace and didn't give a shit about stuff anymore.

Decades later, when Bobby found out that Ray had a daughter named Maggie, he wondered if his friend had named her after the character in that play. Bobby wished he could have asked him—wished he could have thanked Ray, too, for putting into words the thing about the click. But Bobby never told Ray he had gone to see the play that night—it felt weird, especially since they had lost touch and were going to different schools at the time. Maybe being closer to Ray was part of finding the click outside the dojo, Bobby came to believe. Same reason he started seeing Ray's wife for therapy.

But after his session with Dr. Morris that day, Bobby had worried he might never feel the click again. Not even there at Rick Cesare's School of Self-Defense—which, for the last twenty years, had been located in a renovated Chinese restaurant on Reservoir Avenue. Up until the day he died at the age of seventy-five, Rick Cesare had been both the biggest badass and nicest guy Bobby had ever known. And for as long as he could remember, Rick had begged Bobby to take over the school instead of his daughter, Tonya, who wasn't the sharpest knife in the drawer, he always said. Still, ten years after Rick dropped dead of a heart attack one night during class, Tonya was still managing to keep things afloat. Good egg, that Tonya. She let Bobby keep his key, though he was no longer teaching. The fluorescent lights bouncing off the kids' gis hurt his eyes too much and made it impossible to train, let alone get the click.

But that morning, with just the cold gray light flooding in through the dojo's plate glass windows, the only thing keeping Bobby from his click was his lack of focus. He felt tired and easily distracted, and his nose would not stop running. Bobby had learned early on in his training that, rather than just executing a sequence of moves, forms—or *kata*—were only beneficial when visualizing attackers and how his techniques affected them. But after his session with Dr. Morris that morning, Bobby could not see anyone during his forms other than his mother.

Bobby still didn't understand how all that worked—how he could talk to Dr. Morris about Rhonda as Dave but then take away things about Carla as Bobby. Then there was that big gap of time when he zoned out, after which Dr. Morris looked at him as if she knew a secret. *What did we talk about?* Just like last night after leaving Ray's, there were parts Bobby couldn't remember—but his gut told him it was something more than just the usual Dave bullshit. When Bobby was in his early twenties, he and his buddies used to go see this guy Frank Santos, the R-rated hypnotist, who made people do all kinds of whacky shit in his show. Having sex with chairs, singing like Michael Jackson, even made this guy think he lost his balls once. *Did Dr. Morris do something like that? Did she hypnotize me to give me the balls to go to my mother's grave? Is that why I can't get the fucking cunt off my mind?*

Must be. And only after he had been practicing his forms for over two hours, when he understood that he was imagining his mother because Dr. Morris had helped him, Bobby felt the click, and he was resolved. He finished his form with a bow then quickly showered and left the dojo. He drove first to the CVS down the street, where he picked up a bottle of Robitussin, then drove into Saint Ann's Cemetery a few minutes later. He remembered his family's plot was on a corner near a tree, but it took a while of driving around to find it because the cemetery was so vast and, at some point in the twenty-plus years since his grandmother had died, the tree had been cut down. Bobby parked on the side of the narrow lane and turned off his engine. He slipped the bottle of Robitussin out of its box, removed the safety seal, and put on his sunglasses.

Bobby exited his car and walked over to his family's gravesite with the same weightlessness as the breeze. The click was still with him. His hair was wet from his shower, but Bobby was only dimly aware of the coldness behind his ears as he moved to the other side of the headstone to read the names and dates. His mother's information was chiseled below his uncle Domenic's, who had died as an infant from something that no one ever talked about—a hole in his heart, Tommy told him once, but even he couldn't say for sure since it all happened about four years before Tommy was born. Bobby's grandfather was buried on top of Domenic, a fact that used to make Bobby feel claustrophobic when he was a kid. But now, he just thought it strange, a big casket for an adult buried on top of a little one for an infant.

Bobby unscrewed the cap from the bottle and slowly poured its contents onto the place where, to the best of his recollection, he thought his mother had been buried. The viscous red liquid splashed a little when it hit the frozen ground then began to run in little rivulets back toward the headstone. Bobby drained the bottle and stood there watching as the cough medicine slowly soaked into the close-cut dead grass. The gravesite looked like a crime scene, Bobby thought. Like someone had been shot there. Bobby didn't know if the Robitussin was his idea or Dr. Morris's—he couldn't remember ever telling her how his mother used to chug it sometimes—but hey, that was all right. Even if his grandparents could see him, Bobby figured they wouldn't know what the hell was going on anyway.

Chapter Twenty-Nine

It was just after one o'clock when Eddie stood at the window of the small second-floor conference room. The sky was cold and gray, but even with the window cracked, the room was as hot as ever. Eddie could also smell the nearby Dunkin' Donuts wafting in on the icy breeze. He hadn't eaten anything since he'd blown his earlier donut order into Ray's bushes, but just the smell of it now nauseated him. That was what happened when Eddie Sayers puked up something he loved: he became repulsed by it—macaroni and cheese, Oreo cookies, tequila—*please, God, no, not Dunkin' Donuts.*

Then again, it was probably for the best. He wasn't getting any thinner—not to mention, if he had a dollar for every time some douchebag made a crack about a donut shop being next door to the Cranston Police Headquarters, he could've retired a rich man. But Eddie didn't feel retired as he stood there looking down at the parking lot, just as he had done nearly every day for over a decade from the window in his old office down the hall.

Seabrook's team had finished their sweep of Ray's house a couple of hours earlier, after which Eddie and Ray had driven together to headquarters for their polygraphs and toxicology samples. All the evidence had been collected from the crime scene—Matt's car already in the impound lot, his body on some cold metal table at the morgue, Eddie figured. Seabrook had told him they had half the division knocking on doors all over Eden Park, looking for witnesses and a security camera that might have caught something. Eddie figured they had a fifty-fifty shot at that, but the good news was Ray Dawley had passed his polygraph with flying colors. So had Eddie.

"You okay, man?" Ray asked.

They were alone now—Eddie by the window, Ray sitting on the other side of the conference table by the door. Seabrook was following up on some leads, while Costa was still down in Newport, trying to get something out of Shelly. Poor gal had been temporarily admitted to the psych ward of the Newport Hospital on the rec of some crisis intervention specialist. Kids would've been notified by now, Eddie figured, and were probably on their way from wherever it was they went to school. He felt guilty for not being there, but still, he was grateful for this time alone with Ray. He had been struggling with whether he should tell his old friend the reason why he'd splattered Ray's hedges with a dozen half-digested donuts. And after Ray passed his polygraph, Eddie figured, *Who the hell else can I tell?*

"You ever think about that day on the ice?" Eddie folded his arms, leaning with his ass on the windowsill.

Ray clicked off his phone and stuffed it into his hoodie pocket. He had been texting Natalia, no doubt. Still clueless as to what was going on in her neighborhood, in her own goddamn house.

"Yeah, I do," Ray said after a moment. "A lot. I still don't understand how we didn't fall in. That ice should've cracked from the weight of us, at least three times that of Bobby, but somehow, it didn't. I think that's what's been messing with my head all these years. People don't get lucky like that more than once, you know?"

"I'm not following you."

"I don't know, man." Ray slumped in his chair. "It's crazy living in my old house. Things overlap sometimes. The past, the present, who I was back then, and who I am now. I still feel like a kid sometimes. Always worried something bad is going to happen. The ice breaking, some rug pull, know what I mean?"

"You been through a lot. Hana, Connie and the custody shit. PTSD, if you ask me. I think it'd be weird if you never worried about rug pulls."

Ray exhaled sadly and looked past Eddie out the window. "I'm talking about way before all that. I was always scared when we were kids. Things we did, yeah, but also getting close to you and Matt—to let you see who I really was—because I was afraid you might not like me. I wasn't conscious of it back then, of course. I just didn't know how to do it—be close to people, I guess. That's why I was always trying to be someone else. Same reason I got into acting. Coward, I was afraid of growing up, never knew who I was. Anyway, who gives a shit now?"

Eddie swallowed, unsure of what to say. "You were the first one out on the ice that day" was all he could think of.

Ray met his eyes with a plaintive smile. "And it's been downhill ever since. I never had that kind of clarity, that kind of fearlessness again. Not once. Always played it safe, always scared and nervous something bad would happen. I could never just give myself over to anything or anyone. You know, let them feel the full weight of me. Like the ice that day."

Eddie searched his friend's sad expression then looked at the floor. How could he tell him the truth, that the only coward in the room was named Edward Albert Sayers, who just so happened to be a real shitbag of a person too? Would Ray understand if Eddie tried to explain that, ever since that day on the ice, he had done everything in his power to make up for it? To prove to the universe or something that he wasn't the guy who jacked off in Carla Bonetti's panties and then, a few months later, just stood there, perfectly content to let her son drown? Would Ray understand, would he even believe Eddie if he told him that the real reason he decided to become a cop was because he owed it to kids like Bobby, to murdered babies like Jerri Ann Richard, to make sure they never fell through the ice ever again?

Nah, Ray would probably just think him a big bullshitter like Katie and everyone else. So Eddie just said, "Well, yeah, that's what I wanted to talk to you about. I never told you what Bobby said to me after it happened."

"The thing on the ice, you mean?"

Eddie nodded and cast a glance at the small window in the conference room door. No sign of anyone out in the hallway, so he moved to the other side of the table and sat next to Ray. After the polygraphs, Seabrook had shown some mercy and let them wait in here instead of in one of the regular interrogation rooms, which were equipped with security cameras. Cranston PD had two conference rooms, one big, one small, both of which were private. But still, Eddie spoke as if they weren't.

"First day Bobby was back at school," he began, "we were all out at recess. Remember how we used to slide on that big patch of ice beneath the cafeteria windows?"

Ray nodded.

"So yeah, everyone was doing that. I'm standing there, watching near the fence, and Bobby, he comes over to me and says, 'They don't come back.' I'm like, 'What do you mean?' and he says, 'Fish tails. They don't come back when you cut them off.' You know what he was talking about, Ray? What he was referring to?"

Ray's face went pale. "Yeah," he said blandly. "That day down at the pond when you cut off the fish's tail. You wanted to see if it'd grow back."

"Only the four of us were there that day," Eddie said. "You ever tell anyone about that? Not just about Bobby laying me out but about the fish?"

Ray furrowed his brow, looking down as if he were poring over a Rolodex of names on the floor, then he met Eddie's eyes again and shook his head. His expression was oddly reminiscent of that day—the fear, the cautious uncertainty around what would happen next.

"I wouldn't have done the same," Eddie said. "I was such a big mouth back then. Had the roles been reversed, it would've been all over the school. But I was always grateful to you, Ray. And to Bobby, believe it or not. I never forgot how you both kept your mouths shut about all that. Same as I never forgot that day at recess. I swear to you, when Bobby said that thing about fish tails, those blue eyes of his were all pupils, just big black circles—like that hole in the ice."

Ray leaned in closer. "Eddie, what the hell?" He lowered his voice. "Are you telling me you think Bobby Bonetti murdered Matt?"

Eddie breathed in deeply. Ray giving voice to his burgeoning theory made it sound all the more remote, all the more absurd. At the same time, Eddie could feel the old instinct kicking in—amplified, no doubt, because he was back in his old office. He was onto something, and he knew it.

"Just take a step back with me and try to see the bigger picture," he began slowly. "I don't need a toxicology report to tell me what I already know. You and I were drugged. Matt probably was too. If we're lucky, they find a trace of something in that empty Scotch bottle or those pizza boxes—"

"It had to be the pizza," Ray said. "Everything else was mine. The booze, the beer. You saw me. I was drinking more than either of you guys."

"Regardless," Eddie said, "I'm not buying this mob bullshit. Someone wants to get to Matt, he's gonna just put a bullet in the back of his head, know what I mean? He's not gonna go through all the trouble of drugging us."

"That's *if* we were drugged, Eddie. Jesus, just because I threw that out there doesn't mean it's true."

"We were drugged, Ray. You know it as well as I do. And that fish tail, you telling me you don't think that's a very strange coincidence?"

"Yeah, that is what I think, Eddie. I think it's a very strange coincidence."

Eddie clenched his teeth. He knew his theory bordered on convoluted, but still, Ray's tone, the skepticism, the contempt in it, was almost too much to bear.

"Eddie, look," Ray said, "whoever killed Matt had to know in advance that he would be at my house. And the only people who knew that were the three of us, Shelly, and my girls. You telling me one of them called Bobby? My daughter, maybe?"

"Don't be a dick. Bobby could have followed Matt to your house. Maybe he was just looking for an opportunity. He would've known Matt would be in town from seeing the obituary in the paper."

Ray scoffed and shook his head. Eddie fought the urge to slap the smirk from his mouth.

"The hell are you thinking?" Ray asked. "We were all standing outside the church after Jimmy's service when we decided to get together. Plenty of other people were around—Debbie's friends and whatnot—any of whom could have heard what we were saying. Christ, Matt even joked about remembering my address—blurted out my goddamn house number and everything."

Eddie felt overcome by a sudden rush of ridiculousness, as if it had been Ray who'd slapped him in the mouth. He hadn't thought of that.

"I'm not trying to cockblock you," Ray went on, "but what if someone at the funeral overheard what we were saying and, I don't know, intercepted the delivery boy—paid him off to spike the pizza or something so he could get Matt down to the pond? You know, to make a statement?"

"Either way, Matt's killer was inside your house, Ray," Eddie said, aware of a childlike stubbornness in his voice. "Someone planted that bottle of tequila to make it look like we drank it then put that KISS record on and tucked that pillow under my head. How would they know to do that—the record, I mean—unless they knew what we were into as kids? And a fish tail in Matt's mouth, at Blackamore Pond of all places? You really want to double down on that—that it's just a coincidence?"

"But, Eddie," Ray said weakly, "*you* cut off that fish's tail. You were the one who got into it with Bobby that day. Why would he want to murder Matt? We haven't seen him in years. Let's say for a moment that I agree with you—that he could've followed Matt or something—well, why Matt instead of you?"

Eddie felt at a loss, but at the same time, something in him softened—a need, a vulnerability with Ray Dawley that he had never sensed before. Not even when they were kids.

"You have to trust me on this," Eddie said. "I know in my gut that fish tail is connected to Bobby somehow. His uncle Tommy used to be in deep with the Matarese family. You know that? I had only been on the force for a couple of years when it all came out, when they found that body buried on Branch Avenue. I was there that night when they arrested Tommy at his house, Ray. I was outside helping with traffic control when they walked him out. Looked guilty as fuck, if you ask me. Feds couldn't pin it on him in the end, but I knew in my gut Tommy Bonetti was involved. Same as I know now that Bobby is involved in this. And if they're gonna put anything on my gravestone, it's that Eddie Sayers listened to his gut, know what I mean?"

Eddie saw something in Ray's eyes that hadn't been there before. *Regret, is it? Pity maybe?* Whatever the case, Eddie felt a vulnerability, an understanding coming back from Ray too. But before either of them could say anything else, John Seabrook entered the conference room with some papers.

"We got lucky," he said, sitting down across the table. "Kauffman's wife is in pretty rough shape, Costa says, but he was able to get the code for your buddy's phone. He texted back and forth with her around eleven thirty. Made a phone call, too, just before midnight—"

"Wait, so you're saying Matt was awake at that time?" Eddie asked.

"At least between eleven and midnight, yeah," Seabrook said. "This was after you guys said you passed out, right?"

Eddie and Ray exchanged an anxious glance, then Ray nodded tentatively. Eddie couldn't speak. He felt thrown off his game and claustrophobic again, like on Ray's porch—the heat in the conference room oppressive, the air heavy with the threat that everything he had just laid out for Ray was about to unravel. He swiveled his eyes to the window overlooking the parking lot.

I am confident, articulate, and relaxed. Car...

"Okay, so this at least gives us a clearer timeline." Seabrook scanned the report. "You guys sure you don't remember anything? Kauffman said you all were pretty drunk—" He read from one of the papers, "'Hey, babe. Drank way too much. Need to sober up before I head back. Will text you when I leave. Love you and don't wait up.' The Uber app was open on Kauffman's phone. Search history says he was looking up escort services and the Foxy Lady. Late night, were you guys looking for some fun? Foxy closes at one on Sundays—"

Ray chuckled cynically and shook his head. "You gotta be kidding me."

"Fuck no, come on," Eddie said. "How many times do we have to tell you we don't remember shit? Besides, anyone could've messed with Matt's phone—"

"Someone who knew the code, you mean?" Seabrook asked with a contemptuous smirk.

Eddie's stomach squeezed with anger. "Yeah, or someone who opened it with Matt's fingerprint."

Seabrook shrugged, a *mea culpa*—disingenuous, just humoring him, Eddie knew, like he was a child. Eddie repeated his CAR mantra. More than ever, he needed to keep his cool.

"John, listen to me," he began again. "I think Matt's killer was inside the house. I think he laid out that whole scene we woke up to so it would look like we were drinking. Problem is, I'm still trying to work out how the guy drugged us. But I'm telling you we *were* drugged—passed out around nine, nine thirty from what I can tell."

"I'm not saying you weren't," Seabrook said, his tone less condescending now. "And let's say I agree with you, that all this was just some big setup and someone else got into your buddy's phone. Kauffman was not a small guy, at least six feet, two-hundred-plus pounds. It would've taken someone with a lot of strength to carry him out of that house and put him into his car. Never mind drive him down to the pond."

"What," Eddie said, "you're saying Matt walked out of Ray's house on his own?"

"Maybe you guys were passed out and he wasn't. Maybe your buddy wanted to get away for a little action and cover his tracks before heading back to Newport."

"Bullshit," Ray muttered.

Seabrook shrugged again. "We won't know for sure until the toxicology tests come back. But even if the two of you were roofied, nothing right now indicates to me that Kauffman was too—nothing to indicate that someone messed with his phone either."

"So what? You're saying you think Matt roofied us?" Eddie asked, incredulous.

Seabrook shrugged a third time. "All I know is I got one guy dead, strangled, with half a fish in his mouth, and two guys who say they don't remember anything. Two guys who passed a polygraph and who've been cooperative, yeah, but who also, working together, would have been strong enough to carry the victim outside and into his car."

"Jesus Christ," Ray muttered, getting up and moving to the window.

Eddie sat there with his arms flaccid at his sides. He felt as if John Seabrook had just kicked him in the balls. On some level, he understood that his old friend was trying to bring him back to reality—Seabrook was telling him that though he and Ray were their prime suspects, he was doing everything he could to resist going down that rabbit hole. But still, Eddie felt like lunging across the table and punching him. The audacity, the betrayal.

Seabrook leaned back in his chair with his hands folded across his stomach. "You see how this looks, right? You see how convoluted we need to get for the two of you *not* to be suspects? Right now, I got nothing to arrest the two of you on—"

"Un-fucking-believable," Eddie muttered.

"And to be honest, I don't even want to go there yet. Not until all the tests come back and I can corroborate your story—"

"Oh, come on." Ray turned from the window. "Even if those tests come back positive, next thing you'll say is it doesn't prove anything. We could have drugged ourselves after we killed him, right?"

"Maybe," Seabrook said. "But for now, the way I'm playing it is you guys got so hammered you don't remember shit, then for whatever reason, Kauffman walked out of that house on his own and somebody forced him to drive to the pond. That said, you two don't just go booking flights to Europe yet, understand?"

Thank God Seabrook was being somewhat reasonable. But still, the fact that Eddie's old friend, a guy who had worked under him for over ten years, refused to absolve him of a crime he didn't commit stung like hell.

"Well, I want in, then," Eddie said. "I want to be a consultant on the case."

"No can do, old friend—"

"Come on, John, this is personal."

"Which is precisely why I can't have you around." Seabrook leaned forward on his elbows. "Do I think you or your buddy here did it? My gut says no, but polygraphs have been fooled before. Never mind the shitstorm I'd bring down on our heads if anyone got wind I'd brought in a murder suspect as a consultant on their own case. Even if he used to be one of us."

"Then rule me out!"

Seabrook slapped a meaty paw on the table. "Goddammit, Eddie, what the hell do you think I'm trying to do here?"

Defeated, Eddie exhaled and looked up at the ceiling, at the grid of drop-panels that, for the first time ever, reminded him of some giant map on which there were no coordinates to help him plot his course. *What the hell do I do now?*

"You said Matt made a phone call," Ray said. "Who did he call?"

Seabrook fixed his eyes on Eddie's. "His niece. He called Debra Kauffman."

Chapter Thirty

Natalia found three texts waiting for her after her twelve-o'clock patient left.

The first text was from her ex-husband, Tim. Natalia ignored that one and went straight to the second: a cancellation notice from her scheduling app regarding her one-o'clock patient. No excuse, no apology, typical BS move from this thirty-year-old, self-important trust fund baby who was happy to live off her father's millions while at the same time twisting her guilt-ridden ovaries about how hard it was being the victim of such an oppressive capitalist. No biggie. She didn't give twenty-four hours' notice, so Natalia would still get paid. *Viva la capitalista!*

The third text was from Ray. *Rough morning, will explain when you get home, can you just pick up some Chinese food after work?*

Natalia just tapped a heart emoji when what she really wanted to say was *What do you know about rough mornings other than being hungover from partying? When's my party, Ray? When's MY FUCK-ING PARTY???*

Natalia glared at the picture of him above her desk. Baseball hat and T-shirt, barefoot, sitting on some rocks and gazing contemplatively out at the ocean. The shot was usually one of her favorites among the handful that hung in her office's back alcove, but today, all she could see was her husband's self-centeredness. After working all day, *she* had to pick up the Chinese food? *Sure, Ray. I wouldn't want to interfere with your afternoon nap or anything.*

Natalia moved into the bathroom and, flicking on the light, frowned when she spied herself in the mirror. More gray hairs overnight, she swore, not to mention her crow's feet looked more pronounced. Natalia washed her hands. Was she really pissed off at Ray? Or was she still on edge from her session with Dave? She had seen three patients back-to-back since then but hadn't been able to get him off her mind—especially the odd, cryptic identity of Machete, who talked in circles about auras and angelfish and boxes of bees that stung him in his dreams. At one point, when Natalia suggested that Machete should encourage Dave to visit his mother's grave, Machete smiled and shot her with a finger gun. *How's that for rough mornings, Ray?*

Jesus, cut the poor bastard some slack, Natalia told herself in the next breath. *You're really going to be bitter about a boys' night that* you *suggested?*

Natalia dried her hands, turned off the light, and moved again to the picture of Ray on the rocks. Christ, she loved him. Yeah, he could be self-centered sometimes, but maybe she was being too hard on him. Maybe she should be grateful that her husband still had a little of the party-boy alpha-male thing going on. Refreshing, nowadays—especially after her fifteen years of being married to Tim Nowak.

Oh yeah, Tim.

Natalia checked the text from him. Nothing important, just a quick note asking if she would be open to a conversation about adjusting Jeremy's plans for Christmas.

Natalia replied, *Sorry, too late, already planned everything around my parents' visit from Florida.*

That would be the end of it, Natalia knew. Tim Nowak wasn't a man for confrontation. He wasn't a man at all, really—more like a jellyfish who, when he wasn't lecturing their son about the dangers of toxic masculinity, spent his time doing yoga and collecting royalties as the poster boy for beta males with mommy issues.

To be fair, Natalia had understood all that when she'd first start-ed dating him during their doctoral program at Duke. Natalia fig-ured they had some things in common back then, but for the life of her, she could no longer remember what. It certainly wasn't sex, and toward the end of their marriage, Natalia had become convinced that Tim was gay. *Ray, on the other hand...*

Natalia felt her cheeks get hot. She had had more lovers than she cared to admit over the years, all of them disappointing, some even pathetic. But if the kind of sex life she and Ray had cultivated was the reward, it was worth it. Ray was beyond attentive and knew how to both take control and give himself over with such abandon that, when they were finished, Natalia was left exhausted and literally buzzing from his passion.

But she had always suspected it would be like that—ever since high school, when she sensed a faint electric charge in the air when-ever Ray was close, when she caught him looking at her in English, or when his eyes met hers as they passed each other in the hall. They had run in different circles back then, but sometimes, Natalia would watch Ray during art class—the way he would smudge the curves of his charcoal lines with his finger. Slowly, almost sensually, and with such complete immersion that she could almost see the world melt-ing away around him.

Then there was that play he was in senior year, *Cat on a Hot Tin Roof*, in which he'd played the character of Brick.

"You were a wonderful lover," said Danielle Collins, the gal who played Maggie. "Such a wonderful person to go to bed with."

The auditorium of immature high schoolers tittered for all the wrong reasons, but not Natalia. She lay awake that night, imagining Ray touching her like one of his drawings, caressing the curves of her body with his fingertips and getting lost in her eyes. But for a whole host of reasons that seemed relevant back then, the two of them nev-er got together. Fast forward to their first date three decades later, and Natalia knew as soon as she hugged him hello that she wouldn't let Ray Dawley get away again.

Look at me, standing here, mooning over his picture like some hard-up high schooler. The day was getting to her, no doubt. She needed some air.

Natalia bundled up and, a minute later, was outside, breathing in the frigid gray light, the urban street sounds that spoke of escape. But still, she could use a cup of coffee. She headed off down Waterman Street toward College Hill. The café she had in mind was on Thayer Street, a little over a half mile in the opposite direction from the one she usually frequented in nearby Wayland Square. A bit of a hike, yeah, but worth it on the off chance she would run into Jeremy. Natalia didn't dare text him a heads-up, though. That was the promise she had made to her son if he chose to stay local over Princeton. She would leave him alone.

But was that the real reason she was going so far out of her way for a cup of coffee? Maybe it was because the farther away from her office, the farther away she might feel from Dave. God knew she needed some perspective. The encounter with Machete had really thrown her for a loop—in no small part because Machete had implied that he knew something about Gina.

"You got boxes of bees, too, Doc," he said. "In your dreams. Bones of silent sisters that still sting."

Natalia brought back Dave's identity immediately after that. Dave seemed to have no memory of Machete's insinuation, but still, Natalia felt violated. Dr. Natalia Morris never blamed her patients for looking into her background. In fact, she had come to expect it. Even after twenty-five years in private practice, it was not uncommon for a patient to have romantic feelings for her. But Dave Ruggieri, yeah, this motherfucker had crossed a line—not to mention, he had to have sniffed around pretty hard to find out anything about Gina, whose suicide four decades earlier was not mentioned anywhere on the Internet. Nothing, not even a footnote, the whole world moving on as if she had never existed. No, Dave more likely found out via word of mouth—small world, someone who knew her back in the day, typical Rhode Island six-degrees-of-separation bullshit. And *that* was worse. Four decades on, she still bore the mark of the girl whose sister committed suicide—still wore it around her neck like some albatross, like some big scarlet fucking S branded on her chest.

Bones of silent sisters that still sting...

Or had Machete said "swing"? Natalia wondered, and the image of Gina hanging from their father's chin-up bar—eyes bulging, tongue lolling—flashed again before her eyes. Natalia pushed it away and walked looking at the sidewalk. She suddenly felt very cold and tired, and while waiting for the cross signal to change at Governor Street, she almost turned around and headed back. Then she got a whiff of weed and heard the dull bass line of Pink Floyd's "Breathe" coming from a passing car and took it as a sign to press on. Jeremy just loved Pink Floyd.

Natalia tugged up at her collar and quickened her step—past the intersection of Cook, then Hope, and eventually took a right onto Thayer, where the crowded Victorian houses and brick administrative buildings gave over at once to the trendy commercial storefronts of College Hill. She stepped into the small café two doors down. It was hot, mercifully uncrowded, but no sign of Jeremy.

Natalia exhaled and unzipped her parka. She felt foolish for expecting to run into him among all the other students flitting about in between exams. Jeremy was no doubt holed up, studying in his dorm, pissing in empty Mountain Dew bottles, and poking his head out only to pick up his DoorDash. Poor kid stressed way too much and, even back home, was in the shitter a half dozen times a day. Stomach problems because of nerves. Being a local boy, he'd had to work ten times as hard to even be considered for the biology program at Brown. GPA through the roof, all the right extracurricular activities, and he'd won first place in the National Science Fair two years back. Something to do with the effect of Wi-Fi signals on the growth of pea pods. He'd made bank, written his own ticket, and hadn't let up since. Natalia was beyond proud, but still, she wished her son would stop just to breathe once in a while.

She ordered her usual latte macchiato and was about to leave when something on the wall-mounted TV screen caught her eye. Breaking news, a local reporter on the scene. No sound, but Natalia got the gist from the banner at the bottom. *Man found dead in Cranston.* That was all she saw before the broadcast cut to a commercial, and Natalia was left feeling oddly unconcerned and entirely grateful. *Her* man in Cranston was safe, she knew, and that was all that mattered.

Natalia smiled and left the café, humming Pink Floyd's "Breathe" all the way back to her office—where she once again played the part of therapist before picking up her stepdaughter and some Chinese food for her hungover husband.

Chapter Thirty-One

"How come you didn't say anything about the fish?" Ray asked as they pulled up in front of his house. "Back at the police station, I mean?"

Eddie threw his truck into park and sat for a moment with the engine idling. "I don't know. Dose of reality, maybe. You and I are still the prime suspects. The thing about Bobby and the fish would just get lost in all the noise."

"Because Seabrook wouldn't understand?"

"Because Matt calling his niece Debra made my theory seem all the more convoluted. Fucking stupid, really, even to me."

"Then you do think Matt called her? Not someone messing with his phone?"

"That's the way John's playing it for now, so it doesn't really matter what I think. At least not until they rule me out as a suspect."

"Then maybe they'll go for you being a consultant?"

Eddie shrugged. "Not unheard of. But this being so personal, who can say?"

Ray nodded and looked up at his house. When he was a kid, he had always loved this wintery time of day—the warm, safe feeling he got when he arrived home after school, just before the world began to dim. But now, upon his return from the Cranston Police Headquarters, he felt only dread, a sense that the worst, gathering in the gloom at the edge of daylight, was still to come.

"You remember if I shut off the outside light?" Ray asked. "Last night, at some point after the pizza was delivered?"

"No, why?"

"I usually leave the light on until I go to bed, but it was off when you left this morning. Door was unlocked too. Weird that I would've shut the light off and not locked the door, which makes me think it wasn't me."

"So what? You're saying it was Matt's killer?" Ray shrugged. "What then?"

"Maybe it was Matt who shut off the light." Ray turned back to Eddie. "Maybe that call to Debra had something to do with it, and he intended to meet her outside. I don't care how blitzed he was, I don't see any other scenario in which he would have left his phone behind. Not the way Shelly tracks him."

Eddie considered this for a moment. "Seabrook said, from the time stamp, the call didn't last long. Most likely went to voicemail, then the caller hung up. Won't know for sure until they interview Debra and get the phone records—"

"Either way, why would Matt call her? What if Seabrook is onto something about Matt being the one who roofied us?"

"The hell you talking about?"

"Just hear me out. What if Matt slipped us something—you know, left us passed out and his phone behind as cover—so he could go outside to meet Debra or someone she works with. No way that's a coincidence he's googling the Foxy Lady, fucking escorts and shit, then calls her. I read about that prostitution bust there a few years back—"

"Ray, come on—"

"So you're telling me all that's just a coincidence? Him calling his niece, who just so happens to be a waitress at the Foxy?"

Eddie snickered and shook his head.

"I'm serious. What if Matt went outside to meet someone—you know, a connection through Debra. He turns my house lights off in case—I don't know—any stragglers from the Bucs game are still around. Maybe he gets spooked and wants more privacy, so he takes his pro down to the pond."

"Right, then Guido the killer pimp shows up with a fish and strangles him?"

"Okay, so what if it's not about sex? What if Seabrook's right, and there's some drug connection through Debra. Same deal using us for cover, but then things go bad?"

"I don't know, Ray." Eddie sighed. "I'm hungover and tired and can't think straight. The stuff running through my head now. I mean, Matt was no altar boy, believe me, but—" Eddie stopped himself.

"But what?"

Eddie just shook his head and looked out his window. Ray could tell he was holding something back, but instead of pressing him, he turned his gaze toward the passenger-side mirror. He could see little else other than his reflection and the side of the truck, but still, Ray imagined he was seeing the ramp as it had looked when they drove past it a few minutes earlier—down Blackamore Avenue and around the curve up onto Lexington. The whole area was clear now, save for a single length of police tape stretched between a tree and the fence at the top of the ramp. Other than that, no one would ever have known a crime had taken place there. Same for his house.

Despite his mounting sense of dread, Ray felt strangely relieved. More than anything, he hadn't wanted Natalia and Maggie to come home to some bizarre, real-life episode of *CSI*. But still, what the hell was he going to tell them? Especially Maggie.

"Something I always wondered," Ray said, turning back to Eddie. "Guys like you, cops, you ever watch those crime shows about what you do? I don't mean shit like *CSI*, but you know, the documentary ones? Like on the Discovery Channel or something?"

Eddie shrugged and shook his head, and Ray stared off in the direction of his friend's old house.

"There was a time I would've known exactly what you watched," he said. "Pretty much knew what you were doing every second of the day. Same for Matt. The way our lives intertwined—threads, braided together like rope. At some point, though, things began to unravel. We just... drifted apart. Why did I let that happen?"

Eddie swallowed hard and sort of shrugged again. "Not your fault," he said, avoiding Ray's eyes. "That's the way life is. People grow apart, is all."

"They shouldn't, not the ones who matter."

Eddie shifted in his seat.

Ray could tell his friend felt uncomfortable, but Ray refused to be a coward, to let himself be frightened by the vulnerability in the truck between them. He wanted to say something like *I never had friends like you and Matt again. I never understood how lucky I was back then, but even more, how stupid I was to throw it all away. You were like a brother to me, Eddie, but I didn't know how to love you because I was too busy trying to love myself. I still don't know who I am, but I know I love you, Eddie. I always have. And knowing you were always there, that I could just call you out of the blue and that, deep down, you would be happy about it because you love me, too, even if you don't know it... Well, that's what has really kept me from falling through the ice all these years.* All this somehow ran through Ray Dawley's mind in a split second, but in the end, what came out of his mouth was just "Eddie the Anchor."

Eddie gave a feeble chuckle, the two men exchanged "see ya later"s, then Ray was in his house, heading straight for the kitchen, where he quickly began wiping everything down with some Windex and a dishrag. Seabrook's forensic team had already cleaned up most of their fingerprint powder, but traces of it lingered here and there—on the doorjambs and doorknobs, on the liquor cabinet in the living room and pretty much everything in the den. The whole thing took about twenty minutes, after which Ray sat down on the porch and fixed his eyes on the corner of his lawn where he had seen the dog taking a shit the night before.

It was then that Ray became aware of a different kind of anchor, one as familiar as Eddie Sayers because, much like Ray's feelings for his friend, it hung heavily inside him. Ray could actually feel the weight of it in his stomach, an anchor as big as the symbol of Rhode Island itself, the squeeze of its chain winding, cold and biting, around his heart. It was an anchor of blame, an anchor that would drag him under—way, way down into the cold, dark depths if he wasn't careful. If only he hadn't moved back to his old neighborhood, if only he hadn't invited his friends over, if only he hadn't gone through with their boys' night when he made that bet with himself about the guy and his dog, Matthew Kauffman would still be alive. Just like if he hadn't directed *Romeo and Juliet*, just like if Hana hadn't driven down from Boston just to be there for him—

"Fuck you," Ray said, squeezing his eyes shut. *Don't even think about it. Just hang on. The ice will hold. The ice will hold.*

Ray went back inside, made himself a cup of coffee, and Natalia and Maggie arrived home with some Chinese food a few minutes later. Ray kissed his wife and hugged his daughter a bit tighter, a bit longer than usual.

Maggie shrank away from him and whined, "*Dad!*" in that middle-school-girl way that usually annoyed him but today made him tear up as he watched her disappear up the stairs for her coveted daily hour of screen time.

Natalia picked up right away that something was wrong, so Ray led her outside onto the porch, where they sat, and he explained everything. Natalia listened and hardly spoke, and Ray realized—only gradually, it seemed—that the anchor around his heart was chained to her heart too. And *that* was what finally made Ray Dawley cry—openly, and without fear, for the first time that day.

Chapter Thirty-Two

Tommy pulled his gray Ford Explorer into the parking lot of West Warwick Gun and Coin just after five, in full view of the two cameras he knew Pete Scungio had installed outside. Pete was already in the process of dragging the security gates across the windows, but when Tommy slipped out of his car and Pete saw him, he unlocked the door and just stood there in the entrance with an expression of *What the fuck?*

Tommy jerked his chin at Pete to go inside, and Pete's saggy hound dog face went from confused to uncomfortable. He held open the door.

"Your timing is impeccable," Pete muttered as Tommy slipped past him, then Pete locked the door and led him to the main display case.

Tommy had known Pete since they were kids but had only gotten close to him from playing bocce at the Santa Maria Di Prata Club. Tommy had never gone near the store back in the days when it was in Providence—when Pete's father, who they called Petty Boy, was in the business of securing untraceable firearms for the Matarese family. "You don't shit where you eat" was the rule, spoken by every wiseguy as much as any bullshit from *The Godfather.*

But some rules were *unspoken*, which was why Tommy knew Pete would understand why he had driven all the way to West Warwick instead of just calling or texting. Tommy wanted to talk to Pete about something important, something about which he wanted to look into Pete's hound-dog eyes to see if he would lie to him.

Pete went around to the other side of the display case and, exhaling tiredly, made a sort of Vanna White gesture at the various models inside—the first step in a dance that the two of them would perform for the cameras, which Tommy knew didn't pick up sound.

"You see anything interesting?" Pete asked, his tone resigned and communicating that he knew Tommy was not in the market for guns.

Tommy had a record and couldn't buy firearms legally, but he pointed to a gun in the case anyway. "Christmas gift maybe for my nephew."

Pete took it out for him.

Tommy aimed it away from Pete, pretending to test the sight so his mouth was covered. "You ever sell him any Caspers?" he said quietly, barely moving his lips.

Casper, as in the "friendly ghost," was a term the mob had been using for untraceable firearms long before the term "ghost guns" entered the common vernacular.

Pete nodded. "Select clientele. Keep things in the family, know what I mean?"

"Yeah, I hear you." Tommy handed the gun back to Pete. "Okay, man, see you tomorrow at bocce."

"Yeah, bring your A game."

Tommy left the store and drove back to Cranston, stopping first at Dave's market for some sausage, which he would cook with some peppers and throw in a sandwich for his nephew when he got home from his gig at the club. Sausage-and-pepper sandwiches were Bobby's favorite, and now that Tommy knew he had killed Ronnie Matarese—and who knew how many others—with a Casper nine millimeter supplied by Pete Scungio, he figured he might as well soften him up a bit before asking him if he had killed his old friend Matthew Kauffman, the guy Pete's friend on Cranston PD had told him was murdered down at Blackamore Pond. A murder like that had to have been personal. And Tommy Bonetti knew better than anyone never to let things get personal.

Part V: Homecoming

Chapter Thirty-Three

The call from John Seabrook woke Eddie just after six on Tuesday morning. Eddie had been dreaming about his daughters. Emily and Elizabeth were little again—about four and six, respectively—and they were all at Bonnet Shores Beach Club. Until the divorce, Eddie had paid through the nose every year to be a member, mainly because the girls loved it, and he had been going there ever since he was a kid. Not anymore though. The girls were grown, Eddie was too self-conscious about his weight, and the beach was always too fucking crowded.

But in the dream, Eddie was happy to be there. He sat in his chair, watching his girls build a sandcastle by the water. It was sunny, and the brightly colored umbrellas that dotted the sand looked like candy. Eddie thought he could taste them.

"I told you I would show up," he said. "I told you I was a good father."

Eddie looked to his left, expecting to see Katie in her beach chair beside him, but instead, he found eleven-year-old Matt Kauffman guzzling Kool-Aid from a big blue jug.

"Ahhh," he said, dragging his wrist across his red-stained lips. "That's right, Eddie, you were a way better father than ours ever were."

Matt smiled, the Kool-Aid thick and syrupy now, like blood staining his teeth. Eddie was a kid again, too, he realized, turning back toward the water—so were Ray Dawley and Bobby Bonetti, who were now working on the sandcastle instead of his daughters.

The hell are they doing here? Eddie thought, trying to stand. But for some reason, his legs wouldn't work and his knees were all black and blue.

"From sucking dick," Bobby Bonetti said, rising and suddenly older. Sunglasses, black suit and tie, hair slicked from a face somehow both close and far away.

They weren't at the beach anymore, Eddie realized with mounting horror, but in the woods at the edge of Blackamore Pond.

"You like sucking dick, Eddie?" Bobby asked, unzipping his fly, and an enormous fish tail slithered out like an octopus's tentacle.

It twisted toward Eddie, kicking up dirt and blocking out everything with its flapping fins. Eddie tried to scream, but the tentacle was in his mouth now, slithering down his throat and choking him as Eminem's "Lose Yourself" started playing. Eddie's eyes sprang open, and air rushed into his lungs. At the same time, he turned his head and saw the call from John Seabrook glowing beside him in the darkness. Eddie pawed clumsily at the nightstand and answered his phone.

"The fuck," he said, his voice all sandpaper from snoring. "Christ, John, you know what time it is?"

"At least some of us got to bed," Seabrook said on the other end. "How fast can you get your ass down here?"

Eddie rolled over and propped himself on his elbow. "You find something?"

"I can only discuss that with my consultant," Seabrook said.

Eddie could hear the excitement in his friend's voice, barely contained behind a manufactured formality, and Eddie's heart began to beat very fast. "Be there in half an hour."

He hung up and felt something release inside him, a sense of relief that lodged in his throat and almost made him cry. He was no longer a suspect. *But what about Ray?* Eddie had forgotten to ask Seabrook if they'd cleared him too. Still too groggy, couldn't even remember dragging his ass to bed after the takeout Chinese and a few episodes of *The First 48,* a true detective show like the ones Ray had been asking him about in his truck the day before. Eddie usually stayed away from shit like that, but after the conversation with Ray—*well, who knows what made me watch it?* Eddie couldn't even remember what the episodes were about, only vague impressions of trying to stay awake.

Eddie swung himself out of bed and padded to his bathroom. *Must have been really out of it.* He didn't even wake up once during the night to piss—which was even more of a miracle than Seabrook ruling him out so quickly. Still too soon for all the forensic tests to come back, so Cranston PD must've found something pounding the pavement. Eddie was relieved, in a way, that it was all coming down today, now that he could feel the old mental sharpness kicking in. Amazing what a good night's sleep could do for a person.

"Except for you," Eddie's father would have said. *"You were always borderline retarded, even with a good eight hours."*

Eddie flicked on the bathroom light and, with his eyes adjusting, stood at the toilet and took a piss.

"I thought girls sat down to pee," he heard his father say in his head.

Eddie told him to fuck off. That he should be thinking of ol' Rick, who was alive and well with ol' Janet down in Florida, struck him as dismally appropriate, given his dream, the bits and pieces of which remained in his gut like shrapnel. There was Matt and Bobby and the fish tail, too, but what stung the most was seeing his girls—not in the dream, but now, in his mind, when he had time to reflect on what a shitty father he had been.

Eddie Sayers had never laid a hand on his daughters like his father had done to him, but he figured he had beaten them in other ways. Through his absence, mainly, which no doubt left them stinging more than any backhand from ol' Rick. What made Eddie feel all the guiltier, however, was that he had been more than willing to blame his job until it became easier to just blame Katie, to embrace some bullshit rationale that he didn't want the girls to see them fighting or sense the toxicity between them.

And after the divorce, when the girls were older and the distance he felt from them had solidified into something roughly defined as "It is what it is," Eddie took comfort in a sort of moral justification that Katie had poisoned them against him over the years—which was true, but only part of the story. Eddie could count on one hand the times his daughters had stepped foot inside his condo. In the beginning, Eddie had big dreams of making the place homey—hang some pictures, buy some plants—so the girls would feel comfortable when they came over for dinner. Eddie couldn't cook, but he would learn for them. He bought a grill and everything for the patio but never followed through on any of it. He blamed work again, which was a hell of a lot easier than admitting he just didn't care enough to make it a priority. Or maybe he just didn't know how.

That was the hardest part, because Eddie had known all along there were so many chapters of the story he could have rewritten if he had only known how—or if he had cared, *really cared*, enough to learn. How did he let that happen? How could he just wake up one morning with piss dribbling out of him like a leaky faucet and a couple of daughters who didn't need him anymore, who never even called just to ease their guilty consciences? Other than a brief text exchange on Thanksgiving, Eddie hadn't talked to either of them in over a month. Emily was an elementary school teacher, married, trying to have kids. Elizabeth was in real estate with a serious boyfriend—her fourth in as many years. Eddie didn't even know the latest guy's name. *Jesus Christ, how could a father not know his own daughters anymore?*

Eddie shook off the last of his piss and moved to the sink, splashed some cold water on his face, then stood there, looking at his reflection in the mirror. His eyes were puffy, and his white beard stubble made his already-pasty complexion look like the Pillsbury Doughboy's.

That's right, you fat fuck, Eddie said to himself. *And while you're feeling sorry for yourself, maybe you should text Ray a quick apology for the way you just sat there yesterday and let him take the blame for you guys drifting apart. You know goddamn well you let the threads in that rope unravel just as much as he ever did. Maybe you should confess to him how you both loved and hated him over the years, and that eventually, you let yourself drift more toward the hate end because it was easier to let him get away than to fight for something you were afraid of in the first place. Maybe you should tell your old pal that you made the exact same mistake with your daughters because to risk them rejecting you would've been too much for a pussy like you to take.*

Eddie felt a swell in his chest, and he began to weep. He closed his eyes and imagined he was back with his daughters again on the beach in his dream—only Ray Dawley was with them now, eleven years old and helping them with their sandcastle.

Chapter Thirty-Four

"*Bobby? Hey, man, it's me. Wake up.*"

Bobby's eyes fluttered open—morning, still dark outside, he realized as he lifted his grandfather's hunting cap just high enough to see. He must have fallen asleep with it on but didn't remember wearing it to bed—didn't remember much at all, really, after going to the cemetery then to his gig at the club, where he saw on the six-o'clock news that a body had been discovered down at Blackamore Pond. No other information was being made public at the time, but still, Bobby spent the rest of his shift in a daze, doling out drinks and making small talk as more details trickled in—friends of friends with inside information that, by nine o'clock, eventually confirmed what Bobby somehow already knew. His old friend Matthew Kauffman had been murdered.

"That you, Matt?" Bobby pulled the hunting hat over his eyes again, and Matt laughed.

"*No, it's the tooth fairy. Of course it's me! Hey, you asshole, how come you didn't come to Jimmy's funeral?*"

"I can't hang out with you guys anymore," Bobby said. "At least not when Ray's wife is around. I fucked up big time and started seeing her for therapy just to be close to him. Gave her a fake name, and you know, if she finds out I lied—if *Ray* finds out—"

"*Wow, that* is *fucked up. You hear how I died?*"

"Yeah. Strangled with a fish tail in your mouth. Not on the news, though. You know Cranston. Word gets around. You see who did it?"

"I think so, yeah, but I don't remember. Your mom said the angelfish might show me someday, but... Hey, how come you sound like a kid again?"

"I don't know. How come you do?"

"I don't know either. I'm still getting used to it in here. Haven't seen the angelfish yet, but your mom told me I will soon. She looks good. Your mom, I mean. Even younger than when we were kids. Eddie always wanted to bang her. He swore me to secrecy on that, but I don't give a shit about telling you now."

"I hear you," Bobby said. "I don't give a shit about a lot of things anymore either, know what I mean?"

"Yeah, but be careful. Things come back to haunt you. Like me." Matt laughed.

"Do you think I killed you then?"

"I don't know. Do you think you did?"

"Sometimes I forget things, or remember them different than the way they happened. Like the other night, I just remember driving around for hours after casing Ray's house. I could feel something waking up, something alive again, way down there in the mud at the bottom of the pond. Water is so cold, isn't it? Sorry I couldn't do anything to help you before you got sucked in too. I should have stuck around longer."

"It's okay, man. Maybe you can still help me, though. You know, try to find out who killed me in case the angelfish dicks me. Watch, she prolly won't tell me shit. Story of my life, you know? Always getting dicked."

"Yeah, I hear you on that," Bobby said. "I definitely hear you on that."

Chapter Thirty-Five

Tommy sat down at the kitchen table with his second cup of coffee and his eyes fixed on his nephew's bedroom door. He would give him another ten minutes before he knocked and asked if he wanted an omelet for breakfast or just his eggs sunny side up. Bobby was awake. Tommy had heard him talking—no doubt to himself, he figured, since he had never bothered to get a cell. Didn't like talking on the phone was his excuse. Okay, fair enough, but let him try saying he didn't like talking this morning. Let him try to say he wasn't hungry again, like he did last night when he got home. Tommy would tell him to get his ass to the table and eat something anyway. He was sick and tired of Bobby's BS.

Yeah, Tommy had woken up that morning sick and tired of pretty much everything having to do with his nephew. Sick and tired of doing his laundry, which now sat folded on the dining room table behind him. Sick and tired of cooking him shit he didn't eat, like the sausage and peppers, which now sat cold and congealed in the fridge. But most of all, Tommy was just sick and tired of the distance between them—which had been no more apparent than when Bobby had gotten home last night after his shift at the club.

"So, let's talk about that thing on Lexington Avenue," Tommy had said as he took the sausage-and-pepper sandwich out of the oven.

He had toasted it with melted provolone just the way Bobby liked it, but his nephew said he wasn't hungry.

"You kidding me? I made this special."

"I know." Bobby sounded sad and oddly childlike. "But that thing, word's already going around who the guy was. Matt Kauffman, an old friend of mine. I need to sort out how I feel about it."

And with that, Bobby had gone to bed, leaving Tommy in the kitchen holding his sandwich like some rejected housewife. His brief meeting with Pete Scungio had confirmed what he had suspected since discovering Bobby's missing gun. His nephew was doing hits for the DeLorenzos. Problem was this Kauffman guy didn't seem to fit into the whole thing. *Some big shot with Credit Suisse?* Tommy didn't see the connection. No way the Boston mob had suddenly gotten their fingers into international finance. Too risky, too easy for the Feds to track—never mind that even the New York families didn't have that kind of influence anymore. No, the hit on Kauffman *had* to be personal.

But that was only part of what upset Tommy, he had realized as he was wrapping up Bobby's uneaten sandwich. His nephew had been acting strange these last few months. Keeping more to himself, not hanging out as much with his friends. But it was more than that. It was the look in Bobby's eyes—the same look Tommy had first seen while sitting across from him at the visitor's table at the ACI. The dark, hollow look behind the smiles. The cold-blooded look of a killer.

Ever since he'd gotten out of prison in the summer of 1982, Tommy had dedicated his life to extinguishing that look, to kill it with love and kindness, to slay the monster of Silver Lake like some dragon with the sword of his presence. For years, Tommy didn't see the monster at all, and by the time Bobby reached his mid-twenties, Tommy had begun to relax—had begun to think that maybe he had killed the monster for good. Then Carla had to go kill herself, and everything changed.

She had been living in a halfway house in East Greenwich at the time. After over a decade in the loony bin, the doctors had said her progress was promising, new medications for people like her, no longer a danger to herself *blahdy-blah-blah*. It was Bobby who found her—in the tub with her arms slit all the way from her wrists to the crooks of her elbows. A straight razor lay on the bathroom floor beside her. Fuck knows where she got it, but after that, Bobby was never the same. The monster behind his eyes was back with a vengeance—like some dragon breathing fire so hot, so bright that Bobby had to sometimes wear sunglasses.

So yeah, that morning, Tommy had woken up fucking furious at that dragon—who, for the last six months, had been coming around so much that Tommy felt he hardly saw his nephew at all anymore. Tommy didn't think he could slay the dragon with a single conversation, but he would go right for the neck, hacking away at it scale by scale if he had to. No more bullshit, no more dancing around things and keeping quiet because of some stupid code.

When Bobby finally came out of his bedroom to take a piss, Tommy told him to hurry up and come to the table. Bobby didn't give him any shit, so Tommy poured him a cup of coffee and had it waiting for him when he sat down.

"I'll take that sandwich now," Bobby said, smiling, but Tommy didn't bite.

He knew it was the dragon talking with its Bobby mask on, manipulative little prick. "I know you killed the Matarese kid," Tommy said.

Bobby's smile wilted, his face like stone.

"Don't ask me how I know—and you're probably thinking, who the hell is this guy to talk, right? Okay, fair. I understand I got no ground to stand on when it comes to that. But I don't give a shit because I'm not gonna just sit here and pretend I don't see what's going on, what getting mixed up with the Boston crew is doing to your soul. I've seen it happen to too many guys—a fire-breathing dragon that burns everything inside until there's nothing left but a shell. I don't want that happening to you."

Bobby was quiet, his lips slightly pursed and his eyes downcast as if he were considering whether to respond.

"Mind you," Tommy went on, "I'm not lecturing you. I'm not even telling you to leave the life. I guess, what I'm really saying is, either way, I want you to stop shutting me out. Don't let that dragon take over because you got secrets. I'm telling you right now you got a fight on your hands if you keep this shit up. I won't just sit here and watch the kid I love disappear. And if that means you leaving the life then, yeah, okay, I'll help you. I'm willing to do that, to risk the DeLorenzos coming after me, because I love you. More than anything, ever, if you want to know the truth."

As Tommy had been speaking, he remembered something that he hadn't thought about in years—the last time he had spoken to his nephew for so long a stretch. August 23, 1982, the day he got out of prison, when he sat with his nephew in the backyard during his homecoming party and the words had just poured out of him. Tommy had been better with numbers than words back then, but now, he thought it might be the opposite. Because unlike that day, when he had told his nephew he would always be there for him and searched his eyes in vain for a sign that his words had caught fire there—*now*, after all these years, Tommy finally saw it. A spark. The flicker of a flame behind his nephew's eyes that didn't come from the dragon.

Bobby took a deep breath. "Okay, the truth." He held his uncle's gaze again. "The truth is I love you too. Also the truth, you don't need to worry about the DeLorenzos because I'm not working for them. I killed Ronnie Matarese on my own. Because I knew what he would do if I didn't."

"I'm not following you." Tommy's heart beat heavily in his chest.

Bobby was smiling again, but it wasn't the manipulative, mask-like smile he had worn when he sat down at the table. This smile belonged to Bobby, but at the same time, Tommy could still see the dragon—unafraid, out of its lair now and circling above his nephew's head against some black storm clouds in the distance.

"The truth," Bobby said. "You want the truth, so here it is. For almost thirty years now, I've been killing guys from the RITS. Over a dozen of them. You know, real scumbags—rapists, murderers, child molesters. Guys who, if I let them live, would have wreaked more havoc than any fucking dragon. Like you say, don't ask me how I know. Not because I'm trying to hide anything from you but because, if you knew the truth, if you knew how fucked up I really am because of what your sister did to me, the sheer fire of it would incinerate you."

Tommy sat very still, but on the inside, he was trembling. He couldn't remember having ever been so afraid, not even on his first night in prison. Tommy Bonetti had been untouchable back then—no one would ever have thought about messing with a made man. But dragons were different, for some reason, and Tommy could see one coming for him. A dragon breathing truth instead of fire—a revelation, an apocalypse that, if Tommy let himself *really hear it*, would burn down his world until nothing was left but ashes.

"Don't be afraid." Bobby leaned forward. "And for Christ's sake, don't blame yourself. You did everything you could to protect me. But sometimes, no matter how hard we try, no matter how much we love, people fall through the ice and into the cold, dark water. Like Matt Kauffman. You think I killed him, don't you? Trying to figure out how he's connected to the Matareses because I was in the neighborhood that night? Well, truth is, I don't know if I killed Matt or not. I don't think I did, but sometimes, I forget things or remember them different than the way they happened. Either way, I wish I'd never gone back there, and that will haunt me forever."

Tommy felt an ebb in his fear but still couldn't speak. The kitchen had taken on a surreal quality, as if he were in a dream, as if it were perfectly normal to be sitting there across from someone with a dragon of truth circling over his head.

"But guys like Ronnie Matarese," Bobby went on, "they don't haunt me at all. I killed them. A bullet between the eyes or in the back of the head, whatever it took to get the job done, and I never regretted it for a second. I got rid of the evidence—the guns, just the barrels sometimes, yeah, and the shell casings. Tossed it all into Blackamore Pond. Know why? Because that was where it all began—where I learned the truth when I fell through the ice. There are no dragons, Uncle Tommy. Only elves. Only elves."

Chapter Thirty-Six

When Eddie arrived at police headquarters, he found John Seabrook in the small conference room on the second floor. Dan Costa was there, too, along with Lieutenant Detective Brian Rehnquist, who had taken over the Criminal Investigations Unit when Eddie retired. Eddie and Brian had come up together in the academy, but still, Eddie was a little surprised his old friend had agreed to bring him onboard. No laws prohibited civilian consultation in a homicide investigation, but Rehnquist had been in charge of the traffic division during that state police investigation a few years back. Big scandal, some dumbass rookies writing over a hundred parking tickets in less than two days in the wards of some city councilmen who had voted against a police union contract. Ever since then, Brian Rehnquist had been all about optics.

"Like a stray dog coming round for scraps," he said as he rose to greet Eddie. Rehnquist wore a small bandage over the bridge of his nose, the result of a melanoma he'd had removed the day before—which was why, praise Jesus, he had been MIA when Eddie and Ray took their polygraphs. Rehnquist gave Eddie a quick bro hug then jerked his chin toward some boxes of Dunkin' Donuts on the conference table. "Just make sure you leave some for the rest of us."

Eddie felt a wave of nausea but pretended to laugh and gave Rehnquist the finger. Dan Costa handed him a cup of coffee, and Eddie sat at the table between Russell Clancy, the department's expert on digital forensics, and Laurie Woodward, who worked downstairs in the evidence lab. Eddie was happy to see Woodward more than anyone—not just because he'd always had a thing for her, but because her presence meant some of the forensic tests had come back. The only person missing was the ME, Rita Gonzalez, which meant the final autopsy reports had yet to be completed. That was all right. Whatever it was that had exonerated Eddie was already there in the room—on the laptops and scattered papers that sat in front of the others at the table. The blackout curtains were closed, the big viewing screen on the far side of the room was down, and Eddie could hear the fan in the mounted ceiling projector whirring softly overhead.

"Thanks again, everyone, for coming so early," Rehnquist said, "and for all your hard work yesterday while I was out getting my nose hacked off. It's been a long night, so I'm sure we're all grateful for this fresh set of eyes, especially since Eddie was friends with the victim. Let's start by bringing him up to speed on where we are now."

His nausea passing, Eddie sipped his coffee as Dan Costa recounted his interviews with Matt's wife and children—all of which, he said, yielded nothing except the combination for the victim's cell phone and a clearer timeline of when the murder could have taken place. No enemies, his family said. No idea who could've done such a thing. Seabrook had also tracked down the DoorDash guy. Steve Parker was his name. Kid was nervous but cooperative, and no one in the neighborhood saw anything other than what was caught on camera. They would get to that in a moment, Seabrook said, but Eddie knew right away that was why they had ruled him out. Their footwork had paid off. They had found something on someone's security camera.

"What about this Debra Kauffman?" Rehnquist looked at some papers in front of him. "We interviewed her on that Matarese thing the day before yesterday, and now, the victim calls her late at night? Anybody talk to her about all that yet?"

"I caught her in the parking lot before her shift at the Foxy yesterday afternoon," Seabrook said, swiping his phone. "She played me

Kauffman's voicemail, which he left her shortly before midnight. Just ten seconds or so of him breathing and some music playing in the background. Forwarded it to me, already uploaded it into evidence, but here it is for your listening pleasure."

Seabrook played the voicemail on his phone. Eddie could hear some breathing, yeah, but most of it was drowned out by the guitar solo from "Detroit Rock City" by KISS. The hairs on the back of Eddie's neck stood on end. "Detroit Rock City" was the first song on the *Destroyer* album, which Eddie had found propped beside him when he awoke in Ray's den.

"In any event," Seabrook said, "Debra is scheduled to come in and talk to us at eight, on her way to her second job at the nail salon. We'll see if she shows."

"Does this kid even have time to be a suspect?" Rehnquist asked.

Seabrook shrugged. "Girl's gotta pay for her father's funeral expenses. Said her uncle Matthew was a cheap bastard. Loaded, but didn't offer her a dime—" Seabrook caught Eddie's eyes. "Hey, man, I'm sorry."

Eddie felt a bubble of anger in his stomach but just smiled and waved it away.

"Good, then," Rehnquist said. "We got some bad blood there, maybe even a motive." He turned to Eddie. "Your buddy ever talk about money disputes with this gal?"

Eddie shook his head—he was antsy to get to the camera footage.

"What about other things? Search history on the phone shows the victim looked up the Foxy Lady and escort services on the night he was murdered. Did he ever call his niece to hook him up? Girls she works with, maybe some blow when he's in town?"

Eddie exhaled impatiently—Ray had thrown out the same idea yesterday. "I don't see that guy ever paying for sex, Brian. He told me some shit over the years, yeah, but nothing like that. As for drugs, Matt didn't even smoke weed, as far as I know."

"What do you mean he told you some shit?" Seabrook asked. "That he had been unfaithful?"

Eddie shifted uncomfortably in his seat and nodded.

"He had a chick on the side then? Here in town with an angry boyfriend or something?"

"Nobody that I know of, no."

"Victim had a nephew too," Rehnquist said, reading. "James Kent Kauffman, aka JK, aka Jimmy Kahn. Real piece of work, this guy. Juvie record, in and out of prison on various offenses since he was eighteen. Currently finishing up a five-year bid for B and E. Anyone ever cross paths with this chode?"

"Warwick PD got the brunt of his bullshit over the years," Seabrook said. "Dan and I will head over to RIDOC today. Two-for-one deal, since we were scheduled to question him yesterday about Ronnie Matarese but got sidetracked with this. Incarcerated at the time of both crimes, but still, he might know something. Might've even hired someone. Matarese liked beating up on JK's little sister. That one definitely looks like a contract hit. Execution style, single gunshot wound between the eyes, not a clue so far except for the caliber of the weapon. As for Kauffman, completely different MO, but still looks like a targeted hit to me."

"I agree," Rehnquist said. "There was some planning here—someone who knew the victim would be in town for his brother's funeral and seized the opportunity. Eddie, what do you know about this JK clown? Kauffman ever mention him?"

"They were never close," Eddie said. "Matt had a falling-out with his brother, Jimmy, about ten years ago over some property in Warren. Whole thing went down when their father, Kent Kauffman, died. Jimmy took a swing at Matt at the wake. Big scene, hadn't spoken since. Same with Debra and JK. Matt didn't associate with them."

"Good to know about this property dispute," Rehnquist said, writing. "You guys make sure you hit that during the questioning."

Seabrook and Costa nodded and wrote something down too.

"Laurie, you want to take it from here?"

Eddie shifted in his seat again and groaned inwardly. *Just get to the footage!*

Laurie Woodward looked at her laptop. "Fingerprint analysis so far has yielded nothing. Everything taken from the house checks out with either the family or our victim. And of course, our consultant."

Woodward smiled at Eddie in that way that always made his stomach flutter like some goddamn middle schooler. He smiled back and gave her a thumbs-up, praying that he wasn't blushing.

"We're still working on tracking down all the prints from the pizza boxes. On the liquor bottles and what we managed to lift from the beer cans, we got Dawley, Eddie here, and the victim."

"What about inside the bottles?" Eddie asked. "You find anything to prove we might have been drugged? You know, traces of that roofie shit?"

Woodward shook her head. "All the tests we ran came back negative on that. No traces of any kind of benzodiazepine found in the liquor bottles, but the symptoms you described, Eddie—the dizziness, feeling hungover, and especially the anterograde amnesia—all of those are classic indicators that you might have been slipped a date-rape drug like flunitrazepam, more commonly known by its brand name, Rohypnol."

"Aka roofies," Seabrook muttered.

"Right. However, unlike Xanax, Valium, and other widely available benzos, Rohypnol was never approved by the FDA for use here in the United States—only available on the black market or in Europe and Asia. In any event, the Providence lab will need to do a special toxicology test for that. But, Eddie, if they do find Rohypnol or some other benzo in your system, it didn't come from those bottles. Didn't find anything in the glasses, either, but those had been washed."

"It had to be the pizza then." Eddie turned to Seabrook. "The DoorDash guy—what's his name?"

"Steve Parker."

"You said he was nervous when you talked to him. I mean, I know this is a long shot, but you think someone could've paid him off to keep his mouth shut? Someone who could've gotten to the pizzas before they were delivered?"

Seabrook raised his eyebrows and heaved a heavy sigh. "I don't know, Eddie. That's a *huge* long shot. The killer would have to have known the pizzas were being delivered, and then, what, he sprinkles powder or something on the—"

"I know, I know." Eddie waved his hands. "It sounds crazy, but I was drugged. I'm telling you. And it was from either the booze or that pizza."

"Maybe Laurie is onto something," Seabrook said. "Kauffman slips something into your glasses then washes them before he leaves—"

"Let's wait for all the tests before we go down that rabbit hole," Rehnquist said. "What else you got, Laurie?"

"The forensic team is still combing through the victim's car," she said, consulting her laptop, "but we've identified the fish tail as belonging to a species of snapper common in stores all over Rhode Island. Previously frozen, so who knows when or where the killer could have gotten it."

"Any theories as to what's up with that?" Rehnquist asked. "Beyond some Godfather wannabe with a flair for the dramatic?"

Everyone looked at each other, then Laurie Woodward said, "I don't see a connection to the species itself yet. However, as I'm sure all of you know, fish is often associated with the female genitalia. Lends credence to some kind of sexual connection, if one wanted to look at it that way."

The men averted their eyes and shifted uncomfortably in their chairs.

"Noted." Rehnquist wrote something down.

Eddie stayed quiet, resisting changing the mood by offering his theory about Bobby Bonetti. After a good night's sleep, something in his gut just didn't sit right. Never mind Matt's internet activity and the call to Debra, Bobby would have to be a complete idiot to leave such an obvious clue, especially since he had to have known word would eventually get back to Eddie. What was more, Eddie had been there on the night they arrested Bobby's uncle in the mid-nineties, so Bobby had more of a beef with Eddie than he'd ever had with Matt—unless, of course, there was some connection of which Eddie was still unaware. So yeah, until he had more evidence, Eddie would keep his mouth shut. He was only a consultant, and the last thing he wanted to do was lose all credibility by leading everyone down the wrong path—just like he had almost done when he suspected Ray of roofieing him.

"What about the other evidence gathered from the car?" Rehnquist asked, and Woodward consulted her laptop.

"Clothesline was taken from the backyard of the Dawley residence. Cut ends match those still on the hooks. It appears recently severed—clean cuts, possibly with a utility knife on the night of the murder. Providence lab has everything now for DNA analysis, including the tissue found in the back seat."

"What tissue?" Eddie asked.

Woodward punched a few keys on her laptop. "Here." She showed Eddie a picture on the screen—a wad of Kleenex, it looked like, wedged between the rear seat cushions in Matt's Lexus. A yellow evidence marker sat beside it. "No other tissues like it in the car. Given the victim was strangled from behind, we're hoping it belonged to the killer."

"The bit with the clothesline is a classic mob-style hit," Seabrook said. "Use something already present at the crime scene so it can't be traced back to the killer."

Woodward shrugged, then finally, Rehnquist handed things over to Russell Clancy. The digital forensic specialist rose from the table, turned off the lights, then sat back down. In the light from his laptop, Clancy looked like an owl because of the shadow from his glasses. The mounted ceiling projector whirred louder, and a night vision video from someone's doorbell camera began playing on the screen. The tail end of a car could be seen passing by, left to right, from the passenger's side. The camera had missed most of it, but then another, longer clip played from an angle across the street—right to left, from the driver's side. The footage was grainy—the driver, undistinguishable—but Eddie could tell right away that the car was a black Lexus. His heart twisted, and a fresh wave of nausea ran through him.

"Okay," Russell Clancy began, "none of the houses in the immediate vicinity of Dawley's are equipped with security cameras, and of the ten we counted between his house and Blackamore Pond, eight, for whatever reason, did not pick up Kauffman's car at all. This second clip is the better of the two we got"—Clancy had stopped it and now zoomed in on the driver's-side window—"picked up just after one o'clock. You can just barely make out a figure behind the steering wheel, but even with the enhancement I added, it's too dark to tell if the driver is our victim or someone else."

"What about cameras in the opposite direction?" Eddie asked. "You know, that might have picked up someone entering Lexington Avenue from Pontiac?"

"A lot of cars came in and out of the neighborhood that night because of the football games, but we haven't been able to find footage yet that shows any suspicious vehicles around that time. No one on foot either. Not at one o'clock in the morning."

"We're still canvassing Concord and Blackamore to see if we can find anything else," Dan Costa said.

Clancy switched to another video. "Right, but I doubt we'll get anything better than this."

Russell Clancy played his next clip, this one showing some woods and a distant figure dressed in a baggie hooded sweatshirt, face mask, and backpack. Eddie figured the person was in all black, but because it was night vision, they glowed a phosphorescent green as they hopped a chain-link fence and quickly moved out of camera range behind some trees. Clancy quickly rewound the footage and froze it just after the person cleared the fence and stood to their full height. Their mask covered their entire face with no opening for a mouth, and their hoodie was down too low for Eddie to see their eyes.

"Ninja, meet Eddie," he said. "Eddie, this is Ninja, our prime suspect."

"You're kidding me," Eddie muttered. "Where was this?"

"House overlooking the pond at the bottom of Waterman Avenue," Russell Clancy said. "Security camera picked this up at one twenty-seven, roughly ten minutes after the footage of Kauffman's car. The owner contacted us late yesterday afternoon."

Clancy had zoomed in on the figure, but still, Eddie could not make out any discernible features.

"Of course," Eddie said. "We used to cut through there all the time going to school. Fence wasn't there back then, but if this is the perp, they would've hugged the curve from Lexington onto Blackamore, hopped the guardrail there, then cut through the woods to come out on Waterman. You guys search the area for footprints yet?"

"Had to wait for daylight," Seabrook said, "but yeah, team's over there now."

"Gonna be tough, though," Costa said. "The ground's frozen solid. Pond mostly, too, one of my guys texted. Today'll be a cold one."

"Good news, however," Clancy said. "Using that fence as a reference, we can put our little ninja here between five six, five eight or nine max."

"How tall are you, Eddie?" Seabrook asked, half smiling.

So that was why they had ruled him out. The height and weight were way off—not to mention Eddie Sayers hadn't been able to hop a fence in over twenty years.

"I still tell chicks six feet on Tinder," he said, and everyone chuckled. "And Ray Dawley, he's over six feet, I think."

"You can have the honor of telling him he's out," Seabrook said. "But it goes without saying that's all you tell him, understand? We have enough trouble keeping a lid on shit around here as it is—"

"Goes without saying." Eddie made a peace sign.

"So, our suspect is between five six and five nine," Rehnquist said. "Thinner build, it looks like, but hard to tell because of the clothes."

"Almost certain, then, that Kauffman walked out of Dawley's house on his own," Seabrook said. "Unless our suspect is unusually strong, of course. But still, that means he would have gotten inside the house while you guys were partying. I mean, if the bottles show no trace elements of tampering, the only way Ninja Boy could've drugged you guys was to get to your glasses. Then again, if our guy *really is* a ninja..."

The others chuckled, and Eddie swiveled his eyes to the frozen image of the suspect on the screen. The idea that this son of a bitch could have entered the house and drugged them right under their noses was remote, *insanely* remote. Goddamn. It looked as if Matt had more to do with this than Eddie wanted to admit.

"Those date-rape drugs," Costa said, "they mess with your perception of time—make you forget shit, especially if you're drinking. Who knows what time you guys got dosed, Eddie—which would explain why you woke up in the situation you did. You could have kept right on partying and wouldn't remember any of it."

"In any event," Rehnquist said, "we'll need to start knocking on doors again. Expand our search and see if any cars or foot traffic was picked up on security cameras in the vicinity. Timeframe should be roughly between eleven thirty, when Kauffman called his niece, and two the next morning. We know for certain this Ninja prick was in the neighborhood at that time."

"Smart," Eddie muttered. He was startled a second later to find all eyes on him. He didn't realize he had spoken. Eddie cleared his throat. "What I mean is, this is the best way to go in and out of the neighborhood if you're worried about cameras. Park a car down at the bottom of Waterman Avenue then head around the back of the elementary school and along the pond until you hit Aqueduct Road. Fewer houses in that area, and those that have cameras on Aqueduct, the settings will be such they're not going to pick up every car going by. Main thoroughfare, too much traffic."

"So you're thinking Ninja Boy was heading for Reservoir Ave?" Seabrook asked.

Eddie shrugged. "Or Pontiac, yeah, if they don't live nearby. Either way, last I checked, that part of Cranston doesn't have many traffic cameras, am I right?"

A heavy silence fell upon the room, eyes dropping guiltily, as if someone there were to blame, then Rehnquist asked, "What do you mean 'if they don't live nearby'?"

Eddie shrugged. "Seems to me, only someone familiar with the neighborhood would know about cutting through the woods over there. You want to murder someone down at Blackamore Pond and not be seen, that's the way to do it."

"Our ninja could've cased the area in advance," Laurie Woodward said. "Clearly, this took some planning."

"Definitely possible." Eddie nodded. "But the window for all that would've been very small. The killer would've needed to know Matt would be at Ray's that night. And we didn't decide on that until after the funeral, when we were all outside the church."

"Who's 'we'?" Brian Rehnquist asked.

"Me, Matt, Ray, his wife, and Shelly. Ray's daughter was there too. Maggie."

Dan Costa consulted his notes. "Victim's wife has a solid alibi. Checks out with the owner of the B and B. Same for Dawley's wife and daughter. Spoke to them last night. Dawley's mother too. Natalia and Maggie spent the night at her townhouse in Western Cranston. Just like Ray Dawley said from the beginning."

"But a lot of other people were in front of the church too," Eddie said. "So yeah, I wonder if our ninja was at the funeral and overheard us."

Rehnquist leaned forward. "Please tell me there was a guest book at the church."

Eddie smiled. "Why, I believe there was, Lieutenant. I believe there was."

Brian Rehnquist clapped his hands, rose from his chair, and turned on the lights.

"We should be able to quickly narrow down a pool of suspects from that guest book then start throwing out those who don't fit our ninja's body type."

Everybody started collecting their things, and Rehnquist checked his watch.

"Debra Kauffman should be here in about half an hour. John, you get on the horn and tell her to bring that guest book. I'll have a warrant for it in an hour—for her whole goddamn apartment if she gives you any shit."

"You got it," Seabrook said. Eddie stood, too, and Seabrook put a hand on his shoulder. "I assume you're gonna stick around for our interview with Little Miss Sunshine?"

"Yeah, and I'd like to tag along to see Matt's nephew, too, if that's all right."

Seabrook looked at Rehnquist.

"It's more than all right," the latter said, then everyone began to file out of the room.

Laurie Woodward was the last to gather her things, and Eddie stopped her at the door.

"I forgot to ask you. That fish tail, was it salt or freshwater?"

"Saltwater. Why?"

Eddie shrugged and shook his head. "Just wondering what kind of message our suspect was trying to send is all."

Laurie Woodward smiled again in that way that made Eddie's stomach flutter. "I always liked the way your mind worked," she said. "We miss you around here."

She held his eyes, and Eddie smiled back.

But instead of saying he missed her too—*Honestly, more than anyone, Laurie, because I was always too much of a pussy to ask you out*—Eddie just nodded at the Dunkin' boxes on the conference table. "Well, hey, at least you guys get more donuts."

Woodward nodded and smiled—somewhat regretfully this time, Eddie thought—then she left. Eddie turned back to the projector screen—to the reason why he had asked Woodward about the fish, which had dawned on him all at once, it seemed.

Give or take an inch, and maybe a pound or two, the height and build of their suspect could put him around the same size as Bobby Bonetti—*who really is a ninja, Detective Seabrook.*

Chapter Thirty-Seven

Shelly sat in her daughter's car, watching the crow peck at something dead.

The car—its engine running, its heat on high—was parked near the entrance of Newport Hospital. Shelly occupied the passenger seat, the crow to her left, in the grass near some bushes on the small island in the middle of the circular driveway. Shelly had spied the bird through the driver's-side window—its startled black wings catching her attention as Jenny shut her inside. Jenny was talking to Matt Junior by his car, parked behind her. "MJ," as they all called him, had wanted to stay in Rhode Island at least until the autopsy was done, but Jenny had insisted on getting their mother home.

On some level, Shelly knew it was too much to ask of them. Things should be reversed. She should be strong for them, not the other way around. And yet, here they were. MJ had driven down from Boston around noon yesterday, and Jenny from Bennington a short time later. The twenty-four hours since she had learned of Matthew's death had been somewhat of a blur, a cacophony of anguished cries and weeping—some belonging to her children, but most coming from her. The doctors prescribed Shelly something to help her sleep and numb the pain. And now, there was only the crow.

From where she sat, Shelly could see little more than the fur of the animal on which it fed—gray and whitish in spots. A rabbit, most likely—roadkill that the crow had snatched up somewhere nearby. In another lifetime, Shelly might have searched for meaning in the bird's decision to feed so close to her. The child in her would have seen it as something magical—a supernatural test, perhaps, in which the crow wanted to see if it could trust Shelly before revealing to her some important secret. The college student would have seen the bird as a metaphor, something to be used in a story about the brutal, methodical peck-peck-peck of death. The housewife, however, would have just worried that the crows had gotten into her bird feeder again back home, leaving the other birds to starve. The cardinals and the blue jays. The goldfinches and black-capped chickadees. The northern flickers, the Carolina wrens, the fox sparrows, the red-breasted nuthatches, and all the others that hung on through the coldest of New Jersey winters.

Strange, Shelly thought as she watched the crow. So very strange that she had once cared enough to know the names of all those birds. Same as she had once cared to know the person calling her now. Shelly felt the phone buzzing in her hand before she heard it ringing. And because the call was not coming from someone in Shelly's contacts, the name scrolled under the number like spam. Natalia Morris. Shelly stared at the letters for a moment, unable to make sense of them, her brain slow to register, it seemed, that here was someone with whom she would like to be friends.

But caring about things like making friends was from another lifetime. Maybe even a life that had belonged to someone else—someone named Shelly Before. Shelly Before had been married to a man named Matthew Kauffman. Shelly Before had been dedicated to her children, to making a home for them like the one she'd never had. The kind of gal who kept the rooms neat and clean and sometimes cooked things just so the house would smell nice when everyone came home. The kind of gal who only wanted to make memories and cherished a cup of cocoa snuggled up on the couch more than any trip to the Bahamas. Yeah, *that* Shelly had always been there, had been strong, like the birds in her backyard that hung on all winter. Shelly Before never would have let her son officially identify her husband's body at the morgue in Providence while she lay around half out of it in some hospital bed in Newport.

But it was Shelly *After* who had made that decision—that was, if Shelly After were capable of making decisions at all. Shelly After was a widow now and just sort of let things happen around her—just walked through life on autopilot, just gobbled down Xanax prescribed to her by the hospital doctor. Shelly After remembered Shelly Before, and felt, deep down, that she could be like her if she really wanted to. But Shelly After wanted numbness more—needed it like air, every breath of which felt like a dare.

Shelly answered her phone. "Hello?" Her voice sounded hollow and far away—so different than Shelly Before.

"Hi, Shelly, it's Natalia."

"Yes, your name came up on the caller ID. How are you?"

"My God, Shelly, I can't begin to tell you how sorry I am. No words can make this better, but Ray and I are here for you. Where are you? We'd like to come see you."

"Thank you, Natalia, but Matthew Junior and Jenny are here, and we're driving back to New Jersey today. This is very hard, and we all need to be home, in our house, together as a family. We never should've come back here."

A heavy silence came next, in which Shelly could sense Natalia searching for the right response. Or maybe, being a shrink, she was analyzing the detached, almost robotic way Shelly spoke. *No, not speaking, more like leaking,* Shelly thought.

"Please try not to go down that road," Natalia said. "Second-guessing will only make things worse and get in the way of finding out who did this. Any news around that, Shelly? Anything at all that I can help with?"

"Not that I know of, no."

"I don't know if your husband ever told you, but I lost someone too. A long time ago. Someone very dear to me. My sister. I tell you this not to compare our tragedies, but so you know you have someone here who understands beyond her degree on the wall."

"I appreciate that, thank you." Shelly was only half listening now.

Her eyes had drifted back to the crow. The big black bird had torn loose some of the rabbit's entrails and now pumped its beak upward, chewing and working the bloody strands bit by bit down its throat.

Another heavy silence, then Natalia said, "Well, again, we are so very sorry, Shelly. You have my number now. Please take care of yourself, and call me if you need anything, okay?"

"Yes, I will. Thank you, Natalia."

Shelly ended the call, then a second later, Jenny slipped into the driver's seat, blocking her view of the crow. She smiled at Shelly, but her daughter's eyes were still red from weeping. And the little scar on her chin, which she had gotten when she fell during recess in kindergarten, looked whiter and more pronounced.

Jenny took off her knitted cap, tucked it in the seat beside her leg, and unzipped her parka. The cap was off-white with a grayish fur pom-pom, and the parka was light blue. Shelly Before had given her daughter these things for Christmas last year, but Shelly After now thought it silly how conscious she had been of her children's natural coloring when picking out their clothes. Jenny had blond hair and a cute, slightly upturned nose from Matthew's side of the family, whereas MJ was darker featured like Shelly. As for their dispositions, it was the opposite. Jenny was a bit more type A, whereas MJ was more easygoing, though he was two years older.

"Do you think the house is cold?" Shelly asked.

Jenny sat there for a moment, immobile and staring at the steering wheel. "I don't know, Mom," she said after a deep breath.

Her voice sounded tired and tense—from holding back her tears, Shelly understood. Which was why, as they drove off, she did not mention that the pom-pom on her daughter's hat looked like the dead rabbit in the grass. Besides, those kinds of details were meaningless now, and something only Shelly Before would have cared to notice.

Chapter Thirty-Eight

After she hung up with Shelly Kauffman, Natalia tucked her phone in the back pocket of her jeans and, peering out the window in the den, watched the pair of detectives slip into their unmarked car. She had seen them pull up in front of the Mullaneys' house next door about fifteen minutes earlier—right after Ray left with Maggie for school. Same guys who had interviewed her after supper the night before. Natalia couldn't remember their names but had found them considerate, if not a bit cagey, when it came to the details of their investigation. All they had really wanted from Natalia was a timeline of their overnight at Sue's, including what time they all went to bed—around nine, Natalia told them, which they said jived with her mother-in-law's account of events. Apparently, they had already visited her too.

But why were they visiting the Mullaneys again? Natalia wondered as the car spit out a blast of gray exhaust. *And so early in the morning too?* That was what had really prompted her to call Shelly. Eddie had texted Ray her contact information the night before—said he had tried reaching out but never got a response—so in a way, Natalia was grateful that the grieving widow had answered at all. Shelly had sounded out of it, probably pumped full of Xanax or some other benzo. Still, Natalia would've liked to get at least a little bit of information on the investigation. Mainly, if the police were still looking at Ray. *If so, what did Shelly think about all that?*

Natalia turned from the window and slipped on her coat. She shouldn't have come right out and asked Shelly about leads. Probably shouldn't have mentioned anything about Gina, either, but goddamn, those detectives visiting the Mullaneys so early in the morning had spooked her. Natalia didn't see how the elderly couple could be of any assistance. They were in bed every night by eight and didn't have a doorbell cam. So her thoughts had naturally drifted to the worst-case scenario: they were bashing Ray—who, just before Halloween that year, told old Ben Mullaney to go fuck himself after he advised Ray not to give out candy because of all the "spics and gooks" that came around these days.

"I hope you fellas are looking real hard at that Dawley character," Natalia could hear the old bigot telling the detectives. *"Son of a bitch verbally assaulted me not even two months ago!"*

Natalia swiveled her eyes again out the window just as the detectives were pulling away. She chuckled. *I'm worrying for nothing.* Ray hadn't done anything. And after five minutes with the Mullaneys, the detectives would know what they were dealing with—especially Ben's wife, Barbara, who was half senile and always sputtering nonsense. Yeah, Natalia should be grateful the detectives had spoken with the Mullaneys instead of her. She was running late, and the last thing she needed was to get held up answering a bunch of questions.

Natalia fetched her purse and gloves from Ray's writing chair and was outside a few seconds later. Another brutally cold New England morning, but Natalia had used the auto start before calling Shelly, so her Mercedes was already toasty warm when she slipped inside and spied the detectives' car in front of Carl Deware's house three doors down. Carl handed one of them his cell phone through the driver's-side window. Even from a distance, his chubby face looked tense. Carl thrust his hands into the pockets of his parka, waited for a few seconds, then said something while glancing back over his shoulder toward Spring Street. Natalia smiled. No, the Mullaneys didn't have a doorbell cam, but Carl Deware did. He must have flagged down the detectives as they were pulling away—to show them a security app on his phone, Natalia hoped. Maybe his doorbell cam, which was directly across from Spring Street, had picked up something interesting.

Wouldn't that be a relief? Natalia thought as she glanced at the dashboard clock: 7:56. What with traffic, she would be cutting it close if she waited to talk to Carl after the detectives left, and her first patient that day was a real piece of work. Nothing compared to Dave Ruggieri, but still, Natalia needed time to go over her case notes and prepare. What was more, she knew Carl only superficially, and given that a CSI van had been parked in her driveway the day before, he would probably slam the door in her face. True, the local news media hadn't mentioned anything about all that, but who could say what the neighbors knew, especially with the way word got around in Cranston.

The detective passed the phone back to Carl, who nodded and began speaking again. Christ, she was curious what they were talking about. For a moment, she thought, *Fuck it, I'm just going to walk right over there and ask what's going on.* Then the call from her ex came over the car's Bluetooth. Natalia immediately sent it to voicemail, but when she turned back to Carl, he was heading toward his house and the detectives were driving away.

"Thanks a lot, prick," Natalia muttered, glaring at her phone.

She knew what Tim wanted. Same as when he texted the night before, beginning with how the murder at the bottom of her street was all over the news and he was concerned about how Natalia would address it with Jeremy. Natalia told him not to worry about it, but she had opened the door, and Tim immediately pivoted again to switching their usual Christmas schedule for some yoga retreat up in Vermont that he wanted to attend with his new girlfriend. It started the day after Christmas, which was during his usual block of time with Jeremy. Natalia said she would be more than happy to have their son for his entire break so Tim could do whatever the hell he wanted, to which Tim called her self-centered. Unreal. The fucking nerve.

Heaven forbid Tim Nowak should miss out on some downward dog because his ex-wife's parents had planned their entire visit from Florida around their grandson's usual schedule.

Natalia looked down at her gloved hands and closed them around an imaginary rope—perhaps even the clothesline Matthew Kauffman's killer had used to strangle him down at Blackamore Pond. Ray had told her about all that—had choked back tears as he described identifying the body. But it was Tim Nowak choking now, squirming and flailing his arms in a desperate attempt at one last sun salutation while his ex-wife strangled him from the back seat of her mind.

Chapter Thirty-Nine

The camera feed for the interview room began as soon as Debra Kauffman was let inside.

Eddie sat on a small sofa in the adjoining room, watching Debra on the big wall-mounted flatscreen and doing his best not to eavesdrop on John Seabrook, who was on the phone with his ex-wife near the watercooler. Second call that morning, something about their elder son being late for school. Dan Costa was trying not to listen, too, Eddie could tell. The detective stood in the doorway pretending to read through some papers, though he couldn't keep a straight face.

"Okay, okay," Seabrook said, "just tell him he gets no PlayStation for a week. A *month*? Jesus Christ, Monica, come on..."

John Seabrook was recently divorced—amicably, for the most part, it seemed to Eddie—but in a lot of ways, the poor guy had had a rougher go of it than Eddie back in the day. John had fifty-fifty custody of his two boys, twelve and ten, but the older one was not taking it well. Messing up at school, mainly, in addition to mouthing off to his mother and biking over to John's when he wasn't there. Monica had gotten their house in Garden City, and John was renting a dumpy one-bedroom apartment not even a half mile away. Eddie had helped him move and even got him a George Foreman grill—part housewarming gift, part joke because everybody busted his balls about how much he resembled the former heavyweight champ. Eddie hadn't been by John's place since then, because he spent all his free time with his boys—which Eddie admired the hell out of him for.

"For Christ's sake, Monica, I'm at work. Just take the key from him when he gets home and... Well, what else can I do? I can't stop him from going over there and playing when I'm not home."

Eddie leaned forward in his chair and tried to focus on Debra. Gone were the days when detectives had to crowd around a window of one-way glass to observe an interview. Unlike Debra's room, which was little more than a closet with a table and a couple of chairs, Eddie's looked like a waiting room in a doctor's office—small sofa and club chairs, watercooler, and a coffee maker, pictures of light-houses and the Rhode Island countryside on the walls. The "soft in-terview room" had been outfitted to help make trauma victims feel more comfortable, but Eddie thought it made things worse. The rob-bery witnesses, the rape victims, the family members of the deceased all seemed more prone to hysteria these days. Maybe it was just his imagination, but still, there was something to be said for the sobering effect the cold, old-school utilitarian aesthetic had on people—both the victims and the suspects.

But is Matt's niece really a suspect? The camera feed from her interview room was a bit grainy, but still, Eddie could tell the girl looked more tired than nervous. She sat at the table with her eyes closed and her face in her hands as if she might fall asleep. Her sandy-blond hair was pulled back in a bun, and she wore a navy-blue Patri-ots hoodie and sweatpants. A bit rough, but not a bad-looking girl, Debra Kauffman—big blow-job lips and fuck-me eyes that no doubt got her plenty of tips on those ten-dollar cans of beer at the Foxy. Mid- to late twenties by now, Eddie figured, and a goddamn miracle, really, that she'd avoided the path of the crew she came up with. No kids—the result of a botched abortion at sixteen, Eddie had learned at some point—and had somehow managed to kick her heroin habit and get into the local methadone clinic. She was taking criminal jus-tice courses at CCRI and trying to turn her life around, she had told Seabrook when they questioned her about Ronnie Matarese.

Good thing, too, Eddie thought. Despite the number her ex had done on her face, Eddie could tell Debra Kauffman only had a year or two left at the Foxy before they put her out to pasture—the bags under her eyes, the sagginess of her jowls, visible even from a distance on the camera feed. Someone had paid to have her boobs done, Eddie had noticed at the funeral, but the flesh around her pits and on the backs of her arms was already starting to look flaccid—no matter how many tattoos she got.

Seabrook hung up with his ex-wife and moved to Costa. "Kill me now," he said, looking through his partner's papers. "Kid called his mother a queef sniffer. Twelve years old, where the hell he hear something like that?"

Costa chuckled and shrugged.

Seabrook handed him back the papers. "Okay, you know the drill. Remember, she brought the guest book, so go easy on her unless you sense she's dicking you around."

Costa gave a half salute and left. Seabrook closed the door and sat next to Eddie on the sofa. He turned up the TV volume with a remote control that had been affixed to the arm with Velcro, and a few seconds later, Costa entered the interview room on the TV screen with his laptop and a cup of coffee. The camera angle was such that it looked down on them somewhat and showed more of Debra when Costa sat across from her at the table and gave her the coffee. He pulled out his phone and began to record their conversation—backup in the event that something went wrong with the video upload. Brian Rehnquist would no doubt watch the interview later in his office. The detective lieutenant had two homicides on his hands in twenty-four hours and was busy following up on a lead in the Matarese murder.

Costa slipped a pen from his shirt pocket, checked his watch, and wrote the time in his notepad. Seabrook did the same beside Eddie, then Costa began his interview with the usual small talk, asking Debra how she was holding up and thanking her for bringing the guest book and taking time out of her busy schedule to speak with them again.

Eddie figured that if Debra intended to ask for a lawyer, she would have done so already. What was more, Matt's niece seemed exasperated rather than anxious, as if she truly couldn't fathom why they were bothering her again with this bullshit. Whether that came from innocence or overconfidence remained to be seen. It was hard for Eddie to tell without being in the same room, without sensing the girl's energy and breathing the same air. That said, it had been clear to him as soon as she appeared on the TV screen that Debra Kauffman was not the suspect in the security video. A little spitfire of a thing, she was lucky if she clocked in at five-two max.

"You guys don't let up," she said. "Seriously, I already told your buddy I hardly knew my uncle. The fuck he doing, accosting me in the parking lot at work? 'Specially after what happened a few years back. I'm on thin ice there as it is, you know. I don't need people thinking I'm in on another sting."

Debra sipped her coffee, and Costa wrote something. "I know you've been through a lot. We're just grateful to pick your brain is all. Any idea why your uncle, Matt, would've called you so late Sunday night?"

Debra leaned forward and held Costa's eyes. "Maybe to say he was sorry for fucking over my father. Or maybe he changed his mind about chipping in for the funeral. The hell should I know? I was at work, didn't even see I missed his call until after my shift. We can't have our phones on the floor. You heard the voicemail. I forwarded it to you guys. What else do you want?"

"You've been more than cooperative," Costa said, writing. "Can't tell you how much we appreciate it. But you said you got off work that night at what time? One o'clock?"

"That's when my shift ended, yeah, but by the time I closed out my tips and finished my drink, I didn't leave until about two, I guess. On the house because of my father—the drink, I mean."

"Sucks you having to work after his funeral."

Debra sipped her coffee and shrugged. "Girl's gotta eat. And I ain't getting any younger. I'm happy to pick up what I can. Money's good, but nothing like when I worked Friday and Saturday nights. I'm strictly B-team now."

Costa chuckled. "And you went right home after that? Sunday night, after your drink, I mean?"

"To my mother's, where I been staying since I left Ronnie. You can ask her if you want, but she was sleeping. I turned off the alarm, though, so maybe you can corroborate that with the alarm company or something. ADT, I think, but ask her."

"All that true?" Eddie asked Seabrook. "Her alibi checks out?"

"Yeah, but it doesn't mean she wasn't in on it," Seabrook said.

Eddie sat back in his chair and sipped his coffee, as cold and bitter as the girl in front of him. Debra Kauffman had nothing to hide, Eddie sensed. He didn't like where this was going.

Costa continued writing. "Okay, but your uncle, anything you can tell us about what happened? Anyone you know who might've had it out for him?"

Debra sighed and shook her head. "Last time I saw him, before all this, was when he and my father got into it at my grandfather's funeral, ten years ago. So what can I tell you? If he treated other people the way he treated us, I figure he's got plenty of enemies."

"I wanted to talk to you about that." Costa looked through his papers. "I heard your father and your uncle, Matt, had a falling-out over money. Sale of some rental property in Warren, right?"

Debra laughed. "Auntie Shelly tell you about all that? Did she also tell you how they fucked me out of my inheritance? The least the cheap bitch could do is toss me something for the funeral, but hey."

"Your brother, James—Matt and Shelly screw him too?"

"We woulda split our share, so yeah. I mean, that's what my father always said, but who knows now? He prolly woulda blew it all on booze. Still, it was the principle of the thing. Being fucked over by your own flesh and blood, that's what did him in, my father. The final straw. Ever since then, it was downhill. Uncle Matt and that gold-digger wife, I blame them both."

"Why do you blame them? I'm still not sure what happened."

"We're barking up the wrong tree here," Eddie muttered—mind racing, only half listening now as Debra got into the weeds of the dispute. Something about Kent Kauffman giving Matt power of attorney and money being allocated for a bankruptcy. Eddie didn't care to follow the details. Unimportant, since Debra obviously only knew half of some bullshit story her alcoholic father fed her. *Everyone against me, even my own family, blahdy-blah-blah.*

"Tough broad," Seabrook said. "All those years on the needle and working the Foxy, you learn how to play your part."

Eddie shook his head. "Nah, she's no actress. Willing to bet she had nothing to do with this. Doesn't give a damn what she says, not worried about slipping up and keeping her story straight. Just tired of life and doesn't care who knows it."

"Let's just see what happens when Dan shows her the video," Seabrook said. "Keep a close eye on her."

"What about your brother?" Costa asked Debra. "He got a beef with your uncle Matt, too? Pissed about getting screwed out of his inheritance?"

"Prolly, yeah." Debra slumped back in her chair. "But if you're thinking he could kill someone over something like that, I don't know. You need to ask him. I'm sure you know where he is."

She chuckled, and Costa opened his laptop.

"Seriously, though, I've hardly talked to him since he went in five years ago. Trying to get away from those kinds of people. Ronnie, even my own brother, you know?"

"What about Ronnie?" Costa moved his finger on the mouse pad. "He ever mention anything to you? You know, if your uncle was mixed up with any of his people? Guys from Boston, maybe?"

Debra's eyes narrowed, and her mouth hung slightly ajar, as if her brain couldn't compute what the detective had just asked of her. "Wait, is that what this is about? You think what happened to Uncle Matt and Ronnie is connected?"

"We're just talking here—"

"Fuck, wow." Debra shook her head. "Didn't see that coming, but no, Ronnie never talked to me about his bullshit. Are you kidding me?" She laughed.

"Seems to have gotten over her ex pretty quick," Seabrook said.

Eddie didn't see it that way. The girl was in survival mode. So much death around her—her father, her ex-boyfriend, her uncle—all of whom she had mixed feelings toward. If she took on the weight of it all, if she even allowed herself to think about it, she would suffocate.

"Like Ronnie"—Costa turned the laptop to face her—"we're thinking your uncle's murder was a professional hit. And this is our prime suspect."

Eddie leaned forward as Costa played the security footage for Debra, who squinted at the screen and sipped her coffee as if she were reading the morning paper. Eddie watched her closely—especially after Costa paused the video to magnify the suspect's face—but Debra Kauffman's demeanor did not change. Same tired-of-all-the-bullshit attitude, maybe even a bit more irritated now at the ridiculousness of her being involved in all this.

She scoffed. "You can't even tell if it's some dude or a girl, and I'm supposed to know who this person is?"

"Well, yeah, we were hoping they might look familiar," Costa said. "Maybe you'll recognize something if you look closely. Clothes, body type, I don't know, someone who was at the funeral, maybe?"

Debra leaned in closer to the laptop then exhaled and shook her head.

The girl's a dead end, Eddie thought, half-listening again as she went back and forth with Costa about whether anyone at the funeral had mob ties.

"We're gonna run all the names from the guest book anyway," Costa said, "so you might as well tell us what you know."

Blahdy-blah-blah. Maybe they would have better luck with her brother, but more than ever, Eddie's gut told him that would be a dead end too. Seabrook probably thought the same thing, since when his phone rang, he answered it instead of letting it go to voicemail.

"Yeah?" Seabrook was silent for quite some time, nodding and uh-huhing as the person on the other end spoke. Eddie could tell by his friend's demeanor that it wasn't his ex-wife again. "Okay, well, just have them email it to you, then upload everything into the case file when you get back to headquarters. I know. I'll follow up after we talk to the vic's nephew. Right." Seabrook ended the call.

"What's up?" Eddie asked.

"Probably nothing, but three houses down from Dawley's, a doorbell cam picked up a suspicious vehicle. Fella named Carl Deware. He flagged down two of our guys when they were leaving Ray's next-door neighbors. Second time they been over there, couple of old kooks saying they found footprints in their yard. All bullshit, but—"

"What about the suspicious vehicle?" Eddie asked, impatient.

"Doorbell cam is almost straight on with Spring Street. Super sensitive, Deware says, always picking up shit even from across the way. I guess around four thirty or so, Sunday afternoon, this black

Honda Accord pulls up near the corner. Doesn't belong in the neighborhood. Camera is triggered a bunch more times afterward—cars, people going by—and you can see the Accord in the background. Then around seven thirty or so, the camera is triggered again by the Accord leaving."

"I don't get it," Eddie said, splitting his gaze between Seabrook and Costa, who was wrapping up his interview. "What with the games, lots of cars in the neighborhood didn't belong, including mine."

"Yeah, but the thing about this one is, with the camera being so sensitive, the guy figured you should've seen someone getting in or out. But you don't. Looks like the driver just sits there for a few hours then drives off."

"Corner of Spring Street." Eddie thought. "The driver would've had a clear view of Ray's house."

"That's what my guys are thinking, yeah."

"License plate?" Eddie asked, though he figured Seabrook would have told him that up front.

"With the angle, the distance, and the glare, you can't make out the numbers. But we'll see if Russell can enhance it."

Seabrook stood—Debra and Dan Costa were getting ready to go—and Eddie stood too.

"Like you said," Seabrook said, "there were a lot of unfamiliar vehicles in the neighborhood that night, so it's probably just someone there for the game—camera not picking up on them getting in or out. Freezing that night, gotta be crazy to sit in a car that long without the engine running. Speaking of which, you ready to take a ride?"

As Costa led Debra from the interview room on the TV, Eddie turned off the video feed with the remote control on the sofa.

"Yeah," he said. "Let's go see big brother."

Chapter Forty

Ray sat at the table with a glass of milk and some Pillsbury cinnamon rolls his mother had made him because she knew they were his favorite. Sue Dawley lived in a two-bedroom, one-and-a-half-story townhouse in a rural part of Western Cranston—right off Scituate Avenue, in a small cul-de-sac of about a dozen units surrounded by woods and some artfully sculpted retaining walls. Each unit had two residences with adjoining garages and driveways out front. The interiors were mirror images of each other, and the front doors were on opposite sides of the building. The master bedroom and bathroom were downstairs, and a smaller bedroom and bathroom were upstairs off a landing that overlooked a vaulted-ceiling living room.

Frank and Sue Dawley had purchased their townhome in the late 1980s. The small neighborhood had been brand-new at the time, but the architecture, Ray always thought, looked like something straight out of *The Brady Bunch*. Ray's parents had made numerous updates to the interior over the years, but for some reason, Ray always remembered the place as it had looked in the aftermath of Hana's death, when he had haunted the upstairs bedroom like a ghost lost in a fog of grief.

The only ghost in the townhome now, however, belonged to Ray's father, and as Ray bit into his cinnamon roll, he half expected to see him sitting across the table, grinning from ear to ear as he told his wife how much their son looked like the Pillsbury Doughboy himself these days.

It had been almost fifteen years since the lung cancer finally took Frank Dawley. Might have lived a little longer had he opted for treatment. But back then, the stubborn SOB hadn't wanted to hear it. "I'd rather live what little life I have left like a man than go out as half a one." He was dead six months later.

At first, Ray had been resentful that his father hadn't made more of an effort to stick around to meet his first grandchild. But by the time Connie learned she was pregnant, Frank was too far gone to turn things around.

"Strong father, strong daughter" were his last words to Ray from his hospital bed before he slipped unconscious. His labored breathing would last another two days before the life eased out of him for good.

A month later, when Ray and Connie found out they were having a girl, Ray wept. Frank Dawley had somehow known the sex of his first grandchild before the doctors did.

"Please, he was delirious," Connie said. "A fifty-fifty chance of being right."

But Ray knew it was something else. Frank Dawley just seemed to know things that others didn't. Especially when it came to people, most of whom he avoided like the plague—perhaps because he saw something in them like the darkness he once described in Bobby Bonetti.

And after the divorce, when Ray's mother finally felt free to speak her mind about Connie, she told Ray that his father had never trusted her, from day one. It was then that Ray understood his father's last words to him were not just advice, but a warning. Years later, when the shit finally hit the fan, Ray would repeat his father's dying words daily like a mantra, like the battle cry of some ancient warrior summoning the spirits of his ancestors to help him defeat his enemy. "Strong father, strong daughter..."

That morning, sitting there at his mother's kitchen table, Ray Dawley felt his father's spirit more strongly than he had in a very long time. The text from Eddie Sayers had everything to do with that. Ray received it just as he was turning onto Pontiac Avenue with Maggie. He and Eddie had both been ruled out as suspects—something caught on video, his friend explained—but couldn't say much other than he would be working as a consultant on the case after all.

Still, it was enough, and Ray felt his father's spirit descend on him like a warm summer rain—felt his presence there in the car with him and Maggie all the way to school, as if he were sitting in the back seat, nodding in approval at how grounded, how attentive Ray was, though Maggie seemed a bit moody and distant. They made mostly small talk—her assignments, her upcoming choral concert, and the usual middle school girl drama. The only thing that gave Ray pause was when Maggie mentioned something about having fallen asleep in class the day before—said she felt exhausted and almost went down to the nurse. Ray asked how she felt today, and when Maggie told him she was fine, he did not press it—in part because he felt both guilty and grateful that she hadn't asked to come home when the detectives were there.

Ray also felt his father's spirit sitting there with his mother—a sense of being grounded and having the strength to take care of someone other than himself. Sue Dawley had known Matt ever since he was a toddler, had been best friends with Gail Kauffman up until the day she died, but never had any use for her husband, Kent.

Then again, did anyone? Ray thought.

"I still can't wrap my mind around all this." His mother sat down across the table with her iPad. Sue Dawley still had a handful of friends from back in the day—and some hobbies, too, like reading outside on the patio and maintaining her tiny garden during the summers when she felt up to it. But most of the time, when she wasn't posting inspirational memes on Facebook, she just watched

TV or played hearts on her iPad. More than once, Ray had threatened to take a hammer to it just to get her out of the house. But today, all that seemed unimportant.

"Detectives didn't freak you out too much, I hope," Ray said around a mouthful of cinnamon roll.

Ray's mother adjusted her reading glasses and scrolled through her iPad. "Nothing more in the news. And no, they didn't freak me out. Said they were just trying to get a clearer picture of events, but I've seen enough *CSI* to know they were checking alibis. I'm just happy you and Eddie are in the clear. Imagine them looking at you, Matt's friends."

Ray nodded and swigged his milk. He hadn't gone into much detail about the crime scene when he spoke to his mother the night before—after the detectives were done questioning her and she called him half-panicked. And that morning, Ray had no intention of telling her anything other than the thing about the video ruling him out. He had texted the good news to Natalia after he dropped off Maggie, and Natalia responded with a heart emoji and a quick note saying they would talk about it later when she got home. Ray was looking forward to that, but Christ, talking to his mother sometimes was like playing whack-a-mole. Answer one question, and three more pop up. *"I can't believe Matthew Kauffman was into hookers,"* Ray imagined her saying. *"He always seemed like such a nice boy."*

As if reading her son's mind, Sue Dawley said, "Oh dear, that reminds me."

She left him at the table, and a few seconds later, he heard her rummaging through the closet in her bedroom. Some jewelry for Maggie or Natalia, he figured. Ever since he moved back to Rhode Island, more and more, Sue Dawley had been giving them things that "she wanted to pass down among the women"—a ring she had worn as a child, her mother's locket, some earrings an old aunt had given her once. The girls were grateful, but Ray worried that his mother knew something the rest of them didn't—that she was letting go of her life piece by piece in preparation for her final departure. The thought truly terrified him—even more than when he knew his father was about to die with so much left unresolved between them.

Ray had always felt a kind of distance from his father—a subtle tension of not wanting to disappoint him while knowing all along that eventually he would. There were exceptions, of course—moments of closeness when he was a boy that Ray wished he could have bottled and drunk when he was older. Trips to the zoo or watching the Fourth of July parade on Rolfe Street from atop his father's shoulders. Even little things, like when his father would tousle Ray's hair or just walk with his big hand on Ray's back.

As Ray grew older, however, those precious moments became all but nonexistent, and by the time he reached high school and told his parents that he wanted to major in theatre, the distance between him and his father seemed all but insurmountable. Ray's father never said a word about his chosen career path. Only after college did Ray understand why. In the mind of a blue-collar guy like Frank Dawley, who became the man of the house at fifteen when his father died, Ray had been old enough to make his own decisions. So it wasn't without a trace of guilt that Ray pounded the pavement in New York City, rarely calling home to say hi, never mind to ask for money, because it made the pain from his father's judgment all the more acute.

Ray's decision to become a college professor didn't do much to make things better either. It was then that Ray finally understood that the distance between him and his father had always been there—not because they didn't love each other, but because they had never learned how to relate. And after his father died, Ray often imagined their relationship had taken place in a crowded movie theater with his father in the audience—his big, shadowy shape stuffed uncomfortably into a seat much too small for him as he tried to understand a story about someone else's son.

Ray's mother, on the other hand, well, Ray could have told her he wanted to be an underwater basket weaver, and she would have supported him.

"I thought you would like to have this," she said, coming back into the kitchen. "I was going to send it home with the girls yesterday, but what with all the drama of getting Maggie to school on time, I completely forgot."

Ray's mother handed him a framed copy of the "Snow Day Saviors" article from the *Providence Journal*. She'd had it professionally matted and everything. "I used a twenty percent off coupon for that place on Rolfe Street. You all look so happy. Can you believe that was over forty years ago?"

Ray was speechless. He hadn't seen the article in decades—had always figured his mother had kept it but never cared enough to ask. He cared now. Jesus Christ, how he cared. And seeing the grainy black-and-white photograph of his friends, especially Matt, smiling and entirely clueless that, four decades later, he would wind up dead in the same pond from which they had just pulled Bobby Bonetti—well, it was all too much for Ray, and he burst into tears. His mother put her arm around him, offering words of comfort, then when his sobs subsided, she handed him some tissues from a nearby box.

"I'm sorry." Ray blew his nose. "I've been trying to be strong—at least in front of Maggie, you know? But it's all a big show. Just like during the custody battle. I don't want her to ever see me like that again."

"It's okay to be vulnerable in front of her." His mother sat back down on her side of the table. "Better to let her see who you really are—that you're human, I mean—than to have her growing up thinking you're some kind of superhero. Trust me, it'll make things a lot easier on you both when you eventually let her down." Sue shot him a wink.

Ray laughed. "So just set her up with low expectations is what you're saying?"

"Realistic is more like it. Look at what happened with Natalia."

"I'm not following you."

"Yesterday morning," Ray's mother said, scrolling through her iPad again. "Natalia was right to yell at Maggie, you know. I could tell it bothered her—Natalia, I mean—but it's good that Maggie sees all sides of her. It will only strengthen their relationship. I need to tell her that when I see her next. I can only imagine how stressful being a stepmom is—the toll it takes having to perform, especially in front of me. Maybe next time, she'll ask me to join her in that drink."

"I'm sorry, Mom, you had me until drink."

Ray's mother looked up from her iPad. "I meant nothing bad by it. I just assumed Natalia'd had a drink because, that morning, after she and Maggie left, I noticed the door to the liquor cabinet was open."

Ray swiveled his eyes in its direction. From where he was seated at the kitchen table, he could not see the liquor cabinet against the wall in the dining area.

"There's a little trick to keeping the right-side door closed," his mother said. "You have to sort of lift and press it so it catches the other door, or it keeps popping open"—she demonstrated—"like this, you know?"

Ray didn't, but he nodded anyway.

"I just figured Natalia had a little nightcap after Maggie and I went to bed. Well-earned, if you ask me, and no need to feel ashamed. You know I only keep that stuff for guests—don't even remember what's in there—so she's more than welcome to it." Ray's mother smiled and went back to her iPad.

Ray looked again in the direction of the liquor cabinet and felt a ripple of alarm. Natalia was not much of a drinker beyond the occasional glass of wine, so the sleepover must have been more stressful than she'd let on. But there was something else: the thing about Maggie being so sleepy the next day. *Did something happen—an argument or some crisis, maybe, that kept them both up later than they let on? Or was it something more innocent, just some chatter about chick stuff into the wee hours of the morning?* Ray smiled. He could see his wife doing that. Always trying to strengthen that bond with her stepdaughter.

In any event, he would have to ask Natalia about it when she got home that night and he showed her the newspaper article. Ray gazed down at the picture and traced his finger over Bobby's face—which was partly in shadow and slightly grainier than everyone else's. Ray wondered if his father had ever noticed that too—the darkness that he thought hung around Bobby Bonetti recorded for all posterity.

"You think Dad would've liked Natalia?" It wasn't the first time Ray had ever posed this question to his mother, but for some reason, he needed to hear her answer—which he got when she just peered at him over her glasses like he was an idiot.

Ray chuckled and glanced down at the article again, overcome by a sudden urge to pay Bobby Bonetti a visit, just like he used to back in the day against his father's wishes. Ray almost asked his mother what she thought about all that but quickly decided against it. He already knew her answer. After Carla Bonetti went nuts—after *the way* she went nuts, walking down Reservoir Avenue half-naked with her arms all chewed up—Sue Dawley wanted nothing more to do with "those people" ever again.

"Does it ever end?" Ray asked. "The ice breaking underneath you, I mean."

"No," his mother said—her voice flat and certain, her eyes never leaving her iPad.

Ray expected her to say something else—to follow up with some Facebook-worthy words of inspiration—but when she didn't, he stuffed another cinnamon roll into his mouth and looked again at the picture, wondering if Bobby would smile like that again should Ray decide to pay him a visit after all.

Chapter Forty-One

James Kent Kauffman—aka JK, aka Jimmy Kahn—was already sitting there, waiting, when Eddie and Seabrook entered the cramped, dingy conference room at the Rhode Island Department of Corrections medium-security facility.

From the neck up, Eddie thought him the spitting image of his father. Shaved head, slits for eyes, and an upturned, piggish nose that had mercifully skipped his uncle Matthew in the family gene pool. From the neck down, however, he was all hardcore con. Broad shouldered and barrel chested under his tan scrubs. Tattoos of mobsters up and down his beefy arms. Al Capone, Scarface, the guys from *Goodfellas*.

Not your typical B and E douche, Eddie thought.

Those guys were usually skinny and had a squirrely, nervous energy about them. But James Kent Kauffman looked to Eddie more like a tired old bear. He sat with his hands in cuffs and his fingers laced upon the table—his eyes steady yet vacant as he watched the detectives set down their notepads and take their seats across from him.

Eddie had read through JK's rap sheet on the ride over from Cranston PD. Typical low-level nonsense until his last pinch—a botched robbery of some priceless art from the home of a private collector in Bristol. It would have been a legendary score had he gotten away with it, but just like his father's nose, JK had also inherited Jimmy Kauffman's bad luck. The battery of his getaway car died, someone called the cops, and JK was caught red-handed with the stolen paintings in his trunk while waiting for a buddy to give him a jump. Fast-forward five years, and here he was, just like any other inmate at the tail end of a bid. Calm, confident, and exuding that weary air of resignation that came with being just a little wiser.

"VIP treatment." His eyes drifted up to the camera in the corner above Eddie's shoulder. "Just the three of us, no chance of someone paying off that guard outside to snitch. Walls in the old visitors' room have ears, right? Which means you guys wanna talk to me all private-like about Ronnie Matarese."

JK smiled and twiddled his thumbs, and Seabrook exchanged a look with Eddie that said they were in for a ride.

"I'm Detective Sergeant Seabrook. This is retired Detective Lieutenant Sayers. He's a consultant on a different case that may be connected to Ronnie Matarese, so yeah, since you brought it up, what can you tell us about all that?"

JK leaned back in his chair with his hands folded behind his head. "Damn shame what happened. I was hoping to do a number on him myself when I got out. Dumbass couldn't stick around for a couple more months to let me fuck up that ugly face of his."

"Because of how he treated your sister, you mean?"

"Ostensibly, yes."

Seabrook exchanged another look with Eddie that said, *Ostensibly? My, my.*

"So you know what happened, then?" Eddie asked.

"What I hear through the grapevine. Whacked in his bedroom, early Sunday morning. Word came down from Boston, everyone's saying." JK leaned forward with his hands clasped on the table again. "But what I wanna know is why you're even wasting your time with this clown. Let Matarese's people take out their own trash. No one mourning that piece of shit. Not even my sister."

"It's like you're psychic, James." Seabrook mirrored him with his fingers laced upon the table. "It just so happens Debra is the reason we're here. Word on the street is you had it out for Ronnie. No punk of a boyfriend gonna tool your little sister even when you're locked up, am I right?"

Eddie caught a flicker of alarm in JK's eyes, but the con quickly covered it with a smile.

"Fuck me," JK said. "Here I was thinking you were hoping to buy yourself some ears on the inside, maybe even try to roll me for some secret Debbie told me. Shit, two months left on my bid, I was gonna tell you to go fuck yourselves. But now I get it. Wow, I'm flattered you think I got that kind of pull, but man, Cranston PD must be really desperate if you're trying to pin this on me."

"Then you're saying you had nothing to do with Ronnie Matarese's murder?"

"That is precisely what I'm saying. And since I'm psychic, I'll answer your next question too. *No.* As in, no, Detective Seabrook, I have no idea who done it neither."

"What about your uncle, Matt?" Eddie asked, practically interrupting.

He sensed Seabrook tensing beside him—irritated, no doubt, that he had jumped the gun—but Eddie didn't care. He hoped to see that flicker of alarm in JK's eyes again, something that would get them off on the right foot. But all Eddie got back was confusion.

"You know what I'm talking about, don't you?" he asked.

JK shook his head, his gaze never faltering as it locked with Eddie's.

"Your uncle, Matt, was found murdered over in Cranston. You know anything about that, Jimmy Kahn?"

The big inmate held Eddie's eyes for a second longer then looked down at his hands and was silent for some time. Eddie had purposefully left out the specifics of the murder—when and where and how it took place—all questions the answers to which someone with no knowledge of the murder would want to know. But still, he wasn't sure how to read the guy—couldn't tell if JK was trying to get his story straight before he spoke or just letting the news sink in.

"I heard something about a guy in Blackamore Pond, yeah," he said finally. "Never even crossed my mind it coulda been family. Found him in his car yesterday morning. No details, name hasn't been made public yet, right?"

Eddie shook his head.

"Well, you going to tell me what happened, or do I have to put my request in writing?"

Shit, there it was. Eddie took a deep breath. *I am confident, articulate, and relaxed. Car.* "Your uncle was found strangled behind the steering wheel of his car. A professional hit, it looks like. That's all I can tell you for now. But what about you? Can you fill in some blanks for us?"

JK shook his head, and Eddie repeated his CAR mantra.

"We already spoke to Debra," he said. "She told us about the bad blood between your uncle and your father—about the shady shit that went down with the sale of that property in Warren. Seems your uncle, Matt, screwed your family out of some serious coin. I'm surprised your sister didn't give you a heads-up we'd be stopping by to talk to you about all that."

"We ain't been close for a long time," JK said. "Didn't even know she went by Debra now. How sophisticated."

"Come on, you telling me you didn't wanna tap dance on Ronnie Matarese's face for what he did?" Seabrook asked. "We figure it's the same for your father. The way your uncle, Matt, fucked him over—the way he fucked all of you—seems a little payback is in order, am I right?"

Seabrook smiled, but JK—more pensive than anything, Eddie thought—nodded absently and stared down at his hands.

"I coulda applied for a furlough to attend my father's funeral," he said after a long silence. "I decided not to, though, because I didn't want people seeing me like this." JK nudged his handcuffs toward the detectives. "Some con, standing there in leg shackles with a coupla guards breathing down his neck. Figured I could pay my respects, what little I had left, when I got out."

"Why you telling us this?" Eddie asked.

JK met his eyes. "Same reason I wanted to go after Ronnie Matarese—not because of what he did to my sister, but because of how it looked for me. Guys like me, we gotta have a certain amount of respect to get shit done—in here and on the outside—which is why I care more about my rep than my sister, my father, even. As for my uncle, Matt, he didn't fuck anyone over, just flipped the script. Was too smart to let his big brother dick him like he dicked everyone else in his miserable life. Even his own kids."

"Come on, JK," Seabrook said. "You expect us to believe you had no hard feelings toward your uncle? We know you would've gotten a nice chunk of change if he didn't fuck things up. Didn't give your sister a dime for the funeral, either, she said."

"Three sides to every story, as they say, and you didn't know my father."

"Actually, I did," Eddie said. "Your uncle, Matt, and I were best friends. Lived just a few houses away from each other on Lexington Avenue. So yeah, I know a lot more than you think I do, Jimmy Kahn."

Eddie saw another flicker in JK's eyes—recognition this time, maybe. Like he was putting two and two together.

He seemed to search Eddie's face for a moment then said, "One good thing about prison is it teaches you how to be objective—you know, how to not take shit personally and to keep your emotions in check. I don't blame my uncle for how he handled that shit with my father. Don't blame him at all for wanting nothing to do with me and Debbie neither. Guy in his position, that kind of life and his family, I'd be a hypocrite if I blamed him for looking out for his rep too."

"You know how this looks, though, right?" Seabrook asked.

Eddie could hear his doubt—an echo of his own, he thought.

"We got two murders in twenty-four hours," Seabrook said, "and you and your sister got beefs with both the victims in some way."

JK sighed wearily. "Again, I'm flattered, Detective, but I wish I had that kind of pull. Would make things a hell of a lot easier when I get out."

"Yeah, let's talk about you getting out." Seabrook leaned closer. "I bet if I poke around long enough, I can find some quid pro quo going on, am I right? If not with the DeLorenzos, then some local crew. They whack Ronnie and your uncle, then you go to work stealing for them when you get out. Everything copacetic as long as you make sure your car battery is charged, am I right?"

Seabrook was poking the bear—trying to rattle him, Eddie knew—but it wasn't working. JK's expression had gone stony.

"Like I told you," he said, leaning back in his chair, "prison teaches you to keep your emotions in check. So yeah, you go right on busting my balls and barking up the wrong trees. Makes no difference to—"

Seabrook's phone rang. He looked at the number then excused himself and stepped outside to take the call.

As soon as the door latched shut, JK said, "Sayers. Eddie Sayers, am I right? Knew I recognized the name, but didn't make the connection until you said the thing about growing up with my uncle, Matt."

"Oh yeah? Your father tell you about all the wedgies he gave me?"

"Nah," JK said, his expression blank. "One of my old correctional officers. Guy back in juvie we called Machete, but you probably just knew him as Bobby Bonetti."

Eddie's face dropped—he hadn't seen that one coming—and it must have looked like he'd just gotten his bell rung by Mike Tyson.

"Yeah." JK smiled. "He had the same effect on us back in the day. I did eight months at the RITS for jacking cars when I was a kid. The whole time I was there, I only saw one dumbass test him. Some gangbanger from Southy everyone called Sasquatch. Big motherfucker, I'm talking like six six, four hundred pounds, but dumb as a bag of hair. I forget what he was in for, but this prick gets a bug in his ass over something and goes after Machete during this fight in the rec area. All the hacks had come down to break it up, right? And Sasquatch, who wasn't even involved, he rushes Machete from behind. Big mistake, and before you know it—*bam, bam, bam*—fat fuck is out cold on the floor with a broken arm and a broken jaw. Spent over a month in the infirmary and came back to general pop like a bitch."

Eddie forced a smile, though he felt something cold and heavy gathering in his stomach. "Great story. But where do I come in?"

JK leaned forward again with his fingers laced on the table. "Not long after I was processed, Machete shows up at my cell. Typical Rhode Island shit follows next—my last name rings a bell, we make the connection to my uncle, Matt. The whole time I'm at the RITS, Machete stops by now and then to tell me stories about you guys growing up. You know, shit you got into, like the time you all saved him from drowning in Blackamore Pond. What's even more fucked up is I remembered seeing an article about all that on the kitchen wall at my grandmother's house when I was a kid, but I never would have recognized him. You neither."

"Small world," Eddie said.

JK smiled sadly. "Sometimes too small, yeah, but in a good way back at the RITS. Machete took me under his wing cuz of my uncle, you know? Sent a message, too, so no one would fuck with me. I never forgot that, or the names of the friends he spoke about—names that I had seen probably a thousand times in my grandmother's kitchen. My uncle, Matt, yeah, but also Raymond Dawley and Edward Sayers—who was the biggest punk of them all, Machete told me, and wound up being a cop, of all things."

"We were never close." Eddie's heart beat heavily, and he could hear a thinness in his voice. "I'm surprised Bobby mentioned me."

"Oh, he mentioned you all right," JK said, his smile more acidic than sad now. "As a matter of fact, your name came up the last time he ever spoke to me."

"Do tell."

"About six years ago, before I got pinched, Machete shows up at my apartment late one night. Bizarre, right? Hadn't seen him since the RITS. Long story short, he says he's been watching me for a long time and knows what I'm up to—the B and E shit, I mean. Tells me to give him my equipment—says it's time for me to pay him back for looking out for me at the RITS and specifically wants this high-tech magnetic lock-picking device. Has no intention of turning me in, he says, but after I hand everything over—because yeah, he still scared the shit out of me—after I give him what he wants, he puts his hand on the back of my neck, looks me dead in the eye, and says, 'I don't give a fuck who your uncle is. I ever catch you glowing like Sasquatch again, you better pray Eddie Sayers gets to you before I do.'"

"I'm sorry—did you say glowing?"

"Yeah, glowing," JK said, his smile wilting. "The hell that means, I don't know, but it couldn't have been good, cuz I remembered hearing back in the day that not even a week after Sasquatch had gotten out, he was found dead in some playground. One bullet in the back of his head. Drug deal gone bad, rival gang, who knows? Fucked up that Machete would mention that and you in the same breath, am I right?"

Eddie nodded absently, only dimly aware, it seemed, of the inmate's eyes searching him from across the table. Small world, strange coincidence, fucked-up thing to say, yeah, but there was something else—something that unsettled Eddie more than it should have.

However, before he could put his finger on it, the guard who had been sitting outside entered the conference room, followed by John Seabrook.

"Interview's over," the guard said as he moved to the other side of the table.

He motioned for JK to remain seated while Eddie, rising to his feet, searched Seabrook's eyes. *What the fuck is going on?*

"I'll explain in the car," Seabrook said, his tone conveying a need for discretion.

Eddie gathered their notepads, and the detectives thanked JK for speaking with them, but before Eddie was out the door, the inmate said, "You ever run into Bobby Bonetti, you tell him I never glowed, okay?"

Eddie swallowed dryly and nodded. JK smiled, then the detectives were gone—not speaking a word until they reached Seabrook's unmarked five minutes later and slipped inside.

Seabrook started the engine and blew steam into his hands. "What was that about Bobby Bonetti?"

Eddie explained how his old friend's name had come up, after which Seabrook just sat for a moment, staring over his steering wheel as if into space.

"Goddamn," Seabrook muttered. "First the black Honda Accord on that doorbell cam, and now this. Son of bitch must be psychic after all."

"The fuck you talking about?"

Seabrook turned back to Eddie. "Gal over at the lab in Providence owed me a favor and expedited the analysis of the DNA we got off the Kleenex in Kauffman's car. NDIS came back with a match, and you're not going to believe to whom."

"Bobby Bonetti," Eddie said, throat tight and ears buzzing.

Seabrook smiled. "Close enough. Partial match to his uncle, Thomas Bonetti. Guy's profile has been in the database since the nineties. Some murder they tried to pin on him going back like fifteen years earlier or something."

"Mob hit, some prick they found buried behind this old factory over on Branch Avenue, am I right?"

Seabrook nodded. "My gal says the DNA is that of a close biological relative—male, most likely Thomas Bonetti's nephew. He's got only one, and I bet you'll never guess what kind of car he drives."

"A black Honda Accord."

Seabrook smiled and threw his car into gear.

Chapter Forty-Two

At precisely noon on Tuesday, Bobby backed his uncle Tommy's Ford Explorer into a space at the Budlong Pool and sat there with the engine running and his eyes fixed on the entrance to the parking lot.

The pool, which sat empty and choked with grass behind him, had been closed for a few years, but when the weather was right, the basketball courts and the nearby baseball fields were as crowded as ever. That morning, however, what with school in session and it being cold as a witch's tit, the place was all but deserted, save for a handful of adults in the distance skating on Aqueduct Field. The air smelled like snow. The light was muted and gray, but because the Explorer didn't have tinted windows like Bobby's car, he still needed his sunglasses.

Bobby checked his watch—Pete Scungio was late, but that was all right. After the run-in with his uncle earlier, it was nice to sit in silence—though Bobby had been driving around in silence all morning, wearing his grandfather's hunting cap. He had hoped to hear from Matt again—a whisper, maybe even an image that might help him make good on his promise to find his murderer. Even if it had been Machete or Bones who'd killed him, Bobby figured he would remember *something*. But Bobby didn't remember shit and hadn't heard a peep from Matt—or anyone else who was dead, for that matter—since talking to him earlier that morning.

Bobby still felt guilty about the way he had treated his uncle, Tommy—who, after their little chat at the kitchen table, just kept nodding to himself, saying, "Okay, okay," as he disappeared into his bedroom. Tommy just said, "Okay, okay," too, when Bobby told him he was taking his Explorer to meet Pete Scungio. Because of the tinted windows on Bobby's Accord, cops still liked busting his balls sometimes, though he had a medical exemption. The last thing he needed was to draw attention when meeting Pete to "shoot the shit," he had told him on the phone—which was code, they both knew, to make a deal at their usual spot. Bobby had disposed of the last gun Pete had procured for him immediately after he'd used it on Ronnie Matarese. Tied it to a big brick and tossed it into Blackamore Pond from the woods near their old sled run, where it easily broke through the ice and sank to the bottom.

Good thing he never used the ramp, Bobby thought as he watched one of the skaters fall on his ass in the distance. Good thing he picked Saturday night to take out Matarese instead of Sunday too. Timing was everything, which was why Bobby called Pete Scungio that morning, soon after Childhood Matt spoke to him in the hunting cap. Bobby wanted to make sure he was packed in case his old friend spoke to him again and he needed to act quickly.

Bobby slipped a tissue from its package in the console, blew his nose, then stuffed the tissue into his jacket pocket. He gripped the steering wheel and breathed in deeply. His nasal passages felt achy and swollen, and the lining of his grandfather's cap was slightly damp with perspiration. It would be a long winter if he didn't kick this cold. It would be even longer if he didn't make up with his uncle soon.

"But winter is almost over," someone said.

Bobby froze—just sat there motionless with his hands on the steering wheel for at least a minute. But there was nothing else. And when Bobby saw Pete Scungio's truck pulling into the parking lot a few seconds later, he chalked the voice up to his imagination. After all, the voice had sounded like his uncle Tommy's, and only people who were dead spoke to Bobby from his grandfather's hunting cap.

Bobby slipped off the cap and tossed it onto the passenger seat, and in the next moment, Pete pulled up his truck so his driver's-side door was practically touching Bobby's. The men lowered their windows. Bobby handed Pete five hundred-dollar bills folded in half, and Pete handed Bobby a brown paper bag with the gun inside.

"Cold as they come," Pete said, quoting a line from *The Godfather*. His nose and hound-dog face looked red and blotchy, as if he had been drinking. "That's two in as many weeks. Business must be good."

"Likewise," Bobby said.

Pete's eyes played over the Explorer. "You know." He lowered his voice. "Your uncle was by to see me yesterday. At my goddamn store, mind you. Nut-bag move, yeah, but I wasn't about to lie to him."

"It's okay," Bobby said. "He knows everything now."

Pete sighed. "I'm too old to have this kind of shit traced back to me, understand?"

Bobby nodded. "Worry about nothing, Pete."

Pete nodded back, rolled up his window, and drove off. Bobby didn't bother checking the gun. He stuffed the bag with it inside under the passenger seat and put his grandfather's hunting cap back on. He sat there listening for a moment then retrieved the paper bag and took out the gun. He checked to make sure it was loaded and the safety engaged, then he stuffed the gun into his jacket pocket and slipped out of the car. He didn't hear any more voices as he hurried toward the parking lot entrance. Yet, something told him to take a walk through his old neighborhood and stop by Ray Dawley's just the same.

Chapter Forty-Three

Eddie sat in the passenger seat of the unmarked Interceptor, splitting his gaze between the street map in his lap and John Seabrook, who was outside speaking with Sergeant Steve Guillemette and a handful of other kitted-out AR-15-packing officers from Cranston PD's Special Reaction Team.

On the map, the cordoned-off area where they were gathered had been circled in green. This was the staging area for A-Unit at the east end of Salem Avenue. At the west end of the block, where Brian Rehnquist was with B-Unit, was another green circle, and directly behind Bobby Bonetti's house, in the middle of adjoining Hazelton Street, was the green circle for Dan Costa and C-Unit. Two yellow circles at either end of the Hazelton Avenue block indicated that those areas had been cordoned off too. Three green arrows stretched from the staging areas to the Bonetti residence, which sat in the middle of a red circle on Salem Avenue about five houses down the street from where A-Unit was waiting to move. From Eddie's vantage point, he couldn't see their target.

His breath steaming, Guillemette gave the standby order into his shoulder radio and, as Seabrook headed back to the Interceptor, took position with his men behind an SRT van, in which three more officers waited with the battering ram. Eddie hoped to Christ they wouldn't need it—that Bobby would just answer the door and come out peacefully—but his gut told him otherwise as well as making him uncomfortable. The window was cracked, the heat barely on, but despite the freezing cold, sweat pooled in the folds of flab under Eddie's bulletproof vest.

"Sixty seconds until go time," Seabrook said, slipping behind the wheel.

He held out his hand, and Eddie slapped it. Brian Rehnquist had been given little time for second thoughts about Eddie tagging along. Eddie had even less time to consider telling anyone that he had suspected Bobby Bonetti from the beginning. Then again, Cranston PD had little interest in filling in the details until after their suspect was in custody. They had DNA tying him to Matthew Kauffman's murder and video of his car in the vicinity only hours before. That was all they needed for now.

Still, as Eddie sat waiting for the midday raid on Bobby's house to commence, he couldn't help trying to fill in some of the details for himself. *How could Bobby have gotten into the house and drugged us? And seriously? A Kleenex full of snot left at the crime scene?* Then there was the most important thing: motive. Beyond something personal of which Eddie was unaware, given that the Bonetti family had organized crime ties going back to the late 1970s, Eddie figured there could be a link involving Matt that they had yet to uncover. Something connecting Debra, JK, and also Ronnie Matarese, who would've known Bobby from the RITS and might've let him in on the night of his murder. No forced entry, no theft, no sign of a struggle, all classic signs that the victim knew his killer. Or maybe Bobby used the lockpicking equipment he had taken from JK. Maybe Bobby did JK a solid by whacking the guy who was beating up on his sister.

Eddie's fingers played absently over his lips as if they might find a cigarette there. Goddamn, what he wouldn't give for a smoke to settle his thoughts, never mind his nerves. The secret to a successful raid was the element of surprise, but Cranston PD had decided to move fast, because one, Bobby's black Accord was in the driveway, and two, given that information tended to leak from headquarters like diarrhea from a diaper, there would be little chance of catching Bobby off guard if they planned something for predawn the next day or even later that evening.

Still, Eddie was rattled by how quickly things had come together—the intelligence, the warrant, the mobilization of the SRT. In addition to A-Unit, a handful of guys from B-Unit would make their approach from the top of the block, followed by Rehnquist and the standard column of police vehicles, while C-Unit would approach the back of the house entirely on foot through the neighboring yards.

And as was the case with every raid in which Edward Albert Sayers had been a part during his thirty years in law enforcement, everything next seemed to happen at once. The go order came over the radio. There was a flurry of movement—some of which Eddie saw, some of which he only sensed—then it was all over. Not even five minutes from the start to the "all clear" signaling it was safe for Seabrook and Eddie to come inside.

They entered through a side door in the garage and were directed by one of the SRT officers to some stairs in the back. Eddie and Seabrook took the stairs down into the cellar, where they found Brian Rehnquist and Steve Guillemette and a couple of other officers gathered around Tommy Bonetti—who, naked beneath his open bathrobe, twisted slowly at the end of the rope with which he'd hanged himself. The rope had been tied to one of the ceiling beams. A small overturned stool lay at Tommy's feet. And spray-painted in black on the cement wall behind him was the word *ELVES*.

Chapter Forty-Four

Though Ray had entertained the idea of visiting Bobby Bonetti earlier that morning, the last thing he ever expected when he returned home around noon was to find his old friend waiting for him on the porch.

Had Ray been paying attention as he climbed his front steps, he might have seen the outline of Bobby's head against the windows inside. Had he not still been swept away by the framed newspaper article his mother had given him, he might have noticed that the storm door was unlocked and that the heater was on. But by the time Ray realized these things, he was already on the porch with his key held out toward his front door.

"Long time no see," Bobby said.

Ray froze. Slouched there in the chair in the corner and dressed from head to toe in black, Bobby was little more than a silhouette in the dull gray light. He was wearing sunglasses, but it was the hunting cap that alarmed Ray more than anything. He recognized it from when they were kids.

Bobby sniffled, swallowed, and cleared his throat. "I got this bad cold, so I picked the lock on your storm door and turned on the heater." Bobby pulled out a stubby metal cylinder from his coat pocket. "High tech, magnetic, won't damage the lock's internal mechanism. Comes in handy in times like these. Got it years ago from Matt Kauffman's nephew. Talented thief, that JK, but man, unlucky as fuck." Bobby smiled and slipped the cylinder back into his jacket pocket.

Ray stood very still and drew in a long, tense breath. He didn't like how nonchalant and unapologetic Bobby was, as if breaking into someone's house was an everyday occurrence. It was then that, with almost painful swiftness, Ray understood Eddie had been right all along. Bobby Bonetti had broken into his house on Sunday night too. Through the back door, probably, while the three of them were partying. He'd drugged their drinks then driven Matthew Kauffman down to Blackamore Pond, where he'd strangled Matt and stuffed a fish tail in his mouth. And now, he had come back for Ray.

"You look like you've seen a ghost," Bobby said. "Relax, I just want to talk to you. Haven't seen you in—what, like ten years? Since Kent Kauffman's funeral."

"Something like that, yeah," Ray said.

Bobby shifted in his chair, and Ray noticed the bulge in the righthand pocket of his fur-lined leather jacket. Bobby was holding something. Ray could see the outline of it, hard and pointy and pressed against the inside of the pocket.

Bobby smiled as if he noticed Ray noticing it. "Yeah, you should probably sit down. We've got a lot to talk about."

Ray was close enough to the door to make a break for it. If he moved quickly, he might be able to get outside before—*well, what, before Bobby shoots me in the back with the gun in his pocket?* Ray almost laughed at the absurdity of it all. For over twenty-four hours straight, Lexington Avenue had been crawling with cops. *Where the hell are they now?*

"Sit *down*, Ray," Bobby said.

Ray slowly lowered himself into the rocking chair. His legs felt weak, his heart beat very fast, and he had to remind himself to keep breathing.

"What do you have there?" Bobby asked.

Trembling, Ray held out the framed newspaper article, and Bobby took it with his left hand. But it was his right hand, the one Ray thought was holding a gun in his pocket, that still had all of his attention.

Bobby smiled. "Well, what do you know? 'Snow Day Saviors.' Shit, I haven't seen this in years. Still seems like yesterday—in more ways than one. I swear, part of me just stopped growing up that day. Split off from the rest of me and just stayed eleven years old. You ever feel like that, Ray? You know, that part of you is still a kid?"

Ray shrugged and smiled weakly. "Sometimes."

"'Sometimes,' he says." Bobby set the frame on the floor beside his chair and looked around. "Shit, how could you not? Past and present—lines get blurry, I bet, you living in your old house. Must wake up sometimes thinking you traveled back in time. I wish I could do that. Travel back, I mean, to before that day on the ice. Things were never the same after that. Not just between you and me, but all around, huh?"

Ray swallowed hard. "What are you doing here, Bobby?" he whispered.

Bobby shrugged. "I could ask you the same thing," he said, leaning forward. "What are you doing here, Ray? Why did you move back into your old house?"

"I don't know," he said. "A lot has happened since the last time I saw you. Divorced and remarried. Big custody battle, job sucked, so I retired, and... Well, I don't know, timing was right to finally move back, I guess."

"But why back into your old house?"

Ray swallowed again. His throat felt like sandpaper. "I don't know. I guess I'm still trying to figure all that out."

Bobby nodded and sat back in his chair. "Yeah, well, I guess I've been trying to figure out a lot of things too. Like why, ever since you moved back, things have felt like they're breaking inside me. Like different parts of me splitting off into entirely different people, it feels like sometimes. But I didn't realize all that until I started seeing your wife for therapy."

Ray felt the color drain from his face as a wave of nausea passed through him.

Bobby chuckled. "Jesus Christ, don't worry. I use a different name so she doesn't make the connection. Conflict of interest, probably wouldn't see me if she knew that we were friends." Bobby nodded at the framed article on the floor. "*Used* to be friends. I don't know, Ray, what do you think? Would you say we're still friends?"

"Yeah," Ray said quietly. "We're still friends."

Bobby nodded, but with his sunglasses, Ray couldn't read his expression, couldn't tell if his answer had satisfied Bobby. *But my fucking wife?* Had Natalia ever been in danger? Had Bobby ever sat across from her with a gun in his pocket like he was sitting there now?

"Not her fault, though, Natalia," Bobby said. "I pay in cash so she doesn't tie my social to my health insurance. I heard through the grapevine that you'd moved back but never expected to hear from you. So much time had passed. Christ, we haven't kept in touch since junior high. Even at the funerals and shit, it was all pretty surface-like. I bagged out on Jimmy Kauffman's because I didn't want to run into Natalia and blow my cover. I figured going to her for therapy was the only way to still be your friend. Or at least, to pretend like I was."

Jesus Christ, Natalia, Ray thought. She was at work now. *Did Bobby go to see her before me?*

As if reading Ray's mind, Bobby said, "I would never do anything to hurt her. You have my word on that. Have I ever lied to you, Ray?"

"Not that I know of, no."

"That's right. Besides, today's Tuesday, and I see Dr. Morris on Mondays."

Bobby smiled, and Ray swallowed hard. *Dear God, please be telling the truth.*

"Damn," Bobby said, looking around again, "we haven't shot the shit like this in forever, right? Since, what, before my mother went off the deep end?"

"Bobby, I'm sorry—"

"You were the only person I ever told about the shit she did to me. Remember that story I told you when I was sleeping over that time? The one where she almost threw me down the cellar stairs because of the elves?"

Ray nodded blandly. He remembered.

"You ever tell anyone about that? One of your three fucking wives, maybe?"

"Never." Ray's nausea intensified, a sense of panic welling up inside him. "You swore me to secrecy."

Bobby smiled. "You were always loyal, Ray. I was too. One of the things I thought the two of us had in common. Loyalty. Never got that kind of vibe from Eddie and Matt, though. I heard about what happened the other night down at the pond. Word gets around in certain circles. Fucked up, yeah, but the thing is, I somehow got it in me that I need to know more. You know, maybe even try to find out who did it. A favor to an old friend, you might say. So how about you tell me a secret for once, Ray? Just like I told you back in the day. Do you know who killed Matt?"

Ray couldn't speak, but he managed to hold Bobby's gaze through his sunglasses. *Yeah, that's it,* he thought. *Let's play a little game. Let's pretend that I don't know you broke into my house Sunday night just like you did now. Let's pretend I don't know you drugged us and that Eddie didn't make the connection to the fish so maybe you'll think you're in the clear and get the fuck out of here so I can call the police and tell them that Eddie was right all along.* Had Ray been able to put on a better poker face, something like that might have happened.

But instead, Bobby just said, "I'm loyal, too, Ray. I can keep a secret. But I need to know if it was you or Eddie who killed Matt.

Maybe the two of you were in on it together. But let's take it one step at a time. Tell me what happened that night, and maybe I'll just walk out of here pretending to be none the wiser. For old times' sake, Ray, because I've always been loyal to you, not Matt."

If Ray had been scared shitless only seconds before, he was now confused in equal measure. *What, Bobby Bonetti is a vigilante now, paying me a visit because he thinks Eddie and I murdered Matt?* Or was this just a ruse, another frame job because his first one didn't work? Was Bobby trying to scare him into a false confession? Was that a recorder in his pocket, not a gun? Whatever the case, Ray couldn't think straight, so the only lifeline he thought might get him out of this was the truth.

"The cops have already ruled out Eddie and me as suspects." Ray forced a calmness into his voice. "So yeah, I'm telling you the truth. Neither of us had anything to do with Matt's murder. I swear on my daughter."

"So why you all nervous and shit to see me, then?"

Ray held Bobby's gaze and, despite his sunglasses, saw something dawn in his expression.

"Wait, so you think *I* killed Matt?" Bobby asked.

Ray tried to remain perfectly still, but he could feel himself shaking. The confusion was gone now, and the fear was back in full force. What was he doing playing games with this guy? He needed to call the police. He needed to get out of here.

"Holy shit." Bobby shook his head in disbelief. "I had basically this same conversation with my uncle this morning. I can understand why he would've thought that, but I don't get why *you* think so. You mind filling me in on that one, Ray?"

"The night Matt was murdered," Ray began slowly, "someone broke in here and drugged us. The last thing Eddie and I remember before we blacked out, Matt was still alive. But somehow, his killer drove him down to Blackamore Pond and strangled him before rolling his car into the water with a fish tail stuffed in his mouth."

"A fish tail?"

Don't pretend like you don't know, Ray thought, but what he said was "Yeah, a fish tail. A message from the killer. Eddie made the connection to you because of what happened all those years ago at Blackamore Pond. When you laid him out after he cut the tail off that sunfish."

A tense silence hung between them as Bobby, motionless and stone-faced, sat staring back at Ray. The whir of the heater suddenly seemed louder—the air, charged with electricity—and Ray got a sense that things might just very well explode if he didn't explain.

"So yeah, it was Eddie who came up with that idea," Ray said, a spike of anxiousness in his voice. "But as far as I know, he only told me because it seemed so remote and convoluted—you know, wouldn't make sense to the police. Circumstantial, a big leap for them to start looking at you. A connection going back all those years—not just to the thing at the pond, but to what you said to Eddie that time in the schoolyard about fish tails not growing back. You scared the shit out of him, so much so that he remembered it after all this time."

"That was Bones," Bobby muttered—or at least, that was what Ray thought he said—but in the next moment, Bobby's disposition changed completely. "Okay, I get it," he said with a smile. "Given everything that happened, me showing up here like this, well, I can understand why you'd feel spooked. And I guess, since you told me the truth, I should tell you the truth too." Bobby leaned forward again. "I don't know if I killed Matt or not. I don't know why I would want to do such a thing, but like I told you, different parts of me are like different people sometimes. I don't even know why I ended up in the neighborhood that night—I was just sitting there, watching your house for a couple of hours after your wife and daughter left."

Ray's stomach dropped, and his mouth fell open. That must be what Eddie meant when he texted that the cops had found something on video. Someone's doorbell cam, most likely, had picked up Bobby's car. So the police *did* consider Bobby a suspect, and if Eddie knew his car had been in the neighborhood that night, he most likely had told them about the fish tail. Good thing Ray hadn't mentioned Eddie's text.

Yeah, Bobby, how about we make a deal? Ray thought. *I won't tell you you're a suspect, and you won't tell me you did it, okay? Because, if you tell me, then you'll have to kill me, right?*

"I saw Eddie and Matt come over that night," Bobby went on. "I'm not even sure why I was casing your house. Maybe I just wanted to be part of the reunion, even if from a distance. But yeah, like I said, I don't remember anything about strangling Matt. On the flip side, what I do remember from that night, I don't trust. Hard to explain, the things that go on in my head—the different parts splitting off into different people. But hey, that's what Dr. Morris is for, right?"

Ray's phone rang—a classic bell sound, once, twice—but Ray did not reach for it.

Bobby jerked his chin in the direction of the ringing coming from Ray's jacket pocket. "You should check that. Might be Maggie's school."

Ray slipped the phone out and felt his stomach lurch when he saw it was Eddie Sayers. What should he do? Answer and pretend it was Natalia so Eddie would get the message that something was wrong? Maybe he should try to play it straight with the hope that Eddie would pick up something from the tone of his voice, the subtext in his replies.

Bobby made the decision for him. "Let me see."

Ray showed him the caller ID.

"Speak of the devil. Put him on speaker, but don't tell him I'm here."

"Bobby, please, I—"

"Do it." Bobby produced the gun Ray had known was there all along and leveled it at him.

Ray, who had never been so scared in his life, did as he asked. "Hello?"

"Ray, it's Eddie."

"Yeah."

"Listen, I can't say much, but we just raided Bobby Bonetti's house. Rolled the dice, but he wasn't there."

"So he's a suspect, then?" Ray said, heart hammering and eyes never leaving Bobby.

Muffled voices, a sense of commotion and yelling in the background on the other end of the call.

Eddie sighed audibly. "Let's just say we've got a hell of a lot more on him than a fish tail. Looks like he may have been involved in some other shit. His uncle, too, but... Well, it'll be all over the news soon, so you might as well hear it from me. We found Tommy Bonetti hanged in his cellar. He's dead."

A cold iron spike entered Ray's throat, choking off his air as it traveled downward and pierced his heart. Bobby lowered the gun into his lap, and Ray spied a single tear run out from under his sunglasses.

"Ray, you there?" Eddie asked.

The *beep-beep-beep* of a truck backing up followed on the other end of the line. Eddie cursed, and Ray tried to answer him, but the iron spike in his throat only seemed to expand. Same for the tunnel that was forming around Bobby's face.

"Yeah, I'm here," Bobby called out.

And perhaps because of all the noise on Eddie's end, he took Bobby for Ray.

"We got an APB out for Bobby. I'm over at Budlong Pool now. Cranston PD found his uncle's car—they got some units patrolling the neighborhood, but if you see that motherfucker, you call nine-one—"

Quickly, so very quickly, Bobby stood, snatched the phone from Ray's grasp, and tossed it over his shoulder, where it disappeared behind the chair in the corner. Bobby paused for a moment, looking down at Ray, then stuffed the gun into his jacket pocket and tore off his hunting cap. "For old times' sake," he said, nudging it toward Ray.

Ray felt his fingers close around the cap's tattered roughness before he realized he was taking it. His eyes were still fixed on Bobby's sunglasses, in which he saw himself reflected as a boy. And for the first time ever, it seemed, Ray Dawley was no longer afraid.

"I never had a friend like you, Ray," Bobby said.

Ray swallowed. "Same."

Bobby nodded and moved toward the door.

Only after he was gone did Ray notice it was snowing.

Chapter Forty-Five

Bobby's feet were freezing. This was the only thing that seemed to matter, the only thought that had risen to the surface out of all the others swimming down in the muck of his mind, in the cold black bottom of his despair. Uncle Tommy had hanged himself. He was dead now because of what Bobby had told him. Dead because his mind had been unable to wrap itself around his failure to protect his nephew. From the elves, from his sister, from himself. It was all the same now. No more time to figure things out. Winter was almost over.

And yet the cold remained. Bobby's feet were almost numb with it now as he hurried down the sidewalk. He could not remember a day so cold. He could not remember a silence like the one that seemed to envelop him as he reached the top of the hill and began to run. The silence buzzed with a snowfall that stung his face like bees. It nearly blocked out every other sound—his footfalls, his breathing, the police sirens, and the shouts behind him.

"Bobby! Bobby, wait!"

It was Ray, but Bobby did not look back. Others were coming too. He sensed them approaching now with revving engines and tires that scarred the snow-dusted pavement. Blue flashing lights blossomed all around him—faintly at first on the houses at the bottom of the hill, then on the trees and the guardrail as he sprinted past the ramp and around the curve at the edge of the pond.

"Bobby! Bobby!"

Ray's voice, farther away now, was drowned out by a policeman on an intercom, but Bobby could not make out the words. The cold, the numbness had traveled up from his feet to the rest of his body, and he felt almost drunk with the silence, light and dizzy and as peaceful as the falling snow.

This is all I ever wanted, he thought as he hopped the guardrail, dimly aware of a police car, its blue lights flashing and sirens blaring, fishtailing to a stop only a few feet away from him at the bottom of Blackamore Avenue.

"You gotta twist right before you hit the ice," Eddie Sayers said in his head, and Bobby began to laugh—giddily, like when they were boys—as he dashed down their old sled run for the pond. He could see something glowing in the distance up ahead, about twenty feet from shore beneath the snow-dusted ice. Bobby tore off his sunglasses, and the world almost blinded him.

"Bobby, no, don't!"

"Bobby, don't do it!"

Someone else now with Ray—*Eddie,* Bobby thought as he raced past the chain-link fence. Laughter—his own, yeah, but also his friends' from when they were kids. *This is the only thing that belongs here in the silence.*

More flashing blue lights entered his periphery—from a distance, on the other side of the fence near Waterman Avenue. Muffled shouts came from that direction and some policemen, too, their forms hazy in the glare as they approached the fence with their guns drawn. But the laughter was stronger, innocent and as pure as the snow that would soon cover everything.

Bobby fixed his eyes on the glowing spot ahead of him, and in the next moment, he was on the ice with feet like wings, feet that carried him over the dull cracking and buckling all the way to the angelfish. Black eyes staring and mouth pulsing up at him from beneath the ice—ice that was so thin in spots, it should never have been able to hold him. But the ice *did* hold him—there, where the angelfish turned and swam away in a trail of bright-blue sparkles, and all the way out to the middle of the pond, to the place where Bobby followed it. He stopped and turned around.

A bunch of cops crowded the shore now. Ray and Eddie were there, too, out in front and screaming for Bobby to come back. Bobby could hardly hear them above the laughter, but that was all right. The sounds of his childhood were the only things that belonged here. He was happy he had given the hunting cap to Ray, so very happy that he would never hear the voices again—Matt, his mother, his grandparents. He never should have come back from this place. But that was all right too. He was home now.

Bobby waved goodbye to Ray and Eddie and turned his gaze up toward the sky—opened his arms wide and let the light and the snow and the tears he was crying sting his eyes one last time. Then the ice gave way, and he was gone.

Chapter Forty-Six

When Eddie got home that evening, he made himself a mug of instant chicken noodle soup and sat down with it at the kitchen table in the dark. He cupped the soup in his hands and looked out the window. Outside, about thirty yards away, on the far side of the parking lot was a narrow strip of snow-covered grass with some trees that separated Eddie's part of the complex from the main driveway. In the light from a nearby streetlamp, Eddie could see a small snowman over there—branches for arms; rock eyes, nose, and mouth; black ribbons of exposed ground where the body had been rolled.

When it snowed like this, enough to cover everything but not stress him out, Eddie liked to imagine he was a kid again—to pretend, if only for a few minutes, that things might stay this way forever. Pure, unsullied, an empty canvas of possibility. And yet, that night, Eddie could only think about the next morning, at which time the search for Bobby Bonetti's body would resume. Eddie thought it all a waste of time. *Why? Because they don't come back.* Bobby had told him this all those years ago in the schoolyard. He said he meant fish tails, but Eddie understood now that he had really meant people. Even the ones that got out alive, the darkness took something. It always took something.

Eddie closed his eyes and imagined Bobby falling through the ice again. Eddie had felt no impulse to run away this time, no impulse to run after him either. Only disbelief that it was happening all over again, and that Bobby should have gotten so far out onto the ice. One of the cops had tried to follow him but got only a yard or two before he found himself knee-deep in the frigid water. *How the hell did Bobby do it?*

Eddie looked again at the snowman, wondering who'd built it—a father and his daughters, he hoped. Eddie could not remember ever building a snowman with Elizabeth and Emily, but he must have. *Right?* He must have...

Eddie took out his phone and dialed Elizabeth. When he got her voicemail, he hung up and dialed Emily. He got her voicemail, too, and tossed the phone across the table, where it slid off and landed on the chair opposite him. *Probably for the best. What would I say to them anyway?*

Turning back toward the snowman, Eddie remembered something he hadn't thought about in years—winter, ninth grade, this night when he and Matt Kauffman walked around Eden Park, tipping over every snowman they could find.

Eddie was standing by the snowman a minute later. He looked around then tore the head off and hurried back with it into his condo. He placed the snowman's head on a plate and sat across from it at the kitchen table. In the dim light coming in from the parking lot, he noticed that the snowman's rock nose must have fallen off as he was carrying it in. Eddie wished he had a carrot to replace it with, but his refrigerator was practically empty.

Eddie sat at the table for a long time, sipping his chicken soup and splitting his gaze between the snowman's face and its headless body outside. Eventually, one of the rocks for the mouth fell off. Eddie got up, pressed it back into place, then put the head in his freezer. There was plenty of room. Eddie's freezer was practically empty too.

Part VI: The Ghosts of Christmas Past

Chapter Forty-Seven

Until Shelly Kauffman was questioned by the FBI, she'd had no idea her husband had always had a thing for Natalia Morris.

The pair of field agents showed up at Shelly's house the day before the wake. Not the best timing, they agreed, but since Matthew's killer appeared to have ties to organized crime, the case had been kicked up to the federal level and Credit Suisse had turned over Matthew's work computer. Nothing illegal so far, the agents assured Shelly, but some odd things had turned up in his search history, including what seemed to be an unusual interest in a psychiatrist from Rhode Island named Natalia Morris. Could Shelly offer any insight about that? A connection that went beyond their acquaintance in high school?

Shelly—who, since her return to New Jersey, had spent most of her time in a daze—played dumb even as she began to connect the dots to what she noticed a few days earlier in the guest room. The three of them—MJ, Jenny, and Shelly—had been going through some boxes of photographs for the funeral display when MJ dug out his father's old yearbooks. Some of the pages had been dog-eared, Shelly noticed, but never thought to wonder why. A few days later, after the agents had left, Shelly pulled out the yearbooks again and discovered that each of the dog-eared pages contained a photograph of Natalia Morris—class portraits and group pictures of her clubs and sports teams, homeroom, student council, candid shots. Every. Single. Page.

Sitting there on the floor with the yearbooks spread out around her, Shelly racked her brain for something she might have missed outside the church. Some thinly veiled innuendo. A clandestine look between her husband and Ray's wife or maybe a gaze held too long. But there was nothing. Shelly figured Matt had most likely dog-eared the pages when he was younger. *But why had he never told me about his crush? Had he felt guilty because of Ray? Or worse, had he still longed to be with Natalia after all these years?*

It literally pained Shelly to wonder. Too much thinking was like too much weight upon her chest—her unanswered questions, a mountain of crushing, suffocating boulders. Why did they have to go to Jimmy's funeral? Why did she allow Matt to go to Ray Dawley's when she knew deep down that it was a bad idea? Why did she not insist he take an Uber back to Newport that night? Why did that psychopath Bobby Bonetti strangle him and stuff a fish tail in his mouth?

Please, God, anyone, tell me why my dear husband is dead.

No, the only way Shelly could breathe, it seemed, was to numb herself to anything beyond what was required to get her through the day-to-day—which was why, when Natalia and Ray showed up at the wake the following evening, Shelly kept things polite and accepted their condolences with grace. True, the Xanax and the vodka helped with that, but Shelly did not blame Ray for Matt's murder—Bobby Bonetti would have gotten to him sooner or later, the Feds had assured her.

They had also made it clear that there was no evidence of any communication at all between Matt and Natalia. In fact, the only reason they brought up his search history—"And please, Mrs. Kauffman, this is to remain confidential"—was because Bobby Bonetti had been seeing Natalia for therapy under an assumed name. "A strange coincidence that both your husband and his killer had some kind of secret involving her, don't you think?"

Yeah, Shelly thought so too—which was why she could not resist saying something about it to Eddie at the wake. When Ray and his wife were out of earshot, she had cut her eyes at Natalia and said, "Matthew always had a thing for that one." If her husband had told anyone about his crush, Shelly figured, it would have been Eddie Sayers. But when Eddie just blinked back at her blankly, she knew Matt had kept that secret to himself.

How many others were there? That question might have sent Shelly over the edge if she'd allowed herself to keep asking it—might even have sent her screaming bloody murder after Ray and Eddie too. Those Snow Day Saviors, those ghosts of winters past that plagued her husband's dreams until the day he died. Thankfully, neither of them had stuck around for the collation after the funeral. What, with all the pills and the open bar, Shelly most certainly would have let something slip.

And Shelly *did* let something slip a few nights later, on Christmas Eve. The kids had been against celebrating the holiday—too soon, they both thought—but Shelly had insisted their father would have wanted it that way. MJ and Jenny found a tree that morning and spent most of the afternoon decorating it while Shelly watched from the sofa, nursing a bottle of sauvignon blanc. When the tree was finished, MJ and Jenny joined her with some Chinese takeout followed by eggnog for dessert.

Shelly had just dipped into her third—which, like the others, was really more brandy than eggnog—when, out of nowhere, she asked, "What did you guys think of Natalia? You know, Ray's wife, the shrink?"

MJ and Jenny exchanged a confused look and shrugged.

"I, too, have a secret," Shelly said. "Dr. Morris is the star atop our Christmas tree. So many ornaments, so many lights, and still my attention goes back to her..."

The room began to spin, and Shelly had become aware of a slurring, detached quality in her voice. She had been hearing that voice more and more these last couple of weeks. Same as she heard that voice more and more from her mother in the weeks following her father's suicide—which was why, when Jenny suggested Shelly go to bed and MJ helped her up, Shelly did not resist. The only thing better than not thinking was sleeping. *For how long?* Well, that was something Shelly Kauffman didn't want to think about either.

Chapter Forty-Eight

Back in the days before Eddie's parents moved to Florida and his sister still hosted Christmas, like clockwork, just after the coffee was served during dessert, Pam Sayers would tell the puzzle story. Eddie never understood why Pam always picked that particular time or why, out of all the things she could have brought up to bust his balls, she always went for that. But somehow, no matter what anyone else was talking about, Pam always managed to segue into it.

"That reminds me of the time Eddie and I were doing that puzzle," she would begin. "Some castle with a bunch of water around it. You know, lots of pieces that were the same color and cut very similar, especially in the water part. And Eddie—hell, he was only six at the time—he insisted that this one piece should fit, and no matter how much I tried to convince him otherwise, he wouldn't listen. Got so pissed off, he started pounding on the card table, screaming, 'Make it fit! Make it fit!' before flipping out and tipping the whole thing over!"

Cue the obligatory eye roll from Eddie and a chuckle or two from anyone at the table who was listening—especially if Eddie's father followed up with something like "Most retards have problems with impulse control." Eddie figured the puzzle story was probably Pam's way of both busting his balls and complimenting him—a testament to the kind of tenacity that had served him well in his thirty years of law enforcement, though he had been such a little shit as a kid.

Eddie's sister had not hosted a Christmas in over a decade. Childless, an office manager, of all things, and married later in life to this dumbass electrician named Ralph, who Eddie couldn't stand. Pam and Ralph always visited Eddie's parents in Florida now for the holidays, but in the weeks following the deaths of Matt Kauffman and Bobby Bonetti, it was as if Eddie had come up with another puzzle story all his own. Some of the pieces were easy to put together, but others were shaped so oddly that, no matter how hard he tried, Eddie could not make them fit.

Easy pieces first. Bobby Bonetti had murdered Matthew Kauffman. On that, everyone agreed. The toxicology report confirmed that Ray, Eddie, and Matt had been drugged with flunitrazepam, more commonly known by its brand name Rohypnol. Consensus was that Bobby broke into Ray's house through the back door while they were partying, somehow roofied them, then faked the business on Matt's phone before staging the scene and driving him down to the pond. The footage from the doorbell cam and Bobby's conversation with Ray confirmed that he had been casing Ray's house on the night of the murder. The DNA on the Kleenex found in Matt's car placed him at the crime scene, and the video showed someone with a similar build to Bobby's at the pond that night. But what sealed the deal even as it blindsided everyone was the revelation that Bobby had been seeing Ray's wife for therapy under an alias. After some resistance, Natalia had turned over Bobby's case notes. Dissociative identity disorder was her diagnosis. Cranston PD consulted two other experts, who confirmed DID could account for Bobby having no memory of Matt's murder, which was what he told Ray.

Then there was the unexpected piece about the pistols. During the handful of days in which Cranston PD searched Blackamore Pond before it became too dangerous, divers recovered two Glock nine millimeters that had been discarded there. One was in such poor condition that an independent ballistics lab was unable to work with it, but the other, which had been fastened to a large brick, they managed to fire through a suppressor found at Bobby Bonetti's house. Bingo, an exact match to the bullet that had lodged in the wall behind Ronnie Matarese's blown-out skull. Cranston PD was still trying to connect Bobby to organized crime but so far had come up with nothing. As for Bobby's body, they had yet to come up with that either. And once things became too difficult because of the ice, Cranston PD suspended the search until further notice. Strange, yeah, Seabrook had to admit, but it would only be a matter of time before he turned up. The pond was only so deep, after all, and Bobby wasn't going anywhere.

Some pieces, not the least of which was Bobby's motive, were missing altogether. Where were the clothes Bobby wore on the night of the murder? Where did he get the fish, and why were there no traces of it in his home? Why was there no physical evidence at all linking Bobby to the crime scene other than the Kleenex, which had somehow magically wedged itself between the cushions in the back seat?

With some mental gymnastics, Eddie could make these pieces fit. But then there were the pieces that Eddie couldn't fit into his puzzle at all—only two, actually, but both were big enough that he spent many sleepless nights flipping over card tables in his mind. Some nights it got so bad that Eddie found himself in his kitchen, sitting across from the snowman's head again. A little fucked up, keeping it in the freezer, but it helped him to talk through things. And since no one at Cranston PD wanted to hear it, who else was there?

So yeah, the first piece had to do with the narcotic Bobby had slipped them: Rohypnol. Illegal in the US, the drug was becoming harder to find and used less in date-rape cases because things like Ambien and other prescription sleep meds got the job done just as well. Never mind where Bobby got the shit, why bother using it when other drugs were more readily available?

"That's what's been bugging me," Eddie told the snowman one night. "The only reason I can think of for why Bobby used that roofie shit is, unlike Ambien, Rohypnol produces this thing they call anterograde amnesia."

The snowman's black rock eyes stared blankly back at Eddie.

"*Anterograde,*" Eddie said as if explaining it to a child. "Means you can't form new memories after the drug takes effect. That would explain why Ray and I don't remember anything after the Scotch. But here's the thing, Matt's autopsy showed that he'd been given a shot of epinephrine to his thigh before he was murdered, right? Little chance of that happening down at the pond. I mean, Bobby would need to be in the front seat or at least lean over then quickly move back into position to strangle him. Not a lot of time before Matt would come to and fight back. You see where I'm going with this?"

One of the snowman's eyes fell off and onto the table. The plate held a little water now, too, so Eddie began to speak fast. He needed to work everything out before the snowman melted much more.

"What I'm saying is, the more likely scenario is that Bobby stuck Matt with the EpiPen at Ray's so he could walk out on his own. Bobby was strong, yeah, but hauling out a guy Matt's size over his shoulder and leaving no trace of physical evidence? Practically impossible, right? But the problem with this scenario is that, because of the Epi, Matt would've had enough sense about him to recognize his killer. So why the fuck would he willingly leave with Bobby?"

The snowman could not say, so Eddie put his head back in the freezer.

The second piece Eddie couldn't fit into his mental puzzle was *how* the three of them had been drugged. The doorbell cam picked up Bobby leaving the neighborhood *after* Eddie and the others ate the pizza, so the timeline for him to get into Ray's house and drug them that way didn't jive. And since all the beers had been sealed and no traces of Rohypnol were found in the bottle of Bowmore, the only possible avenue was the glasses, which had been mysteriously washed.

"Things are a bit fuzzy, yeah," Eddie said to the snowman during another sleepless night. "But I'm telling you, there is no way that shit was already in our glasses when Ray poured those drinks."

The snowman's head now leaned to one side because it had melted a little during previous conversations, and because of the angle and the light, its eyes seemed to regard Eddie skeptically.

Eddie threw up his hands defensively. "Yeah, I know the den was kind of dark. And yeah, I know Laurie said it wouldn't take a lot of that shit to do the trick, but you're missing the obvious. Even if Bobby could've tampered with the glasses in the living room while the rest of us were distracted, how the hell did he know Ray would offer us Scotch, let alone use those exact glasses?"

Once again, the snowman could not say.

Yet, for his mental puzzle to be complete, Eddie had to make these pieces fit. He might have been able to do so, too, had Shelly Kauffman not said something very strange to him at her husband's wake.

Two weeks after Matthew Kauffman's murder, Eddie drove down to New Jersey and met Ray and Natalia outside the funeral home. Seven o'clock, a decent number of people were there but not a long line. Matt had been cremated, so only a box of his ashes and a picture of him were surrounded by some flower arrangements at the front of the visitation room. Ray and Natalia were ahead of Eddie, and given that everything had gone down at their house, Eddie braced himself for a shit show as they approached Shelly to express their condolences.

Fortunately, it was the opposite—hugs and tears all around.

"Thank you for coming."

"If there's anything you ever need."

But when it was Eddie's turn, Shelly leaned in close to him and, with her eyes on Natalia, whispered, "Matthew always had a thing for that one."

Eddie just blinked at her blankly, then Shelly smiled and thanked Eddie for coming before moving on to the next visitor.

After the service the next day, Eddie kept playing over Shelly's words in his mind during his return to Rhode Island. As far back as he could remember, Eddie and Matt had been trading stories about their love lives—their childhood crushes, their trips around the bases, the salacious details of their adult affairs. Eddie even confided in Matt how he'd jerked off into Carla Bonetti's panties. And in all that time, never once did his best friend mention "a thing" for Natalia Morris. Eddie found it hard to believe.

So where was Shelly getting that idea? Just the paranoid, lunatic ramblings of a grieving widow?

Maybe, but Eddie's gut told him something else—a sense of another puzzle on a card table across the room. The box had no picture to go by, but Eddie knew if he could get closer and start turning over the pieces, he would eventually put things together—which was why, after Seabrook told him about Natalia's starring role in Matt's search history, Eddie accepted Ray's invitation for Christmas Eve.

Natalia Morris was half-Italian. Her mother made sure Eddie was aware of this as soon as he arrived for dinner and proceeded to tell him about each dish on the menu for their traditional Feast of the Seven Fishes. Eddie had never been a big fan of seafood—and especially not now, after what had happened—but he lied and said he was excited. A total of eight people sat around the table that night. Eddie, Ray and Natalia, Maggie and Jeremy, Sue Dawley, and Natalia's parents, Anna and Stan Morris, who had flown up from Florida to celebrate their daughter's first Christmas in her new home.

Her new home. That very place where Eddie's best friend had been kidnapped before being murdered at Blackamore Pond. *Surreal being back here,* Eddie thought, but thankfully, the mood around the table was lighthearted. And yet, he kept coming back to his puzzle—not the one Pam always talked about, but the one in his mind. He stood over the card table now with the pieces spread out before him. He just needed to start turning everything over.

Eddie got his chance at the end of the night—out on the porch, while shooting the shit with Ray and Natalia over beer. Sue Dawley had left, and everyone else had retired upstairs—the kids to their rooms and Natalia's parents to the master. Ray and his wife would be sleeping on the pull-out sofa in the den, Ray told Eddie—"Just like we all used to do as kids in the summer, remember?"

"'Course I remember," Eddie said. "Bet you never thought you'd be sleeping in there with such a hottie, though. You're way more of a catch than I ever was, Natalia."

"Yeah, but you cuddle better, Eddie," Ray said.

All three of them laughed, and Eddie sipped his beer. He had a good buzz going and felt pretty chill, but he quickly ran through his CAR mantra anyway to help him focus.

"Crazy, the shit that came out of our mouths," Eddie said. "Me, you, and Matt back in the day. Can't believe he never mentioned anything about what Shelly said."

Ray and Natalia questioned him with their eyes.

"You know, when we were in line at the wake."

The couple exchanged a confused look and shook their heads. Eddie knew full well that they hadn't heard what Shelly said to him, but playing dumb—something his father would have said came naturally to him—had always worked well for Eddie Sayers when attempting to catch a suspect off guard.

Ray chuckled. "What are you talking about?"

Eddie was sitting on the love seat—Ray to his left in the corner chair and Natalia to his right in the rocker by the door—so he could only pick one of them to focus on when he turned over the first piece of his puzzle. *I am confident, articulate, and relaxed. Car.*

"Shit, I'm sorry." Eddie glanced back at Ray before fixing his eyes on Natalia. "I just assumed you heard what Shelly said about Matt always having a thing for you."

There it was—the flicker of alarm in Natalia's eyes that told Eddie she knew what Shelly was talking about. And Natalia knew that Eddie saw it, the two of them reading it in each other's faces before Natalia scoffed and hid behind another sip of beer. Eddie looked back at Ray and saw nothing but a good-natured, slightly drunken expression of bewilderment. So that was it then—the first piece of the puzzle turned over. Natalia knew something of what Shelly spoke, and Ray did not.

"Get out of here," he said. "I never knew that. Did you, Natalia?"

Natalia smiled and shook her head. "Hell, no. And good thing too. I only ever had eyes for you, Ray Dawley."

"Me too, Ray," Eddie said.

They all laughed again, and the conversation quickly turned to something else. But still, Eddie kept thinking about this new puzzle. And just like when he watched the interview with Ralph Richard almost four decades earlier in his old house down the street, Eddie knew Natalia Morris was lying. He would start turning over more pieces ASAP—first on his own, then after Christmas, with the help of John Seabrook. *Hopefully.* Eddie was still a civilian, and Cranston PD was certain they had their man. He would need to be careful or risk getting shut out completely.

But those were things Eddie Sayers could figure out later, when he was alone with his puzzle, the pieces of which felt so heavy to him now that even the strongest of card tables would surely buckle beneath them.

Chapter Forty-Nine

After Eddie left, while Natalia finished loading the dishwasher and straightening up the kitchen, Ray went upstairs to wish his daughter and his stepson good night.

He could hear his father-in-law snoring behind the master bedroom door before he even reached the top of the stairs. Jeremy's door was closed, too, and the crack underneath was dark. Poor guy was probably exhausted from enduring the adults at the dinner table all night. Smiling and nodding and pretending to be interested when all he really wanted to do was get lost in his music or maybe even text some chick from Brown.

Not like he would ever tell anyone, though. Jeremy was private—quiet, respectful, sort of just go with the flow on the outside, but he swallowed a lot and thought way too much about things. That last bit was something they had in common, Ray thought. Same for their love of music and movies. For Christmas, Ray had bought Jeremy some vintage blues albums, which he would give him tomorrow morning before he left to spend the day with his father. His plan was, when Jeremy came home, they would spend some time listening to the albums in the den. Hopefully, they would talk about the artists' influences on the music Jeremy was into—a lot of rap and indie rock. Despite the distance Ray often felt from his stepson, he wasn't ready to give up on forging a bond between them. Hopefully, after a semester at Brown, the kid would be a little more loquacious.

"Merry Christmas, buddy," Ray whispered outside his stepson's door, then he padded to the end of the hall.

Maggie's door was open halfway, and Ray could see the lamp next to her bed was on. He knocked softly and entered to find her bleary-eyed and blinking back at him. She had fallen asleep reading in bed—a children's version of *A Christmas Carol*, Ray discovered as he sat beside her. Santa had given it to her a few Christmases ago. The box from South Carolina she had pulled it out of was on the floor nearby.

Maggie yawned. "We didn't watch it this year."

Ray's heart clenched like a fist. Ever since Maggie could sit up straight in front of the TV, they had watched *A Christmas Carol* together on Christmas Eve—the surreal, darkly animated, half-hour TV version that was released in 1971. Scrooge was voiced by Alastair Sim, who gained fame playing the same role in the classic live-action version twenty years earlier. Son of a bitch was hands down the best Scrooge of all time, Ray thought. The only actor who ever got both the bitterness and the joy of redemption at the end. That was what all the other Scrooges missed—the joy of redemption at the end. What with everything that had happened, Ray had forgotten to make time for it. *Just one of many things when it comes to Maggie,* he thought, and in the next moment, the tears overflowed.

"Jeez, Dad, you drunk or something?" Maggie asked, and Ray laughed.

"No, sweetheart." He took a deep breath and wiped his eyes. "I'm just sorry is all. I haven't been a very good father, have I? The move, everything happening so fast, I'm afraid you think you got lost in the shuffle—you know, maybe felt like you didn't matter as much because of Natalia or the new house. But you know you matter to me more than anything, right? Do you know that?"

Maggie rolled her eyes. "Yes, Dad. You're too hard on yourself. And I know you've got a lot on your mind. Especially lately."

"Yeah, well..."

"Seriously, it would've been weird trying to watch it with everyone else around. I'm just glad it worked out, me being here for our first Christmas together as a family."

Ray felt the clenching fist in his chest again. As a result of the custody battle, Connie got Maggie every other Christmas. This time next year, Maggie would be out in California. Ray did not want to think about that—did not want to let his ex's looming black cloud of a presence rain on this kid's parade any more than it already had. *But I've done my share of raining, too, haven't I?* He'd introduced his daughter to a whole new set of worries and disappointments—leaving her friends and the only home she had ever known, a new school, blending their families—Christ, what had he asked of her? How often had Maggie lain awake, staring up at the same ceiling Ray had stared at as a kid, wondering if her father still loved her as much as he used to when it was just the two of them? *How could I have ever let such a thought cross her mind?*

Ray gently took the book from her and, with another deep breath, willed the fist in his chest to open. "I got an idea. How about we get up early tomorrow and watch it in the living room on the laptop? New tradition, just the two of us before everyone else wakes up for presents. Might be kind of nice in there with the tree and all."

Maggie smiled and nodded. "Just promise to brush your teeth," she said, yawning again.

Ray chuckled and set the book down on the nightstand. "You got it." He kissed Maggie on the forehead. "Love you and sweet dreams."

"Love you too."

Ray turned off the lamp and moved to the door.

"Dad?"

"Yeah?"

"That friend of yours, is he ever coming back?"

"Eddie?"

"No, I like him. He's funny. The other one, I mean. The bad one."

Something cold and heavy settled in Ray's stomach. "Bobby?" Some light was spilling into the room from the hallway, and Ray could see Maggie nod. "No, of course not. What made you ask that?"

"I overheard Jeremy talking to one of his friends on the phone yesterday. Said they still haven't found his body yet. You think he might be alive?"

"No, sweetheart," Ray said, moving toward her again. "Bobby Bonetti is dead. I was right there. I saw him drown, and the only reason they haven't found his body yet is because it's cold and dark down there and the pond is frozen solid now."

"And his ghost?"

Ray detected a spike of fear in his daughter's voice that had not been there in a long time—not since the custody battle, when Maggie would make him promise every night before bed that she wouldn't have to go live with her mother.

"It's not like *A Christmas Carol*, right? Ghosts don't come back—not even at Christmastime?"

"No, they don't come back." Ray kissed Maggie's forehead again. "Now get some sleep before Santa passes us by."

Maggie giggled and rolled over on her side. "Merry Christmas, Dad."

"Merry Christmas, kiddo."

Ray left the room and hurried down the hallway into the bathroom, where he closed the door and vomited in the toilet. He then moved to the sink, splashed some cold water on his face, and stood there looking at himself in the mirror. *You lied to her, you piece of shit. Ghosts* do *come back. They walk among us, sometimes for decades, just like Bobby Bonetti before he fell through the ice a second time—ice that should never have held him but did because... well, because ghosts are much lighter than the rest of us, right, Maggie?*

Ray squeezed his eyes shut and dug the heels of his palms into his temples. It literally hurt to think about that day, to play over in his mind what he witnessed from the shores of Blackamore Pond—the moment when Bobby, as if offering himself up to the darkness, disappeared through the ice, never to be seen again. What really messed with his head, though, was that Ray could have stopped him. He had known as soon as Bobby gave him his hunting cap where he was going. How Ray knew this and why he let Bobby get so far ahead before he ran after him, he could not say. But it was the guilt of that knowledge, driven daily into his skull like nails, that made life a hell on Earth now.

Ray had resolved not to tell anyone about it, not even Natalia. He was an actor, after all, and just like when he was on stage, he would play his part. He would speak and behave like the character of Ray Dawley until it all felt real—or as close to real as life could ever feel again. This empty stage, this pretending he hadn't let go of his best friend any more than if he had let go of him all those years ago on the ice. Bobby had serious mental health problems, Natalia had told him. *It's not your fault.* But was it Bobby's fault? Bobby told Ray he wasn't sure. And the more Ray thought about it, he wasn't so sure either. But Ray must *pretend* to be sure. And maybe if he pretended long enough, he would someday believe. *Because if not Bobby, then who?*

Yeah, that's it, Ray. Just keep lying to yourself, just keep lying to everyone like you did to Maggie. Play your part, you actor, you two-bit fraud, you glorified community theatre hack. Strong father, strong daughter. Strong father, strong daughter...

Ray splashed some more cold water on his face, brushed what was left of the vomit from his teeth, then went downstairs and set up his laptop on the coffee table in the living room. He got *A Christmas Carol* ready to go on YouTube, set the alarm on his phone, turned off all the lights in the house except for the Christmas tree, then slid under the covers next to Natalia in the den. The springs of the old pull-out sofa squeaked noisily, and Ray winced. Natalia was lying on her side with her back to him. Ray had thought she was asleep. She wasn't.

"Everything okay?" she asked.

Ray leaned over and, kissing her cheek, felt her stiffen.

"Thank you for a wonderful first Christmas Eve," he said. "I know it must have been stressful with your parents here, but—"

"Next time we host a holiday, can you do me a favor and not invite anyone without asking me first?"

The abruptness of her reply, the iciness in her tone chilled Ray as if she had thrown open the window above his head. He should have seen this coming. The comment Eddie had made on the porch pissed her off. No use playing dumb about it. Or arguing.

"Okay," Ray said quietly, but before he could add an "I'm sorry," Natalia snapped at him again.

"Matter of fact, don't you think it's time you moved on from that guy? I know you think this whole Matt Kauffman thing has brought you back together, but don't forget why you guys drifted apart in the first place. You've nothing in common anymore, so please don't make it a regular habit, having him around here, okay? Being talked about like that. I swear to God, some things never change. 'Always had a thing for you.' Who the fuck does he think he is? Like I'm a piece of meat, some car you idiots want to take out for a test drive. Asshole. I never liked that guy. Sure as hell, I never did."

"Ghost of Christmas Past," Ray whispered, the words passing his lips, it seemed, before he realized he was even speaking.

Natalia whipped her head back at him. "What did you just say?"

Ray swallowed hard. He had never seen her so mad. "Ghost of Christmas Past. I was just talking to Maggie about that—the *Christmas Carol* we always watch. I forgot about it this year. Guess that's why it slipped out."

Natalia huffed and turned away from him again. "Whatever. Merry fucking Christmas, Ray."

He lay there awake for a long time after that, staring up at the ceiling with nothing but the darkness reflected back at him in his head. Eventually, Natalia's breathing leveled off, and she began to lightly snore. Slowly and without a sound, Ray slipped out of bed and padded down the hallway into the kitchen, where he fished out Bobby Bonetti's hunting cap from the top shelf of the coat closet. Ray put it on then went into the living room, where he sat on the sofa and stared all night at the Christmas tree until his phone alarm signaled it was time to wake up Maggie for their movie.

Chapter Fifty

First thing Christmas morning, Eddie stopped by John Seabrook's apartment with a bottle of Goldschläger. Seven o'clock, early as hell, but Eddie had pretty much been up all night, talking to the snowman, and wanted to catch Seabrook before he headed over to his ex's to watch their boys open their presents. John and Monica were trying to keep things as normal as possible for them this Christmas, especially since their oldest had gotten suspended from school for fighting right before break. The kid was still having a hard time with the split, which was why John would be staying for dinner too. Eddie couldn't imagine coparenting like that with Katie back in the day. *More power to them.*

As for the Goldschläger, that was a little inside joke. Back before John's boys were born, on the rare occasion he and Eddie partied together, John always downed a shot or two of "Goldy" at the end of the night because he liked his cigarettes and the hot and spicy cinnamon schnapps hid the taste from his wife. "If not for the Goldy, my boys would've never been born." Luckily, Eddie already had an untapped bottle on hand. Perfect excuse for a visit.

"In case Monica throws you a pity fuck," Eddie said when Seabrook answered the door.

The big guy was in his T-shirt and held a small towel, which he used to wipe some shaving cream from his face. Beaming, John took the bottle and offered to make Eddie a cup of coffee, but Eddie declined.

"I know you got shit to do, but I just wanted to stop by and wish you Merry Christmas. I really appreciated you letting me tag along on that Bobby Bonetti thing. I owe you one."

"Yeah, man, maybe we can tap this sometime."

"You know it. You hear anything else about that, by the way? You know, the thing the Feds were looking at between Matt and Ray's wife?"

Seabrook smiled. "I knew you didn't come over here just to play Santa."

Eddie smiled innocently.

"And no, I haven't heard shit. Feds took their ball and went home."

"Yeah, I figured as much," Eddie said. "Gotta say, though, weird coincidence, don't you think? Bobby seeing Natalia for therapy and Matt googling her two, three times a week going back who knows how long?"

"Coincidence, yeah," Seabrook said. "How many times have you ever done a deep dive on some chick you wished you'd gotten with back in the day? That's all it is. Midlife crisis, obsessed with the one that got away. Been there myself from time to time."

"Yeah, you're probably right," Eddie said. "Just curious, though, if I wanted to take a look at some traffic cam footage from the night Matt was murdered, you think you might be able to hook me up with that on the DL?"

Seabrook narrowed his eyes. "What's bugging you?" he asked, his voice flat and devoid of sarcasm. "Something I should be aware of?"

"Probably nothing," Eddie said. "But I don't wanna waste my time if they already dumped the footage—or if you're gonna cock-block me before I even get to first base."

Seabrook smiled. "Give me a holler after the holidays, and I'll see what I can do."

"Thanks, man."

Eddie and Seabrook exchanged a quick bro hug, wished each other Merry Christmas, then Eddie left. He spent the rest of that morning taking different routes from the bottom of Waterman Avenue, where Cranston PD believed Bobby Bonetti had parked his car on the night of Matt's murder, to Sue Dawley's townhouse in Western Cranston, where Natalia Morris had supposedly spent the night. *Supposedly.*

Yeah, from the moment Eddie realized Natalia was lying about Matt, he had begun to entertain the possibility that she might be lying about other things too. So the first thing he did when he got home from Ray's the night before was to sit down with the snowman's head at his kitchen table. He began their discussion with the premise that maybe Natalia's relationship with Bobby went beyond professional.

"Not an affair, necessarily," Eddie said, "but maybe she told him something about Matt, then maybe Bobby murdered him on her behalf."

Silence as Eddie imagined the snowman replying.

"Yeah, you're right," Eddie said. "If something like that were true, Bobby's visit to Ray and his actions afterward don't make sense at all—never mind what he said about not remembering."

That caused Eddie to go down this whole *Manchurian Candidate* rabbit hole, in which Natalia somehow brainwashed Bobby into carrying out the murder for her because of his DID. That would explain why he didn't remember it.

"But could something like that really work?" Eddie asked the snowman. "Especially since no one knew about the get-together at Ray's until a few hours before?"

Eddie imagined the snowman shrugging then put the head back in the freezer and went to bed, where he tossed and turned for about an hour. Eventually, he tried to settle his mind by fantasizing about Laurie Woodward. They were back in the conference room at police headquarters—Laurie bent over the table, panties off and skirt hiked up around her waist as Eddie took her from behind and spanked her. And it was that image, a reddened palm print on Laurie's ample ass, that made him remember something she had said during their meeting a couple of weeks earlier—something so obvious, Eddie couldn't believe he and the others had overlooked it.

The Bowmore. Only Ray's, Eddie's, and Matt's prints had been found on the bottle—which Eddie subsequently confirmed when he leaped out of bed and checked the case file he had downloaded on his laptop.

"But hadn't Ray said that Natalia had given him the Bowmore as a belated wedding gift or something?" Eddie asked the snowman.

The head was on its plate beside him at the table, its black rock eyes pointed at the laptop.

"Shouldn't Natalia's prints have been all over the bottle too?"

"Not if Natalia had given Bobby another *bottle,"* Eddie imagined the snowman saying, and the light dawned on him like some heavenly sunbeam breaking through the clouds. Having *two* bottles of Bowmore would've been the simplest way to drug them—especially if Natalia had been hoping for no blood and urine tests, which was probably true given how things were staged to make it look like they were partying.

"You're a fucking genius," Eddie said to the snowman. "Natalia could have easily spiked the Scotch before she left—Christ, she even told Ray to break it out for us. Then, when everyone was passed out, Bobby could've entered through the back door, switched the bottles, and slapped their prints on the stand-in. Bobby's prints, however, would be missing because he was wearing gloves—just like the person in the security footage."

"But what if the person in the security footage wasn't *Bobby?"* the snowman asked. *"What if it was Natalia? She's about the same height, isn't she?"*

Eddie thought about this for a long time—so long that when he looked at the snowman again, the water on the plate was almost over-flowing.

"If Natalia carried out the plan herself," Eddie began, "that would explain the EpiPen and Matt leaving with her. Especially if they had a history. Matt waking up half-dazed, being so obsessed with her—like a dream come true, he must've thought."

"But what about Bobby's DNA at the crime scene?"

"What if Bobby blew his nose during one of his therapy sessions like I do? What if Natalia fished out the Kleenex from her trash can with the intention of framing him—especially if she knew about his side gig as a hitman."

The snowman agreed that was the most likely scenario but also reminded Eddie that he had no physical evidence yet tying Natalia to the crime and thus would have a hell of a time convincing Brian Rehnquist to take another look based on just a bunch of "what ifs." What was more, Cranston PD was not only certain they had their man, but they also now suspected him in at least a half dozen oth-er murders. Punks, lowlifes that Bobby would have known from his days at the RITS.

"Then there's the thing with the fish," Eddie said, moving the snowman's head back to the freezer. It had melted quite a bit that night—was looking smaller and a bit misshapen, and two of its mouth rocks had fallen out. Eddie pressed them back into place then stood at the refrigerator, speaking to the snowman with the freezer door open. "Ray swore that he never told anyone about me cutting off that fish tail, but maybe he forgot. Or maybe he was lying. Either way, if I can catch Natalia in a lie—if I can poke some holes in her alibi and put her someplace other than Sue's that night—well, that would be an entirely different kettle of fish, now, wouldn't it?"

Eddie imagined the snowman chuckling at his pun then closed the freezer door and went back to bed—maybe slept for an hour before heading over to Seabrook's with the Goldy then to Blackamore Pond.

Unfortunately, that Christmas morning, Eddie found at least a dozen routes Natalia could have taken to avoid the handful of traffic cams on the way to Sue's. One of them might have caught her car, but if not, Eddie would have to roll the dice anyway. Better to wait until after the holidays in that case. Rehnquist would be more receptive then and not so quick to get rid of him.

Eddie spent the rest of Christmas Day eating McDonald's, drinking beer, and watching football. His original plan had been to drive down to Florida the week before to visit his parents, but after everything that had happened, he didn't have it in him. His girls were spending the day with their boyfriends' families, which left Eddie on his own. But that was okay. He didn't feel much like socializing and was happy to bounce ideas off the snowman until the next day, when he got the call from Ray Dawley around noon.

"Hey, man, you got a sec?" he asked.

Eddie could hear the tension in his voice. "Yeah, of course, what's up?"

"This crow at my mother's. Christ, Eddie, I feel like I'm going crazy."

"Whoa, slow down. What do you mean, 'this crow'?"

And so Ray began, and Eddie listened.

Chapter Fifty-One

The day after Christmas, at a quarter to midnight, Natalia Morris parked her husband's Honda Civic in a brightly lit space about twenty yards from Eddie's door. She slipped off her gloves and, with her husband's phone, texted Eddie.

Hey, man. Been driving around and saw your light was on. You alone? Okay if I come in for a second?

As Natalia waited for Eddie's reply, she wondered if her parents had replied yet to the text she had sent from her phone back home. *Going to bed soon, phone on silent, just let me know you landed safely, okay?* Their return flight to Florida had been delayed by almost three hours, but Natalia figured they must have landed by now—figured Jeremy had gone to bed early at his father's, too, since he never replied to her text saying good night. Either way, her phone—the texts, the cell tower pings—would support her alibi that she was home when Eddie Sayers was murdered.

Ray's phone, on the other hand...

Hey, yeah, of course, Eddie texted back. *Just let me throw on some clothes.*

Natalia gave Eddie a thumbs-up then quickly put her gloves back on and wiped down the phone with a rag from the glove compartment. *Why am I rushing?* It had been only an hour since she'd poured Ray the glass of wine laced with Rohypnol. After that, Natalia had gone upstairs to shower for their romantic evening and came back down to find the glass empty and Ray out cold in the den. Maggie would be at Sue's all night, so no need to spike her hot chocolate again as she had a couple of weeks earlier. Natalia hadn't needed to work her magic on Sue Dawley that night. The wine and the meds Natalia had prescribed for her mother-in-law's insomnia the year before had done the trick just as well.

Natalia stuffed the phone into the pocket of Ray's oversize parka, adjusted her surgical mask, slipped on Ray's sunglasses, and pulled the parka's hood over her head. She slipped the nine millimeter off the passenger seat and, pulling her sleeve down over it, exited the car and made a beeline for Eddie's condo, which was a first-floor corner unit with two entrances—one from a patio, which was under a couple of decks for the upper units, the other from an outdoor hallway that ran through the center of the building.

Natalia kept her head down. She wasn't sure if there were any security cameras around, but she would make a point to drive through a gas station on the way home—which was why, in addition to Ray's parka and his sunglasses, she had worn his Tufts sweatpants and his Timberlands. The boots were so big on her that they made a squishing sound as she hurried across the parking lot to Eddie's patio door. Natalia knocked, and a second later, the light flicked on, and Eddie opened it. His eyes bulged when he saw the pistol pointed at him.

"Inside," Natalia said.

Eddie backed away with his hands up, and Natalia shut the door behind her. She flicked off the switch for the outside light, motioned with the pistol for Eddie to move into the living area, then told him to sit. Eddie did, and with the pistol leveled on him with one hand, Natalia removed her sunglasses with the other. She stuffed them into her jacket pocket then pulled back her hood and tore off her surgical mask. A little dramatic, but Natalia wanted to see the look on Eddie's face when he realized who it was—just like he had wanted to see the look on her face, no doubt, when he mentioned the thing Shelly had said. And yeah, it was worth it, all right. The stupid son of a bitch looked as if he were trying to understand quantum physics.

"So many questions," Natalia said. "I'm tempted to answer them just so you can see how stupid you were to test me."

"Test you?" Eddie asked, his voice flat.

Natalia laughed. "Don't play dumb, Eddie. I know why you dropped that hint on the porch. I saw it in your eyes. You knew it was me, didn't you? Same as Matthew knew it was me when I popped him with the EpiPen. But he didn't go with me willingly because he had *a thing* for me, as you and that widow of his think. He went because he felt guilty."

Eddie sat back and held her eyes. "Guilty about what? I mean, you're right when you say your reaction got me thinking about you and Matt. But I didn't consider you a suspect. Not right away. Just that there might have been something between you back in the day—"

"Something between me and Matt?" Natalia snapped, moving closer. She didn't like how calm, how smug Eddie was acting. "You really are an idiot, aren't you? There was never anything between me and Matthew Kauffman. But my sister..."

Eddie's expression dropped. He understood.

"Oh, you remember, do you?" Natalia went on, smiling bitterly. She could feel the heat of her blood in her cheeks. "That's right. My sister, Gina. She was only in eighth grade at the time. Can you imagine that kind of pain, how much she was suffering? Of course you can't. You didn't live in that house with my father. You have no idea about the toll it took on her. He would have killed her, probably all of us, if he ever found out what your best friend had done to her."

Eddie's face was all fear now—he was dreading what was coming, Natalia could tell—but she would make him listen. She would make him understand.

"That's right. Matthew Kauffman worked his charms on my sister while on his paper route. Figured she was easy prey, I'm sure. Lonely, depressed, parents never home, and me working my job at fucking Burger King to help make ends meet. Told her he loved her, wanted her to be his girlfriend just to get in her pants, then threw her away like a piece of garbage. Not the kind of thing you brag about to your friends, especially when you knock up an eighth grader. Matthew said she couldn't prove it was his—said he would start rumors about her being a slut if she didn't keep her mouth shut and get an abortion. That's what sent her over the edge. My mother and father, good Catholics, would never allow such a thing. Gina was too terrified to go to them, too terrified to even live. She told me all this the day before she hanged herself. But I never said anything—at first, because I wanted to avoid a scandal and preserve my sister's memory. But in the end, it was because I wanted to make Matthew Kauffman pay. Can you imagine the kind of drive, the kind of patience it took to keep me going all these years?"

"So that's why he was googling you so much," Eddie muttered. "Shelly thought he had a thing for you when the Feds investigated his search history."

"I don't know anything about that," Natalia said, aware of the tremor in her voice. She hated that Eddie might see how the talk about Gina got to her, so she forced herself to speak calmly and deliberately. "All I know is that, as the years passed, I must've come up with a thousand different ways to make it happen. However, when I learned Matt would be in town for his brother's funeral—when I realized how, after all these years, the pieces were finally falling into place—I couldn't pass up the opportunity. I mean, how poetic, right? What better place to murder that bastard than where the three of you learned just how cruel and cold the world can be?"

"Blackamore Pond," Eddie said, and Natalia nodded. "So, that's how you knew about the fish tail? Ray told you what happened all those years ago?"

"Unwittingly, yes. You see, not long after he relocated to Rhode Island, we tried some ketamine to help him deal with his trauma from the custody battle."

"What the fuck is ketamine?"

"A dissociative anesthetic medication that, when administered properly, can produce a psychedelic experience that helps people with things like treatment-resistant depression. Cutting-edge, recently approved by the FDA for therapeutic use in small doses. Ray said a lot of things he has no memory of during his session. Unfortunately, he did not like it enough to do it again. He doesn't know what's good for him sometimes."

"And the Rohypnol? You give him that for his own good too?"

Natalia smiled. "No. I get that on the DL from a British colleague. She gets me all kinds of goodies that you can't get in the States. Same chippie that got me the Bowmore at a very good price."

"Two bottles, am I right?" Eddie asked. "You drugged the first one before you left then switched the bottles when—what, after you came in through the back door?"

Natalia fixed her eyes on Eddie's. He was so cocksure, so proud of himself, that she had to fight the urge to slap his face, to hack that look from his skull with the butt of her pistol as if it were a hatchet. Did he not understand why she had come? Did he not believe her? Or was he just in denial—the shock of it all too much?

"Well done, Detective," Natalia said, forcing herself to stay calm. "I had been storing one of the bottles in Sue Dawley's liquor cabinet. I wanted it to be a regular thing to commemorate our honeymoon but didn't want Ray being tempted. Never thought I'd be using a five-hundred-dollar bottle of Scotch as part of my revenge plan, but it all came together so quickly when I learned Jimmy Kauffman had died. I got lucky you guys agreed to the boys' night. Got lucky, too, with the fish. Sue Dawley just happened to have one in her freezer.

Cut off the head and tossed it in the woods out back with no one the wiser."

"You got lucky with the doorbell cams too," Eddie said. "The way you were all ninja'd out, amazing none of them picked you up walking back to your house from the bottom of Waterman Avenue."

"Oh, they probably did." Natalia smiled. "But I wore a wig and Ray's Patriots hat and hoodie, so I'd blend in with pretty much everyone else who was around that night. Backpack underneath so I'd look like your typical Cranston fatty." Natalia giggled. "But yeah, good thing Mrs. Feldman didn't have a security camera. She lives directly behind us on Blackamore Avenue. I cut through her yard, hopped the fence, and came in through the back door. Took my own sweet time changing and setting things up while you were all passed out. Waste of time in the end. I had hoped to confuse you with all that—make it look like Matt had roofied you and had something shady going on. Trust me, when I found out there was video of me down at the pond, I almost shit myself. That was a mistake, yeah, but lucky for me, Bobby Bonetti and I are around the same size. Or at least, it looked that way, given my getup."

Natalia smiled, but still, the son of a bitch seemed unfazed—just leaned with his elbow on the arm of the sofa and rubbed his chin as if he were considering what to order for takeout. Swear to Christ, it took everything not to pull the trigger right then and there.

"So, you framed Bobby Bonetti for Matt's murder," Eddie said. "My guess is you snagged a Kleenex he used in your office during one of your sessions together and planted it in the back seat of Matt's car, knowing they would trace the DNA back to him."

"Winner, winner, chicken dinner," Natalia said, but underneath her anger toward Eddie, she was starting to feel rattled—not only because he was acting so calm, but also because none of this seemed like news to him.

"The only thing I don't get," he went on, "is why you kept up the charade with Bobby for so long—why you pretended to buy his Dave Ruggieri routine. You must have made the connection between him and Ray at some point."

"Because he was suffering from DID," Natalia said. "What difference does it make if he knew Ray when they were kids? He needed my help. But when I learned what he had done—you know, to guys like Ronnie Matarese—I must admit I was intrigued. Maybe even prescient, on some level. The idea of having a murderer, a fucking killing machine, at your disposal? Who wouldn't find that attractive?"

"So you knew about all that other stuff he was into?"

Natalia smiled. "Don't need ketamine to get a guy like Bobby Bonetti in a dissociative state. Came by it naturally from his bughouse mother. He told me all about his childhood and his hit jobs but had no memory at all that he'd spilled his guts. Same when I planted the idea in his head that he should drive by the church and case my house. I hoped some cameras would pick him up. I could not task him with Matthew's murder—not enough time to brainwash him to do something like that. But something he *already* wanted to do—"

"So you did this when?" Eddie asked. "During one of his sessions, what, the week before or something?"

"That's right. I came up with my plan a couple of days after I learned the date of Jimmy Kauffman's funeral. I couldn't guarantee you guys would bite for the boys' night, but I needed to guarantee Bobby was in the neighborhood just in case. Imagine my relief, then, when—unknowingly, mind you—he told me during our next session that my little inception plan had worked. Bobby had been in and out of the neighborhood in the precise window I gave him. Made my frame job all the more believable. Same with that fish in Sue Dawley's freezer. An insurance policy, in case the tissue with Bobby's snot wound up in the water. I had a feeling you or Ray would make the connection, and I was right—about so many things in the end. Hell, the way everything played out, it was almost as if it was meant to be, don't you think?"

"Almost, yeah," Eddie muttered.

Natalia gritted her teeth. *Come on, you fat ginger fuck, show some emotion.*

"Shame what happened to Bobby, though," Natalia went on. "His uncle too. Then again, given their track record, I'd say they both had it coming. Just like you, Eddie. You have it coming, too, don't you think? Ray told me your wife left you for her boss at the DMV. Why was that, Eddie? You fuck around on her like pretty much every other cop I know? I've had my share of you blue boys sitting across from me over the years—shitbags like you, who use their shitty jobs as an excuse to be a shitty person. Shitty husband. Shitty father, too, I bet."

Eddie shrugged and dropped his eyes. "Yeah, you're right," he said blandly. "I am a shitty father. Shitty husband, too, I guess. Not like Ray, though. Which reminds me, what are you going to tell him? I mean, texting me from his phone, driving his car, and wearing his clothes—what, you roofie him before you came over to frame him for—"

Eddie nodded at the pistol, but Natalia kept her eyes fixed on his. The cold, calculated manner as well as the swiftness of her decision to frame Ray Dawley for the murder of Eddie Sayers had surprised even herself. Unfortunate, yes, but necessary, she decided in the end. There really was no other option, no telling how much Eddie knew and what he might have already told the police. Natalia refused to wait around to find out. Sure, she would miss her husband—and Maggie, who would no doubt end up living with her witch of a mother out in California. The kid would have a hard time going forward. Again, unfortunate. *But, hey, sometimes you gotta break a few eggs to make an omelet,* she might have said had Eddie not spoken first.

"That pistol there," he said. "Ray told Cranston PD about it when they were searching your house. Loaded, kept in a safe in the bottom drawer of the nightstand next to your bed. Got it after you divorced your ex. You shot it only once, Ray said."

"Don't worry. I'm a natural."

"Even if there's a crow?"

"What do you mean, 'a crow'?"

"The crow Ray saw at his mother's today."

Natalia's heart had begun to beat very fast, and she could feel the blood in her cheeks again. She quickly eyed the safety to make sure it was off and moved closer to Eddie with the pistol pointed at his head. "Don't play games with me."

Eddie sighed. "Normally, I'd be nervous, even with an unloaded gun pointed at me. No such thing, as we say in law enforcement. That's why, when Ray called me earlier today saying he saw a crow with a fish head on his mother's patio, I not only told him to empty your clip, but I also instructed him on how to remove the firing pin when you were taking your parents to the airport."

Natalia pulled the trigger, and her breath hitched when the pistol did not fire. She tried again—once, twice—then Eddie stood. He slipped a small digital recorder out of his back pocket and showed it to her. He had been recording their conversation the entire time.

"Ray called me again after you left to say you were on your way. I mean, I know I ain't too bright, but if I'm gonna roofie someone's wine, I would make sure they drank it before I took my shower."

A groan of panic escaped her throat—for a moment, Natalia almost bolted for the door—but then she saw the flash of police lights coming from outside, and all at once, she knew it was over.

Epilogue: Snow Day

One month, two weeks, and three days after his wife was charged with Matthew Kauffman's murder, Ray Dawley woke up to a snowfall unlike any he had seen in years. About twenty inches when all was said and done. Not as much as the Blizzard of '78, he told his daughter, but impressive nonetheless. School was canceled all over Rhode Island, and after Sue Dawley cooked them breakfast, Ray and Maggie bundled up and went outside to build a snowman in the backyard. The world appeared to him much the same as it had as a child—his troubles, the heartache from Natalia buried so far below that he could almost forget about it. Almost...

Even before he saw the crow, Ray Dawley had suspected his wife might've had something to do with Matthew Kauffman's murder. It began with a general unease, a knot in his stomach when Maggie mentioned how tired she felt the morning after the sleepover at her grandmother's. That unease became mistrust when Ray asked Natalia if she had seen the backpack for his laptop—a flicker of alarm in her eyes before she covered with a shrug. And when Ray asked about his missing Patriots hat and hoodie, Natalia became downright indignant. Ray would not understand his wife's behavior until he listened to Eddie's recording, after which he went searching for the blond wig Natalia had worn to a Halloween party a few years back. It was missing too. Same for his old Boston Bruins hat with the ski mask, which his mother had kept in a box all these years.

As for what Natalia did with everything after the murder, she wasn't saying and had hardly spoken much at all beyond a quick "not guilty" during her arraignment. Ray had not seen his wife since her incarceration, and Natalia had not tried to contact him—never even offered an apology to Jeremy, who had visited her a handful of times before giving up.

"Too painful, and what was the point?" he asked. "Since all she does is sit there staring down at the floor."

Ray suspected it might all be an act—something to bolster a defense, maybe, that she had committed murder because she, too, suffered from DID.

As for the attempted murder of Eddie Sayers? Ray wasn't sure how his wife would play that one, either, but Eddie said he doubted the whole thing would ever go to trial. The case was too strong. Then again, one never knew—especially since Jeremy told them that Natalia's defense team had contacted him about being a witness. They'd even tried to imply that Ray was an abusive husband, to which Jeremy basically told them to go fuck themselves. Christ, he could only imagine what the poor kid was going through. Jeremy ended up taking the semester off and moved in with his father. Ray texted and talked to Jeremy almost every day—tried to see him a couple of times a week and even took him to his therapy appointments—but the kid was still as withdrawn as ever.

Maggie was taking things hard too. Never mind that her stepmother had turned out to be a murderer, her biological one was on the warpath again. "What the hell did you get her into, Ray? That is no place for a child. She needs to move to California now!" Ray couldn't blame Connie—he would feel the same, no doubt, if the roles had been reversed—but thankfully, Maggie's new therapist had advised that the last thing their daughter needed was the trauma of being uprooted again, especially since she wanted to stay with her father. Still, Ray figured another court battle was on the horizon. But that was all right. He would get through it for his daughter—just like he would get through this, the mother of all rug pulls, for Maggie too.

Had it not been for Ray's mother, his suspicions about Natalia might never have been confirmed. The day after Christmas, Ray and Maggie had stopped by Sue Dawley's to return a casserole dish, and while they were there, Ray ended up fixing a leaky trap under her kitchen sink. His mother had been using a bucket to catch the water, and when Ray went to throw it out the back door, he startled a large crow on the patio. The crow cawed loudly and flew away, and Ray saw that the big bird had been picking at a large fish head—frozen, mostly bones now, and missing its eyes. Ray picked up the fish head with a plastic bag and tossed it in the trash. And that might have been the end of it had he not mentioned the incident to his mother soon after.

"What is it with these fish around here?" Sue Dawley said, and Ray asked her what she meant. "Well, when I found out Natalia's mother was making the traditional Italian dinner for Christmas Eve, I thought of that snapper in the freezer. Bob Pelletier two doors down gave it to me last summer after his annual fishing trip with his son. Perfect for those appetizers, I was thinking—those little fish pies your grandmother used to make in the muffin tins. Anyhow, I swore the snapper was still in there—I remembered seeing it at Thanksgiving, when I froze all that leftover soup I made. But for the life of me, I couldn't find it..."

If his mother said anything else, Ray did not hear it. He felt as if the wind had been knocked out of him, and his ears were ringing. Somehow, he managed to hide his distress and went out to his car to call Eddie, who proceeded to tell him of his suspicions. Ray spent the rest of that afternoon in a daze as he carried out Eddie's instructions—the weight, the horror of his discovery threatening to drag him under with every breath. A snapper tail had been found three weeks earlier in Matthew Kauffman's mouth. And now, the head of that same snapper most likely had been found by sheer luck on his mother's back patio. *Natalia,* Ray knew at once. On the night of

Matthew Kauffman's murder, she had taken the fish from his mother's freezer, cut the head off there in the kitchen, and disposed of it in the woods, never dreaming that a crow would drop it on Sue Dawley's patio three weeks later like some belated Christmas present.

The insanity of it all was so overwhelming that Ray felt like screaming. Still, he somehow managed to do what Eddie asked. He retrieved the fish head from his mother's trash bin and met Eddie over at Cranston PD, where Eddie gave it to a friend of his in the crime lab—Laurie was her name. The analysis would take some time, she said, but if they could tie the fish head to the tail found at Blackamore Pond, then a judge would be more apt to issue a warrant for Natalia's arrest. She was the same size as the suspect in the video, after all, and would have had access to the fish on the night Matthew Kauffman was murdered.

However, all Ray could think about was Maggie. Innocent or guilty, he did not want her around Natalia—who, as luck would have it, had taken her parents for a quick trip to L.L. Bean on their way to the airport. And while she was gone, Ray hurried home and packed Maggie's things. Eddie instructed Ray on FaceTime how to unload and disable the pistol but told him to leave it in the house so as not to spook Natalia, in case she went looking for it before the tests came back for the fish head. Eddie also had Ray go looking for the Rohypnol, but before he could find it, Natalia returned home, and Ray played the rest of the night by ear.

Ever since the thing with Eddie on the porch, Natalia Morris had been a first-class bitch to her husband, but her mood did a one-eighty when he told her Maggie would be spending the night at her grandmother's house again. Natalia suggested they share a bottle of wine and have a romantic evening just the two of them, and Ray knew at once that she was up to no good. She poured him a glass in the den and told him to drink up while she took a shower, after which, she promised, she would give him a blowjob right there in his chair before going upstairs.

As soon as Ray heard the shower turn on, he dumped the wine down the kitchen sink and, returning to his chair, pretended to be asleep with the glass tipped over on the floor beside him. His only plan at that point had been to see how Natalia reacted when she found him passed out. He heard her come downstairs about twenty minutes later. She slapped his cheeks a few times, fished his phone out from between his thighs, then Ray heard her in the kitchen—rinsing out the wine glass, he discovered when he glanced down and saw it missing. Natalia left through the back door shortly afterward, but only when Ray dashed upstairs and discovered the pistol was missing did he figure she was headed for Eddie's.

Ray called him from Natalia's phone, which she had left on the night table. Ray's boots and his jacket were gone, he discovered as he and Eddie spoke. His car was gone too. Eddie figured she was up to another frame job and told Ray to let him take it from there. The plan was to call John Seabrook if and when Natalia showed up at his condo and have him on the line listening. The code word for Cranston PD to make their move ended up being "crow," which Eddie managed to throw out *after* he recorded Natalia's confession. A certified genius, that Eddie Sayers...

Ray arrived at Eddie's complex just in time to see the police escorting Natalia out in handcuffs. He met her gaze only briefly, upon which she looked at him as if he were a stranger—her expression blank, her eyes vacant as the cops stuffed her into the back of a police cruiser and drove away. John Seabrook took a statement from him, during which Ray almost lost it a half dozen times, but after he listened to Eddie's recording that night, he felt something in him change. A hardening in his heart, a determination that, in the days that followed, began to feel more like healing. Ray could almost feel a new kind of blood pumping through his veins, like some high-octane fuel making him stronger, making him feel more alive than he had felt in a very long time. Most of all, Ray Dawley was no longer afraid.

Sure, Connie was making plans to take him back to court, he figured, but Ray started making plans too. There was the therapist for Maggie, a written evaluation, and a treatment plan that entailed her staying in Rhode Island. Then there was Ray's new job as an academic counselor at Providence College, which he would start after the first of March. The unexpected vacancy wasn't the best-paying position, but decent enough to get by with his pension and his online gigs. There would also be help from his mother, who ended up moving in with him a couple of weeks after the New Year. She already had three offers on her townhouse—all profit, a nice chunk of change that would take care of Maggie's tuition until she graduated. Ray didn't think he would have to drop much on the divorce either, as Natalia would have no choice but to go the uncontested route. Ray was in the process of setting all that in motion too.

So yeah, that was the plan for now. *That's how to be strong for your daughter,* he kept telling himself. *You make plans, you prepare for war, you work hard to ensure your kid stays far away from the front lines so that when you see the enemy on the horizon, you're ready to hit them back with everything you have without collateral damage.* But it was also important to make time to play, to get lost in it with abandon—like a child on a snow day. All the worries buried far beneath the pristine white.

Eddie was probably thinking the same thing, Ray figured, when he stopped by that morning. Katie was still giving him a hard time about his pension, but Ray would never know it from the smile on his face. Ray and Maggie had just finished rolling the base for their snowman when Eddie pulled up with a plow attached to the front of his truck.

"Roads are brutal, but that never stopped us from sledding back in the day." Eddie had brought along three toboggans. "Got them on sale after Christmas," he said. "I figured we could start a new tradition before Maggie gets too cool to hang with us."

They all piled into Eddie's truck and drove across town to Roger Williams Park, where they spent the day sledding on the big hills near the Temple of Music. But still, Ray imagined himself at Blackamore Pond, twisting just before he hit the ice, as Bobby Bonetti watched him from the darkness below.

About the Author

Gregory Funaro is a *New York Times* best-selling author of stories for both children and adults. His books have been translated into more than half a dozen languages and have received starred reviews from *Kirkus Reviews*, *School Library Journal*, and *ALA Booklist*.

Gregory lives with his family in Rhode Island, where he is busy working on his next novel.

Read more at https://www.gregoryfunaro.com/.

About the Publisher

Dear Reader,

We hope you enjoyed this book. Please consider leaving a review on your favorite book site.

Visit our site to find more quality books!

Read more at https://RedAdeptPublishing.com.